My Jane Austen Summer

3/11

"When one has read the six great Austen novels, and been throug ... and then reread ... ny of others ... *mmer* fills t ... g, a wonde ... uliar heroir ... t. By loving ... wins my aw ...

"A bea ... nex- pected ... eeply honest ... ny on a litera ... xim: Book ...

"Auste ... en- ture a ... ey could ...

"An i ... vill have ... ves a ve ... nd scene ...

"A delightful story that takes us for a romp through the English countryside and into the wonderful world of Jane Austen. You can't help but root for Lily Berry, a refreshingly real heroine, as she searches for herself in a novel and finds something quite unexpected."

—Shilpi Somaya Gowda, author of *Secret Daughter*

"*My Jane Austen: A Season in Mansfield Park* is a loving tribute to the timeless appeal of the world created by Jane Austen. A delightful and imaginative coming-of-age story of a young woman's search for romance, acceptance, and belonging, with some help along the way from Jane Austen herself."

—Kathleen Kent, author of *The Heretic's Daughter*
and The Wolves of Andover

My
Jane Austen Summer

By Cindy Jones

My Jane Austen Summer

My
Jane Austen Summer

A SEASON IN MANSFIELD PARK

Cindy Jones

WM

WILLIAM MORROW
An Imprint of HarperCollinsPublishers

MY JANE AUSTEN SUMMER. Copyright © 2011 by Cindy Sundermann Jones. All rights reserved. Printed in the United States of America. No part of this book may be used or reproduced in any manner whatsoever without written permission except in the case of brief quotations embodied in critical articles and reviews. For information address HarperCollins Publishers, 10 East 53rd Street, New York, NY 10022.

HarperCollins books may be purchased for educational, business, or sales promotional use. For information please write: Special Markets Department, HarperCollins Publishers, 10 East 53rd Street, New York, NY 10022.

FIRST EDITION

Designed by Diahann Sturge

Library of Congress Cataloging-in-Publication Data is available upon request.

ISBN 978-0-06-200397-3

11 12 13 14 15 OV/BVG 10 9 8 7 6 5 4 3 2 1

For George

Synopsis of

Mansfield Park
by
Jane Austen

Young Fanny Price is sent to live at Mansfield Park, the manor home of her wealthy Aunt and Uncle Bertram, where she grows up neglected and abused, and secretly in love with her cousin Edmund. But Fanny is the obvious dark horse in any competition for Edmund's affection, especially after the arrival of Mary Crawford, a witty and engaging husband hunter.

Edmund is so charmed by Mary Crawford that he abandons caution and agrees to act in amateur theatricals while his father is away—mischief! As expected, the relaxed decorum of the stage inspires Mary's brother, Henry Crawford, to flirt with both of Edmund's sisters, one of whom is engaged to be married. When Uncle Bertram arrives home unexpectedly, the stage is shut down, but the scene is already set for disaster.

Without theatrics for amusement, the players are left to their own devices. Edmund's sister marries her rich buffoon, and Henry Crawford blazes uncharted territory: he will make Fanny Price fall in love with him. Henry convinces everyone, perhaps even himself, of his reformation. But Fanny has seen Henry in action and she steadfastly refuses his marriage proposal, even though it makes everyone mad at her. Uncle Bertram hopes an extended visit with her birth family in gritty Portsmouth will allow sufficient leisure to rethink her impertinence.

Henry pursues Fanny to Portsmouth, where he maintains his good behavior, ingratiating himself by overlooking her mother's slovenly housekeeping and her father's coarse manners. At the moment when even the reader thinks perhaps Henry *has* changed and perhaps Fanny should reconsider, news arrives that Henry has committed a sin of the first magnitude; he has run away with Edmund's sister, a newly married woman. Mary Crawford's casual response to her brother's barbarous behavior clues Edmund to Mary's real character. His infatuation destroyed, Edmund is free to discover his affection for Fanny.

In the end, Fanny's tenacity in the face of competition and steadfast resistance to artful guile win her the love and happiness generally reserved for witty and charming heroines.

Mansfield Park was published in 1814.

My
Jane Austen Summer

One

My spirits always lifted the instant my car started. Abandoning the grocery store pretense, I backed out of the driveway and headed in the familiar direction of my ex-boyfriend's house, driving the same direction I'd driven the previous three, eight, or perhaps thirty-eight nights. Passing through familiar neighborhoods: ferocious Highland Park, sleepy SMU, earnest M Streets, stopping for lights, I played the protagonist careening toward destiny, Anna Karenina rushing to Vronsky, or Marianne seeking Willoughby. One soulful connecting glance and Martin would confess he'd missed me. We would share his blue denim sofa like the old days, Martin watching ESPN, me reading a novel. But Martin didn't expect me anymore; I was no longer a part of his life.

At the red light a mile from his house I opened the book on my passenger seat: Jane Austen's *Unfinished Novels and Juvenilia*. Having read all six novels, I now trolled her minor works desperate for the sort of Jane Austen fix a book like *Sense and Sensibility* offered. But instead of reading a few sentences at the red light, I studied the postcard doubling as a bookmark: a postcard promoting a summer literary festival in England where people enact Jane Austen's novels. Vera, owner of my favorite indie bookstore, gave me the postcard the day I bought *Mansfield Park*, saying, "I think you're ready for this."

The light turned green and my stomach lurched. This drive-by spying thing wouldn't be happening if Jane Austen hadn't died so young. I'd started reading *Persuasion* aloud to my mother shortly after her cancer diagnosis, kept reading *Emma* as her faculties deteriorated, and finished *Mansfield Park* alone. I read the last three in a state of denial and hit the wall after *Pride and Prejudice*, confronted with the stark reality there would *never* be any more Jane Austen novels. The sequels and prequels failed me; no amount of fan fiction could bring her back to life in my mind. All other books paled; I reread random pages from *Mansfield Park* for days, postponing the inevitable withdrawal, jilted by Jane Austen. If only Austen were still alive and writing, I wouldn't have to stare at the walls of my bedroom, studying the Braille-like texture under the paint, as if the clues to my failure hid there.

Or stalk my ex-boyfriend.

At first, I drove by his house late at night and saw the blue light flickering in the front room, Martin operating the remote from his sofa. Once, on a Saturday evening in early spring, I drove down his street of stately trees and found him outside, his back to me, relaxing with a beer in his hand, talking to a neighbor. As much as I loved seeing his familiar male legs and broad shoulders, the close call scared me into staying home the next two nights. But great windows of free time opened up after my termination, allowing me to drive by earlier and more often, lured by the notion that discovering Martin's secrets would reveal my own missing pieces.

Lately, he'd been up to something. Last Wednesday evening Martin had not been home. His car gone, windows completely dark, the dog didn't even come to the fence. Thursday I drove by a little later and he was gone again. But the dog was home. On Friday, stopping just beyond his driveway, lurking in my dark car as if *I* were the secret, I noticed an unfamiliar bicycle leaning against the garage wall. I told myself he slumbered alone, tired from the busy week, but the unfamiliar bicycle troubled me.

At home, I tidied up my kitchen and went to bed with Henry James, unable to engage *The Wings of the Dove* no matter how many times I started over. Did Martin sleep alone in that dark house? I reviewed the clues: the bike, the pattern of absence, the missing dog. Saturdays were the critical night. I could barely function, couldn't even stare at the walls for the anxiety of Saturdays because, if Martin was going to have a date, he would have it on a Saturday.

Turning off Mockingbird Lane, my pulse quickened, driving through the neighborhood where I'd long imagined Martin and I would eventually reside: mannerly Tudors with yard signs announcing births, advertising remodeling projects, or proclaiming enrollment in elementary schools, private or public. The closer his house, the more nervous I felt, but nervous was so much better than the desperate loneliness of sitting at home wondering whose bicycle had moved in.

My mother had said Martin wasn't my type and I should let go, but she just didn't like him because of his commitment problem and his habit of sometimes closing his eyes when he talked to you. I reminded her Martin was the first guy who would ever agree to a date in the bookstore on Saturday night.

I missed the way I could always find him in the magazine department reading *Car and Driver* when I was ready to go. Now, the scorching pain of my emptiness was unbearable. I began the final approach to Martin's street; one more turn and I would see his car in the driveway. Twenty feet farther, the dog would recognize me. Adrenaline surged as my car accelerated into the turn, putting me on the street that had been mine. My heart stopped for just a moment because there, on the sidewalk directly in front of me in cargo shorts and flip-flops, was Martin. I'd never seen Martin walk the dog. Too late to backtrack; I was nailed and he wasn't alone. Stopping the car, my mind raced for excuses.

Martin contemplated his cargo pockets and then fixed his gaze on the air just over my head, waiting. The woman holding his hand turned and stopped speaking when she saw me. The dog, straining on his leash, stopped pulling. Stepping out of my car, ankles teetering on my optimistic stilettos, keys jangling in my trembling hand, I tucked my hair behind my ears and smoothed my stalker-black sheath as if I had a purpose in interrupting their walk. Martin adopted the expression one saves for door-to-door magazine salesmen, but the woman smiled warmly, as if unaware of our adversarial position as well as her advantage.

"Hi, I'm Ginny," she said; her hand twitched as if she had considered extending it, and I could tell she knew everything. I tried not to study her dark blond Afro, her T-shirt advertising a hunger walk four years ago, and her lack of any of the *Car and Driver* curves Martin found interesting. My replacement was so contrary to my expectations I began to think I'd completely misread Martin.

"Hi," I said, looking at Martin. The dog sniffed my legs, pulling the leash Ginny held. Martin had never walked the dog with me.

"Scout," Ginny whispered, coaxing the dog to her side.

Martin glanced down the street as if help might be coming. "What's up?" he said.

Tucking the hair behind my ears again, unfortunately using the hand holding my keys that tangled and pulled out several long brown strands, I prayed for inspiration. She was down-to-earth, ordinary, and apparently sweet, not a single quality I could claim for myself. Is that what he wanted? I'd been struggling with cosmetics, lingerie that guaranteed cleavage, and sheaths selected to accentuate all things slim, when, all along, he had preferred Mother Earth. *I* could have done *earth* for him.

"Scout, please," Ginny said, "remember what we talked about?"

We waited for Scout to answer.

"Ginny works in a vet's office," Martin said.

I found my perky face and smiled, then changed the subject. "I just wanted to let you know"—I cleared my throat—"that I'm going to England for the summer." This was news to me, too.

"England?" Martin directed his face at me, but closed his eyes. He'd been expecting a hormonal rage or paternity test results.

Ginny stood apart, reminding the dog about not jumping on people.

"Yes," I said, trying to remember the words below the English manor house on Vera's postcard: "Featuring *Mansfield Park*, June through August." Vera's invitation was thoughtful, but did she understand my utter dependence on salary and benefits? "I'm going to a lit fest," I said.

"What's a lit fest?" Ginny asked, smiling, way too familiar.

I shook my hair and stared meaningfully at Martin: my Countess Olenska to his Newland Archer, urging him to indulge his true passion or be sorry. "Literary festival," I said slowly. The postcard said, "Literary escapes in rural England: A novel approach to the study of literature." "They feature a Jane Austen novel every summer."

"Oh, I love Jane Austen," she said, handing the leash to Martin like a wife passing a baby off to the husband.

"Really," I said, disconcerted by the friendly hand rubbing Martin's back and the way Martin took the rubbing for granted.

"And what will you do there?" Ginny asked.

"I don't know yet." Leaning on my car, I crossed my arms over my chest, unable to bear the idea of sharing Jane Austen, as well as Martin, with her. Jane Austen was *my* new best friend. Even with the age difference—me twenty-six, Jane eternally forty-one—we understood each other and agreed on everything. Ours was a possessive relationship. I crossed my legs at the ankles and gave Martin the look that always brought him closer. "I'm still working out the details." Like whether to toss the postcard in the trash.

"What about work?" Martin asked. "They giving you more vacation?" He took two steps backward, aware I had exhausted my vacation time watching him ski.

"Work is not a problem."

Martin nodded, taking two more steps away from me.

"I quit my job." I pursed my lips and gazed upward.

"Really." He stopped walking away.

Ginny raised her hand. "Nice to meet you," she said. "I'm going to get Scout a drink of water." Then I witnessed an exchange between them, a look so packed with understanding and implying such a depth of intimacy I had to glance away. Ginny walked to the house, leaving Martin to me.

"So," he said, blinking rapidly.

"Now you know," I said, remembering how my boss caught

me reading *Northanger Abbey* in my cubicle, my lunch hour so far in the past that even the fumes from my tuna sandwich were history. Phones, copiers, and printers resumed business while I danced in Bath. I made a show of tidying my lunch bag while my boss counted the five other novels stacked in my corner. "You've been busy," he said. Then, using his chain saw voice, he informed me that I'd cost the company over ninety-two thousand dollars misrouting payroll tax deposits. As my boss explained termination benefits, it occurred to me that books should come with a warning from the surgeon general: *Literature can be dangerous to your mental health and should be indulged in moderation. Read in excess, fiction may blur the line between fantasy and reality, causing dysfunction in personal and professional relationships. Readers should refrain while operating heavy machinery or driving automobiles.* Or working in offices.

"So what are you going to do?" Martin asked.

"Move home, of course," I said. "As you know, my duplex is two doors from annihilation." I'd complained to Martin for a year about the McMansions invading my street, moaning about moving, but he'd left me to the wrecking ball rather than propose marriage. "And my dad needs me."

"How *is* your dad?" Martin asked. His concern might have been touching had he not ditched me in the wake of my mother's death, exercising his option while I grieved, optimistic that one more hit could hardly matter.

"Not good," I said. "He has a girlfriend. Twenty years younger."

Martin's eyes bulged. "Really."

"I'm not happy about it."

"Doubt your mom would approve."

The last time I saw her, my mother had been dead ninety minutes and the look on her face conferred anything but approval. Rather than the peaceful repose I'd been promised in books and movies, her jaundiced features were frozen in tension, her cheekbones raised, and her mouth slightly open as if she'd died in pain. Eyes were closed but her head tilted up, giving the impression she had been trying to raise herself as she died. I bent and kissed her forehead as she had kissed mine all those nights I pretended to be asleep clutching the still-hot reading light under my covers. Her forehead felt chilly under my lips and she no longer labored over the ragged breathing that sustained us halfway through *Mansfield Park*. In spite of these powerful indications of death, I wanted to believe she was pretending, as I had once pretended with her.

"Well," Martin said, raising a hand in farewell, taking steps away from me. "Have a great time in England."

"Martin," I said, perhaps too loud.

At the sound of my voice, Ginny and the dog closed the front door behind them. Martin halted in his tracks and slowly returned, his head bent. "Let's not have tears," he said. His eyes scurried up and down the street, waiting for someone to turn our page. His porch light came on. "You need to go home."

A car passed behind us.

"Martin, look at me."

He reluctantly focused on my face.

"Is it really over?" I asked. "Is this what you want?"

Martin shook his head. "Ginny's not needy." He raised his hands in supplication. "If you can't stay away, you need to get help." He enunciated as if I were dense. "We've seen you drive by. Even Ted's seen your car." He gestured at Ted's window, especially damning since Ted's eyes never left his video screen.

"I can't believe we're saying these things. Martin, how did we get to this point?" He took a breath and closed his eyes and I knew he was considering whether to reveal a painful truth. I braced myself for the hit.

"I let it go on way too long," he said, stepping away.

"Wait." I reached out.

"Are you listening?" he whispered. "You're a lost dog." He shook his head. "Go home."

At home, my phone was ringing and I raced to answer it, expecting a remorseful Martin.

"Hi, Lily." It was Karen, my sister in Houston. I'd never had much use for her growing up except during tours of my house I gave my six-year-old friends. I'd fling open her bedroom door to reveal a real live teenager in bedcovers; we'd scream and run if she moved.

"I'm so glad to hear your voice," I said. "Do you think I'm needy?"

Karen hesitated. "No," she said.

I waited in case she wanted to elaborate. "You don't sound good," I said, clutching the gold cross around my neck and twisting the chain around my finger.

"I just got off the phone with Dad." Karen inhaled sharply; the news was bad. "And I'm counting on you not to fall apart." In the early stages of Mom's illness, Karen had counseled me not to jump to conclusions. She reminded me that the doctor hadn't ruled out tuberculosis. Or bird flu. We clung to the hope of bird flu. Now, I sat on my kitchen floor, preparing myself. It hadn't been bird flu and Mother had died within six months of the diagnosis.

"What happened?" I asked, wishing for a tissue, wiping my nose on the dishtowel hanging from the fridge handle as I felt something slither around my neck, into the dishtowel, and then onto the floor. My necklace lay sprawled on the linoleum—the necklace my mother had made for me when she knew she would die. I couldn't bear to let it touch the ground, much less lie there broken. "Oh my God," I said. "My necklace just fell off." Karen had one, too, a cross, made from the melted gold of our mother's wedding rings. It wasn't just a necklace to us, and my dad's girlfriend knew this, so I always made sure the cross hung outside my shirt in her presence. "Hang on," I said, bending to gather the cross and chain from the floor, making sure none of the tiny links had skittered off under the fridge or stove. "Things are really falling apart," I said.

"Is it the chain?" Karen asked.

"Yes," I said. "But I think I got all of it. Don't worry, I can fix it."

Karen sighed.

I braced myself for the bad news.

"Lily, I talked to Dad."

"Yes?" I held my breath, staring at the legs of my breakfast table, fuzzy dust freeloading in the curves of the woodwork.

"Dad and Sue are going to be married."

I remembered then where I'd seen The Look Martin and Ginny exchanged. My father shared the same exclusive look with his new girlfriend, Sue. A look that telegraphed secret communication—about me—and conferred privileged status to the gold digger sucking the life out of him. The pain was exquisite, razor-sharp surprise from a dark corner, completion of the outrage that began with my mother's senseless death.

I'd puzzled so long over the mystery of Sue's sudden arrival in my father's house that I wondered if she found him in the obituaries. She would have seen my mother smiling from the newsprint, her face cropped from the family portrait we'd taken right after Karen's second was born. Sue shed no tears over my mother's life story, the Great Books Club she ran for the library, her term as president of her garden club, or the years Mother spent touring children through the Butterfly Garden. Sue skipped instead to the list of survivors, underlined my father's name, and marked her calendar for one week after my mother's funeral, the standard grace period in her business. Sue gave us a week to say good-bye. The bridge club, Mother's Bible group study buddies, and her hairdresser all paid respects, dropping off food, hugging my sorrowful dad, and lending support in the funeral home. But then everything changed. The day Sue appeared in my mother's house, my dad met me in the front hallway. He stood in front of Mother's antique armoire we named The Monster, stopping me with his eyes as if I'd committed a mistake entering his house without knocking, something I'd done every day of my life and would continue to do when I moved back home. When I asked him who was talking on our kitchen phone, he said it was "Sue." I asked if Sue was from hospice, noting she'd collected my mother's unused meds from the counter and loaded them into a box.

"Lily?" Karen said. "Are you there?"

"Yes," I said, my voice breaking. I cleared my throat.

"So, what will you do?" Karen asked, knowing I'd soon be homeless.

"I'm going to England."

"You don't have a job, how can you afford England?"

"England *is* a job," I said. "I'll get paid." I pulled a bottle of Chardonnay from the fridge, kicking the door shut. Vera had never mentioned pay. "How did Dad tell you?" I asked.

"I don't remember and it's not important," Karen said, unwilling to feed the old dysfunction.

"But did he use the word *love*?" I asked, recognizing early stages of fresh turmoil like a black wind howling inside me.

Karen sighed. "Don't make me say these things to you. I'm not the bad guy, Lily."

"But I just want to know what happened to my father. I don't know this man who's taken over his body." Where was the father who held me up on ice skates, who loved me enough to punish my white lies and celebrate my report card? "What did he say?"

Karen sighed. "He told me Sue had been cleaning out the garage to make room for her stuff. It went from there."

I found a glass and slammed the cupboard. "It makes no sense. How could he care about someone so different from Mom? I can't even stand to look at her, those eyebrows tweezed to death and hair teased like a rat's nest. She is so opposite of everything Mom was. I can't stand by and watch him do this to our mother," I said. "Can you?"

"He's an adult." Karen paused. "You know, this really isn't a good time for you to be making big changes. Is there someone at church you could talk to?"

"No," I said, pouring wine, spilling on the counter. "I know what I have to do." The important thing was to get off the phone, hide my car keys from myself, and focus my energy on figuring out how to get to England. There, I could start over without all this mess. My mother would want me to go, her well-known desire to travel unfulfilled because Dad objected; he traveled too much for work. "See the world," Mom had said, offering me *A Passage to India* when I was twelve, teaching me to escape the confines of my life through literature. "I've got to go," I told Karen. I hung up, gripped by new fear of the many potential obstacles, financial and otherwise, between me and *Mansfield Park*.

I had to see Vera.

Two

The next morning, I crossed the river and drove toward Oak Cliff. My mission: to accept Vera's invitation to her literary festival. Once I decided to go to England, my recent failures stopped looking so bad. In fact, they began to seem like necessary groundwork for a possible turning point in my life. If I hadn't failed, I'd still be failing.

Posters crowded the bookstore window: "Breastfeeding Mothers Welcome Here," "Winter Solstice Ceremony at White Rock Lake," and "Holotropic Breathing Workshops." Tangled in a roaming philodendron, a hand-lettered sign reached out to me: "Dallas Office of Literature Live." An Oriental brass bell announced my arrival as the breeze from the open door blew stacks of free newspapers, their pages fluttering against the red bricks placed to ground them. Colorful fliers advertising yoga teachers or seeking lost exotic pigs hawked phone numbers on tear-off tags. A portly cat patrolled the entryway and I thought of Aunt Norris.

"Is Vera here?" I asked. A fragrant candle burning near the register encouraged my hope as the cashier, my gateway to England, processed the question. I tried not to stare at her pierced face: her eyebrows, a nostril, and the corner of her mouth. I could barely think, wondering about her tongue. Her name tag said Chutney; surely her mother had not named her Chutney. The woman shrugged and I feared I'd missed Vera; she'd already left for England. But Chutney nodded toward the back. I hurried through stacks rising on either side of me like narrow canyons, the atmosphere cooler and quieter among the shelves. I grew excited by the musty paper smell and the promise of a different kind of future. I'd always wanted to live in a novel, a living cosmos bound by cloth covers, awaiting a reader's attention to launch its narrative. Attending a literary festival seemed very close to my dream of living in a book.

I sensed a gothic villain on my trail and quickened my pace, passing Tolstoy, Wharton, and Zola. Frida Kahlo's eyebrow glared at me from a poster on the end of the next stack. At the turn, I collided with Rochester's mad wife, a small Asian woman reading while she walked, scaring us both. Shouldn't they post that warning from the surgeon general in here?

Stepping into the office doorway, my heart still pounding, I found Vera at her desk, surrounded by books. She peered at me over her reading glasses, reminding me of the silver-haired bookmobile lady from my elementary school who placed her hands on my shoulders almost twenty years ago, gently turning my body away from the childish picture books to behold the novels. "I think you're ready for these," the bookmobile lady had said. A mighty chorus filled the air and an intense beam illuminated dust motes as I reached for my first chapter book.

"You all right, Lily?" Vera asked, her finger resting on the last word she'd read, her voice so soft and inviting I wanted to sit next to her and read whatever page she was on. Last time we talked, she'd said we were kindred spirits, swallowing mid-sentence, confessing to the same dream of living in a novel. I'd asked if participating in her husband's literary festival was like living in a novel and she said it depended on one's approach.

I cleared my throat and spoke. "I accept your invitation to the literary festival." When Vera first invited me to the lit fest, the books in her office listened politely, knowing I couldn't afford the flight. Now that I wanted to go, books stacked on the floor and covering every horizontal surface held their musty breath awaiting her response. Vera lifted her glasses to the top of her head where they rested on her gray Georgia O'Keeffe braid.

"You accept what?" She marked her page and gently closed her book.

Why did she ask? We'd talked about this.

She pointed to a chair. "Please sit."

Her reaction surprised me; Vera pretending not to understand, as if we'd never discussed me going to England. Navigating piles of books, I walked around her desk and lifted a box of paperbacks from the old dinette chair. Had I read too much into her invitation? Suddenly, the reasons they wouldn't take me multiplied: I had no passport, I spoke no foreign languages, and my literary skills were limited to turning pages. "You gave me the postcard for Literature Live. You said I was ready for it."

Vera shrugged. She smiled at her desk and willed the phone to ring; a woman in the act of backpedaling. Had she used the same line on everyone in the store that day? "Are you planning to be in England this summer?" she asked.

I wasn't imagining things. Vera had said I was ready. She

said I should go to England and leave my problems in Texas. Staring directly at her, I picked a ragged cuticle on my thumb, resisting the urge to bite. Perhaps projects excited her as long as they remained in the abstract. Practical considerations, like what I would *do* and who would *pay*, killed her buzz.

"For some reason I thought you were planning to travel," she said.

"I'm *planning* to change careers," I said. "And when we talked about your husband's literary festival, we were talking about *me* needing a *job*." I leaned forward. "Can't I audition," I asked, pressing my hands together, "for a small part?"

"Audition? I wasn't aware you were an actress," Vera said.

I ticked off high school musicals on my fingers: *The Music Man*, *Camelot*, and *Fiddler on the Roof*. Nothing in college. "And I volunteered with Dallas Community Theatre." I passed out programs when I first moved to Dallas, before I had friends. The sorry smile on Vera's face stopped me from launching into my living-your-literature-like-living-your-faith philosophy. "What?" I asked.

"Auditions were held months ago." Vera frowned.

I held my thumb. "What about a nonspeaking part?"

"You don't understand." Vera shook her head and then revealed the major obstacle lurking beyond the range of my hope. "Visitors don't do the acting," she said. "Visitors watch productions and attend lectures."

I bit my cuticle and blood gushed.

"The festival hires professional actors who perform for the paying public." She tapped her pen on a pink message pad. "But, you know," she mused, pointing her pen at me, "I like your idea. Firing the salaried actors and replacing them with the paying public is an interesting approach." Vera pushed her chair back and offered me a tissue for my thumb. "Let's fire the actors. I wonder how that would work."

I wrapped my thumb in the tissue. "I don't think you would fire all of them," I said, accepting credit for the business concept she'd converted from my misunderstanding. "You'd keep a couple of professionals to coach the amateurs."

Vera's eyes grew wide. "We'd save money."

We stared at each other, not blinking.

"So, can I go?"

"I'm thinking." Vera put the pen down. Something about firing the actors had changed the dynamics and she began to seem like her old self.

"Do you have any other jobs?" I asked.

"Like what?"

"I have a business degree. I could help you in an administrative capacity."

"We have Claire for that." Vera bit her pen.

"I can take tickets."

"You'd have to fight the volunteers for that job." Eventually, she folded her arms and spoke slowly. "We do have one sticky situation you might help with. Let me call my husband and see where he is with that. Hold on." Vera picked up her phone and dialed England, home of her husband, executive director of the lit fest. "Let's fire all the actors," she mused, punching numbers twice before getting an answer. "Nigel dear, any word from Her Ladyship?" Vera swept a few stray hairs off her forehead and I realized what a big adventure this would be, the very word *Ladyship* opening portals of newness for me.

"I was hoping she'd have executed something by now," Vera continued. "No, I don't think it means anything other than she's busy and we're low priority." Her tone changed when she said, "Nigel, how's this for an idea?" Vera looked at me as she spoke. "Have you ever considered firing the actors and allowing visitors to perform the enactments?" The air-conditioning cycled on while we waited for Nigel's reaction. "Exactly," Vera said. "Not this year, of course." Then Vera smiled at me. "I'm sitting across from the breath of fresh air, even as we speak."

I smiled my breeziest smile.

"Listen, the main reason for the call is to ask where we are on the Miss Banks Situation." Vera wobbled the pen between her fingers. "I want to know if we have a Plan B in the likely event Elizabeth Banks no-shows, because the breath of fresh air sitting across from me is also a lovely young actress." Vera smiled at me. "Think of a young Anne Elliot, brunette, blue eyes, who could fill that opening *and* help us in the Randolph Department."

The Randolph Department?

Vera waited. "No, this is not another of my adoptions." She rolled her eyes. "Although she is a worthy candidate." Pause. "I know. Not only does she have a business degree but she's studied theater in college and performed musicals in Dallas."

Whoa.

Vera winked at me.

I wondered. Was professional acting any harder than high school productions? Acting is acting.

"She's prepared to devote all summer." Vera nodded.

I nodded back.

Chutney stuck her pierced head in the door and listened until Vera waved her out. "I'll discuss that with her. Yes. I'll take my chances with Magda."

Magda?

When Vera finally hung up, she looked at me.

"So?" I asked.

"Assuming Elizabeth Banks fails to show up," she said, "and assuming we get you past Magda, you are in." Vera took a deep breath. "You'll have to pay for your flight."

"What's the Randolph Department?" I asked.

"Randolph Lockwood, Eleventh Baron of Weston." Vera paused, perhaps considering how much to tell me. "He recently inherited the manor where we stage our productions and he's very interested in bottom lines—if you will."

"And you need help with *him*?"

Vera leaned in to confide, "Yes."

"What happens if Elizabeth Banks shows up?" I stopped breathing.

Vera smiled and shook her head. "She won't show up."

"But what if she does?"

"We'll have a new problem." Vera straightened and pressed her index finger on the desk, getting down to business. "You've read *Mansfield Park*," she said.

"Of course."

"And you are familiar with the criticism." Her eyes narrowed.

"Some," I said, considering the introduction I'd saved for last, wondering where I could find more criticism to read—quickly.

She pressed her lips together and lifted a book off the floor. "You'll love this." She handed me a biography of Jane Austen, her gesture conjuring my mother: a gauzy childhood memory where I'm nestled in my mother's side listening to a story about twelve little girls in two straight lines. My mother saved my childhood books in an antique chest and when I read them I can still hear her voice. "And read this," she said, handing me another. "It includes a few essays on *Mansfield Park*."

I took the books. "Vera," I said, locking eyes with her. "Thank you."

She looked startled. "You're welcome." And then she smiled. "You know, you remind me of myself," Vera said. "I don't often come across amateur readers with such a passion for literature. Jane Austen's prose spoke to you, just as it spoke to me."

I had a feeling that, were Jane Austen present, she would ignore the amateur readers in the room and speak directly with the Randolph Department. Perhaps I should exert more diligence.

"When do I leave?" I asked.

Three

Once my bags were checked and my boarding pass tucked into *The Mysteries of Udolpho*, nothing but a series of long corridors remained between me and my plane to England. Every step I took in my tailored pantsuit, looking more like a flight attendant than an actress, keeping pace with business travelers power-walking to their flights, took me one step farther from my father's wedding and closer to my rebirth in a Jane Austen novel. I wondered if my father even knew I was leaving the country. "Teach him," I muttered silently, hoping my lips hadn't moved. I avoided tripping over rolling carry-ons as I changed lanes, desperately seeking a bathroom to relieve myself of the coffee I'd been drinking all morning. What if we had no bathroom in our *Mansfield Park* house? I'd better go while I still could.

Ducking into a ladies' room, I took my place at the end

of the line, advancing to the rhythm of flushing toilets and banging Band-Aid-colored doors. I checked the mirror for the same blank look everyone else wore that morning. I did indeed look like a lost dog—or the plain women they get to play the secondary characters in the films of Jane Austen's books. Brown hair, blue eyes, medium height. When I looked happy, there was a certain spirit in my eyes. I gave up on the mirror, first in line now, alert for the next open door.

Perhaps men who actually liked secondary Jane Austen character types existed out there. Maybe the person who played the pompous Mr. Rushworth would like me. I tried to hurry, conscious of the impatient line, but once locked inside the stall I indulged self-pity as I remembered my new grief. In the chaos of the yard sale I held to finance the purchase of my airline ticket, I lost the box of books my mother had collected for me. But not just books; I'd lost my mother's voice. And I'd lost her voice through my own carelessness.

Outside my stall, the persistent tapping of heels on tile floor and the starting of hand dryers pushed me forward. I washed my hands, hoping my appearance had transformed, unsurprised to find the secondary character still in possession of my mirror. The traffic in the corridor pushed me toward my destiny once again, people walking while talking on phones, listening to iPods, pushing strollers, and pulling backpacks. I wished Martin could see me now.

"You should let it go," Karen had said in the wake of my breakup. Married with two kids and her own neighborhood association, she'd forgotten about lonely Saturday nights.

"I am letting it go," I said to no one as I stepped out of the path of a golf cart transporting people to their gate. I was letting *everything* go.

★ ★ ★

Vera waited at the gate for the flight, her wrinkles and liver spots more apparent in the airport light. I'd camped out in Vera's office several times to pose pointed questions designed to understand Literature Live, but each time Vera would disclose a beginner detail, like, productions are staged in Newton Priors, an English manor house restored to the period, and Monday and Tuesday are the days off. Then she would dart off on a tangent about how whales were getting whacked out by the navy's sonar. I liked Vera immensely, but she distracted easily. I removed the ridiculously heavy bag of books she used to save my seat. "A little light reading." I groaned, pulling a random sample out of the bag: *Real Estate for Dummies*. "What's this for?"

Vera focused through the bottom half of her glasses. "Oh, that's so I can figure out how to do the extension."

"What extension?" I asked. Extension implied *expiration*. Did they *not* have a lease? Did I dare board a plane to fly into a novel that might have no setting? With one foot in Dallas, the other on a departing plane, I would do the big-time splits or splash into the Atlantic. And be eaten by sharks. "Do you *not* have a lease on your venue?" I asked, my voice pitched higher than normal.

In a gesture of nonchalance meant to downplay any potential drama implied by my tone, Vera shrugged. "We *have* an agreement," she said, uncrossing and recrossing her legs away from me.

"When does it expire?" I sounded like the parent.

"Sometime in May." Vera cringed as if expiration dates were distasteful.

"The *May* that comes before June? The May that already happened?"

Vera rolled her eyes. "I'm sure I told you we need an extension of our agreement to use Newton Priors, the country house where we have held our festival for the past thirty years."

I paused to reconsider the security of an empty apartment in Dallas. "How long before we're thrown into the street?"

"Don't be silly, Lily." She smiled at her rhyme and then straightened and faced me. Her hair pulled back, she resembled a ballet master. "You know neither Lady Weston, our patroness, nor the history of this organization. Don't fret about matters you don't understand."

"I took a real estate class, so I understand more than you think."

"Well then, you can help me figure it all out." Vera opened her novel. "An actress with a real estate degree, interesting."

A fat couple holding hands watched CNN, Starbucks balanced on their armrests. A businessman with a heavy briefcase took the last seat opposite me. "Does the Randolph Department have anything to do with this lease renewal?"

"Yes. And it's not exactly a lease. It's an agreement."

I pictured terms of the festival's use penciled on a paper napkin. The businessman across from me spoke on his cell phone, his grown-up manner reminding me of Karen's husband. "FYI, Vera, I took one class, not a degree." She'd blown things up—for the second time. Which brought me to my newest worry: Did Vera *believe* I was a professional actress? I had misled her about my acting background, but she had distorted what I said beyond recognition. I asked her. "You know I'm not a professional actress."

Her eyes went to my necklace. "Nice cross," she said.

I repeated myself. "You know I'm not a professional actress."

"Nice cross," she said again.

"Thank you." I pulled the newly repaired chain out of my scarf. "The last gift my mother gave me."

"Oh." Vera looked closer.

"Before she died, she had her wedding band and some other jewelry melted down to make two crosses, one for me and one for my sister."

"How lovely," Vera said.

My mother began letting go of me the day she gave me the box with the necklace inside. She had been home under the care of a hospice nurse for about a month. I visited every day after work and we spent my visits reading aloud, taking calls from Karen, and making jokes about my dad's cooking. Regular obligations went into suspense, allowing us cozy oblivion while the illness retreated to the background, as if it might leave altogether. But everything changed the day Karen drove up from Houston; my mother must have decided the time had come to say the things she needed to say to us. I wasn't prepared. Her calm acceptance of death frightened me; my throat hurt from the effort to restrain emotion. Karen and I fastened the chains around our necks, listening as she told each of us in turn how much she loved us. The days we were born were the two happiest days of her life. Karen sat close to me and our knees touched Mother's bed as she addressed each of us separately. She reached first for Karen, her hand strangely bare without her wedding rings. "Take care of Lily," she whispered. When she took my hand, I was unable to stop the tears, unable to articulate what I wanted her to know. "My good girl," she said to me. "Everything a mother could want in a daughter." Karen held a tissue to her face; my hot tears flowed as I caressed my mother's hand. When I could speak, I said, "Don't go."

Without the books, the necklace assumed the full burden

of my memories as well as the connection with my mother; I could not let myself lose it. I centered the cross on my neck as they announced our group ready for boarding.

I stowed my carry-on, and rested with *The Mysteries of Udolpho* in my lap, watching passengers wrestle overhead bins. Vera opened her book, turning pages as the plane taxied down the runway. Sun blazed in the window as the aircraft turned, permitting one last look at Dallas. I looked at my open book, reading the same sentence in an endless loop, wondering what sort of person Lady Weston might be, imagining a top-heavy matron smuggling Corgis into restaurants. "How do you know Lady Weston?" I asked.

Vera placed a fingertip on the word she'd just read. "She's a patron of Nigel's from back in the old days. She knew him when he waited tables, dreaming of creating a literary festival. She offered to partner with him. Her contribution is the use of her manor house." After a slight pause, as if she'd debated further disclosure, "At least, it used to be her house. Well, that is, her husband's house."

"What happened?"

"Her husband died a year ago."

"So?"

"Her grandson inherited the house and the title."

Randolph? "Did Randolph inherit the Jane Austen festival as well?" I asked.

"No." Vera looked into the aisle. "But Lady Weston is a Janeite," she whispered. Noting my blank expression she added, "An enthusiastic admirer of Jane Austen's works."

"Is that bad?" I whispered back.

"Only for Nigel, when he has to reconcile Lady Weston's conservationist approach to Austen with the progressive theories of the academics involved with the festival."

I learn something new every day.

Vera leaned in confidentially. "My poor husband, caught between Fanny Wars and a costume ball."

"Fanny Wars?" I asked.

Vera looked at me. "Did you read the essays I gave you?" she asked.

"There was nothing about Fanny Wars in those essays," I said. "That's the sort of thing I'd remember." Vera frowned as air forced its way through circulators, smelling like cheap perfume, blowing wisps of hair into Vera's face. "You're afraid they'll meet at the lease signing and start a Fanny Fight in spite of your husband's best efforts," I said.

Vera returned to her book.

As we climbed into the sky, I imagined Lady Weston duking it out with Professor Plum over the meaning of Fanny's opposition to theatricals in *Mansfield Park*. I spent at least fifteen minutes staring at page 127, wondering how this had happened to me; and then wondered if Professor Plum was married. "So," I said. "The new lease will have to be negotiated with the so-called Randolph Department, and Randolph is not a Janeite. Therefore you are afraid of losing the house for good."

"I am not afraid of any such thing," Vera said, turning off her reading light and closing her eyes.

Staring uncomprehendingly at the pages of my book, I imagined myself as Fanny Price, the poor cousin, brought as a child to live in the home of her rich uncle. I have always loved Fanny Price. Of course, I knew I wouldn't play the lead, but I kept imagining myself in the part. Whenever I read, I always assumed the protagonist's part. This assumption held the mere date of my birth responsible for my present mediocrity. Had I been born in an earlier century, when people appreciated special qualities like mine, I would be beautiful and confident, and travel in higher circles. Edmund would have fallen for me.

The moment to test this idea was fast approaching. A clean slate and the opportunity to reinvent myself lay before me. Nobody here knew the old me. Even with the lease problem, a new world lay ahead where I would finally fit. Surely I'd done the right thing.

Four

On the first page of my new life, I met my first Janeite. She stood inside the entry to the residence hall, a dormitory on loan to the festival where I would reside for the summer. She checked participants off her list and passed out brown envelopes and keys. Like a Greek statue, classical in her beautiful white Regency dress trimmed with red, her ensemble included a sleeveless overgarment that buttoned once just below her bodice. Her hair peeked from beneath a plumed military-style hat, perfect spit curls coiled on her brow. Gloved to her elbows in pure white, she reached out to straighten the hand-lettered sign on her table, "Welcome to Mansfield Park," as the two people in front of me approached her. In spite of slight pressure behind my eyes and a haze of fatigue, the remote possibility that Elizabeth Banks might show up kept me on my toes. I read every name tag that passed, looking for Miss Banks, waiting my turn, leaning against the wall for support. The temperature disoriented me; the bracing chill from open windows rather than air-conditioning led me to believe that in crossing the ocean we'd traveled over a seasonal divide, from summer into fall.

Gary, a twentyish Middle Eastern student who had fetched us from the airport, offered to find me a chair, but he'd done enough already, lugging my bags up the front steps, holding a sign for us in the terminal, and driving us in his itty-bitty car on the wrong side. He kept his window open through the endless repetition of London's fringes and beyond, but closed it on the motorway, a charming turnpike where only flat-faced trucks and undersized cars participated in traffic. Driving between villages, I'd seen spires and hedgerows through my mental fog and imagined people foxhunting. No billboards anywhere.

Vera touched my arm and nodded for me to move forward. She looked a bit nervous, but when I stepped up to the check-in table, the Janeite looked past me at Vera. "Vera," she said, "I didn't see you come in!" She extended her gracious gloved arms, a tiny fringed bag dangled from her wrist. And then I put it together. In order to proceed, we had to get past this woman who held the official list in her possession.

Vera cleared her throat. "What a beautiful dress," Vera said.

The Janeite stepped back and held her skirt for us to admire. "Oh, this is my Emma dress," she said. "But I had the pelisse made"—she indicated the overrobe—"the year we did *Persuasion*. Do you remember? My Anne Elliot pelisse." She smiled, unbuttoning the single button of the pelisse for a better view of the dress. "Oh, Vera, you know how I love this festival and dressing for Dear Jane. From the minute I leave London, all the way on the train, and till the moment I'm home again, every stitch of clothing on my body is Regency." The Janeite glanced at me, still dressed in my flight attendant pantsuit.

"For 'Dear Jane'?" I asked.

Vera said, "Mrs. Russell, I'd like to present Lily Berry." And then to me, "Lily, Mrs. Russell is a very important member of our volunteer staff."

Mrs. Russell bent to raise her skirt, revealing a scrolling design just above the ankle that would have been a tattoo except it was woven into the thick white stocking that covered her legs like something surgery patients wear.

"Lovely," Vera said.

Mrs. Russell straightened, reaching for her heavy hat whose thick ribbons might choke her if the hat were allowed to fall. "Wait till you see my ball gown." And then her face grew serious. She took Vera's hand, moved closer, and whispered, "Magda says we're not to plan a ball. She says the ballroom is booked every evening of the season and we're not to disrupt the schedule."

Vera stood silent, frowning, while people behind us rolled suitcases across the floor.

"You know what this means to us," she said, tilting her head so plaintively I couldn't help but sympathize. "Nigel promised a ball this year but we can't seem to find Nigel anywhere and Magda won't budge."

I wanted to help the Janeites win their ball; there was nothing I wanted more than to dance in a white gown and gloves. But I could understand Nigel's reluctance. A costume ball would be a big distraction. Dresses or discussion?

"I'm so sorry," Vera said as a suitcase thumped up the stairs.

Mrs. Russell whispered, reaching again for the hat with a life of its own, "And as you know, if we don't have the ball this year we may never dance in Newton Priors. Ever." Vera patted Mrs. Russell's gloved hand and I felt a twinge of jealousy over this Janeite's relationship with Jane Austen. Like sibling rivalry.

"Why don't you start small?" I asked. "Have a tea. Then work up to a ball."

Mrs. Russell turned her gaze on me and her expression warmed. "A tea? That's a wonderful idea."

"Well," Vera said slowly. "I'll see if I can't find Nigel and sort things out." Then she added meaningfully, "But first things first." She looked at me. "Let's get Lily into her room. Is Lily Berry on your list?"

"Oh, let's have a look." Her pen traveled up and down the column of names as my uneasiness grew and I knew my name would not be found. A zealous reader of The Six, I'd never considered dressing in costume for "Dear Jane." In fact, I knew nothing about Regency gowns and less about scrolled stockings. But "Dear Jane's" real fans were apparently far more devoted to their passion. As for me, I'd fallen behind in my duty, shown up for the first day completely underdressed and not on the list.

"Hmm, your name doesn't seem to be here."

"Is Elizabeth Banks on your list?" Vera snapped.

Mrs. Russell looked up. "Magda doesn't like us to mix things up."

"Is Miss Banks on the list?" Vera repeated.

I held my cross, twisting the chain around my finger.

Disinclined to entertain the question, she looked again. "Yes, here it is." The pen made a tiny blue dot next to "Banks, Elizabeth." I would have thought she'd use a quill.

"That will be Lily's room," Vera said. "The Banks girl won't be here."

Mrs. Russell hesitated as if considering the angle to her advantage. Magda or Vera? Ball or no ball?

Vera looked at her watch. "Nigel is expecting me," she said, with meaning.

And then Mrs. Russell cautiously handed me the key, clearly on the promise of Vera's proximity to Nigel.

"What about the packet?" I asked, having seen the arrivals ahead of me leave with a brown envelope.

"Oh dear, you can't have her packet." Mrs. Russell smiled, as unyielding as the marble statue she resembled.

"Why not?" I asked, a mere newbie wearing pants.

"Well"—she smiled—"it contains personal compensation paperwork for Miss Banks."

Vera assumed her ballet master pose. "Could you have them prepare a packet for Miss Berry? By tomorrow," Vera suggested as we turned to go.

"Don't forget the tea." Mrs. Russell nodded at me.

If the Janeites considered themselves an exclusive sorority, the guardians of the Jane Austen grail, perhaps I could pledge. Like siblings clamoring for attention, I didn't particularly want to share My Jane Austen with them but I most certainly felt they should share theirs with me. All the same, I wished for a white gown. And gloves.

Climbing the stairs, I noted cream-colored molding painted so many times the crisp edges were gone. The building was probably older than anything in Texas. And Jane Austen's presence felt so much stronger here. She hovered in my periphery now, a gauzy, ethereal being. If I attempted a direct look, she darted to the other side like the floaters I sometimes get in my eyes. Her fragile dress of faded lavender might have come from a dream or a 1950s prom rather than the Regency. Her dark hair fell in loose curls and she favored red lipstick, the color my mother wore when I was very young. When I read her books, Jane Austen spoke to me from the place between the lines of her fiction and I recognized my best friend, as if we'd shared a porch swing on summer evenings and traded confidences in another realm of time and space. She agreed that Martin would change if I was patient. She agreed that my boss was a total jerk and I deserved better. She never looked away to see if someone more interesting had just walked into the room. Through all the long days I spent staring at the walls after Martin abandoned me, she waited patiently, never ditched me out of boredom. Whereas in Texas she'd been confined to remote reaches of my imagination, here in her homeland she grew stronger, commanding a nearer presence in the periphery of my thoughts. Not quite a ghost, more like an imaginary friend.

Gary and I dragged my bags up two flights of stairs, through cavernous halls, over creaking wood floors smelling so musty they diminished the power of Gary's very strong aftershave. Transom windows flared open above doors, and damp air gave me a chill. My simple square room offered two beds with bare mattresses, two closets, a large bureau, and a very old sink with rust stains. Gary set my bags on the floor and hesitated, expecting a tip or a good night kiss. Did he sympathize with the women in period dress or the academics?

"Bye," I said, opening the door, calculating the cost of a custom pelisse. Gary left and I hoisted my large suitcase onto my bed and unloaded the contents. Did everyone here own a pair of snowy white gloves? My hanging clothes took only five inches of the closet bar and my folded clothes filled less than two of the eight dresser drawers. Tiptoeing around, checking out the table, opening a window and a bureau drawer, everything seemed so new to me, bordering on mysterious, hardly related to the books I'd read and the novel I expected to live in. There was even something odd about the light switches and door handles I couldn't resolve.

★ ★ ★

A knock rattled my door and I jumped out of my skin.

"It's me, Gary," the voice of my driver who'd left me less than ten minutes ago called through the open transom. Only it sounded more like, "Ees me, Gahr-ree."

I opened the door a tiny crack and peeked. Gary offered me a small white bakery bag.

"Arabic cookies. For you. Ees very goot."

"Oh, thank you." I reached out and accepted the bag. "That's sweet of you." I gave him the unencouraging smile for door-to-door magazine salesmen.

"I make dem," he said, planting his large brown foreign student sandals closer to my threshold.

"You made the cookies?" I peeked into the bag.

He nodded. "Middle Eastern Bakery in Hedingham. My job." He said something in Arabic, and then translated for himself, smiling, his white teeth contrasting with his swarthy skin. He could be a young Omar Sharif except for the accent. "You going to the pub?" he asked.

"Not yet." I backed away. "I'll see you later," I said as his face fell. "Good-bye." I waved, closing the door, listening as the muffled creak of his footsteps faded.

When I was sure he was gone, I walked over to the pub alone.

From the steps of my residence hall I enjoyed a perfect view of the town below: a double row of antique limestone buildings situated parallel to the river. Double-decker buses tottered up the hill, and tourists, my future audiences, wandered among faded pastel shop doors. An unfamiliar chill sparked the air, and clouds clogged the sky. The pub, a whitewashed two-story stucco building with multiple chimneys and abundant creeper, stood between the main street and the river. A charming shingle on the street announced: "The Grey Hare." Flaming carriage lanterns, smaller than those on Texas McMansions, flanked the door illuminating a hand-lettered sign proclaiming, "Literature Live Staff Night." That would be me, I thought proudly. Inside, a horseshoe-shaped bar dominated the room, its pewter countertop patched and polished. Behind, a sign on the mirror proclaimed "Bloody Mary Bar Every Sunday" with a price I couldn't yet convert in my head.

Searching among the bare boards, wooden panels, and high-backed settles, I sought a familiar face, all the while scanning name tags for the dreaded Miss Banks. A stuffed rabbit collection crowded a shelf behind the bar, illustrating the pub's name: the Grey Hare. On the wall next to me hung a familiar portrait of an old man in a powdered wig, labeled "Dr. Johnson." Below, someone had handwritten, "The Grey Hair." Several other gray-hair portraits hung around the bar. I ordered a glass of ale, proud to be there, surprised that no one was in costume. How silly to think of finding a Janeite in a pub.

Some guys next to me at the bar spoke to each other in erudite phrases like "the origins of informality." One struck me as a grad student, having mentioned his thesis; the other couldn't have been over nineteen. Their conversation flowed around me until I cleared my throat rather conspicuously and asked what they were talking about. They said, "incorporeal hereditament" as if I should have understood from context. When I asked what that was, they said, "intangible rights that are inheritable."

"Oh, that." I sipped my ale thoughtfully and imagined myself in an improv exercise. During a break in their dialogue, I mentioned Lockley's interesting theory on the roots of incorporeal hereditament in *The Approach of Modernity*, title and author invented by me. I made sure to turn away before they could ask to borrow my copy. But as I turned, I found myself looking into the eyes of a short, dark man in wire-rim glasses. His name tag said Omar.

"Are you new here?" he asked, obviously Arabic like Gary, dark hair, dark skin, no trace of the Middle East in his accent, but maybe a hint of New Jersey. I felt drawn to his open face, his diminutive size, and his generous regard. "I overheard you talking with those friendly guys," he said. I warmed to the sarcasm in his voice. "What are you doing here?" he asked. He raised his glass, pausing midway to his mouth waiting for my response.

"I'm an actress," I said. "And you?"

"I'm an English teacher," Omar said. "I help prepare the scripts and teach a writing workshop."

"The scripts?" I asked. Maybe he knew what part I would play.

"I adapt Austen's novels for Literature Live," Omar said, emitting a titter of insider animation.

"Which novel is your favorite?" I asked.

Omar sipped from his mug. "Personally, I don't have one," he said, his jaws locked, making his remark sound especially snooty. Surely, he was gay.

"Really?" I said.

"I'm with Mark Twain, I'd like to dig Jane Austen up and hit her over the head with her own shinbone." Omar stole a sideways glance, then turned to me and whispered, "Austen's work doesn't adapt well or easily."

"Why?"

"Well, because"—Omar assumed a serious expression, a teacher explaining to a student—"when you adapt Austen's novels for stage, you lose the interiority, the sparkling narrative if you will, which, in my opinion, leaves us with nothing but a dreadful romance. Think of the films." Omar leaned toward me again. "Shaw's my field of study."

I nodded.

Omar invited me to join him at a table in the back where the noise level and general animation increased. Unfortunately, no one in the large group wore a name tag. Omar raised his voice to seize the group's attention. "I would like to introduce a fellow actress"—he put his hand on my arm and read my name tag—"Lily Berry."

They all looked at me expecting something, so—I waved. Then a man with a beautiful smile stepped forward and extended his hand.

"Damn glad to meet you," he said. "Name's Hamlet." Hair randomly bleached, buttons on his plaid shirt misaligned, his smile so contagious I wanted to laugh at *whatever* he was saying whether I could hear it over the din or not. Hamlet's eyes locked with mine even as his arm rose in a professional flourish, indicating the man on his right, "Allow me to present Veal Cutlet." Hamlet's other arm extended like a conductor calling on the brass, toward the couple at the end of the table. "Country Ribs, there." A tall, lanky man nodded at me gravely. "And his little Pork Chop." The woman turned to her partner, selected a finger, and began gnawing.

I enjoyed the joke and his lovely British accent until Hamlet's mischievous eyes met mine, expecting me to reciprocate in kind. "And *you* are?" he said, and I knew I was supposed to be some sort of meat. No time to unwind the jet-lag gauze straitjacketing my brain, I smiled. "I'm *still* Lily Berry," I said, adding, like a beauty contestant with a Southern drawl, "From the great state of Texas," applying specific gusto to the word *great*. I couldn't read the expression on Hamlet's face. Fearing he might expose me for a fraud, the suspense was unbearable. I looked to Omar for a cue but he had started a conversation with someone else. Hamlet raised his arm again and I flinched like a needy dog expecting to be hit. To my utter astonishment he opened his mouth and began singing to me. Conversations halted and heads turned as his rich baritone filled the pub; even the people in the front looked to see what was happening.

"*Oh I wish I wa-as in the land of cotton,*" he sang, pausing to savor the full effect of the longing he expressed. Some began singing harmony. "*Old times there are not forgotten.*" He took my hands in his as if this were a love song. "*Look away, look away, look away Dixie land.*" He immediately segued into "The Yellow Rose of Texas," but mixed it up with "Yankee Doodle." Omar winked, as if Hamlet serenading me were normal behavior. The bartenders looked mildly pleased, as if this sort of thing happened when you associated with actors. But I felt myself on fire because, as an actress, I would be expected to improvise something original, soon.

"*The Yellow Rose of Texas is the only gal for me,*" Hamlet continued, swinging me around in a little colonial do-si-do. Others joined the act, humming the accompaniment. Country Ribs and his little Pork Chop performed backup vocals; another actor played his air guitar, closing his eyes for the more challenging riffs. Veal Cutlet on percussion used spoons to beat the table as one of his mates played the air trombone. Others provided vocal accompaniment and stomping feet; the whole front of the room improvised to Hamlet's crazy medley while I scrambled for an idea. Unless I thought of something quick, it would be very obvious who was *not* an actress in the room.

Hamlet went down on one knee and seated me on the other. I managed to smile and raise my arms in a little shimmy, my butt bones digging into his thigh, ideas racing. Although I never played a lead, I memorized all the solos and sang them to my bathroom mirror. I stood and launched into "People Will Say We're in Love," as if I'd come straight from Broadway, the breath released from my diaphragm, flowing over my vocal cords exactly the way my voice teacher had taught me years ago. I felt like a pro and Hamlet crooned his part, making up words as he sang. We held hands as if we really were Curly and Laurey.

Then I heard the words of *Oklahoma!* coming from the sidelines, gaining momentum, the beat growing stronger, wind sweeping the plains, hawks flying in circles. My heart swelled and I wanted to laugh and cry as I joined in, singing the harmony when I could find the note. We sang and danced, arms in the air, feet stomping; I felt such a sense of belonging in this moment with these people, right up to the final okay!

Hamlet cradled me so far backward I had no sense of balance and no ability to right myself. Then he planted a real kiss on my mouth. He tasted bitter, like ale. Huge applause erupted, encouraging my inner protagonist. When Hamlet prepared to stand, I pulled him back and wrapped my arms around his neck for another kiss. And kicked a leg in the air. The room loved it.

"Well done, Lily," Hamlet whispered. We bowed and then Hamlet took my hands in his. "I think I'm in love." He snapped his fingers. "Let's improvise. Omar, get a pen, this will be good."

A new group of people entered our section of the room and chatter resumed.

"Lily," Hamlet said, slightly breathless, "I have an idea. Let's work up an act. You and me."

I smiled; no idea what he was talking about but I liked the way he said "you and me."

"Shall we have a go at the follies?"

"Yes," I said. The arrival of the new people interrupted the flow. Hamlet let go of me as a striking woman approached him lips first. He held her in a tango dip and I watched their bodies move, so precise and fluid it seemed they must have practiced earlier. I hoped she already had a partner for the follies. After that, people moved around and old friends greeted each other.

I asked Omar, "Is Newton Priors far from here?"

"About a mile."

"Can I go there?"

"What for?" He made a face.

I felt very comfortable with Omar. "I want to see it before we're evicted."

"What are the follies?" I asked, approaching Newton Priors in the mounting gloom of half light via a narrow path lined with tall shrubs on both sides.

"The follies," Omar said, "is an evening in late July when alumni visit and we present a talent show among ourselves."

"Like playing the piano or singing a song?"

"Not exactly," Omar said. "It derives from the impulse of Jane Austen's family skit nights. Most acts have something to do with her." Omar told me that Hamlet's real name was Sixby Godwin, a professional actor who studied at the Bristol Old Vic Theatre School, currently auditioning with the RSC, the Royal Shakespeare Company.

"He's auditioning? What about Literature Live?" I asked, locking my jaws to stifle a jet-lag yawn.

"When he gets on with the RSC, he'll be out of here. And he *will* get on, you can depend on it. He's very talented."

I knew that. "But why leave?"

Omar smiled patronizingly. "Darling," he said, "surely you don't expect him to go down with the ship." Omar extended an arm. "Prepare to feast your eyes," he said.

Trees and plump shrubs on either side of the path still obscured the view. Only a hint of red brick peeked through the leaves. A sign appeared on our right announcing Newton Priors, open to the public the first Sunday of the month. "Open to the public?" I asked.

"They get a tax break for sharing," Omar said, and stopped walking.

There before us, the grand house rose from the earth in majesty.

"Queen Anne in the English Baroque style." Omar gestured.

"It's lovely." The main door centered between two wings curved gracefully at the ends, constructed of deep red stone, face full of tall windows and lovely bays rendering the house more vulnerable than the Palladian boxes with their perfectly square corners. The central tower climbed three stories, crowned by a filigreed stone balustrade filtering the sky. But mostly I got a sense of serenity, very still and very quiet. Soft green grass surrounded the house, reaching out to the place where the lovely gardens began. Soft and fine like the grass on a putting green or a carpet. "Look, bats." I pointed at winged specks flying from the roof. A steeple rose not far from the house. "Does the church belong with the estate?"

"Yes, St. James's Church. The tower dates from the early sixteenth century and the bells from 1350. The Weston family rebuilt the rest of it in the late 1800s."

So wonderful to have my own personal church so close, like having a bit of my mother at Literature Live with me. The problem: how to give Omar the slip and indulge a solitary church visit. I felt my neck for the cross but it wasn't there. Sheer panic seized me before I remembered I'd placed it in my jewelry pouch for safekeeping.

Omar said, "Conservationists are toiling around the clock

to get ready for opening day. Just don't expect them to fix anything." Omar's remarks came with a side of sarcasm.

"Who is Magda anyway?" I asked.

"More like *what* is she." He laughed. "We're *sure* she's not human. We *think* she drinks Janeite blood. We *know* she can smell fear. And Archie loves her."

"Who's Archie?"

"Her immediate supervisor."

"Oh."

"Here's some good advice: Avoid eye contact with Magda."

"Is she from the Middle East?" I asked.

"Lebanese." Omar held a gate open, admitting me onto the immediate grounds. "She was once a student of Archie's but she currently resides in Ann Arbor, where she intimidates freshman English students."

"You know her from there?"

"Yes, we're in the same department. Archie worships her." I waited.

"When he's not at home with his wife and children in London," he added, offering his arm as we reached the steps.

"Oh," I said.

We climbed the oversized sloping stone steps, worn from age and moisture, to the formal double-door entrance.

"And don't let her catch you smoking," he said. "Her friend died of lung cancer—a nonsmoker—last year, and she takes smoking as a personal affront. If you see Archie smoking, look the other way quick." Omar held the door for me. "After you."

"I don't smoke."

Inside, the wide planks creaked and sloped. A marble placed on the floor would roll into a corner. The door handles weren't where I expected them to be, and paint on the ceiling medallion peeled and flaked onto the floor. This wasn't a stately mansion where you pay $16.50 for a tour of immaculate rooms decorated in Smithsonian perfection. But I could feel My Jane Austen in this place. Omar became my tour guide, occasionally abandoning sarcasm to teach me something.

"Please note the whimsical fault lines over the doorway to the ballroom. Repairs were last attempted in 1920." My eyes ascended the fourteen-foot ceilings, taking note of the cracking plaster, the first thing to greet patrons upon arrival. The walls needed paint. Omar showed me a bald spot in the hallway where, in the 1960s, an official of the Historical Society had gouged a sample of the plaster to test for composition.

Omar gestured to dark, somber portraits in gilt frames, suspended by wire from a line of molding. "Ancestors, mostly," he said. On the opposite wall, floor-to-ceiling lace curtains dressed the windows like spinsters left over from the Depression. I sensed an attitude of flexibility in our production, a handmade flavor to the house.

Omar noticed my glance at the floor. "The rugs have been taken out for a beating." We entered a small room off the front hall. "This is the Freezer," he said. "Your greenroom where you will escape the scrutiny of patrons while you spend quality time with fellow actors cramming for the next scene. Or checking your e-mail."

The Freezer reminded me of an oversized coat-check room furnished with mismatched contemporary sofas better suited for a fraternity house, a lime green area rug, and faux Danish modern end tables; it was the only room lacking a fireplace. A noble mahogany library table and sideboard waited here, slumming while a better placement was scouted.

"That's Magda's desk," Omar said, pointing to a surface buried in papers and books. "And that's everyone else's." He indicated a table, bare except for a previous-generation computer and monitor. I could imagine actors lounging with scripts in this room, memorizing Jane Austen's prose. Or checking their e-mail.

"How long has it been since anyone really lived here?" I asked, following Omar back to the entry and turning left at the archway.

"Nineteen forty-five," he said. "And this is the ballroom."

"Wow." I gazed into the cavernous hall. A couple in deep discussion sat at a folding table erected just inside the door.

"Hello." Omar waved. The middle-aged man waved in our direction without looking up. Omar whispered to me, "The scenes are presented in here, some of the lectures, and all of the big meetings. The ballroom is one of the few rooms in the house wired for electricity." I imagined actors performing against the backdrop of the raised-panel wall, patrons seated in rows of folding chairs.

"No electricity?" That explained the orange electric cords snaking along the floor, taped over thresholds; powering the rest of the house. Surely the cords would be less obvious by opening day.

"That's Archie," he said, waving to the man with the gray comb-over ponytail and facial hair. "And Magda," a woman who looked young, twenty-nine or thirty, did not wave but kept talking to Archie, her hand on a stack of paper, obviously the same Magda who was giving the women in period attire so much grief over their ball. Magda wore a scarf covering her hair but the rest of her clothing was typical college garb: black jeans and T-shirt. She was strikingly beautiful, even partially hidden by the scarf. Her lack of visible hair called attention to her clear brown skin and perfect white teeth. At the moment she looked rather agitated, thumping the pages in front of her, speaking with a pronounced Arabic accent.

Omar whispered, "Magda and Archie run the enactments."

"Is that the script?" I whispered back.

Magda hit the stack of paper with the flat of her hand. "I don't get it." Magda leaned away from Archie as if to see him better. "Are you backing off?" She waited. "You said I'd have complete freedom to interpret in accordance with my reading." Her words came out clear and distinct, as though the accent was the proper pronunciation, obviously a teacher.

Archie closed his eyes, reminiscent of Martin. "The radical approach doesn't bother me," Archie said calmly.

"Then what is it?" Magda asked, her mouth open.

"It's the blatant lack of consideration for over half our constituency."

Magda jumped in, "I don't give a rat's ass for the Janeites."

"You should," he said. "They're paying the piper."

Magda reared her head back. "I said I'd babysit Miss Banks for the summer, but I won't compromise." Magda sighed. "Next you'll tell me you love Fanny Price."

"I love Fanny Price," I said this to Omar, but they all heard me and turned to see who had spoken so precipitously. Magda's gaze expressed absolute wonder.

"What did she say?" Archie smiled, not sure he heard correctly.

"Never mind." Magda raised a hand.

"She likes Fanny Price?" Archie turned to focus on me but Magda snapped her fingers at him.

"Brave woman," he said, and I smiled back. At the time, I was oblivious to the passion inspired by *Mansfield Park*'s protagonist. But any hope of aligning myself with these two was now dashed; I might be killed in a Fanny War.

"Would you excuse us?" Magda asked, glaring at me.

"No problem," I said, flashing the indulgent smile I reserved for childish adults.

Omar was already in the hall.

"Miss Banks isn't coming, is she?" I asked, fearing the worst. "Vera told me she wasn't."

"I've no idea," Omar said, steering through a dark room. "Lady Weston locked these doors in 1945, after the war, and moved to modern digs in Kent. She kept up visits in the summers, hoping her son would eventually restore Newton Priors as his residence, but that didn't work out."

"Why not?"

"He got himself and his wife killed while driving in the Cotswolds."

"Driving in the countryside?"

"Have you seen how they drive on country roads? Nope," he said, as we walked, "they died young, leaving two darling orphans for Grandma to raise." Omar paused by the door. "No one has had the time to redecorate or change anything. No central heat or air."

I stopped walking and asked, "So Randolph Lockwood is one of the children Lady Weston raised?"

"Yes; and his sister, Philippa. I'm sure you'll have an opportunity to meet them soon. This is the music room," Omar said, indicating a parlor, another tall boxy room with a fireplace where a ratty sofa kept company with an antique piano. A small bust of Mozart sat on a bookshelf. "You will find drawers and shelves in this house still full of household detritus from 1900 and earlier." Suddenly, I was Catherine Morland snooping through drawers to discover the dead mother's last letter to Randolph.

"Nothing interesting, I've looked." Omar pointed upward where curling shreds of yellowed paper dangled in the dim upper reaches. "Please note the original wallpaper," he said.

I looked up and felt a burst of excitement, ready to begin my new life among musty drawers and peeling wallpaper.

"Oh, and Alex brought his old record player." Omar pointed out the antique stereo plugged into an orange cord, a stack of records nearby, "so you can listen to vinyl LPs in your spare time." Bach topped the pile of albums.

"I'll remember to do that." I followed Omar through a narrow hallway leading to a room where dusty books crammed the shelves. "Why don't they replace the wallpaper?"

Omar laughed, then without answering he stopped and stared at me. "What are you looking for, Lily?"

His question surprised me, and for a moment, I wondered if he *wasn't* gay. "What do you mean?"

He adjusted his glasses. "What do you expect to get out of this summer? Expand your repertoire? Develop an accent?"

"Oh." I had to think. "Yes. Expand my repertoire, exactly."

Omar waited.

"Actually"—I gestured with both arms—"I'm interested in working among actors who also read books; who understand the meaning of *only connect*." This was important to me.

Omar winced.

"You know, E. M. Forster, *Howard's End*," I said, holding my breath.

Omar folded his arms in concentration. "As in, 'connect the beast and the monk; the prose and the passion'?"

Now it was my turn to be confused. I'd read the book long ago, actually seen the movie more recently. Perhaps I should brush up before holding forth to English teachers. "Yes," I said, vowing to find the book at my earliest opportunity. Maybe there was a copy of *Howard's End* in here somewhere.

Omar walked; I followed. Shells, rocks, stuffed birds, and a statue of a shepherd boy kept company with the books on the shelves, all collected by someone long gone, the house a living relic, a repository of the Weston family, their spirit lingering like dust on the books.

"From a photo taken in the 1920s, it is clear that nothing, down to the peacock feathers in that urn over there"— Omar pointed to the corner—"has been changed in nearly a century."

I had a strong feeling right then that My Jane Austen walked the rooms with us and that rather than old and dusty, the place was green and growing, full of hope and possibilities of fulfillment. Another passage led us to what appeared to be a kitchen, tacked onto the end of the house.

"This room was added at the turn of the century." Omar pointed to a pair of odd faucets, connected to metal pipes snaking over the wall's surface. "The sink hasn't been used since 1945." My eyes found a patch of light where settling had caused a gap in the wall large enough for a hand to reach through. I thought of Fanny Price exiled to her shabby home in Portsmouth. The room had no counters, just dark bare wood, shelves holding pale china, and racks for towels. Baskets gathered dust and a rack of old teacups hung on the wall. Mrs. Russell and her volunteers would have a hard time making tea in here. No wonder Lady Weston's daughter fled. Again, My Jane Austen flitted through my peripheral vision, looking pale in her lavender dress.

"What do you understand *only connect* to mean?" Omar asked. "I'm not sure I follow."

"Oh." I cleared my throat, wondering if he could sense Jane Austen in the room or if it was just me. "It's like *really* connecting," I said. "Connecting in an emotional, rather than worldly, sense." Sounded plausible to me. "The way readers connect with books, actually; on the higher plane of ideas. I hope to find people here with whom I can connect, on that level."

"Oh." He pushed his glasses up and folded his arms. "That's not what I understood it to mean."

"Oh?" I braced myself.

"No, I understood Forster advocating that people connect what they profess to believe with their actions." Omar looked up at me. "This requires self-knowledge."

"Oh."

"Which is why I was confused you would come *here* to meet people who understand." He walked out of the kitchen back into the hallway. "Actors? Literature Live is the Grand Central Terminal of disconnected personalities," he said. "And this place is Fantasy Island for Janeites."

I thought of Mrs. Russell wearing her costume on the train.

"You've got your work cut out." Omar chuckled, which seemed better than lingering on my misunderstanding. Omar led us back into the ballroom, where we found a man jumping on the stairs.

"Hey, John." Omar waved. Omar introduced me to John Owen, the project's conservationist. "A friend of Nigel's."

"Don't mind me," John Owen said. "I'm only testing the stairs."

Omar put his hands in his pockets and we watched the man bounce on one step, and then move down to the next. I noticed he was wearing an odd combination of clothing: pants from an old office suit, a dingy soccer shirt, and sneakers with Velcro fasteners. "What do you expect to find?" Omar asked.

We strained to hear him whisper, slightly breathless, "A noticeable bounce may mean structural problems."

"Is it bouncing?" Omar asked.

He stared past us in concentration. "Not sure." He went back up to a previous step. "There may be something here." He examined the steps, going from one to the other, jumping and trying again.

We took the stairs to the second floor while Omar explained that John Owen had been part of the original deal with Lady

Weston. "He putters around all summer with his crew of grad students who think they're having a symposium, fixing things, making sure the place isn't falling into irretrievable disrepair, in return for Literature Live's use of the property."

I smiled. "The students *think* they're having a symposium?"

"And they pay for the privilege." Omar gestured to a lot of closed doors in the second floor hallway. "None of this is open to the public. Some of these bedrooms serve as private offices for Archie and Magda and the lead actors, and since I'm not sure which are which, I just stay downstairs unless summoned." As we walked down the hallway, Omar grinned, nudging me with his elbow. "I don't think John Owen grasps the meaning of *only connect*, do you?"

"I think you're making fun of me," I said, "and we've only known each other since six."

Omar touched the handle of another narrow door and explained about the third floor. "Off-limits," he said, "just a lot of dead furniture up there, not interesting."

I sensed My Jane Austen touching the handle from the other side of the door.

"Do you think we'll get a lease extension?" I asked, imagining the first real lines in my novel life interrupted by a real estate broker with a sign and a hammer, wondering if Omar had felt anything because he was holding his own hand.

"Depends. The taxes are exorbitant, and the new lord needs the cash to finance his bar bills." Omar started down the stairs. "The offices are over here in the east wing." Omar led us down a curving hall and opened a door but we didn't go in. "Nigel's office, the conference room, and library. Not interesting, just the admin heart of the festival." Omar turned and bumped into me. "Let's go, it's dark," he said.

"But we must have seen less than half."

"Tomorrow is another day, Scarlett. You can't see anything in the dark anyway."

The great wooden door, not locked as feared, responded to my push, admitting me into the chilly stone nave of St. James's Church. I'd gently disengaged Omar by professing a need for more exercise, although he likely sensed I was up to something. Pulling the door shut, I waited for my eyes to adjust, dim evening light filtering through the ruby and cobalt of stained glass, delighted to sense that My Jane Austen was still with me.

Tiptoeing carefully over uneven stone to a dark wooden pew, I sat, breathing the musty air deeply through my nose, exhaling through my mouth, a visitor in a quiet tomb. A narrow shelf built into the pew before me held the diminutive Book of Common Prayer, the English version, smaller than those back home. The regular size hymnal hung over the shelf's edge, too big to fit. A needlepoint cushion hung from a hook below. Near the front of the church, stone effigies, perhaps the First Baron of Weston and his wife, slept in a bed of marble, their hands clasped in prayer these many years. I tried to be quiet but the pew creaked with every movement. Another entombed body lay prone in the far corner, all alone, facing the wall with the great window. Lifting the needlepoint cushion from its hook, I knelt and whispered the words from the funeral liturgy: "All we go down to the dust; yet even at the grave we make our song. Alleluia. Alleluia." I repeated the phrase over and over, with a special heartfelt emphasis on "yet even at the grave." Usually the repetition would begin to soothe me and I would become lost in the words, but it wasn't working for me now. I kept thinking about the ancient sleepers and the universal smell of mustiness and how it smelled old but still alive. Still present among the living, but separate. At times like this, the utter permanence of death came home to me like a thick iron wall that closed forever between my mother and me. I could never tell her about Sue or ask her advice about my father or anything else. Death did not negotiate.

No longer whispering, I tried speaking quietly, "All we go down to the dust." Unable to focus on the prayer, I surrendered to the excitement growing in my spirit: the feeling of being in deep communion with a great mind. *Even if* the volunteers were a sorority of secret stockings like those of Mrs. Russell, and *even if* the academics were mostly incoherent to me, this festival was all about the book, *Mansfield Park*. I thought I knew everything there was to know about Jane Austen and her book. But here was a whole new rich, promising world opening up for me, something I hadn't been aware of two days ago. The novel was alive. This was what I had meant about living in a novel. We were all alive *in Mansfield Park*. This could never have happened in Texas.

And from this great distance, I could see clearly that Martin didn't *get* me. He'd never read Forster; he thought *only connect* was a dot game. Being married to Martin would mean sharing him for weekends of hunting and paintball. His ideal vacation would be scuba diving with the guys in some oversubscribed Central American destination. Perhaps I generalized, but it seemed Martin, as well as all the men in my social circle, relied on the same slim catalogue when choosing interests and vocations. We met in a bookstore, yes. But he wasn't buying books. He was checking out the chicks who bought books. I kept squeezing myself into underwhelming romances with men like Martin because I wanted one so badly. But they never had enough gravitas to survive on their own merits. In these relationships, we parked in each other's lives until something like holiday travel interrupted the flow, and when we got back into town, we couldn't remember where we'd left our cars.

Something creaked. I held my breath, and waited for a repeat of the sound I'd heard. Something besides me had moved. Although I thought I was alone in the dark, I couldn't really be sure. It sounded like something alive in another pew but I saw no one. The creak happened again. I sat up straight. My scalp tingled and fear gripped me. What if the tombs opened up? Too late to hide. From the front of the room, a dim figure rose from a pew, Heathcliff hiding in the dark. I scooted closer to the wall, bumping an overhanging hymnal on the shelf in front of me, sending it to the floor with a mighty resounding thud. He looked over at the disturbance and our eyes met. Young and serious, thirty by my guess, wearing jeans and T-shirt, probably frightened by my chanting and afraid to be in the same dark church with me. He had been lying on the pew. Now he stepped over the dead interred in the stone floor, in a church where protagonists had brooded for centuries, their rich stories lingering in the damp fertile air, encouraging all forms of yearning and despair, perhaps in my very pew.

I'd arrived at a place in the cosmos where I could connect, at last.

Five

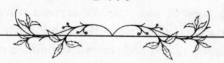

*T*hose arriving at the orientation meeting were forced to squint as morning sun cast white rectangles of light on the wall above the massive stone fireplace. As they squinted, I took a good look at their name tags, bracing myself for the possible arrival of Miss Banks. Urns of coffee exhaled a cozy morning smell and green plastic yard chairs crowded around small tables facing the stage where, in a few days, actors would perform for the public. A staff person tested a microphone while someone placed water bottles at each place on the table behind her. So far, no Banks.

I'd been awake since 3:10 A.M., impatient to begin my new life. I couldn't wait for costumes and scripts so I could start protagonizing in a British accent. My Texas life seemed so far away, and I wondered if the man from the church would be at the meeting. Vera waved to me from her table across the room where she sat with a group of seniors. A man with billowing gray hair and hiking boots, his collar turned up rakishly as if he might be famous in literary or academic circles, sat next to a woman in a flowery skirt, a dog at her sandaled feet. Perhaps these were the founding board members Vera had mentioned. They drank coffee and gazed fondly at the arriving participants. Surely each board member held a position on Fanny Price.

The noise grew as more people arrived consulting their orientation packets, fetching coffee, and settling at tables where one person talked and the others nodded or expressed amazement. A ponytailed guy with a clipboard approached and asked, "Are you Anne?" A flustered woman dropped a heavy book bag on the floor at the table next to me and told her companion, "I looked everywhere." Accumulated sound traveled up to the top of the high ceiling, and then down again. I wished people would settle so we could get started. Everyone had an orientation folder except me. Was it obvious I wasn't a real actress?

I scrunched a plastic chair into the circle around a table, having recognized Pork Chop from last night's improv at the pub. Her name tag said Nikki. My chair arms touched chairs on both sides of me as I listened to the conversation concerning the lease renewal, and how someone believed Philippa Lockwood, Lady Weston's granddaughter, held all the cards regarding the festival's future at Newton Priors. Nikki consulted her watch. "Wasn't this meeting set for half eight?" she asked the group.

"My schedule said eight-thirty," I said.

They all looked at me; no one blinked or smiled.

"Oh," I said, "right."

A group of excited children sat together, three girls and two boys, and none of their name tags said Banks. Proud mothers hovered over the child actors who surely played the young cousins in early scenes. Gary the Middle Eastern driver brought more plastic chairs and Omar appeared in the doorway. I wished I could sit with him.

The people on the stage greeted each other and stalled. Sixby sat next to the tango dancer he'd kissed in the pub. Hard to believe he asked me to perform in the follies with him. Magda wore not just a scarf, but an entire full-length caftan and black robe. She and the staff person huddled over an enormous key ring like characters from Tolkien's Middle Earth.

"Why is Magda dressed like that?" I asked Nikki, who maneuvered her chair to face the stage. I could understand wearing it if you *had* to, but she'd been dressed in jeans last night.

Nikki frowned as if this was something I should have known. "She wears the abaya to be in solidarity with women who are forced to wear such attire in the Middle East and North Africa—and to raise *our* consciousness of that fact."

I nodded.

"Actually, her university is considering her proposal for a seminar on Islamic feminism." Nikki unscrewed her water bottle. "You've met Gary? Her brother," she said. "Real name's Gamal and he's seeking a visa extension"—Nikki smiled—"in case you didn't know."

The sound of metal against glass caught our attention and the buzz of conversation faded. My stomach jumped; the moment had arrived at last. This was it. I wanted to listen. I wanted to know everything all at once.

"Good morning, and welcome to the thirty-first season of Literature Live. For those of you I've not met, my name is Nigel Saintsbury, and I am the founder and executive director of Literature Live." So this was Vera's husband, a white-haired man in patched tweeds who looked as though he might don wellies and walk the moors with hunting dogs.

He winked at Vera—The Look. They were fond of each other. Why didn't they live together? "You are very welcome here," he told us. "We know your work: actors, writers, and teachers."

They must have some kind of atypical marriage. Vera visits Nigel in the summer.

"You are the cream of the crop. We had to turn away people we'd like to work with."

Nigel's gaze traveled to the back of the room and we all turned to see a balding but confident man walking in, making his way through the tables. The guy I'd seen in the dark church walked in with him. The one from the church hit his head like a comedian and the other smiled, but I had a feeling the dynamics between them were usually reversed. "Today, I have the pleasure of introducing our patron," Nigel said. "Although we deeply regret Lady Weston's illness, we are delighted that Randolph Lockwood, the Eleventh Baron of Weston, is present to bestow her annual welcome."

The Randolph Department. But which man was Randolph? The guy from the church or the one with the deeply receding hairline? Everyone applauded and I experienced great relief that it was the hairline guy. Casually dressed in jeans and blazer, his white T-shirt peeking over the V-neck of his sweater, he smiled, walking to the podium as if he did this sort of thing a lot and his premature lack of hair was our problem, not his. I'd met his type before. The fact that he was not handsome in the accepted sense didn't bother him in the least. His profound powers of attraction stemmed from enormous confidence and intelligence: his type rarely played the straight man and never found himself at a loss for words.

Randolph cleared his throat, summoning gravitas. "On behalf of my grandmother, whose health prevents her from being with you today"—he was the prince now—"I welcome you to Newton Priors, my family's ancestral home, for another season of Literature Live." I imagined him mocking us in a bar later. "Her Ladyship is a person of many and varied interests," he said, "but none so capture Lady Weston's enthusiasm as the enactment of Jane Austen's novels. It has been her greatest pleasure to know you are here and to visit you each year at Newton Priors." I'd never seen an aristocrat. He was perhaps on the young side of thirty-five and spoke with a lovely accent. Probably a great dancer.

I glanced back at the guy from the church, curious to see his expression. His brow indeed furrowed attractively in concentration, a knowing smile on his lips betrayed familiarity with Randolph's remarks. I felt My Jane Austen in the background, taking notes, writing on her little squares of ivory fastened like a fan, the eighteenth-century word processor.

"Her Ladyship wishes to acknowledge deep appreciation for the financial support of the Banks Family Grant, as well as the dedication of time and talent on the part of so many staff members and volunteers who enable the festival's continued operation." I noticed he didn't thank the expensive actors. "And of course, the festival would not exist without the leadership and vision of Nigel Saintsbury, for whom we are most grateful." Everyone applauded, but it seemed Nigel had been added as an afterthought.

"To change course a bit"—he paused a moment while we adjusted our headings—"Vera will be taking a look at operations this summer, generating ideas to upgrade and maximize the utility of Newton Priors."

I sat up straight.

"And I invite all of you—Vera has mentioned that some of you have interesting ideas—to share your thoughts."

Had Vera told Lord Weston my ideas—about firing the expensive actors and selling lecture subscriptions?

"We mustn't rest on our laurels," he continued. "Even Jane Austen can stand a fresh approach every thirty years or so." This got a laugh. "Please know that we have the utmost respect for your talent and dedication," Randolph said. "And will carefully consider the ideas you bring to the table concerning the festival's future."

I sensed a threat of endangerment.

"And now," he said, raising his hands in princely benediction, "with all best wishes from Lady Weston; my sister, Philippa; and myself, let the season begin." Randolph shook hands with Nigel and a few others, darting looks to the left and right, aware that paparazzi lurk everywhere. The church guy waited in the back of the room, arms folded across his chest, and once Randolph reached him they departed the way they had come, taking some of the energy from the room when they left.

Nigel introduced Sixby, the lead actor and assistant creative director for Literature Live—my Hamlet from the pub and follies partner—who stood to open the meeting with a reading. In Texas, we'd be getting a prayer.

Sixby read from near the end of *Mansfield Park*. "'Timid, doubting, anxious as she was, it was still impossible that such tenderness as hers should not, at times, hold out the strongest hope of success.'"

I hung on the turn of Sixby's head, the way he said *hope*. He took my breath away; I wanted to get inside the words with him. Austen's prose never sounded so beautiful in my head. Where did he get the ideas for the inflection? Goose bumps prickled my arms and legs, and I wished he would go on, but he stopped, and everyone clapped thunderously. I made a mental note to get the book and read that part again—in his accent.

"Close as he could get to a love scene in *Mansfield Park*," Nikki snarked.

Nigel looked at the floor, showing us the thinning hair on his crown as we took a breath with him. When he looked up, he said solemnly, "We gather every summer—in this place— brought together by the work of the great artist Jane Austen." He paused after each phrase to allow his words to float down and settle on us like snowflakes. I felt certain My Jane Austen enjoyed this as much as I did. "When I explain to others what we do, I like to borrow the words of John Burroughs: 'Literature is an investment of genius which pays dividends to all subsequent times.'" He paused. "Jane Austen gave us her genius. We are simply the clerks whose job it is to pay out dividends to *our time.*

"We return to the text again and again," Nigel continued, "in order to penetrate the meanings with which Austen charged her books." I stopped breathing in order to concentrate on his point; did his returning to the text idea include Magda and her radical interpretation of the subtext? "The words are the medium through which Austen expresses her particular vision of what it means to be a human being in the world we share. Two. Hundred. Years. Later. We continue to return to her text."

I felt my heart swell, my mind raced on the adrenaline of Nigel's comments. I was with him. Someone chose that glorious moment to walk into the room and noisily pull back a chair. Heads turned to see the young woman sit next to Omar. How could anyone be late? How could anyone disrupt our communion with Jane Austen? And I feared it was *her.*

Nigel introduced several other staff members, including Suzanne Forbes, the wardrobe director, who instructed all cast members to schedule fitting appointments after the meeting or suffer bleedings.

The latecomer sat too far away for me to read her name tag. Archie Porter, the hip, middle-aged managing director in torn jeans and a gray ponytail, took the stage, his forearms resting on the podium.

The latecomer didn't look like she belonged here.

His words struggled to keep up with his rapid neural connections. He spoke to the floor and then looked up at us. "You know"—he pointed—"it doesn't matter if you like your Austen straight or with a twist of politics, whether *Mansfield Park* is about society's limits on individual spirit or about slavery, incest, and lesbianism, it all comes down to . . ."

I sat on the edge of my seat wondering what *it all came down to*, thrilled that he might reveal a delicious new insight.

The latecomer wasn't paying attention.

But Magda rose from her seat and interrupted Archie, silently handing him a clipboard. Archie's next words sprang not from his brain but from Magda's clipboard. We looked at the sticker on the back: a cigarette in a red circle with a line through it. His other hand raked his hair, and when he resumed speaking, he stuck to the mundane details of our orientation, never sharing what *it all came down to*. Perhaps Magda didn't want us to know.

Archie said, "No one is ever to enter the gates in civilian clothing. Cast members must be in costume and staff must be dressed in black at all times." *I wanted to schedule my fittings.* "Rehearsal for all actors will begin immediately," he said, and "the schedule for the season is in your packet." *I wanted to rehearse.* Archie warned us, "Treat maids kindly; they are paid, but not much." *I wanted the latecomer to go away.*

Then Archie made a goofy face, alerting us to an inside joke as he reminded us, in a falsetto voice, to prepare ourselves for the annual Founder's Night Follies, an evening of homemade entertainment commemorating Jane Austen's half birthday, sort of. "And *you* will be there," he threatened, "or you will miss Magda's impersonation of Aunt Norris." Magda gave him a look and he shrugged.

Maybe the latecomer was one of Omar's writing students.

The staff woman, Claire, jumped up and reminded everyone "how thankful we must all be that the Banks Family Grant has agreed to finance this summer's budget shortfall." Banks family? Then Claire made it final by looking directly at the latecomer. My worst nightmare had arrived and taken a seat among us. Miss Banks ignored Claire, pulling the cellophane off a pack of cigarettes. Miss Banks, present and accounted for.

"And for those of you who may not know, Literature Live is an independent operation. I can't really think"—Claire, the staff woman, looked at the ceiling—"of any other festival or conference that operates without university or corporate affiliation." She pointed to herself. "I'm the accounting department. You're looking at the accounting department."

Laughter, solid like one dense sound, rose and receded.

She listed on her fingers, "The tuition from the writing program covers staff, our endowment from wills and bequests covers part of the actors' salaries, but we will not be here next year unless a new dedicated funding source is found."

Was this true? I looked at Vera, her jaw clenched, gaze fixed straight ahead. Had she seen Miss Banks? Claire, the staff person, might have had more to say, but Nigel thanked her and she returned to her seat.

A low murmur rumbled through the room and Nigel raised his arms to quiet us. "You may have heard rumors," he said, "concerning our lease renewal. Please don't gossip about it." His hands went into his pockets. "Vera and I have known Lady Weston for over thirty-five years. That relationship, along with Her Ladyship's commitment to sharing Jane

Austen's voice with the world, will ensure our lease is renewed and Literature Live thrives well into the future."

Again, the low murmur from the room.

"Your job is *Mansfield Park*." Nigel put one finger in the air and spoke over the noise. "Your job is to exercise your gifts of writing and academic inquiry in this safe place." He raised another finger in a peace sign. "Your job is to dazzle with your performances." Nigel pleaded with his arms, "Bring Jane Austen's words to life."

Yes, I said silently.

"Leave the renewal of the lease to me and Vera."

Vera closed her eyes and nodded.

I could wait no longer. People were going through the papers in their envelopes, consulting each other and raising hands to ask questions. *I had to know*. My pulse raced as I approached Vera.

"Is that Miss Banks sitting over there?" I asked. "The Miss Banks that wasn't supposed to show up?"

"Oh dear," she said, looking over her shoulder. She appeared older in this light, and I wondered if she and her table-mates were seventy, some pushing eighty. "This makes no sense," she said. "Come with me."

Conversations buzzed and spun around my head. People with questions approached the stage and Nigel yelled over the din for anyone with payroll issues to consult Claire. Nigel touched Vera's arm fondly and leaned in to listen to her question. What was it like being married to him? Then he straightened, looked at me, and shook my hand.

"The great American reader; I've heard of you." Nigel winked; he looked much older up close. But I loved him and feared for his approval already. Surely he could fix the Miss Banks problem.

"Nigel." Vera grabbed Nigel's arm and pulled him close, a

look of restrained hilarity on her face. "Don't look now," she said, "but Mrs. Russell is at eleven o'clock, headed this way." Heedless, I looked up and saw the Janeite from yesterday's check-in table. Still dressed as if she'd just stepped from the pages of *Pride and Prejudice*, ribbons from the military hat still straining her throat, she made her way over.

"Oh damn," Nigel said. "Give them a ball and they'll be back in two ticks demanding a séance."

"Run." Vera pushed Nigel. He managed to escape, but Mrs. Russell was no lightweight. She snagged me instead.

"Oh, Miss Berry," she said in her singsong voice, standing on tiptoe. "Have you set a date for the tea?"

"Every day at four." I waved a napkin as Vera pulled me in the opposite direction.

"Let's check with Archie," Vera said.

"She showed up," Archie said, shrugging.

This was *my life* he was shrugging about.

"We made a decision." Vera insisted, her nostrils flaring. "We gave Lily the part. Would it be so hard to just find another part for the Banks girl?"

Archie shook his head and, at that moment, I had a perfect image of him lying to his wife, throwing another stick on the fire threatening his marriage. Then he pulled Vera into an embrace and spoke so close to her ear I heard only the word *Magda*. I felt my forehead. My hand was cool, my forehead burning. Watching them, I felt the possibility of Literature Live slipping from my grasp, the presence of the immortal Jane Austen closing down again. Had I been mistaken to believe I could find my niche in this place? Feeling faint under the burden of my accumulated failures, I pulled out a chair and reproached myself: Literature Live was an exclusive club I could not join; Newton Priors somebody else's house, and *Mansfield Park* a novel I'd never live in. Leaving Texas had been so final, and Literature Live my happily-ever-after. This couldn't be over already; the universe was running out of places for me to fit in.

"Are you okay?" Omar asked.

"It seems there's no part for me." I looked up at Omar.

"No kidding," Omar said. "You're not a professional actress, am I right?"

He nailed me.

Nikki chatted behind us with an acquaintance from previous summers, laughing, touching the place over her heart, finally letting the other person talk.

"I'm a human resources level five specialist," I told him. "Or I was before they fired me." I began to think writers were the new psychologists. I'd been wary of psychologists from a young age, afraid they had a power like X-ray vision, capable of infiltrating the defenses guarding my deepest private meanings. Karen thought a therapist or minister could penetrate my grief, I'm just glad she never thought of putting a writer on the job; Omar would have nailed me in the first session.

Omar sniffed. "Vera's done this before, for your information. Her M.O. is to adopt an innocent young reader like you and expose her to this world, her own little Pygmalion operation. We all know she does it but you're the first she's tried to pass off as an actress."

My mouth hung open. "What happened to those women?"

"Not much, a little admin work, a minor flirtation with our resident aristocrat, and back home. Nigel fixed the problem by hiring a staff person."

"You mean Claire?"

"Yes. Vera knows the drill here. They hire professional actors."

"What about Elizabeth Banks?" I asked. "She's not a professional actress."

"Oh." Omar smiled. "Right. They *will* hire amateurs that belong to families of board members that come with big donations. And she's related to the Westons. Elizabeth Banks and Randolph are cousins." Omar nodded to the door by which Randolph had left.

"How do you know all this?" I asked.

"I read the newspaper." Omar smiled.

"It's hopeless." I slouched in my chair. "Do they counsel rejected cast members in the church?" I asked, thinking of the guy meditating in the dark.

Sixby, my Hamlet, walking by at that precise moment, interrupted. "He looks busy," Sixby said of Omar. "*I'll* counsel you. Just come to *my* office. In the pub. Second booth on the right. Plenty of ale for what ails you." And then he was gone. And then someone grabbed Omar. Everyone was so busy.

Vera approached, scowling and pulling on her black shawl. I stood to meet her, hoping she'd made progress on my case. "I'm so aggravated," she said, coming very close and whispering, "Did you argue with Magda?"

"What?" I asked. "I've never spoken to Magda." And then I remembered. "I said that I love Fanny Price in her presence. Would she hold that against me?"

Vera's hands flew up. "Who knows? Elizabeth Banks decided to show up. You're in Magda's bad book. Archie caved."

I couldn't let it be over before it even started. "I want a part," I said firmly.

"I'm working on it," Vera said, irritated.

I crossed my arms, staring at Vera, wondering what to believe. Was Vera a good witch or a bad witch? And then I remembered Randolph's comment. "Vera," I said, "did you talk to Randolph Lockwood about firing the actors and letting tourists enact the novel?"

"Yes." Vera brightened. "I gave you all the credit, if that's what you're curious about."

"What did he say?"

"He's interested," Vera said. Her eyes raced back and forth. "Randolph wants everything in writing." She touched my arm. "Can you write a business plan?"

"What?" I dimly recalled a business plan for a made-up company I'd written as a requirement for a class in college. How did I do that? Something about strategy and goals.

"That's what you'll do here. Help me," Vera said.

I would not live in a novel but instead be swept into the current of history, another casualty of Vera's Pygmalion operation, business plan version. Magda swooped in, her black robe billowing as in Miss Clavel, *Something is not right*, her arm locked with a disinterested Miss Banks. "Here's the Lily," Magda cooed. *The Lily*. Magda said to Vera, "Your friend charmed *everyone* at the pub." She placed her long, muscular hand on my arm and I knew she would never lift a finger for me, evident from the way she mocked my name. I studied Magda up close, her perfectly shaped eyebrows above her fine nose, her hair hidden beneath the sea of black fabric, her voice oddly sandy—like a smoker. "This is Elizabeth Banks," Magda said, gesturing to the implausible goth groupie on her arm. "You two are roommates. For now."

I extended my hand and in the instant of introduction saw that the necklace Elizabeth Banks wore was mine—the cross from my mother. I started to speak but I felt someone pull on my arm and turned as Nikki the actress said, "See you at rehearsal." When I turned back my roommate was gone.

My Jane Austen had seen everything.

In my room, I was surprised to find Gary seated at my table and my roommate—who bore no resemblance whatsoever to a Jane Austen character, secondary or otherwise—lying on a batik spread, a cell phone attached to her ear. I looked, but did not see my necklace on her neck. Her shaggy black hair, too blue-black for nature, covered her eyes and contrasted her light bulb–white skin. She raised a hand that looked like a greeting until I realized she was begging off to finish her phone conversation. I tried to look busy while monitoring her speech for signs of professional training, waiting for her to get off the phone so I could ask about my necklace. How could she care about Jane Austen? Gary stared at her, but did he understand what she said?

Suitcases waited, piled on the floor, enough for a Princess of Monaco, some still loitering in the hall. On the table, a pack of Gauloises sat unopened. Oh God, a smoker. The books I'd left on the table had vanished, replaced by her stuff: a small television and a boom box. She dug her fingers under the thick pile of black bangs, her eyes focused in a cell phone stare beyond me. A matching batik bedspread lay folded on my bed, her large flat box hid under my bed, a crate of toiletries dominated my shelf, and an abundance of black clothing hung in my closet. A recent memory of my father's girlfriend surfaced, the one where she discarded all my mom's old refrigerator magnets: the pizza ad, the library hours, even the broken angel magnet that protected us from pigging out since I was nine. When I complained to my father, my heart pounding and my breath too ragged to power my voice, saying his girlfriend had no business throwing our magnets away, he'd said, simply, "Your grief is upsetting Sue."

"Cellmate darling," my roommate put her phone down and crooned in a husky voice, the accent completely American. Just then, I discovered my books sitting in the windowsill; displaced, not destroyed.

"I'm Lily Berry." I extended my hand, feeling the roly-poly

syllables of my name, almost certain my mother named me after the tragic Lily Bart. My sister says nonsense. Perhaps now would be a good time to switch to Lillian.

"I'm Bets," she said, adding, "Short for Betsy, which is short for Elizabeth."

"Can I see your necklace?" I asked.

She looked surprised, and then perhaps embarrassed. She pulled my cross out of her shirt.

"That's mine, right?" I asked, recognizing the custom design as well as the chain.

"I got it out of that drawer." Bets pointed and shared an endearing smile, perhaps the key to her life's progress thus far. "Don't be mad at me," she said.

"I'm not mad," I said, "but that necklace is very important to me and I need it back."

She didn't move.

"Now," I said, my voice calm. "I need it now."

"I'm so glad you're here, my fellow American," she said, reaching behind her neck to unfasten the clasp. "My mother's a Brit but my father's from New Jersey. Where are you from? Oops." She looked on the floor and then at me. "It just slipped off."

I fell to my knees and searched. She reached under her bed, exposing a spiked leather band around her wrist, the rest of her attire too short, mismatched, and torn. She must be really rich. Her shoes, electric blue stiletto pumps, bared white toe cleavage. "I found it."

"Oh good." I sighed. She handed me the cross and then the chain.

"Do you know Gary?" she asked, gesturing to the silent driver watching from his seat at the table. The familiar white bakery bag lay on Bets's bed next to an open package of potato crisps.

"Yes," I said, standing, working to put the necklace together. "The link is gone," I said, tripping over one of her bags.

"Oh, I'm so sorry for being such a hog with my things." She waved a lazy hand in the air and offered the charming smile again. "Do you want me to move my stuff?" Her eyes glanced at the box stored under my bed.

"It's okay," I said, automatically retreating, vowing to accept her second offer, although the second offer never came. I would draw the line at smoking, though. "I really need to find the link." I returned to my knees and resumed searching.

"I'm so sorry," Bets said, standing over me. "Please let me get it fixed for you. I know a really good repair shop in London."

"That's not necessary," I said. "I can fix it if I can find the link." Bets seemed truly sorry and I didn't want to hurt her feelings. "Congratulations on your part, you must be very excited about the summer," I said, sweeping the floor with my hand.

"Oh, terribly," she said, lifting one of her suitcases.

I waited. I still needed help finding the link and she'd moved on to something else.

"It's just that my life is my band," she said, throwing the suitcase on her bed and pulling out a pair of black pants. Bets reached for the zipper on her skirt, about to strip. Quickly, Gary stood, shielding his eyes with his hands, and walked toward the door. "Bye, Gary," Bets called. "Thanks for the cookies."

While I sifted through dust bunnies seeking a tiny gold circle of metal, Bets explained how she did odd jobs for a soon-to-be-appreciated band. They specialized in emotionally intense pop rock with a Teutonic edge, thanks to a talented guitarist from Frankfurt.

"So you're leaving the band to do this?" I asked, exploring a small pile of grit.

"That's the problem." She zipped the pants. "The Wallet made a deal that if I came here for the summer, he'd finance the band for another year."

"The Wallet?"

"My father. He's on the board of this place and he thinks three months away from the band will cure me."

"Wow," I said. "I bet the band appreciates the Wallet." I sat up; unable to find the missing link.

"Let me get that fixed for you," Bets said.

"No." I waved her off. "Thanks, but I'll take care of it." I slipped the broken chain and the cross back into the jewelry pouch and closed my drawer. "I can pick up a new link in town." I would not let her take it for repair, regardless of her sad expression. What part could she possibly play in a Jane Austen production? I asked her. "What role are you assigned?"

"I am"—she put her fist in front of her mouth, and cleared her throat—"not sure." She pointed to a brown envelope on the bureau. "It's all in there, but I haven't looked."

"Which Austen book is your favorite?" I asked.

She was caught in the headlights. Silence. "Um. The one about the guy who marries the nanny?"

"Yeah," I said, nodding. I hoped My Jane Austen was getting all of this.

Her phone rang and she hissed into it, "Just tell him to call me," and snapped it off. Then she moaned, "I'm not very good at this sort of thing."

"What sort of thing?"

She lifted her hands in helpless supplication and moaned dramatically, "Take my cell phone away and lock it up somewhere; it's so distracting." She smiled again.

"Okay," I said, reaching to take it. But it rang, and she spoke.

"Tommy." Her voice thick, I pretended not to hear. But before I could find anything to pretend to do, she pulled the phone away from her ear, looked at me, and squinted. "Would you mind?"

"Excuse me?" Certain I'd misunderstood; the fog in my brain had clogged something.

"I'm sorry but I need to have this conversation," she said, pointing at the phone. "Could I have some privacy?"

A little put out, I walked into the hall. Through the open transom, I heard one side of the whole argument and gathered the deal with the Wallet accounted for only part of the reason Bets had shown up at Literature Live. It sounded like Tommy wanted Bets out of the way so he could concentrate on writing music; Bets was a distraction. The angst of the argument drained my remaining energy and I slumped against the wall. After a while, I left the dorm and walked toward the town, where I discovered the quaint pastel doors merely fronted for the usual suspects: The Gap and Victoria's Secret. My Jane Austen stayed behind in the room to listen, of course.

A note waited on my pillow when I returned, "Gone to London." I turned the paper over and wrote my response, "Please move your things out of my spaces ASAP." I put the note on her pillow and stood alone in the room. Bets and her cell phone gone. Just me and her brown envelope alone in the room. Unable to restrain myself, I grabbed the envelope, unfastened the clasp, and removed the stack of papers welcoming Elizabeth Banks to Literature Live. I flipped through a schedule, calendars, directories, and a welcome letter signed simply, "Weston." Was that a legal name? Could he sign that name on credit card receipts? A note from Magda Habibi offered Bets the part of Mary

Crawford. Wow! Having a father on the board didn't hurt her in the casting department.

I flipped open the script, and read:

Mary Crawford: *Selfishness must always be forgiven, you know, because there is no hope of a cure.*

I straightened the papers and pushed them back into the envelope, refastening the clasp and placing it exactly where I had found it. What if Bets didn't come back from London? She seemed like the type who did whatever it occurred to her to do. Not a team player. I imagined myself in the role of Mary Crawford.

Before retiring for the night, I opened the drawer where I kept the jewelry pouch, feeling the need for a reassuring look at my cross. But the pouch lay open and my necklace—the last gift from my mother—was missing again.

★ ★ ★

From: Karen Adams <karen@adams.net>
Sent: June 10, 6:22 A.M.
To: Lillian Berry <verryberry7@hotmail.com>
Subject: Helloooooo!

Hi Lily,

How's it going? Same old here. The kids have vacation Bible school this week so I am taking time to sort through Mom's Christmas ornaments. Sue vacated Dad's house long enough for me to go through some things last weekend. It was heartbreaking and only the tip of the iceberg. What I really need is a kid-free week and a truck. Wish you were here to help since I'm afraid Sue will take it upon herself to dispose of our inheritance. I'm dividing the ornaments equally, giving you all the ones you made in preschool, of course. I'll store them here for you.

Met Mr. Darcy yet?

Don't forget, I love you.
Karen

From: Lillian Berry <verryberry7@hotmail.com>
Sent: June 10, 7:58 P.M.
To: Karen Adams <karen@adams.net>
Subject: Re: Helloooooo!

Karen,

I may be coming home. I can't believe I came all the way over here to find out they only take professional actors . . . or large donations. You were right about quick moves. I am so disappointed. I'm also rooming with a punked-out kleptomaniac who took my necklace. I'll explain later. I may need a place to live until I can find a job, etc. Kiss your babies for me. Funny, when I was in preschool laminating my face into angel ornaments, I thought I was making them for both of my parents.

Love,
Lily

Six

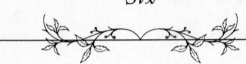

The Literature Live offices in the east wing of Newton Priors included a room full of books called the library, furnished with two mismatched hand-me-down tables. I was in the library affixing address labels to invitations on the morning Bets was scheduled for her costume fitting.

How hard would it be to organize a tea party for Janeites?

Vera had given me some administrative donkeywork, including mailings for the Founder's Night Dinner and Follies, and reminded me to get started on the business plan. I'd written a business plan in college. If I could only remember how I did it. Vera said she would pay me something. Omar, my new best friend, leaned back on two legs of the library chair—his feet perched on his toes—chatting about the national mood toward historic preservation. Wagging a pen, Omar said, "Politicians are campaigning to respect *all* cultural identities, not just those identities belonging to stately manor homes."

"And what does that have to do with us?" I removed ten labels and stuck them on the table's edge.

We would need hot water for tea, of course.

"The national mood matters to us to the degree tax policy is influenced."

"Oh?"

And scones.

"Whoever is steward of Newton Priors will care about tax policy."

"I see." I thought of Randolph's receding hairline and how it would look furrowed over tax policy as I slapped the ten labels on envelopes in rapid succession.

Cucumber sandwiches.

Tax policy sounded like something to address in a business plan, which I would know if I had paid more attention in school. When I had asked Vera if not having a part meant I would eventually have to go home, she assumed her impatient tone and told me to "write my own part." She warned me not to be hasty. With my future tied to the bottom line, I'd better generate some persuasive ideas to employ myself if I wanted to stay. As in: the Business Plan.

"Actually," Omar said, "Lord Weston and his sister are cozying up with the Architecture League these days. Parties to save car parks."

"Car parks?" I imagined Randolph's picture in the paper, published in black and white society pages, laughing over wineglasses in a greenbelt for cars.

"Parking garages, to you."

Then, with no warning Magda blew in. We both flinched and Omar fell off his toes. Magda had spent two solid days in the ballroom fussing at actors, writers, and conservationists, bangles making a racket, her own personal Middle Eastern turmoil. Now she scanned the library as Omar made a hasty exit. I could rest in peace knowing she wasn't seeking me; I'd already been cast off by her. I cringed anyway.

"Lily," she said.

I wondered if her toes were as long as her fingers and what she could possibly want with me. "Yes?" I said.

"Where is Bets?" she asked, looking at my stack of invitations.

"I don't know," I said, sticking the last label. "Probably London."

"Are you aware she missed her fitting appointment?"

I stacked the pile of envelopes on Claire's desk, angry that Bets had taken my necklace to her London repair shop even though I'd told her not to. She'd smiled and asked me not to be mad, a pretty good indication of how she interacted with the Wallet. I glared at Magda. "I haven't seen her."

The next day, I was folding Founder's Night invitations, stuffing them into the envelopes I'd already labeled for Claire.

What china would we use for the tea party?

Omar was tipped back in his chair holding forth on one scholar's suggestion that Jane Austen was an incestuous lesbian, when Sixby entered wearing a cap turned rakishly backward. "Have you seen Bets?" Sixby asked as My Jane Austen yawned.

"No." We both shook our heads.

Sixby nodded toward the conference room. "We're getting ready to start a read-through," he said. "She's missed each one."

I felt a secret thrill, another step in the right direction.

Omar asked, trembling theatrically, "Is Magda coming?"

"No, she's at the visa office with her brother; I'm running the read-through." Sixby started for the conference room and then hesitated, remembering to ask Omar, "Are the scripts ready?"

"Oops." Omar's chair returned to ground level and he jumped up to complete his task at the copier.

In light of Bets's irresponsible behavior, Vera's remark about not being hasty began to make sense. "Sixby," I said, "if Bets doesn't show, can I read her part?"

"Absolutely," he said.

Bets didn't show and I joined the cast, sitting next to Sixby at Nigel's conference table where everyone waited for Omar to finish copying scripts. Nikki the actress demonstrated plummy diction for me. "Like your mouth is full of plums and you have to talk around them."

I tried to copy her, imagining big balls of fruit displacing my jaw; the actor next to Nikki laughed.

"No, actually that's much better," Nikki said.

Enjoying my place in this group, I felt hope revive. Omar arrived panting; his arms full of paper, his glasses sliding down his nose as he circled the table distributing the scripts, running out before Sixby got one. "I thought you kept the revisions from yesterday," Omar said, adjusting his glasses.

"I'd like a fresh script," Sixby said, drumming his fingers.

I'd gotten my copy from Omar earlier and slid it over to Sixby, scooting closer to share with him. I watched as he crossed out all the italicized acting directions associated with his lines, words like *gently* and *loudly*. Perhaps he didn't need anyone telling him how to act. I read my lines in what I hoped sounded plummy—My Jane Austen mouthed them painfully with me. When I looked up, Nikki nodded and Sixby whispered, "Excellent. Don't forget we're partners for the follies," and he patted my arm. My Jane Austen took a deep breath. How could I forget? He didn't coach me as he did the others, probably because I was just standing in. We were reading the scene where Mary Crawford is recruited to join the theatricals, and in the middle of reading my line where I say, "What gentleman among you am I to have the pleasure of making love to," the door opened. Magda's terrible presence filled the room and she interrupted me. Had an actual plum been in my mouth, I would have choked to death.

"Thank you, Lily," she said. "You aren't needed here."

She couldn't even let me finish my line. My blood boiled and stress shaved moments from my life as they continued reading. No one watched me walk out.

That evening, I took a seat next to Omar in the conference room where a small audience gathered for an impromptu talk entitled, "*Mansfield Park*: Convention or Invention?" A lecture idea born at lunch over a bottle of Cabernet Nigel drank with his friend, a professor from a women's college near London. All the writing students were here as well as a representative in Regency attire who occupied the front row, strategically positioned to snag Nigel for a word about ball dates as soon as the talk ended.

Where would we get enough china for a tea party? Paper cups were not an option.

No actors were present since Magda was rehearsing them to death in the ballroom, the opening only two days away. Nigel and the speaker, a white-haired gentleman with watery eyes behind round tortoiseshell spectacles, sipped red wine from oversized glasses.

Omar leaned toward me and said, "Magda was looking for you."

"Me?"

Claire closed the conference room door and gestured for Nigel to begin the introduction.

Omar whispered, "Maybe she has an opening for you."

"Right." I nodded. Everyone applauded the speaker.

"So what are you going to do, stuff envelopes all summer?" he asked as the speaker adjusted his spectacles.

"Or go home," I said, not wanting to chat, looking forward to this lecture. I couldn't go home now, couldn't leave this world where every new thing took me one step farther from my old life. "I'm going to write a business plan," I whispered. And organize a tea party. And get my necklace back.

"Business plan? For what?" Omar whispered back.

The speaker cleared his throat.

"Literature Live."

Omar pointed at the floor. "This place?"

I nodded.

"Do you know how?"

"I wrote one in college."

He grimaced as I turned away to listen.

The professor began his talk, building his case that today's thoughtful reader often applies twenty-first-century issues to *Mansfield Park*, such as slavery and feminism while dismissing the issues of Austen's contemporary society, concerns like amateur theatricals, ordination, and "family values" (air quotes his). The speaker had just introduced Austen's contemporaries: Walter Scott, Frances Burney, and Maria Edgeworth, when the door opened behind me. I ignored the disruption, concentrating instead on the disturbing news that "*Mansfield Park* was written using plot and structure of the sentimental novel that Austen inherited from her literary predecessors."

Say it isn't so, Jane Austen.

The professor put his hands in his pockets and rocked forward on the balls of his feet. "In 1814," he said, "women writers wrote about education, love, and marriage."

I jumped as a set of gold bangles entered my peripheral vision, headed for my lap. Omar saw them and looked up.

The bangles were attached to Magda's arm. Magda's face came close. She dropped a note and touched my shoulder, miming the word *tomorrow*, and turned away. Unfolding the paper, I lost track of the speaker's thread.

> *Make sure Bets gets to her fitting appointment at 9:45 tomorrow morning.*
>
> *Magda*

She didn't even say please or thank you. I offered the paper to Omar; he looked at it but gave it back without a reaction, too intent on the speaker's thread. The nerve of Magda assigning me to be Bets's keeper. I sat there fuming as the speaker went on. "All the characters," he said, "engage in self-deception except Fanny Price. Is it unusual in 1814 to have a character who examines her motives?"

I couldn't answer his question because a really good reason to deliver my roommate to the fitting appointment presented itself: if I helped Bets select her costumes, I could be sure she took one that would fit me. I imagined a white gown trimmed in blue with a matching pelisse and reticule.

The professor touched the stack of his newly published books he'd brought to sign. "Jane Austen used the eighteenth-century novel conventions. But she invented a protagonist who struggles for self-knowledge. *Mansfield Park* dramatizes the emotional pain and reward of endurance."

Everyone clapped; the talk was over.

★ ★ ★

To: Karen Adams <karen@adams.net>
Sent: June 13, 7:38 A.M.
From: Lillian Berry <verryberry7@hotmail.com>
Subject: Helloooooo!

Karen,

Is there such a thing as *Business Plans for Dummies*? Could you FedEx a copy to me ASAP? It turns out they need help with administrative work for the festival and, thanks to my business degree, I've been drafted to help develop a business plan. However, I'm clueless where to start.

Thanks,
Lily

"We need to hurry," I said, headed for the fitting appointment. "We're late." Bets and I passed an actor walking to rehearsals wearing headsets to help memorize lines. Once the word got out that I didn't have a part, the cast ignored me; I might as well have been invisible. When I ran into Alex, the actor of the antique record player, he said, "I thought you were gone."

Bets stopped to light a cigarette the minute we hit the pavement and waved to Gary, who walked on the other side of the street hauling supplies for Claire. "There's Gary," Bets said, exhaling, adjusting the sunglasses she wore even though it was completely overcast.

"I see him," I said. "Do you know your lines?"

"No," she said. "Why don't you wave? He'll think you don't like him."

"Where's your script?" I asked.

"Not sure." She yawned. "I think it's in your JASNA bag."

"*My* bag?" The bag Vera gave me when she sold me *Mansfield Park*. My Jane Austen Society of North America bag.

"At Tommy's."

"I've been looking for my JASNA bag everywhere, Bets." And then I asked, "When will I get my necklace back?"

"Oh!" she said, clapping her hand to her mouth and then feeling for it around her neck. "I must have left it at Tommy's, too."

"You *took* my necklace after I asked you not to and then *lost* it in London?" The brazen entitlement.

"I can find it," she said. "And in the meantime, you're welcome to anything of mine." She gestured grandly.

"You have to get it back to me," I said. "And my JASNA bag."

"Maybe the bag's in my car." She threw her cigarette on the cement; I stopped walking and faced her as she stepped on it.

"I'm serious, Bets. That necklace is one of the few things I have to remember my mother. She gave it to me; she's dead. She can't *ever* give me another necklace." It made me sick to think I might never see that necklace again, not only a necklace; but her wedding band, a gold pin she won in high school, and a baby ring, all melted down and reformed into the shape of a cross, a reminder for my sister and me of what our mother found to be important at the end of her life. Not a necklace; but my mother.

"Tell you what," Bets said, lighting another cigarette. "If I can't find it, I'll give you my mother."

Suzanne, the tiny wardrobe lady, presided over the damp and musty second floor warehouse of costumes inherited from various sources, various sources being a euphemism for dead volunteers in period attire. She pulled an armful of dresses for Bets to try, while another actress changed behind a screen, throwing gowns into separate "take" and "no take" piles. Bets handed me her six-hundred-dollar designer purse and disappeared behind a screen. Maybe Bets could persuade the Wallet to rent china for our tea. Or sentence Bets to another season of Literature Live in exchange for china.

"I can't wear this." Bets laughed. "I look like Granny in Little Red Riding Hood."

The phone rang in Bets's purse.

"Would you mind answering that?" Bets yelled, throwing a rejected gown over the screen.

"She can't come to the phone right now," I said, rifling through the contents of her purse for anything I might recognize as my own.

"Who is it?" Bets asked.

I put the phone away. "Tommy," I said.

"Shit, give me the phone." Bets charged out from behind the screen, reaching for her bag, the dress around her waist.

The wardrobe lady said, "Oh dear," covering her mouth with her little hand.

Bets swiped her purse from my hands. Her body featured artwork that no Jane Austen character had ever sported: a Celtic cross tattoo permanently inked above her left breast. "Forget this," she said, stepping completely out of the dress and leaving it on the floor while she pulled her shirt over her head.

The wardrobe lady reached into a drawer and pulled out several very large white kerchiefs. "You'll have to wear these," she said, "like a shawl," but too late. Bets zipped her jeans, slid feet into her shoes, and ran out the door.

"What about the dresses?" Suzanne called after her.

Suzanne hauled the dresses out and between the two of us, we compared the remaining dresses to the one Bets had tried on, deciding which to take. I held each dress to my shoulder and looked in the mirror, pretending to admire the style and artistry but slyly appraising my own fit, calculating how much time Bets would need to reach the parking lot. I left with an armload of dresses, most of which would surely fit me, imagining Bets in her car. Walking back to my room, I

gauged how long it would take her to get through the main
drag of Hedingham. Opening the door to my room, I said a
little prayer: Please let my roommate be AWOL.

Inside, there was no sign of Bets.

To proceed with my plan, I needed a copy of the script. For
this, I walked to Newton Priors, all the while considering my
favorite scenario: Bets goes to London, gets totally smashed,
and sleeps through opening day. I would play Mary Crawford
in her place, they would all realize how much better I was,
and reassign Bets to play Chapman, the maid. The more I
imagined, the more possible it seemed that with a little maneuvering from me, her part might be available tomorrow.
But first, I must learn her lines. In the office, I lifted a script
off Claire's credenza when she wasn't looking. Next, I needed
a quiet place to memorize.

I set off for the great church at the other end of the town
where I had planned to go anyway for a little self-therapy.
I could hide in the back row and stay as long as I pleased,
communing with my mother, memorizing lines, escaping
into Mary Crawford's character, without having to worry
about meeting anyone I knew. I passed carriage lanterns and
window boxes spilling creeper into the walk, strolled through
a market where cheese, fish, and flowers were sold, and walked
among people on foot, bicycle and open-top double-decker
tour buses, toward the Anglican church whose spire towered
over the town.

Beyond the church's enormous wood door carved with
shields and symbols, the cool air soothed and the upward
momentum of the vaulted ceiling effected the sort of transcendence I experienced hearing Sixby's stage voice. People
moved, coming and going, kneeling, consulting guides,
oblivious to the liturgy, oblivious to the rapture occurring in

the young woman staring at the ceiling. Walking over dead bodies under stone slabs, I slipped into an empty back pew and listened to the service in progress, seeking my favorite passages, but the sound was obscured by the time it reached the back of the enormous nave, competing with the white noise of air circulating through the mighty space.

Kneeling, I recited the funeral liturgy in my head, *All we go down to the dust*, but I was unable to concentrate. Chips of colored glass jumbled together in the tremendous windows and Latin proclamations littered side walls. A stone body lay atop a bier in the midst of the crowd, hands clasped in prayer. How odd that this enormous structure, across the ocean, older than time, smelled just like my neighborhood church, musty as any Baptist basement back home. Yet I was unable to feel my mother's presence in this place. And since it would be really bad manners to actually pray for Bets to get smashed and sleep through opening day, I rested my elbows on the seatback in front of me, sat my rear on the edge of my bench, and evaluated my neighbors' accessories, one pew forward. *Would the church loan us their china?* My Jane Austen frowned at me, and I returned to my knees. Focusing forward, a little shock brought me to attention. In spite of my great distance from the front of the church, I sensed a familiar face. My memory sought an association. Gloomy setting laced with romantic hope? St. James's Church. Behind the rail of the sanctuary stood my church man. The same man who'd walked into the orientation meeting with Randolph— but now dressed in white robes and the collar of a priest. Was this church an extension of Literature Live, my church man playing Edmund at this moment? I was confused momentarily between reality and theatre.

Who was this man?

He came forward to read the Gospel, still too far away to

see me. His reading voice sounded dignified and weighty, not dramatic like Sixby's. For just an instant, in the glare of the ancient words, the whole idea of Literature Live and enacting scenes seemed silly. My script lay abandoned on the pew while I tried to reconcile this priest with the guy lying on the pew in the dark church and the man with Randolph at orientation. The recessional hymn started and he slowly approached my row. He sang the hymn as he walked, but he looked preoccupied as he had looked in the dark church. The woman ahead of me lifted her bright red purse and he looked our way. Our eyes met for an instant.

Time was running out to learn Bets's lines. I walked back by way of Newton Priors, hoping to find a secluded place to memorize lines. What I found was John Owen, the stair-jumping conservationist, holding court near an exterior window of the great house. Several students huddled to hear his urgent whisper, one of them trampling a lavender bed. Flourishing a penknife, John Owen plunged its tip into the undersurface of the window's sash where, to everyone's horror, it stuck. "What we have here, gentlemen," he whispered, "is paint failure."

One of the students shook his head.

"An open invitation to water," John Owen said, "and rot."

Raising his binoculars, John Owen gazed upward beyond the second and third story windows toward the roof. Perhaps there was a quiet place up there to learn lines. Passing binoculars to the student on his left, he pointed to the roof, and our collective gaze traveled up. "A sound roof is the first line of defense against the number one enemy of an old house, which is"—and several of his students moved their lips as he whispered—"water."

"Did water cause the damage around the chimney base?" one of the disciples asked.

John Owen grabbed the binoculars. "Rot can be arrested," he said, looking carefully upward. "Let's go." The group followed John Owen up the fire escape—a symposium field trip. As they climbed, I noticed an orange electric cord hanging outside the building, emerging from a second floor window and entering a window on the third floor, the attic.

Once the posse left, their bodies no longer blocked my view through the wavy glass and I could see the cast rehearsing in the ballroom. They appeared to be on break—or stuck. Magda yelled about rats' asses again. Upon closer inspection, my roommate appeared to be the cause of the fuss.

Bets was still here. She hadn't gone to London.

I wouldn't be able to take her part at the opening.

I would never get my necklace back.

And as I stood there, gazing in the window, Magda approached from the interior side, a furious bunch of nerves, her long finger curling, beckoning me to enter. Why would she invite me in? I walked around to the front, daring to suppose someone had quit and they might offer me the vacated role.

My Jane Austen and I passed each other in the entry; she walked out in a huff as I walked in. The cast slumped on the stage furniture; Nikki lifted her Regency skirt to catch a breeze from the window, all of them waiting for Bets to get something right. Magda pointed to a chair in the audience and I sat. Bets finally got it and they moved on.

Fanny Price: *Sir Thomas, what can you tell us about the slave trade?*

Whoa. I sat up straight. *That's not in the book.* I listened as Sir Thomas provided details he didn't get from Jane Austen concerning the income from his Antigua estate and the number of slaves in his employ. Not in the book. Magda must have written the slavery remarks herself, or made Omar write it. No wonder My Jane Austen walked out.

I watched the entire rehearsal. And then watched it again. The other actors were so good they didn't need to be coached, but Magda fed lines to Bets over and over. Whenever Magda interrupted, "Hey!" to stop the action, the actors sagged, the tension immediately drained from their bodies. Starting up again, their bodies sprang into action. They reminded me of professional outfielders between plays in baseball. By the time they finished, I knew everyone's lines.

When Magda finally indicated the reason for my attendance at the rehearsal, darkness had descended outdoors. "Don't let her out of your sight." She handed me another script. "Work on these lines until she has them down cold, all night if necessary."

"What about sleeping?"

"You don't want to know what I think about sleeping. Have her here at eight-thirty, in costume, ready to perform."

"Me?"

"You are here to help with the festival, no?" Magda stared back. "You are her roommate. The festival needs your help."

"The *festival* is welcome," I mumbled, walking away.

Later, in our room, Bets watched a British reality TV show where women in bikinis ate maggots.

"I thought you went to London this morning," I said.

"I never got away." Bets stuffed potato crisps into her mouth. "Magda caught me and made me sit in the Freezer all afternoon, repeating lines." She offered me some crisps.

"No thanks," I said. "Let's work on your lines."

"No thanks," she said.

"For your own good," I said, removing my shoes and setting them inside my closet, where her clothes lay on the floor. "Did you wear this?" I asked, holding up a pink and white striped T-shirt, thinking it clean, not meant for the dirty clothes hamper.

"Put it back on the floor," she said. "You're not my mother." She increased the TV volume, adding, "I want to go home."

When I returned from the bathroom, the prisoner remained on the premises; a wadded tissue lay on the floor near her bed. "Are you okay?" I asked.

"No," she said, her eyes red and her nose stuffy the way it gets from crying. "I'm allergic to literary festivals."

"Would you like to study lines now?" I asked. Perhaps I should offer her more understanding; even punked-out kleptomaniacs have feelings.

"No." She blew her nose.

She watched her TV and I read her script, working on the lines myself, although it hardly seemed worthwhile given the heightened security. The prisoner remained on the premises and I studied her lines until I fell asleep in the blue haze of the TV.

When I woke the next morning, it was still dark. I slowly surfaced, remembering where I was, placing myself in the day—opening day. And then it all came back to me: Bets. My prisoner. I looked over. Her bed was made. She wasn't in it. Cautiously hopeful she hadn't just gone to the bathroom, I walked down the hall. Not there, either. With great swelling hope and trepidation, I looked out the window. Her car was gone.

Yes.

Seven

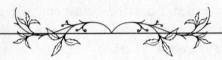

$\mathcal{Q}$uickly, I opened the closet and counted Bets's gowns. All seven costumes hung there. All six Regency shoes waited on the floor. How much time did I have? I pulled the script out of my purse but threw it down; the first objective was to get permission from someone other than Magda. Vera. I must find Vera. My hands shook pulling my door shut behind me.

I ran down the still hallway, descended the stairs, and entered the common area of the dorm, strangely quiet after having been so highly charged with energy the last few days. The first scene of the season would begin in less than one hour and Vera sat at a little table talking with Claire, the staff person. I didn't have time for Claire, who was squinting with the effort of persuading Vera, emphasizing her words by chopping the side of her hand on the table.

"Yes, I see your point." Vera shook her head gently, then smiled at me. "But I'm not convinced of the strength of the connection. In experience and temperament they were quite unalike. Jane Austen was a satiric novelist; Mary Wollstonecraft was not." My Jane Austen listened thoughtfully.

"But," Claire said, "to get back to my original point, perhaps losing the lease on Newton Priors would be a good thing. With a new sponsor, Nigel would be freed from Lady Weston's brain-dead shackles and Literature Live could make a real go of things."

"Vera, could I speak with you?" I said.

"Just a minute, Lily." Vera faced Claire, speaking quietly. "Nigel must have complete control of the organization if we are to preserve the relationship with Lady Weston." Claire began to speak but Vera cut her off. "Save political interpretations for your next job. Nigel will run Literature Live without readings from Mary Wollstonecraft. If you want to help, be quiet and let Nigel work. Lady Weston's happiness is extremely important to the future of this organization. We cannot afford a misstep." Vera looked at her watch. "Speaking of go, it's time," she said, and then glanced at me. "What is it, Lily?"

As soon as Claire was out of range I told Vera about my wish to take Bets's part.

"You'll have to act quickly," Vera said as we hurried to my room. "Believe it or not," she said, "Magda is on the roof of Newton Priors at the moment."

"The roof?"

"John Owen has persuaded everyone the chimney is on the verge of collapse and Magda is meeting the building inspector on the roof, asking him not to shut down the house before the opening. Your best chance is to get permission from Archie while Magda is still on the roof."

Vera helped me slip one of Bets's dresses over my head, our hands running into each other and catching in folds, my pulse racing.

"What was all that about Mary Wollstonecraft?" I asked, standing as Vera zipped.

"Nothing more than Claire demonstrating she's read her latest assignment in Lit 403. She's taking classes, you know. Wants to be Magda when she grows up."

Still, I wondered what the point had been; perhaps *I* should read Claire's assignments.

"Ah," Vera said, "it fits you perfectly." She fluffed the sleeves. I skipped on the Regency underwear, opting for my own, and grabbed a pair of knee-high stockings out of Bets's drawer, remembering her generous offer to help myself to anything of hers—her opening day acting assignment, for example. The Banks Family Grant must have been colossal.

"Where's your bonnet?" Vera asked, finishing my sash.

We grabbed Bets's bonnet and flew down the hall and out the door, the dress rustling between my legs. "The script," I said, as Vera handed it through the window of the carriage, the old horses attracting flies. Too late to walk, I would have to pay the carriage, a private local business operated separately from Literature Live, to transport me to Newton Priors.

"When you get there, sit in the Freezer and calm yourself," Vera said, handing the driver my fare. "You'll be fine, don't worry."

"Aren't you coming?" I asked, afraid to go without her.

"I'll be over in a bit—with Nigel."

A surprisingly long line of patrons waiting in line with tickets watched me rush off, fingers pointing, speaking to each other in French and Japanese. I looked out the window; this was my first journey into a novel, as my carriage traveled through space and time. I looked at my eighteenth-century shoes peeking from beneath my muslin hem, and tried to believe. I looked at the trees and sky framed by my carriage window and tried to believe. I remembered how it felt to read *Mansfield Park* and I tried to feel myself traveling among characters in Jane Austen's world. But something gnawed at the edges that I never thought about when I pictured this moment. The trees and the sky and my shoes refused to stop being real; they wouldn't transform. Everything about me was the same as always, and I couldn't feel any different, too worried to leave my worldly concerns. I didn't know the blocking. Where was I supposed to stand on the stage? Indeed, I feared failure and pain today. Just like real life.

"Have you seen Archie?" I asked an actor in the Freezer.

"Probably in his smoking jacket," Alex said, without looking up from his crossword puzzle. "Look behind the Carriage House."

I ran, but a family of five blocked my path: a blond Texas Hair woman holding a map, followed by a man and three rambunctious children, progressed in a tangle of limbs and barks like naughty puppies.

"Excuse me," the hair woman flagged me down.

I turned my upper body to answer her question, still speed-walking, imagining Magda had sent her to keep me from talking to Archie in her absence, hired them to load me into their monster SUV and take me back to my gray cubicle world of colossal freeway billboards and Nike swoosh sensibilities; a place where My Jane Austen would not thrive.

"Can you tell me where to find the candle-making demonstration?" she asked.

Patrons detoured around us, camera bags slung over their shoulders, maps and guidebooks open in their hands. A Muslim woman wearing a severely modest black outfit, pants

and an overdress, strutted—not a bit oppressed—alongside
her man in Western dress. I must focus or Archie would disappear before I could find him. I didn't have a chance if he
was with Magda. Shading my eyes, I looked up and saw the
group still huddled around the chimney, but who knew how
much longer they'd stay up there?

"The candle-making demonstration is over there," I said,
a bit heavy on the plums. *Ovah theh*.

"Ovah theh?" The woman looked at her map, and then
in the direction I pointed, as if she didn't understand. I ran
toward the Carriage House.

Two enormous old mares parked outside swished flies with
their tails. The dirty Carriage House windows concealed a
graveyard for broken antiques: tables on end, chairs without
upholstery, bed frames and slats, stacked in all directions. No
room for horses or carriages in the Carriage House. And no
Archie. Walking around the side of the building, I encoun-
tered a well-worn path through the high hedge. I followed
the path, squeezing sideways through the bushes, and suddenly found myself looking into the sheepish grin on Archie
Porter's face, one arm stretching to reach a ledge high above
his head.

"You smoke?" he asked, lowering his arm and shaking out
a cigarette in one practiced motion.

I started to say no reflexively, and then considered my case.
"Actually, yes, please."

As Archie shook out another cigarette from a pack of
Camels, not even the filtered kind, I began to hope I would
get what I wanted. Putting it to my lips, he lit a match. "Getting on okay?" he asked.

"Swimmingly," I said, returning the long look, examining
the crow's feet around his eyes and the gray in his ponytail. I
imagined I was smoking with John while Yoko met lawyers.

I'd never seen him so relaxed. "Where's Magda?" I asked innocently.

"Patching the roof." He smiled as if we knew each other. "One of an assistant director's many and varied festival responsibilities."

"Well then. Since she's busy, I'll ask you." Just one puff had made me dizzy; I couldn't inhale these things. The smoke sat on me, lodging in the pores of my skin, permeating hair follicles.

"Ask me." Archie blew dragon smoke out his nostrils as the American children from the lawn barged into our hiding place, giggled, and ran out. The little girl loudly reported what she'd seen.

I said, "You may not be aware that Bets—the actress playing Mary Crawford—is not here."

"No, she is not here." Archie smiled, lifting a branch of one of the bushes that concealed us, nearly brushing My Jane Austen's skirt.

"No, I mean, not in Hedingham. Not at Newton Priors. She's in London."

He took another long drag. "I see. You were supposed to keep track of her?"

"Yes." I looked him in the eye.

"A case of Magda putting the fox in charge of the henhouse."

"I'd like to take her part in the scene today."

He gave me an extra long sideways glance. "Who else knows about this?"

I took a short but dramatic drag, sensing what I once sensed when Martin was about to kiss me. "Does anyone else need to know?" I asked, smoke curling around my face.

Archie pulled on his cigarette, his eyes closing. "Nobody I know of needs to know about anything."

I threw my cigarette on the ground and stomped it out. "Then we're all set."

"You know the part?" he asked.

"Yes," I said.

I had turned, just about to leave the enclosure, when Archie said, "You know what?"

"What?" I twisted to see his face and braced myself.

"You worry too much."

"Me?"

"Relax." He pulled a package of nicotine gum out of his pocket and punched one through the wrapper, slipping it into his mouth. "Want one?" he asked.

"No." The last time I relaxed around a professor, his hand visited my thigh beneath a table.

"Don't be so worried," Archie said. "Fanny Price is safe."

In the Freezer, I sat at the table among empty Diet Coke cans; the vacant computer screen stared at me as I read Mary Crawford's lines, "Oh! Yes, I am not at all ashamed of it. I would have everybody marry if they can do it properly," when Archie, who had just returned, his spearmint breath proclaiming his innocence, lifted the script from my hands and turned the page.

"We're skipping the second scene today," he said. "Start here."

I resumed my studies, struggling to focus, but couldn't get traction because people kept opening the door and I kept looking up, afraid Magda would walk in. Each person whispered to Archie and I tried to hear what they were saying. I wondered about checking my e-mail but Archie rattled a box of antique keys, to my complete undoing. He left the box next to me where I was free to examine keys, of every shape and size, at my peril. My pulse raced. Little time remained until the scene with the children would end, and even that was running out. My script lay open while I studied the jumble of rusty skeleton keys, wondering which key Lady Weston had used to lock the manor in 1945. This felt more like exam day than literary transcendence.

Just as I finally got traction with the script, the junior cast, three girls and two boys who played the children in the first scene, arrived noisily, congratulating each other on their performances. Their adult chaperone beamed at Archie, "Weren't they wonderful?" Archie pointed at me and shushed the kids. But they couldn't shush. I gave up the script and pulled the computer's keyboard out, typing my e-mail password and clicking "check mail." The connection seemed slow. The children giggled and the mother took one boy to a separate seat. Karen's name stood out from the spam; her subject line read: "Please call." I clicked on the subject; something must have happened. Was it Dad or her children? The page was so slow to come up. The mother raised her voice and the children squealed. The door opened again.

> **To:**   Lillian Berry <verryberry7@hotmail.com>
> **Sent:**   June 13, 6:03 A.M.
> **From:**   Karen Adams <karen@adams.net>
> **Subject:** Please call
>
> Lily,
>
> I don't have a phone number to reach you and we need to talk. I was planning to wait till you return but Greg thinks you should know. I found something that leads me to believe Dad knew Sue before

Mom died. Before you fall apart, please call me so
we can talk about it. It's not the end of the world.
   If I'm not home, call my cell.

I'm sorry and I miss you,
Karen

Archie called my name. I turned and looked at him but I
couldn't understand what he wanted, Karen's words reverberating like thunder through my skeleton. Sabrina Howard
in full Regency costume—the lead actress who was playing
Fanny Price—beckoned me. Time for my execution.

"Mary." Sabrina reached for my hand. "Come with me,"
she said. "Everyone is waiting." Archie waved us out the door
and I left the Freezer for my rebirth into *Mansfield Park*, passing the tall case clock, its sharp points radiating from its face
as mighty storm clouds gathered in my spirit.

Sabrina smiled as we walked, linking our elbows; maybe
we could be friends, supporting each other through personal
crises. "I'm Lily," I whispered, not sure she knew my real
name. Sabrina's face changed channels. She shook her head
once, and clicked her tongue; Mary Crawford had never been
Lily a day in her life.

We walked through the entrance hall where portraits of
stern men in gilt frames testified to their part in siring the
Weston line, while the women who'd borne their tiresome in-
fidelities watched bravely from their own elaborate frames. A
smaller butler-type hall led actors to the ballroom where the
performance was about to begin.

The door through which I would soon enter was cracked
open enough to see the audience, people who paid actual
money to watch me sort through my personal shock while
reciting Mary Crawford's lines. The stage might as well have

been an operating room where they perform amputations. The front row hosted an aging fan club decked out in full cleavage-busting Regency costume, their plumage and fans blocking the view of those seated behind them. Olive-skinned women dressed in saris, veils, and a variety of robes and head coverings made Magda's scarf look like something Katharine Hepburn would wear in a convertible. A portly man with a camera around his neck leaned back and nudged his wife to look at the medallion in the ceiling. Perhaps it would fall and kill all of us. Oddly, Vera and Nigel were not in the audience.

Sabrina took my hand and led me to the stage to perform the scene where, while touring the chapel at Mr. Rushworth's estate, Mary Crawford makes snarky comments about clergymen before learning that Edmund plans to be ordained. If I followed Sabrina, we'd make it through the scene. I knew I was safe during the long part where Sabrina, as Fanny, expresses her disappointment over the chapel to Edmund.

"This is not my idea of a chapel," Sabrina said. "There is nothing awful here, nothing melancholy, nothing grand."

A streak of lightning flashed behind my eyelids, followed by a bone-rattling crash of thunder. *My father knew Sue before my mother died.* Sabrina bumped into me as if I stood in her place. I moved without any idea where to go. *How did Karen know?*

"No banners to be blown by the night wind of Heaven," Sabrina continued. "No signs that a Scottish monarch sleeps below." Sabrina gestured to the same chair whose outward scrolling arms supported Sir Thomas in the previous scene.

Mrs. Rushworth said her line: "Morning and evening prayers were always read by the domestic chaplain," she said. "But the late Mr. Rushworth discontinued the service."

"Every generation has its improvements," I said, as another flare of lightning illuminated My Jane Austen's pale figure.

Were they intimate when my mother was alive? Shaking my
head dramatically for no apparent reason, I moved so Mrs.
Rushworth could take my place. I concentrated to deliver my
long line about heads of the family requiring housemaids and
footmen to attend chapel while inventing excuses for themselves to lie in bed for ten more minutes, but the chandelier
glittering overhead distracted me, and the Prussian blue paint
on the walls had "failed" and for the life of me I couldn't
imagine *what had brought Karen to her horrible conclusion.* The
sight of brown Currier and Ives china, donated to the production by a helpful volunteer, would forever strike terror in my
heart.

Ah! I knew where we would get enough china for the tea.

I glanced at Sabrina, whose smile reminded me of Karen's
when Karen first suggested I might need professional help.
I imagined Archie pulling me off-stage with a long hook.
My father would never have an affair. Petrified I would miss
my line, I caught my startled reflection in one of the gilded
mirrors across the hall, envious of the dumb marble bust reflected beside me on its pedestal. "Ordained!" I said. "If I
had known this before, I would have spoken of the cloth with
more respect."

And then thunder rumbled again. Magda entered the ballroom from a side door and stood against the opposite wall
with Archie. Our eyes met. I experienced the sensation that
occurs just before a car accident or a failing grade: *I'm actually going to die now.* Panic surged and I couldn't remember
where I was supposed to be standing. I looked at my shoes,
the carpet, the upholstery tacks attaching gold fringe to a
footstool, beseeching them to help me recall my blocking, but
Magda's scornful expression undid me and my memory vanished like yesterday's tourists. If only I could talk with my

mother one last time, pierce the veil of death for one question.

After I left the stage I heard Sixby. "Well, Fanny, and how do you like Miss Crawford now? Was there nothing in her conversation that struck you, Fanny, as not quite right?" The audience laughed. So much for my part in the follies; Sixby would never mention that again.

Archie waited for me in the hall near a sofa where two Asian tourists with backpacks and empty water bottles either napped or had died. His brow furrowed, Archie gestured and I followed him to the Freezer, where he would feed me to Magda. The portraits scowled, Lady Weston could have me deported, and I took no comfort from the breeze wafting in the open windows. Outside, patrons trained their cameras and video recorders on smiling families, catching other photographers in their pictures, along with the house and grounds. I wanted to run away from him, find a phone and call my sister, anything to stop the squall in my soul.

Claire snagged Archie at the Freezer door so I entered alone to await my doom. Magda was not present. But Bets was. Dressed in costume and ready to perform.

"Hi, Cellmate," she said, returning my JASNA bag. "How'd it go?" as if the horror had been according to plan.

Speechless, I took the bag and stared at her. Bets looked different, perhaps her hair caught up in the cap, maybe she'd been crying.

"You got what you wanted," she said. "And take this," she said, handing me her cell phone. "Lock it up where I can't find it."

At first I thought she meant giving me the phone was what I wanted—because at the moment, I needed a phone to call Karen. "Where have you been?" I asked, sounding like her mother again.

"Tommy's," she said.

"Did you bring my necklace?"

She shrugged. "I forgot."

"Oh, Bets. It's not just a necklace." I imagined my necklace hanging on a bedpost or dropped behind a dresser in some slovenly bed-sit. My mother, left in a tangle near a grimy sink, splattered with water and toothpaste. What nasty rocker was wearing it now? "You've got to get it back."

"It wasn't my first priority," Bets said.

"Next time it needs to be first," I said.

"There is no next time." Bets hesitated. "Tommy needs space." Her voice turned to a whisper; her tough bravado and tattoos weren't much help to her now. "He wants us to take a month off from each other."

"Is he seeing someone else?" I asked.

She shook her head. "He's working on a new song." Bets sniffed. "He got the idea from my script."

"A song about *Mansfield Park*?"

"About Fanny Price," she said.

Her phone rang and I looked at the caller ID. "Bella," I said.

Bets grabbed the phone out of my hand, "Stop calling," she said. "I can't talk for a month." Snapping the phone shut, she handed it back to me and wiped her nose on her white gloves. I might never see my necklace again.

"Bets!" We both turned to see Magda, hissing from the doorway, gesturing for Bets to join the cast.

"Do you know your lines?" I whispered, slipping Bets's phone into my JASNA bag.

"Some of them." She shrugged, walking into Magda's out-stretched claw.

"You," Magda said, pointing her bangled arm at me, "wait."

★ ★ ★

When Magda returned, Archie and Claire came with her, Archie talking seriously into his cell phone. All three looked very concerned, as if they had not discovered a punishment severe enough to fit my crime.

"That's serious at her age," Archie said into his phone. "She may go downhill really fast." *Rilly fahst.*

Archie sat on the arm of a sofa; Magda stood staring at him. She began to speak but Archie raised his hand; his irritation flashed at interruptions, even from Magda. "Are you going to try to see her? Get something signed?" The phone conversation wasn't about me after all. Archie was talking to Nigel and something had happened to Lady Weston.

"Keep us updated." And then he said, "Here's Magda, she wants a word with Vera." Archie handed the phone to Magda as my stomach swooped; he and Claire left the room without looking at me.

"Vera," Magda said. "I know you've got a lot on your plate at the moment but I need to tell you we're having our own disasters over here with the corps of amateurs. Thank you for trying to help, I know she's a personal friend of yours, but I need to be consulted before decisions are made that affect the production."

I slumped onto the sofa, pulling out the crossword puzzle magazine I'd sat on. My Jane Austen drummed her fingers on a bookshelf.

"But Vera, with all due respect, I don't understand why you're taking this stand. It would appear you're allowing sentiment to override artistic and professional considerations at a very critical time."

I found a pencil. One across: animal smaller than horse. Three letters.

"What you are asking the organization to accommodate at this moment is not reasonable. Bets simply cannot handle the demands. I'm shifting the cast around and giving her a smaller part. And I'm sending Lily back to you. You can keep her or send her home, I don't care."

My heart dropped. Home. The wedding. There *was* a punishment cruel enough to fit my crime.

Magda gestured, her bangles clanking. "I appreciate your spirit and I hope you are able to introduce Jane Austen to more and more ordinary citizens, but right now we're trying to produce *Mansfield Park*, and if Jane Austen were present this morning, she'd eat your Lily for lunch. And shut us down."

My Jane Austen *was* present and she was writing her next book based on the persecution of Lily Berry by the tyrannical literary person wearing a head scarf. After Magda clicked off the phone with her long thumb, she smiled at me, and I recognized the expression my boss used when he fired me, the same delicious regret Sue expressed whenever she had the pleasure of saying no to me. Magda folded her arms, silencing the bangles, and I felt my insides crushed to pulp, the end of the line for me.

"Surely you are aware that you are in over your head," she said without expression.

I sat there, absorbing the hit, a misfit at this festival; too bookish for home, not bookish enough for here.

"And I can't imagine you're enjoying this." She rolled her eyes and raised her hands in supplication, waiting for me to speak, but I was so close to tears that one false move would put me over the edge. I determined not to cry in front of her.

"I performed with almost no preparation," I said.

"True." Someone opened a door on the noisy hall and Magda waved them out without looking to see who wanted in.

"I know my lines. I can learn the blocking."

"Listen to me," she said. *Lee sen to mee*. "Don't expect Vera to wave her wand and fix your life by bringing you here." Magda looked directly into my eyes, stabbing her finger into her palm. "Even if she could, she has her own problems right now. She's not thinking clearly." Magda sighed and spoke more softly, almost pleading. "Why don't you get a Eurail pass and travel? Do something good for yourself."

"But I want to do *this*," I said, knowing My Jane Austen far preferred the literary festival to any train trip.

She shot back at me, "Teaching you to act so you can participate here is completely outside the scope of this organization's mission. I'm not paid enough to train you; we have no money for theatre directors. I'm an English teacher who does this for the privilege of spending the summer with other English teachers."

I considered her privilege, one of spending time with a married man in a manor house.

"Archie and I are not theatre directors but we have done enough theatre to pull off what we do here. But we must have professional actors who know what they're doing. Am I clear?"

"What about Bets?"

Magda narrowed her eyes at me and held up two fingers. "Two important qualifications Bets has that you don't: She's related to the Weston family, and her parents are donating funds to cover this year's operating deficit. Any more questions?" She raised her eyebrows and glared at me, waiting.

Could the Wallet cover our scones?

When I said nothing, she continued. "If you insist on remaining at this festival, you must stay in Vera's office. There is nothing for you on my stage."

Bets's phone rang in my bag. "I want a part," I said.

"Good-bye," Magda said louder, competing with the noise of the phone. A staff person with a bucket of tar asked Magda a question from the doorway, and they both left.

I had not escaped my life when I left Texas. There was no escape for me. This organization was another version of reality, just as populated with human appetites and dynamics. If I would act on a stage at Newton Priors, or live in any novel that took place here, I'd have to get past Magda to do it.

Eight

I needed a private place to call my sister. Not in the hall crawling with nosy patrons, nor the busy office. The timid English sun briefly appeared in the fan window above the door, coaxing my gaze upward. Omar had mentioned a third floor. "Off-limits," he'd said. The perfect place. I moved quickly, avoiding Mrs. Russell selling tickets in the foyer.

On the second floor, surrounded by doors, I turned a random knob seeking stairs to the third floor but found a closet stuffed with yellowing roll-up blinds and rotting drapery fabric. The closet smelled musty like My Jane Austen. I chose another door, opened it a crack, and peeked inside. Too dark to see anything, I opened a bit wider and light shone onto a narrow staircase. Ascending carefully, the prehistoric steps not deep enough to accommodate my entire foot, I climbed, balancing in the dim light by touching the naked brick wall. Chilly air at the top smelled of damp decomposition, a likely habitat for unquiet spirits. Moldering boxes and furniture skeletons, paint cans, and rolls of carpet barely left a path from one end of the vast attic to the other. I spied movement out of the corner of my eye but it was only My Jane Austen looking particularly dead in the dim light. "You scared me to death," I said aloud.

The torn side of a box revealed papers tempting me to explore its content. Omar said he'd been through the household stuff and found nothing of interest, but had he been up here? I touched the torn box, imagining a bundle of love letters straining a once-lavender ribbon, glad I'd discovered this part of the house before being extradited to Texas. But then I remembered Karen and her devastating news and the reason I'd initially sought this attic. Pulling the phone out of my JASNA bag, I sat on the top stair and dialed her home number where it must be late afternoon. I listened to the phone ring in my right ear.

"Hello," a man's voice called. But I heard him in my left ear.

"Hello," I responded, the phone still ringing for Karen in my right ear.

"Sorry if I frightened you," the voice said in my left ear.

Karen's machine came on. "You have reached the Adams family," Karen said, followed by the TV theme song. I stood, leaning into the room where I could see a man, ominously back-lit, sitting behind an open laptop at a table near the far window.

I blinked. "If you want to leave a message for Karen, press one." I powered off the phone as excess adrenaline wandered my arteries asking what happened.

"I should have said something to let you know I was here," he said, rising. "But I thought you were one of the inspectors who've been in and out this morning." Tall and serious, dressed in a priest's white collar and black shirt, he was such a perfect gothic specimen I expected him to speak Brontë. Immediately, I recognized the man I'd seen in the dark church, serving at the altar, and in the company of Randolph at the orientation meeting. "Lots of activity up here today." He smiled. The way he closed his laptop with both hands made me think of a coffin lid. "Willis Somerford." He stepped around the table and offered his hand as if this were all completely normal. I told myself that if he was one of the restless spirits in this attic, I wouldn't feel anything when we touched. But his handshake felt firm and warm, his face looked gentle.

"I'm sorry to bother you," I said. "I'm Lily Berry." The area near the window had been cleared for the table where his work-in-progress lay open. His black suit jacket hung over the back of a wooden chair, papers peeked out of several manila files, and a stack of books layered mountainlike, suggesting an ascent into ideas. "This must be your office," I said, imagining him writing sermons on Paul's letters, or an impenetrable book of theology.

He glanced at his desk and then watched me as he spoke, the way Martin observed pedestrian women from his driver's seat, appraising from behind as he got closer and then, after passing, observing their faces in his rearview mirror. Martin's conversation always lacked focus until he'd driven beyond range. Willis squinted at me. "Weren't you in St. James's Church the other night? Did you see me? It was dark."

"Yes, I saw you there," I said, "and at the orientation meeting and the church in town."

"Ah, then we've met," he said.

An open book lay facedown on his desk, *A Midsummer*

Night's Dream. Books stacked on the floor reminded me of the six I'd maintained in my office cubicle, although Willis appeared to read more widely: *The Backpacker's Manual*, *1000 Places to Visit Before You Die*, and *Getting Started in Sailboat Racing.* The orange electric cord hanging outside the house belonged to him. Entering through a crack in the window, it snaked over the plank seat and onto the floor, powering his laptop.

"I gather you're with the festival," he said, gesturing to my costume. Again, he looked at me intensely, like a man too much alone. In a world full of choices I failed to inspire much interest; but apparently, in a lonely attic, dressed as Mary Crawford, I commanded attention.

"Yes, but I'm afraid I've made a mistake coming here," I said.

"Actually, you've only gone as far as the third floor, not too far from where you started."

"No, I don't mean *here*," I said, gesturing to the attic. "I mean England." My toe dug into accumulated dirt and I warned myself to stop, change direction. "You must be a priest," I said, recalling Mary Crawford's insensitive line I'd butchered an hour ago.

"Not yet," he said. "I'm a deacon in the Anglican church."

"So you *will be* a priest?" I sniffed.

He smiled and broke eye contact. "That's a very good question," he said, turning and walking behind his desk. "You're not the first to ask," he added, digging in his pocket. "But you came up here to be alone." He handed me a tissue. "I'm intrigued." I wiped my nose as gracefully as possible while he gallantly diverted his gaze out the window.

"Where to start," I said, stalling, not wanting him to think less of me for being fired by Magda. He gestured to the plank

window seat and pulled the chair from his desk to face me
as I sat. He waited so patiently, a technique learned in priest
classes, no doubt. The longer he waited, the more I felt compelled to answer his question. After all, Karen had suggested
I speak with clergy. Willis planted both feet on the floor and
propped his elbows on his knees.

"Do you know Magda?" I asked.

"No."

"She's the assistant director, and she has it in for me."

"Pity." He shook his head, not without irony. "Did she say
why?"

"Because I like Fanny Price."

"Who is?"

"The protagonist in *Mansfield Park*."

"Ah, I thought the name sounded familiar."

Gathering courage, I told him a sanitized version of how,
covering for Bets, I'd messed up on the blocking. He listened
as intently as he observed. "Do you know what I told myself
before I came here?" I asked.

"What?"

"That Texas didn't *get* me."

"Really. Not get *you*." He smiled as if he knew better.

"I was so certain England would get me. That Literature
Live would get me; that we would all *only connect*." An odd
look crossed Willis's face, reminding me that Forster's *only
connect* did not mean, as I had mistakenly believed, relating
to others with greater gusto. "But the truth is"—I dug myself
in deeper—"I can only *only connect* with people who are dead
or fictional, and can only be happy in places that exist in an
author's head. My best friend is—" I gestured to where My
Jane Austen would be if she were there listening as I felt she
was, but stopped myself and turned back to him.

"I'm sorry?" he said.

"It's nothing." I crossed my legs; wild horses could not force me to tell him about My Jane Austen.

"So," he said, "you're a reader." Then Willis shrugged and looked sideways at me. "Ever consider ditching all this and living in a novel?"

I blinked. He might be pulling my leg, hard to tell. I considered this attic full of junk, murky light struggling through the dirty window, this conversation with a handsome Brontë icon in a house reeking of Jane Austen, and him *getting it*. It seemed increasingly less likely I was conscious. Perhaps I was dead, this was heaven, and murder should be added to Magda's crimes against me. "Yes," I said, leaning forward.

He smiled at me. "Life in a novel would be so much easier than this constant necessity to sort things out for oneself, don't you think?"

Whereas my life had been going from left to right in a general clockwise motion up until that moment, everything suddenly came to an abrupt stop—and resumed a fraction of a second later in the completely opposite direction—with a marked increase in tempo. As if I had crossed the prime meridian or the Continental Divide, suddenly there was a new way for everything to be. Looking into his eyes, I said, "When I was ten I wanted to *be* the Witch of Blackbird Pond."

"A witch." His eyes lingered on my face, and for a second, not only did we share The Look, but I really felt like a witch. No one else had ever come close to understanding such thoughts. Not Martin, not my friend Lisa, certainly not Karen, not even my mother; no one but My Jane Austen. I felt so comfortable with this man, as if we were resuming a conversation we'd been having in a previous life. He appeared to feel the same energy.

"But then authors would be God," he said.

"Ah." I sat up straight. "In that case, I could live my literature the way religious people live their faith." I flinched inwardly as I said "religious people"; Mary Crawford came so naturally when I wasn't on stage.

"Interesting," he said, with emphasis that made me feel brilliant. Willis folded his hands behind his head and propped his feet on my bench. Just as he opened his mouth to speak, Bets's cell phone, incarcerated in my JASNA bag, began to ring. Willis's mouth froze open, his next word unsaid.

"I'm so sorry," I said, rummaging for the phone. Bets had annoyingly left a lot of her stuff in my bag. I found the phone and turned off the power. "My roommate's phone," I said, slipping it back in the bag, wondering if the caller was Karen. Willis looked different when I returned my attention to him. His body remained in the chair opposite but his face was somewhere else, seeing something I couldn't see.

His feet hit the floor as he looked at his watch. "I'll have to excuse myself." Those were not the words he had been planning to say before the phone interrupted. "I've got to run," he said, standing, thrusting arms into his jacket.

I held my ground, watching his face, hoping to grab him by the eyes, but he did not look at me. Instead, he pushed his laptop and some papers into a case. He slung the strap over his shoulder and paused for a moment, drumming fingers on the table, apparently trying to remember what he needed to take.

"A pleasure meeting you," he said to his desk.

"Are you associated with the festival?" I asked. I'd just met my other half; I didn't want it to end. Would I ever see him again? Stumbling upon him in the attic would only work once.

"No," he said, followed by a pause during which his eyes glazed, giving the impression he couldn't think and talk simultaneously. He stuffed pink message papers from a drawer into his pocket. "I'm not with the festival." He looked at me, finally. "Enjoy your time here," he said, smiling politely.

"I'm sure I will," I said, following him out, hoping to continue talking as we walked. But our interview had ended, perhaps forever. I stepped over damp cardboard and tripped down the uneven steps trying to keep up, but Willis walked so fast I lost him after the second floor.

Nine

*H*ow do you know it's Dad?" I asked Karen, talking from a bench in the rose garden behind the manor. The "evidence" Karen had found was a picture of my dad with Sue. I looked up as a patron snapped my photo, *Portrait of Regency Girl Talking on Cell Phone*. My talk with Willis in the attic had changed my perspective, like sun shining inside me after a violent storm, and I didn't feel like dealing with my dad's bad weather. For a change, I was taking Karen's cautious approach, pushing bird flu and TB.

"He's wearing the shirt you gave him for Christmas," Karen said.

"The red plaid one?"

"Yes," Karen said. "And the banner behind them says 'Happy New Year.' They're obviously at a party."

"Do you recognize anyone else in the picture?" I touched a pink rose and bent to sniff.

"No." Karen sighed. "Not a one."

"So," I said, touching the chilly stone robe of St. Francis. "What does this mean?"

"A couple of things," Karen said. "It means they knew each other before Mom was sick."

A thorn pricked my back.

"And someone wanted me to know they knew each other." Karen had already told me she'd found the picture on the counter near the kitchen phone. Sue had put it there on purpose. I could see Sue sorting pictures, choosing one for its power to convey specific information, and then placing it where she knew Karen would see it. "Was Sue there when you found the picture?"

"Yes."

Sue would watch Karen pick it up, maybe holding it in better light as she talked into the phone, the information in the picture too ridiculous to connect with what she knew. But the shock would gradually take hold as she struggled to finish her conversation with her husband or friend. All the while Sue would be watching, just like the old man in the car. The man asked me for directions. I was ten years old, walking home from the playground. He watched my expression as I realized his pants were open. Karen would take her children and leave the house in shock, exactly as Sue planned.

Karen sounded so tired. "I just can't believe Dad would have an affair. I just can't believe it."

"Well, maybe it wasn't an affair," I said. "Maybe it was an office party or something and Mom was there, too." I remembered how my dad would accompany me to the park after the exposure incident, protecting me, even though I continued to go alone when Dad was away on business.

"Lily." Karen paused. "They're kissing."

"What?"

"On the lips."

The weakness came into my arms first. I felt the trembling and my breath choked in my chest. "You didn't tell me that." I slumped down on the pea gravel, my forehead pressing too hard against the base of the statue, *Regency Girl Petitions St. Francis.* "And I didn't tell you about the last time I saw him," I said.

"When?"

"The night you called to tell me they planned to marry."

"Oh, Lily."

"I couldn't help it," I said. "When you told me Sue cleaned out the garage to make room for her stuff it was like a bomb exploded inside me." I told Karen the story of how, that night, I'd hung up the phone and run to my car. I could barely catch my breath, knowing in my heart it was too late. Driving as fast as possible through darkness, neighbors' urgent flaming carriage lanterns lit my way like torches in a Romantic horror version of my life. My mind raced and I imagined Sue walking through my parents' garage, touching things, peering inside boxes where bits of our family life lay in storage. Standing on the balls of her feet, the toenails painted deep burgundy to complement the purple veins in her always-bare legs, she would have pulled boxes from shelves.

The light turned red, forcing me to stop. I opened my window and groaned at the empty street as I imagined Sue touching my mother's Christmas wreath that lay in storage, or the antique chair waiting to be re-caned. My stomach swooped and my arms felt weak as I pulled into my dad's driveway, headlights illuminating the path through his side yard, past his dark house, to the garage entry. My door clicked open and keys still in the ignition sang their warning as I crossed the grass, dew soaking my bare feet, crickets yapping. Entering and reaching for the light, my hand trembling, I felt everyone telling me to stop—go home, get help. But I couldn't stop. I needed the pain to hit me full force.

I hardly recognized the garage. The floor previously covered with boxes, tools, and expiring lawn furniture lay bare. Nothing but overlapping oil stains. I searched the rafters. The Christmas wreath and the old tent, both in storage last week, were gone. Paint cans in residence since my high school art projects were gone. Even the boxes of toys kept for Karen's kids vanished. I searched on the chance she'd taken pity and kept our things—in a new location. But Sue had erased us from the premises. My family never existed in this garage.

I sat on the concrete floor, holding my knees to my face.

"Lily." My father, slumped in his bathrobe, stood just inside the door. A sob wracked my chest and all I could manage was a high-pitched moan while he stood there, hands fumbling for pockets he couldn't find.

"Our things are gone," I said.

He turned sideways in the door. "I don't know anything about that," he said, annoyed. "And it's too late to be rattling around here looking for more hurt."

"I'm not looking for hurt," I screamed, emotions spinning out of control. This, too, was somehow my fault. "Why did you let her throw away our stuff?"

"You need to go home." He stepped outside the garage but I couldn't bear for him to leave. I screamed at the top of my lungs, scorching my throat, stopping him in his tracks. "Where is our tent?"

For just an instant, he feared me. "You know, Sue thinks you need help; your mother's death has been a shock for you." He sighed. "I think she's right." His hand left the door and he walked away.

Sitting on the hard floor, the soles of my bare feet touching an oil stain, I cried until I couldn't cry anymore. She dragged our stuff to the curb to be sure the garbage truck collected it before my dad could interfere. Like a hearse, the garbage truck hauled our things to a dump outside of town. A family's life rots beneath a sea of coffee grounds and eggshells in a county landfill near some prison.

"The universe no longer functions rationally," I told Karen. "Mother is lucky to be dead."

I heard the sharp intake of Karen's breath, and knew she was crying. "It's not the end of the world."

"You keep saying that."

Back in my room that evening, Bets sprawled on her bed watching TV. Gary, who had replaced me in the job of shadowing Bets, preventing any sudden trips to London during the workweek, parked at our table, eyes glued to the little TV. Bets's car keys sat in plain view.

"I'm not playing Mary Crawford anymore," Bets said during a commercial break.

"No?" I pulled books from my JASNA bag, wondering how I could read with that nonsense blaring.

"Just get a new color highlighter and start learning Maria Bertram's lines." She shrugged. "Sorry, I know you would have preferred the bigger part."

In the office two days later, I sat at my desk calculating the optimum time to abstain from Willis's attic—that moment beyond which my absence would provoke not fond memories but no memories at all. I had decided my next move would be a return appearance in the attic, but Claire's nervous bouncing made it hard to think. Every time someone approached

our door, she popped up. Then she interrupted my calculations to announce, "I have a meeting." She grabbed her clipboard. "But I'll be right back. I need to see Nigel when he
gets here."

Claire was up to something. When she and Magda weren't
engaged in covert phone conversations, Claire sat hunched
over a stack of top secret papers. She clicked into her screen
saver if I walked by, covered papers she was working on, and
stopped me with her eyes if I got too close. I waited five minutes before visiting her desk to use her stapler. While there,
I stealthily lifted the books obscuring her top secret papers.

She'd been working on a grant proposal. Looked like a
grant proposal for Literature Live. What's so secret about
that? Just to be sure, I dug deeper into the pile but found
nothing of interest. Suddenly, I froze, sensing a shadow on
my arms, an approach from behind. Looking down, I saw
stealthy white satin slippers, the sort that move over wooden
floors noiselessly. Turning, I stared into the needy eyes of
Mrs. Russell, black curls escaping her mobcap.

"The ballroom is free on Wednesdays from four to six,"
she whispered.

"Good," I said. "Can each of your volunteers furnish four
place settings and a teapot from their personal china?"

Mrs. Russell hesitated. Her face brightened. "How lovely,"
she said breathlessly. "A room full of china patterns." She
looked at me. "Like a china shop."

"Will they do it?"

She considered. "Some will want to bring more than one
pattern." Her eyes darted back and forth. "They'll have to
take turns."

"We need scones, sandwiches, and cookies," I said.

"We've made assignments."

"Clotted cream, sugar, and lemon."

"That's all under control," Mrs. Russell said, raising her palm to stop me. "I'll handle the food if you handle the entertainment."

"What entertainment?" I asked.

"I don't know. That's your department."

"Yes, of course. I'll do the entertainment," I said.

After she left, I sat at my desk contemplating tea entertainment. Tea-theatre. When Nigel finally arrived, Archie came with him and they closed themselves in Nigel's office. With the door shut, I couldn't hear anything. When Nigel's door was open, I heard everything he said on the phone, in meetings, and in casual exchanges. By simple osmosis, as long as his door remained open, I was privy to the ins and outs of Nigel's concerns, my finger on the pulse of the festival. I learned *who* was making the keynote address at which important upcoming conference, *which* distinguished scholar would edit the next important volume of *what* British novel, and *where* Nigel stood on many issues. Things he could not endure: elegiac yearnings and transgressive assumptions. I regularly consulted the dictionary on my desk for unfamiliar words in Nigel's conversations, *Elegiac: expression of sorrow for something now past*. Thereafter, I watched the costumed Janeites, cutting roses or pouring tea, for signs of sorrow. If they were sad for something now past, I would be more sympathetic. The few times Nigel closed the door, I felt cut off, aware of missing something good.

When Archie left, I stepped into Nigel's office.

"The volunteers would like very much to have a tea in the ballroom," I said.

"They told you?" Nigel feigned surprise.

"Yes," I said, glad for his indulgent mood. "And I was wondering if they could do it, with my help, on Wednesday at four."

"I don't see why not," Nigel said, "especially if that will satisfy their ball cravings." Nigel looked past me and I turned to see Claire standing in the doorway. "You'll keep track of the details, I assume."

"Yes," I said. "Income and expenses, volunteer hours and all that."

"What is it, Claire?" Nigel asked, less indulgently.

Claire approached the desk tentatively, a book in her hands, willing me to exit with every step. But I held my ground, thrilled to be in the right place at the right time to learn why she'd been so anxious to speak with Nigel. Claire gave me one last dirty look before proceeding.

"I've discovered something very interesting," she said, handing Nigel her highlighted text, her eyes flashing *stop* in my direction. Nigel looked at the book and passed it to me, as if Claire had meant it for show-and-tell. In the acknowledgment section of *Jane Austen's Letters* edited by Deirdre Le Faye, Claire had highlighted, "There are a few letters still in private hands, with whose owners it has proved impossible to make contact."

"And your point?" Nigel waited as I returned the book.

Claire's expression dimmed at his failure to grasp the importance of unexamined letters written by Jane Austen. She looked as though she'd lost sleep on account of the highlighted words. "Why are these letters being held?" she asked. "Is someone keeping a secret from the world?"

Nigel sighed. "What do you hope to discover, correspondence concerning Jane Austen's secret marriage?"

"Of course not," Claire said. "I just wondered if you knew of any attempts to force those letters into the public domain," she asked. "Don't we have a right to read them?"

"The letters are not being kept secret; they are simply private property of people who don't wish to share. They will become public someday," Nigel added, straightening a sheaf of papers. "The owners will die and the heirs will cash in."

Claire pressed her lips together and looked at her book. "But what if those letters explain what she meant when she wrote the novels."

Nigel paused and I hoped he might suggest she check her twenty-first-century filters at the door, or launch into Jane Austen's opinion of women whose imaginations overcome their reason. But he said, "Jane Austen reveals us to ourselves in many ways in her novels, revelations that require neither act of law nor detective to access."

All the same, I couldn't wait to tell Mrs. Russell about the missing letters, fairly certain Literature Live owned another copy of Le Faye's book. Claire gave up and I didn't shadow her further because I spent the rest of the morning planning my tea-theatre.

Omar explained Claire's squirrelly behavior over lunch. "Magda is plotting a coup," he said.

"What?" The pub was noisy.

"And Claire is helping her." He swallowed. "Magda's seeking permanent funding for Literature Live and promoting a year-round format, and she's dumping the typing and copying on Claire."

I remembered Randolph's request at the orientation meeting for ideas but never considered someone else—particularly Magda—would hear that call and beat me to the business plan. A year-round operation would be great if you could pay for it. "How will she do it?" I asked.

"She's soliciting her Michigan contacts, seeking university affiliation for the festival."

Why hadn't I thought of that? A year-round format would solve a lot of problems, including my employment status. But who was I kidding? There would be no place for me in Magda's plan for the future. "Do you think the Westons would allow Americans to fund their British project? Wouldn't that pose a problem?"

"The *problem* is Magda would be in charge." Omar pointed his spoon. "The *problem* is Magda is a bitch."

I agreed.

"Fifteen minutes of Magda, and Lady Weston would throw us out of her house, the actors would quit, and the tourists would go home," he said, running his spoon across his plate and licking. "Who wants to be bossed around on their vacation?"

Magda would surely sneer at me when she learned of the tea-theatre. I told Omar about the plan. "Will you write a script? I was thinking we might perform a condensed version of *Lovers' Vows*," I said, the same play the *Mansfield Park* Bertrams produce in their father's absence. "And we'll cast it with all amateur actors. Amateur tea-theatre."

Omar looked over his shoulder into the room.

"Will you take a part?" I asked.

"No. I can't act," Omar said.

"Oh please. I'll teach you."

"No."

"Will you write the script?"

"Only on the understanding that I will not act in it."

"Deal," I said, crossing my fingers under the table.

"I wonder if I could get any more of this applesauce."

As Omar approached the bar for more applesauce, I looked at my watch. It had been fifty hours. "Do you know Willis Somerford?" I asked when Omar returned with a small bowl.

"No," he said. "Why?"

"Just wondering." I folded my napkin, resting it on the

table, pleased to have exceeded the forty-eight hours I'd calculated as the maximum effective attic abstention period.

Standing outside the door to the attic, I checked the hall to make sure no one watched me disappear myself into the attic stairwell. What if he wasn't up there? What if he *was* up there?

"Hello, Willis," I called. "It's me, Lily." I hoped my name would ring a bell. I clutched the copy of Shakespeare's comedies, as if the gift were a casual afterthought, as if I hadn't agonized all morning over which edition of the many falling off our shelf he'd like best, nor nursed a mild obsession since our last moment together, waking up in a world that held him, looking for him in every room, most thoughts related to resuming our conversation under his sensual gaze.

"Lily," he called back. "Come up."

The musty, damp smell, the choking dust, the table, and the orange cord all welcomed me back.

"You've brought your book," he said, closing his laptop. "Shall we have our own literary festival?"

"Actually," I said, handing him the book, "I brought this for you."

"Thank you." As he took the book, his face fell ever so slightly and it seemed he flipped the pages to avoid looking at me.

"There's a reading at the pub tonight," I said to cover my embarrassment.

"Oh?" He looked up.

"Students from the writing workshop." Omar said they need a gentle audience. "I thought you might like to come."

He scratched his head. "I'd love to but"—he gestured to his desk—"I've got so much work to do."

We both looked at the closed laptop. Among the many

books on his table only one lay open, a large photo essay titled, *America's National Parks*. "Maybe another time," I said. Perhaps I'd read too much into our first meeting.

But he was still watching me.

"Yes," he said. "Another time."

I gave him something to watch. I pivoted the way I'd been taught in my department store charm school, arms floating gracefully at my sides, gently gliding into steps all the way to the window where I sat and slowly looked up at him. "You know"—I took a breath—"I've been thinking of all the fictional people who live in this house."

"Such as?" Willis asked, hooked.

"The Bertrams, the Crawfords, all the regulars."

"Ah." Willis nodded.

"They'll still be here, long after we're gone"—I shrugged—"moving the same plot forward century after century. If they wrote Christmas cards, they would never have anything new to report. Fanny would always win Edmund's love and Mary Crawford would always be hunting a husband."

"Literary afterlife."

"But what if"—I pointed—"I could take Maria Bertram back to Texas where she could start over with a clean slate in a place where no one knew her?"

"You'd have to guard your husband."

I smiled. After a pause, I said, "I'm planning a tea-theatre."

"A what?" he asked, leaning forward.

"A tea party where volunteers in period dress serve refreshments and Lily performs on a stage." I stood. "Will you take a part? You can have the lead."

He laughed. "Thank you for thinking of me." He shook his head. "I'm not an actor."

"I knew you'd say that." I took a deep breath. Who was left to play a male role, Gary? "Pity you can't make it to the reading," I said breezily, "*or* the tea." I walked past him toward the stairs. "Someday we'll all be famous and we'll be able to say we got our start at Literature Live."

"Good-bye, Lily," he said.

I floated away from him without a backward glance, hopeful that he appreciated the bounce in my step, wondering if I still had whatever it was he found interesting.

At the pub, I drank lukewarm ale and struggled to follow the heavily accented reading of an Indian woman's story about a long distance e-mail relationship. But I kept zoning out and returning to the attic. Maybe I should have waited one more day before returning. The fellow workshop writers took the reading very seriously so I followed their cue to know when to laugh, which was not often. Although we occupied a cozy back corner of the pub, people were coming and going, chairs scraping the wood floor just beyond our gathering.

I looked behind me once and my stomach jumped because Willis was there, standing at the edge of the group. Suddenly, the room was alive and breathing. Our eyes met and I gestured for him to bring a chair to our crowded table but he shook his head and squinted toward the reader. I understood him to mean he would wait for a break, not disrupt the reading. I turned back to the front but could not concentrate knowing Willis was watching me from behind. At the next break I would help him move a chair and we'd sit together. The idea of being a couple excited me. I loved the pub, loved the sound of the woman's voice reading, the smell of food cooking somewhere in the back.

But the reading went on and on. My Jane Austen yawned and left the room. I cautiously turned to check on Willis. He looked bored. Pages kept turning and I strained my eyes at each turn, looking for white space in the manuscript that would indicate the end. No one else seemed the least bit aware that this woman was going on way too long. I found a chair with my eyes and visually relocated it to my side. Better yet, Willis and I could sit at an outlying table by ourselves.

I was busy imagining all the reasons Willis might have decided to join me there when the woman's pace suddenly became halting. She read a few more words and then looked up, smiling shyly. She had reached the end. Everyone clapped and I immediately turned to join Willis. But he wasn't there. Searching the pub, he wasn't near the bar, didn't come out of the men's room. He wasn't anywhere. He'd vanished. I walked back to my dorm alone but instead of fretting about Willis, pondered how we would heat water to make tea.

Ten

The next day, *I* waited nervously for Nigel, mentally rehearsing my disclosure of Claire's plot to undermine the organization with her grant proposals. As I waited, I carefully tracked Claire's covert activities, noting each mission to the copier, watching as she loaded her stapler, determined not to miss anything. My Jane Austen sat in the corner oblivious, reading *Jane Eyre*. The memory of Willis standing at the back of the reading room interrupted my reconnaissance efforts at ten-second intervals. Why had he left the reading?

By the time I returned from my chore of planting a water bottle at the podium for the speaker lecturing on "Edmund's Multiple Incumbencies," Nigel's office door was open and Vera was leaning over his desk, dropping multicolored capsules into a pillbox. The pillbox doors for the various days of the week were open like baby bird beaks and Vera dropped pills, shutting each door as she went.

"It's Lily." She smiled.

"And how is our favorite reader today?" Nigel asked, looking especially tired.

Me? "I'm fine," I said, remembering how my mother's medicine all disappeared when Sue arrived.

"You look worried," Vera said. "Is everything okay with your tea party?"

I closed Nigel's door, cutting Claire off; then folded my hands and took a breath as they both watched me, concerned. "I heard yesterday that Magda is seeking university affiliation for this festival," I whispered.

Vera picked up another prescription container and Nigel leaned back in his chair.

"We know," Vera said, and then pointed at Nigel. "You see?" She shook her head and dumped pills into her palm. "I've been telling him," she said to me, shrugging. "He won't listen to anything I say. I think we need to act—*now*."

"I refuse to bother a sick woman," Nigel said, rubbing his eyes.

"She's not sick, she's dying," Vera said, passing him the refilled pillbox.

"All the more reason." Nigel shut the pillbox in his desk drawer.

"All the more reason." Vera stood. "If you won't go with me, I'll take Lily." Vera looked at me. "Lily understands business. Did you know Lily has a real estate license?"

"I don't have a license," I said, rolling my eyes.

"I'm sorry, Nigel," Vera said, fluttering a hand, "but I'm not about to stand by and watch the ship go down with you in it. Lily, we'll need to prepare a new lease," Vera said. "Ask Claire for a fresh copy."

Right. I wasn't asking Claire for anything.

★ ★ ★

When everyone was gone for lunch I acted against my better judgment and began the impulsive walk that would end in the attic. I had second thoughts upon reaching the second floor. What was I doing? But as I stood outside the door to the attic stairwell, preparing to disappear myself, the click of a latch and the squeaky whine of door hinges resonated down the hall. I was nailed. Sixby called out to me from his room.

"Ah, 'tis the sun," he said. "Just the starlet I wanted to see. Come," he beckoned, reopening his door. "I have something for you."

I scurried down the hall. Fearing Willis would choose that moment to emerge from the attic stairwell, I entered Sixby's room more willingly than under normal circumstances. Costumes lounged on horizontal surfaces and his wardrobe stood open displaying a poster of the Royal Shakespeare Company's *Romeo and Juliet*.

"What happened to you?" he asked, gracing my hand with a theatrical kiss—didn't mean anything. "I haven't seen you around." My Jane Austen flipped through the little black date book on his table.

"I've been working in the office," I said. Claire was probably looking for me now, hands on her ample hips, wondering how her work would get done with me running around the festival like Fanny Price on Prozac. "And I'm organizing a tea-theatre." I described the plan, knowing I needed him to play a part, working up to the request, keeping my back to his unmade bed. "Since Magda won't allow me in her production, I'll just have to produce my own."

"Lily, let go of what happened on the stage," he said.

"Magda says she's not paid to teach me to act."

"The words of Mercury are harsh after the songs of Apollo." Sixby looked down at me, dark roots visible along his hairline. "So I'll help you." Willis would *never* highlight his hair. "First thing is: the Book." He pointed.

Books had piled up in here just like in every other room in the great house. I lifted one from the stack on the floor. "Where did all the books come from? I've never seen so many outside of a library."

"Nigel's dead friends."

"That's nice."

"AIDS, you know."

I dropped the book back on the pile.

"Mostly English teachers and writers, some theatre people. Great collection of books but some of it's getting a bit dated. Ah, but not this one," he said, pulling the very small book from a pile on the shelf. "*Acting.*" He handed it to me. "Thank me no thankings."

Ancient and frayed, the cellophane cover disintegrating, the book fell open and stayed flat in my hand, no resistance left in its binding. A previous reader had underlined the soft yellowed pages in pencil, and its smell reminded me of my lost childhood books. "Isn't it funny," I said, "how old books smell the same?"

Sixby took the book and sniffed. "A rose by any other name."

"It doesn't matter what library they come from," I said. "They all smell the same."

"Lily, you may be on to something." Sixby handed the book back. "But after you finish smelling it, give this book a proper read."

Gripping the book in both hands, I looked Sixby square in the eye. "Sixby," I said carefully, "will you play the lead in my production?" His expression lost all trace of theatrics; my request obviously triggered stress. At last, the real Sixby stood before me.

"I don't think that's a good idea," he said, squinting. "Magda and all."

"Yeah." I nodded, slipping the book under my arm. "I guess you're right."

"But I'll be there for your opening. When is it?"

"Next Wednesday at four. I hope," I said.

"Fantastic," he said, much brighter. "And don't forget we have an act to plan for the follies."

"The follies." I hugged the book.

"We need a good idea," he said. "So think of something: music, dancing, a little Shakespeare."

"Parting is such sweet sorrow," I said, deadpan. "That's all the Shakespeare I know."

"O, speak again, bright angel!" Sixby's rich voice captivated me, just as it had at the orientation meeting. He stepped toward me and took my arms as if his messy bedroom were a stage and I his leading lady. "For thou art as glorious to this night, being o'er my head, as is a winged messenger of heaven." The artful way he said *thou* and *glorious* lifted me out of myself. "Unto the white-upturned wondering eyes," he said as I felt myself airborne, soaring on the beauty of his modulation. "Of mortals that fall back to gaze on him when he bestrides the lazy-pacing clouds and sails upon the bosom of the air." I closed my eyes and imagined exercising my diaphragm to respond in kind. The words spun in my head, reverberating, sound falling on me like dazzling snowflakes as I raised my arms and touched fingers with Sixby, the power of his delivery endowing me with the belief that if I opened my mouth, words would come out to match his in depth and timbre. I *was* Juliet. I felt the emotion; if I knew the lines I could speak. But then Sixby's lips touched mine. I opened my eyes; footsteps approached in the hall. Before I could move my mouth away from Sixby's, Omar stood at the door with an armload of paper.

"From Magda," he said, handing the stack to Sixby.

Sixby groaned.

"Do you have time for lunch?" Omar asked me.

"What's up with you and Sixby?" Omar asked, sitting across from me, waiting for our sandwiches, the pub especially noisy, thanks to a group of men drinking their lunch.

"He's helping me," I said, the acting book tucked in my JASNA bag.

"Helping himself." Omar laughed. "Must be smitten with your inexperience."

"Acting lessons," I said, wondering if Omar might be jealous. I'd caught him watching Sixby at odd moments.

"Acting Lesson Number One." Omar's index finger stabbed the air. "Teach Only Naive American Girls."

"That would be me," I said, over the din of laughter from the men at the next table.

"Acting Lesson Number Two," Omar said. "The Importance of Rehearsing Love Scenes."

"Not in Austen," I pointed out. "No danger there."

"Well," he said, "revisionism is rampant at Literature Live. Just be careful." Omar pulled a folder from his satchel. "Here's your script," he said.

"Thank you, Omar. That was quick." I opened the folder and scanned the first page. *Lovers' Vows, Condensed for Lily's Tea-Theatre*. Seven characters: two women and five men. "Where will I ever find five men to play these roles?" I looked up at Omar, who was watching the table of noisy men. "Omar."

"No."

"Please?"

"I cannot act."

"That doesn't matter. I'll teach you."

"No." Omar stood. "I'm going to get our sandwiches now."

"You can have the smallest part. Oh please. If you say no, I'll have to *beg* Sixby and who knows what will come of that."

Omar laughed. "You'll be good as Agatha."

"I'm Amelia or nothing. I'm in charge, remember? You can play Anhalt." I took his hand and pressed it to my cheek. "Please?"

Omar rolled his eyes. "Maintain your dignity." He took his hand back. "I'll do it—*only if*—you can't find anyone else."

"Oh, thank you! Thank you!"

As Omar brought our sandwiches from the bar, I brought up the subject of Magda's funding initiative. "It seems that Nigel's in denial."

"Yes, Nigel is in denial on many fronts."

"What do you mean?" I asked, speaking over the din.

Omar looked at his watch. "How much time do you have; I'm not sure where to start."

"Approach it alphabetically."

Omar ticked off on his fingers. "A," he said. "Austen's global, Actors are expensive, Attention spans are shorter."

"Okay, okay."

"Banks family bails out, Cash flow dries up, Death claims Nigel."

"Death?" I asked. The table behind Omar shouted a toast.

Omar put his hands down. "Surely you know he's sick."

"No." They clinked glasses and drank.

"HIV positive as long as I've known him. And he's going downhill this summer."

My hand flew to my mouth. How could I not know this?

"I'm surprised Vera didn't tell you."

"No, she didn't." But now I knew what she carefully sorted

and lovingly dropped into his days of the week, hunched over the pillbox, the desk littered with prescription bottles. How sick was he and how much time did he have? One of the men at the next table slammed his empty mug.

At my request, John Owen, the conservationist in charge of maintenance, accompanied Mrs. Russell and me to the kitchen for the purpose of turning on the water. According to my calculations, we needed twenty gallons of tea, and none of our volunteers would haul that much water into the house dressed as Regency ladies. We had no servants, other than me, and I had pressing responsibilities elsewhere. "We need to fire up the stove as well," I said to John Owen, who crouched below the surface, grimacing as he applied his wrench.

"Blow us all up, won't you?" he said.

"Oh no." Mrs. Russell clutched her fringed shawl, she hadn't figured on explosions. She lowered tools to John Owen and his helper, a shirtless grad student by the name of Stephen Jervis, Caribbean judging by his caramel skin and Rastafarian plaits lining his scalp. Perhaps he had roots in Antigua. Stephen and Mrs. Russell, who carried the wrench, went outside; we could see and hear them through the big hole in the wall. Mrs. Russell giggled from a place deep in her chest right before Stephen gave the go ahead to turn the faucet. Globs of water spit and spurt into the sink before easing into a smooth rush.

"Hooray!" I said. "Can you try the stove now?"

While my helpers continued working, I ran back and forth between kitchen and office. Sorting through files, I found the expired agreement. A napkin-quality document, I marveled they'd kept it. While they tested the gas, I typed up a new version using the same casual language but adding the title

"Lease Extension" and a line for Lord Weston's signature. No telling how much longer Nigel would be around to use his IBM Selectric. Desperate to beat both Magda's grant applications and Nigel's terminal illness, I rushed around, filling the copier, hunting paper clips, the thought of Willis in the attic beeping like a private snooze alarm.

Mrs. Russell was standing outside the kitchen looking tense when I returned. "Don't go in there," she said in an unfamiliar chest voice. "We have leaks. Stephen has gone for new pipe."

Stephen. I covered my nose.

"What's that smell?" I turned to find Magda bearing down on me. "We can't have this horrid smell. The next scene starts in thirty minutes."

"We have everything under control," I said calmly, glancing about to make sure all the windows were open. "Don't worry."

"Are you responsible for the water coming out of the second floor bathroom?" Magda asked me. "I don't want it raining in here."

"Not a problem," I said. When Magda was out of earshot I asked Mrs. Russell, "Do you know how to turn off the water?"

I didn't have enough information to complete the lease. Nor did I have enough ideas to start a business plan. What university would give *me* funding for the festival? And in spite of my compelling concern for Nigel and his festival, I kept one eye on the clock, my adrenal glands dumping on several false alarms when tall people in dark shirts walked by. By the time we got the water and gas turned off again, Mrs. Russell had recruited Stephen Jervis to join our theatre. I decided that a short attic break would send me back to my projects with renewed energy.

★ ★ ★

"What happened to you last night?" I asked. Willis sat at his desk. The laptop closed, he'd been reading *Living Abroad in Belize*.

"Nice to see you, too." He smiled.

I walked to the window and sat on the plank bench, feeling my bones on the hard surface. "You vanished."

Willis turned his chair to face me and I felt his eyes, studying me. "Life is too short for bad writing," he said.

He'd listened to the workshop story. While I was oblivious, thanks to him, he'd had the presence of mind to comprehend what she read. Now he focused that same level of inspection on me. I didn't want to come up lacking. I didn't want to end up ditched as bad writing or bad flirting or bad anything. Nervous, I launched into mindless chatter of the sort that would surely have me thrown out for bad conversation. My Jane Austen closed her eyes and slashed her throat as I chattered about the water and the gas leaks, Magda's takeover, and Nigel's illness, willing my pulse to settle as I described my urgency to get something signed by Lady Weston before the kitchen exploded. "Vera wants me to accompany her to the hospital and ask Lady Weston to help us get a lease extension signed," I said. "Soon."

His expression gradually changed from happy interest to mild censure as he stood to fetch a book from the stack behind his table. "I don't think that's a good idea."

I slumped against the window. "Neither does My Jane Austen." No sooner were the words out of my mouth than My Jane Austen stopped breathing and stared at me. I froze, touching my fingers to my lips. Did I feel the vibration of a kitchen explosion two floors below or was that my stricken heart? Had he heard what I said?

"What do you mean *your* Jane Austen?" Willis asked.

I inhaled. "Sit down," I said.

"I'm sitting." He smiled, joining me on the window seat.

"Everyone who reads The Six . . ." I went slowly to make sure he was with me.

"Six Jane Austen novels." He nodded.

"Yes. Believes they know Jane Austen personally. In our secret heart of hearts, each of us believes that she speaks to us personally in her writings. My Jane Austen just happens to follow me around most of the time," I said very slowly.

"I see." Willis bit his lip.

"She's here now."

"Where?" He glanced into the room.

"In the corner." I nodded toward the murky fringes of the room without looking directly. Willis looked directly. "She's like a floater you get in your eye. If you look at her she'll dart off to another periphery."

"Inconvenient," Willis said.

"She's not real." I reached for Willis's arm as if he might be the one with the mental problem.

"Okay." He looked at the hand touching his arm.

"This is all make-believe, Willis. You'll have to stretch the imagination here a bit."

"No, I'm with you. Go on."

In an expansive rush, I told Willis what I'd never told anyone—couldn't even imagine telling anyone. "She's not beautiful. In my mind, she looks like the sketch Cassandra made of her, perpetually irritated, a bit of a bully. She died young so she's eternally forty-one years old, and gray runs through her dark brown hair. Her face is pale with a hint of blue. Sometimes she reminds me of a vampire in a Romantic sense, sucking the experiences out of people to fill her pages."

Willis leaned toward me as I continued.

"But her strongest representation for me is Patron Saint of Thoughtful Women." I paused, brushing a strand of hair from my eyes. "She believes that women whose inner lives dominate their personalities, reserved women who take a backseat to the witty, charming Mary Crawfords of the world, should marry for love." I glanced at him. "Secondary types, like me and Fanny Price, are the protagonists in her stories."

Willis looked at me in a way that made me stop talking.

"What?" I said.

He didn't answer, but took my chin in his hand, raised my face to his, and kissed me.

"Sorry," he said. "I was overcome by all that."

Eleven

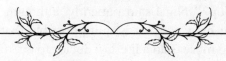

tea-theatre conflicts directly with our productions and the poor quality will reflect badly on this festival." Magda stood near my desk addressing Nigel while Omar stared at the floor. "Amateur hour is not what we need at this moment when we are trying to take the festival to the next level." Magda raised her hands. "Who will seriously consider funding something so unprofessional?"

They all glanced at me walking in. Then Nigel ushered Magda and Omar into his office and shut the door. I strained to hear but could distinguish only the occasional rising of Magda's voice, no actual words. As if I needed more distractions. After my last session with Willis I could barely think; the limits of my resources became clear as I struggled to gain traction with *Business Plan for Dummies*. I finally gave up and stared blissfully into the space over my open book recalling the Kiss, during which Willis slowly bent his neck, touching his lips to mine, his hand gently lifting my chin, as if he were the Prince and I the Fair Maiden. I was about to relive it from the beginning, when Vera arrived. She paused in front of Nigel's closed door and glanced at me.

"Omar and Magda," I whispered.

"Oh yes." Vera frowned, remembering. Then she let herself in, not bothering to shut the door behind her.

"A cover-up?" Nigel said patiently, although I heard exasperation in his voice. "It is quite possible that the trip to Antigua is no more than a literary device to get the father out of the house and further the courtship plot. Put yourself in 1814, Magda."

"I have," she shot back. "And in 1811, the Slave Trade Felony Act was introduced. Austen knew this; her readers knew this. Fanny Price was an abolitionist."

"Really?" Vera said.

My tea-theatre was not the subject of discussion.

Nigel sounded weary. "I simply ask that you not tamper with what is explicit. Don't alter the prose."

Omar spoke for the first time. "So," he said in a careful monotone, "are you saying to cut those lines where Sir Thomas provides details of his slave ownership to Fanny?"

I still felt a little shock, thinking of Sir Thomas owning slaves.

"Yes," Nigel said. "Suggest larger political issues—for God's sake, use Mrs. Norris's green baize to imply whatever you like, but keep it implicit."

Magda interrupted to voice an objection but Claire rose from her desk to close the door, shooting me a glance.

At my first opportunity, I went to the attic.

"Hello, Willis," I called up. No response. I called again.

Everything remained as we left it, except his laptop which he had taken with him. A stack of telephone messages accumulated beneath his collection of pens and the books waited unmoved. The room felt incredibly lonely and even spooky without him. I sat at the window while My Jane Austen read his phone messages. The loneliness grew so oppressive that I left her there, crossing the floor to the stairs in haste, tripping loudly as if she chased me down the stairs. I didn't stop until I found myself outside the second floor bathroom where John Owen continued to wrestle with our plumbing issues.

The next day Willis was still not there and I began to feel slightly desperate. After my third trip up the stairs to look for him, I decided to try the church. I sat in the back, allowing the powerful words entry, giving myself up to calm meditation and deep breathing. My Jane Austen paced an empty row behind me but I ignored her, focusing instead on summoning the necessary blend of reserve and aggression to deal with Willis. He couldn't see me and I felt like a spy, watching him listen to the homily from his seat in the sanctuary.

After the service, Willis stationed himself with the clergy in the entry, shaking hands, wishing everyone a good morning as they left. He saw me before I reached him so when we shook hands my presence was no longer a surprise. He smiled and said, "Good morning," but anyone watching could tell from our smiles that a secret joke existed between us. I struck the tiniest, nearly imperceptible flirtatious pose. Almost immediately, I felt the connection. I kept it light. "Do you have time for coffee?" I asked.

He watched me. I didn't move. If he wanted more, he would have to join me.

"Yes," he said.

Willis didn't want to sit by the window so we carried our coffee to the back of the small café; Willis nodded to an empty table, placing his hand on the small of my back to guide me. I was what's-her-name to his Maxim de Winter, falling for each other in a quaint dining room. He rested his arms on the table and stared at me.

I whispered, "Are you aware of the slavery issues in *Mansfield Park*?"

He sipped his coffee. "No," he said, "tell me."

Appropriating a breathy voice, I told him about the conversation I'd overheard in the office between Nigel and Magda, the explicit references to slavery I was aware of, and Omar's forced adaptation. Willis listened, sipping coffee, his back to the room. We drew attention, people curious about the woman confessing her sins to a priest in a coffee shop, which explained why Willis chose a secluded table.

"But I thought she restricted herself to writing about a few country families," Willis said.

Two things about talking with Willis. With Martin, I could make it up as I went; no facts, no problem. Not Willis, he had a background in this stuff and he listened critically; he would be on to me in a heartbeat. The other thing: I might as well have been describing in minute detail how I planned to disrobe later that evening. He studied me as if every word were an intimate revelation, a window into my deep personal places. "Some people, Magda for instance, believe the novels are charged with political meaning," I said.

"What does *your* Jane Austen say?" he asked, his slow smile an invitation to deeper confidence.

But then I saw a familiar face ordering coffee at the counter. "Oh, look," I said, "there's the woman who read her story at the pub the other night." Willis didn't turn to look. I recognized others from Omar's writing workshop, and then Omar came in. I waved as he came to my table.

"This is my friend Omar who leads the writing workshop."

Willis reluctantly turned to shake Omar's hand. I could barely focus on Omar's entertaining explanation of the writing group's field trip to the coffee shop because Willis had turned his back on Omar and was crumpling his napkin in his fist. He stood, taking his coffee cup with him, and looked at his watch.

"I've got to run," he said. "Pleasure meeting you," he said to Omar as he abruptly departed.

I watched until he was gone.

"What's up with him?" Omar asked.

This would become our routine. Willis would listen carefully as I updated him on tea-theatre progress: water now flowed from the kitchen sink without flooding other parts of the house, but the stove was still dangerous. We had china, teapots, scones, and tablecloths, but no gas. Then he would express wonder as I shared the things I learned at Nigel's door every day. The term *critical vocabulary* opened a whole world, the mere word *traduce* expressed a big idea in only seven letters. I became addicted to the daily dose of attention from Willis; craved his deep and penetrating gaze. But he would not have lunch with me. Too much work.

I spoke of elegiac yearnings and whispered the terrible truth that Jane Austen's fans couldn't face—that in spite of their perpetual search for details, they would *never* really know Jane Austen. Willis appeared genuinely moved. But not enough to relocate to the pub for happy hour.

Collecting bits of wonder during my working hours, I saved them to tell Willis: how Jane Austen's sister, Cassandra, had censored hundreds of letters with her scissors, like shredding documents, consigning their secrets to eternity. I explained there were only two likenesses of Jane Austen, both sketches by Cassandra, from which all other images had sprung; artists adding feminine ruffles, curls, or cosmetics, depending on the time and context of the artist.

But when asked personal questions, he always steered the talk elsewhere. He declined invitations to lunch, dinner, readings, and lectures, unwilling to budge from his desk. He always seemed engaged in our conversations, but never enough to kiss me again. I couldn't figure him out and didn't know what to do.

One day when Nigel and Vera were gone to London and Claire was free to work on nonfestival matters, Claire asked me to introduce the speaker for "Sexual Repression in *Mansfield Park*." I forced Willis out of my head and marshaled every particle of concentration to craft a coherent introduction from the speaker's résumé. If I didn't do a good job, she'd hear about it and never give me another chance. Nonetheless, as I sat listening to the lecture an idea took root. My idea grew while the speaker analyzed the scene where Edmund helps Mary Crawford dismount Fanny's horse, while Fanny watches. By the time Mary Crawford had made her apologies, I had a plan.

Willis sat at the window, staring listlessly into the darkness in a way that made me fear he might be bored. The impulse fueling my plan deflated and I considered that a sensible person might say good night and retreat to her room or attend the performance in the ballroom. Not me.

"Hello, Lily." Willis patted the plank next to him.

"We could really use some cushions up here." I joined him, removing my sweater and leaning in, pretending to look out the window where the glamorous moon lit the night stage presenting tree branches in silhouette, a quiet couple sitting in the herb garden. I wished I could open the window and smell the night air, forgetting it would be cool, not hot and dry like Texas.

"Do you know Mrs. Russell?" I asked.

"No." Willis smiled and turned to me.

I sat up very straight. "She's in charge of the volunteers," I said, "the women who pass out programs and sell tickets. And she's cochair of the tea-theatre."

"She wears a costume," he said.

"Period attire," I corrected him. "Anyway, she announced this afternoon that she wants to play Amelia in the skit. And Stephen Jervis will play Anhalt."

Willis shifted his legs. "Is that bad?"

"Well, *yes.* I'm sure that I am not going to play Agatha, her mother. *I'm* Amelia. And *Omar* is Anhalt." I felt his regard penetrate my face, going in through the eyes, seeking a comfortable place near my heart. "I think she's up to something with Stephen Jervis. Maybe the tea-theatre was a bad idea; we should have continued pushing for a ball. I don't understand why Nigel is so opposed to a ball," I said, talking, while I cast about for the optimal moment to activate my plan. I sensed My Jane Austen in a dark corner, working on "A List of Silly Girls." She'd gotten as far as Lydia Bennet.

"It's not the ball, really," Willis said. "Rather a preference for the way his festival addresses the study of Jane Austen." He looked into my eyes as I ran my fingers over the hem of Bets's black blouse that buttoned up the front. "Professional academics have rules for the study of literature which the fans tend to ignore."

"Such as?" I asked.

"Well." Willis looked down, and I wondered if he knew where I was going with the blouse. "The fan club treats characters as if they were real people and speculate on their lives outside the text."

I sat up straight. "Go on."

"Study requires analytical skills and specialized knowledge that professional academics spend their careers acquiring."

"Well, that automatically excludes a lot of people." My heart beat faster.

"Lady Weston and Nigel chose to work together to elevate the study of Jane Austen, to provide self-taught readers access to the academic research in a manor house setting."

"You must know the Lockwood family," I said, recalling Willis with Randolph at the orientation meeting.

"Yes," Willis said, clearing his throat.

Inasmuch as he knew what he had just told me, how could he *not* know the fun facts I'd been sharing at our daily wonderfests? Maybe he was pretending not to know just so he could listen to me talk. I took a deep breath, gathering courage from the scent of Bets's spicy perfume I'd sprayed on my neck and wrists, and placed my fingers on the top button of my black blouse. The top button slipped out and my fingers traveled down to the next.

"What are they like?" I asked, my voice breaking, the second button freed and my fingers on the third, the top of Bets's black bra visible. Willis exhaled, his eyes on my cleavage as I opened the fourth button and slowly pulled the blouse apart. Moonlight cast a white sheen on my curving flesh as I considered releasing the bra's front clasp. Willis didn't speak but I could hear his breath. He took my hands, pushing them down to my lap, and held them there. Maybe he wanted to look at me in the moonlight. But then he touched the blouse and, starting at the bottom, he buttoned one after the other until all were closed.

Then he held my hands again. "We don't know each other, Lily," he whispered in the darkness. I turned away, fearing this was what Martin meant by needy, feeling I'd been censured, feeling embarrassed and confused, too ashamed to look at him. I would have stood but he had my right hand and held it tight. I looked away, all the bad feelings melting the snow inside me to a grimy slush and I wanted to lie down and drown in it.

"Tell me why you're so sad," he said.

No one had ever asked me that question; I didn't know what to say and if he hadn't been holding me and talking to me the way he was, I would have run away.

"Hmm?" he murmured, his mouth close to my head, his other hand on my chin, lifting my face to look at him.

Even I didn't understand my deep sadness, with me as long as I could remember. My earliest memories were of being sad, different from everybody else; perhaps the reason I never fit in. Grave and serious like Jane Eyre, or Catherine and Heathcliff, or Anna Karenina. I understood exactly how they felt, and nobody in real life shared that kind of pain with me. No one, not even my mother, had ever known about my sadness. I'd been so worried about psychologists, and now writers, penetrating my defenses, when all along deacons had the power. I didn't know where to start—from my deep and powerful identification with *The Secret Garden* in fourth grade, to the loss of my mother, the books, the necklace, or everything in between. "My mother died," I said, tears filling my eyes, "last September."

"I'm sorry," he said.

I felt a rush of gratitude, my face crumpled like a small child while he searched his pockets and handed me a tissue.

"You need help with that grief," he said.

"I've had some help. I chose the Episcopal church, mostly because of the Book of Common Prayer; you know—the exquisite beauty and power of the words." *Manifold sins and wickedness* came to mind. "But after she died, my father do-

nated her body to science and we had a lunch in our back-
yard. He wouldn't talk to the priest; he never went to church
with us."

"Why is that?"

"He says God isn't interested in religion." Telling Willis
brought it back to me, that sudden vacuum of emptiness—
even with all the usual suspects gathered at our house. I told
Willis about "the bossy aunts breaking into my mother's
china cupboard, the black sheep opening the fridge for another beer."

Willis sat perfectly still.

"Everyone was there except my mother," I said. "She
would have asked my cousin questions about grad school and
whispered for me to get the silver tray out of the bottom shelf
for the meat. I kept expecting her to walk into the room. But
she wasn't there. Her place was empty." I stopped to compose
myself.

"Yes," Willis said.

"After she died, I couldn't cry. Not until her best friend,
who traveled from Ohio to see me, walked into our kitchen." I
could still recall the sound of her black pumps on the linoleum
floor, the jangle of her keys hitting the kitchen counter, and
the rustle of her slip against her black skirt as she opened her
plump arms to me. "We've both lost our best friend," she said,
holding me tight while I sobbed into her shoulder.

"That's actually a normal reaction," Willis said.

"How normal is sneaking into random Episcopal funer-
als?" I held the tissue to my lips, recalling the words I craved,
*All we go down to the dust; yet even at the grave we make our
song.*

"Less so." He nodded.

"My father wasn't home much when I was growing up. He
traveled a lot for work and I never felt close to him. Still, I was

surprised when, about a week after everyone left, he started seeing a woman."

Willis closed his eyes.

"Even absent as he had been, his behavior didn't correspond to anything I expected from him or understood about my life and I didn't know what to believe. I still don't. My sister thinks the affair started before my mother died."

"Did you talk to him about it?"

"No. And he told us not to speak of our mother in front of his friend because our grief makes her uncomfortable."

Willis waited while I dabbed my nose.

"I lost the childhood books she saved for me and now I've lost her last gift to me, a cross necklace she made by melting her wedding ring," I said, shaking my head. "I feel like she's slipping away from me."

We were so quiet I could hear a scratching noise and leaves rustling outside.

"No one knows what it's like after we die." Willis looked into my face. I wadded the tissue in my hand and wished for another. "I imagine the soul becomes part of that great eternity beyond our understanding of place and time, with us always, just as God is with us."

"Oh no." I thought of my mother following me around like My Jane Austen.

Willis smiled. "Not in the judgmental *human* way of seeing you."

I accepted another tissue. Willis touched my hand and we sat silently for a while, listening to the house creak and things fluttering in the rafters. "Are you ready to go?" he asked.

"No. I want you to tell me why *you're* so sad," I said.

"I'm not sad." Willis patted my hand.

"Then, what is it?" I asked.

Willis squirmed. "English reserve." He smiled. After a silence, he got up and went to his desk to gather his books and I turned to look out the window. I wanted us to leave together and stay together for the walk back to my dorm. He would not get away from me this time. Closing a book on his desk, his movement jarred the table, and the computer screen came to life.

"A light in the darkness," he said, then turned and opened his arms to me. "I'd like to hug you," he said, "if you'll promise to keep your shirt on."

I was grateful he made light of it; thankful he'd found a different way for us to be.

"One more button and I'm afraid I would have been overcome," he said.

I went to him gladly, my arms about his waist, my head on his arm, saving up the sensation so I could recall it in the morning. Close enough to see the computer screen, I absently read the words over his arm, expecting a sermon or a page from his thesis on moral theology. But the words didn't fit my expectations, forcing me to shift mental gears. It took a bit of reading to comprehend what I saw.

"Willis," I said, stepping away from him.

He looked from me to the screen and I recognized the "stopping" look my father flashed at me when I found Sue in his kitchen.

I touched his arm. "There's a vampire story on your computer." The page heading said, "Vampire Priest."

He looked startled, as if the vampire text surprised him, too.

"You're writing a vampire story. Can I read it?" I asked.

Willis hesitated. He swallowed while I stood completely still, waiting, sensing a crack in his mighty reserve.

"Yes," he said.

Twelve

I read from Willis's laptop screen, deep into the night until I finished what he had written thus far, the story of a vampire priest who preaches the Gospel after dark and falls in love with a symphony cellist. Luna meets him at the stage exit each night, her white neck a terrible temptation in the moonlight.

Had we just enacted the neck in the moonlight scene?

In the morning, I got out of bed and looked in the mirror, imagining Luna emerging from the back door of the performance hall, unbuttoning the front of her dress, finally and forever offering him her neck. Father Kitt stares for a moment and then buttons her back up to her chin saying, "Luna, we barely know each other."

"Bite me," I said aloud to the mirror.

"What is wrong with you?" Bets moaned from her pillow, back from wherever she'd been for the last two days, mascara smudged below her eyes more than usual. "It's impossible to sleep in this place."

"Where is my necklace?" I asked. I always checked her neck, just in case my necklace reappeared; now I would check for bites.

"Stop it," Bets growled, dragging herself out of bed to the window, slamming it shut.

"Get my necklace and I'll leave you alone forever," I said.

She went down the hall to use the restroom and I opened the window again, readmitting fresh air and noise from the outside world. No need for air-conditioning in our building; the thick walls performed as a refrigerator. I could see Gary in the distance, walking toward the dorm, coming to fetch Bets as he did every day. Bets hadn't gone missing on his watch, which made me think they were up to something. Bets wouldn't cooperate without an angle.

Bets returned from the bathroom, dropped her towel in a heap on the floor, and walked naked to the dresser, squinting, hopping on one leg and then the other as she adjusted a thong. Bets didn't do Regency undergarments.

"Where is my necklace?" I asked.

"What necklace?" she asked, slipping the ivory gown with blue trim over her head, the same one she always wore. "Oh, the necklace that reminds you of your mother."

I waited.

"I told you," she said, walking to the door. "I don't know." Bets opened the door and ran smack into Gary. "Oh my God, you scared me."

I climbed the attic stairs several times that day, first to return the laptop, then to tell him how much I liked the story. He was never there. On every visit, I sat looking out the window and breathed deeply to calm myself, reminding myself to hold back, we barely knew each other. But we'd known each other forever, hadn't we met in a secret garden in a previous life? An elderly tourist was pushing a walker over uneven ground three stories below my window, when I finally heard feet on the stairs. "Willis?" I called, each footfall coming closer. I'd be lost without him now.

Willis placed several books on the table, slightly breathless. He came around to sit next to me on the window seat. "What did you think?"

I smiled at him, willing him to touch me. On the leg or the arm, just something. "I absolutely love your novel."

He leaned back. "Oh, I'm relieved. I've been worried you'd find it too simple."

"I love it," I said.

"I'm so glad. It's not Jane Austen, of course." Willis shrugged. "But."

"I know you so much better now," I said, "having read your book."

Willis's expression turned serious on me. Just like the time I'd brought him the book or when I asked him to join me in public. He looked straight into my eyes and spoke slowly. "You don't know me."

My Jane Austen's billowing skirt appeared behind me. Reassured by her presence, I ventured a question more probing than usual. "What do I *not* know?" I asked softly. I imagined a witness protection program, weird political secrets, or a mafia connection forcing him to hide in the attic.

Willis shifted, leaning against the window's frame. "I have a lot on my mind." He paused, perhaps deciding how deep to go. He held one ankle over his knee. "I came here to think, and make decisions."

"Here?" I asked. "As in this attic?"

He nodded.

"Is that why you were brooding in the dark church?" Perhaps he was conflicted over the final ordination, trying to decide whether to break the vows he'd made as a deacon. There must be so much pressure to complete the process once begun.

"You're quite a distraction," he whispered, but he didn't look happy about it.

My stomach flipped; I was not a mere sheep of his flock. Yet I couldn't stand to see him so conflicted. "Should I stop coming to the attic?" I asked. During the long pause, I imagined how I would feel if he said yes.

He shook his head. "I like you."

I broke eye contact and touched his knee. That was enough for me. I would find the patience to wait; I was good at waiting.

"I like you, too," I said.

On the tea-theatre's opening day, I felt uplifted by the joyful news that Willis liked me. Not *Cosmo* me or *earth* me—but the real me: the original me that had been too weird to introduce to any other boyfriends. The *me* I wouldn't have been able to invent. The *me* that now walked the halls as if I were Elizabeth Bennet, mistress of the tea-theatre. No more wrong turns into closets, I solved the hot water problem by borrowing an electric hotplate and reconfiguring the orange cords. I trained Gary to play the part of Count Cassel, recruited a volunteer's husband to play the baron, and talked John Owen into playing the rhyming butler. I was the person in charge; the volunteers all wanted face time with me. When asked to do something, they responded with brisk action. Tickets sold out and our waiting list grew. I began to believe that I was no longer needy, having outgrown that character flaw before it had a chance to scare Willis away.

When our time came, as the last scene of *Mansfield Park*

ended and the room cleared, I gave the go-ahead for volunteers to roll out tables and set them quickly with their wedding china. Tables featured every sort of pattern from understated metallic bands to profusions of blooming wildflowers. We walked among the tables, a china garden, lifting plates to read pattern names: location names like India and Monaco, or female names such as Juliet and Guinevere, or expressive titles like Celestial Platinum and Crown Sapphire. My mother's china, Ivy Flowers, would fit in nicely here, if it weren't being held hostage by Sue, or worse, trashed.

Once the cast sequestered themselves in the music room, volunteers admitted the audience into the china garden for tea.

Omar arrived at the last possible moment dressed in his black staff clothes.

"Where's your costume?" I asked, restraining the alarm in my voice.

"Look, I said I would do this," but Omar did not finish speaking since Magda interrupted, poking her head in the door, sunglasses on, purse slung over her shoulder.

"Gamal," she said, then spoke rapid Arabic.

Gary looked up from adjusting his pink satin cape. He responded in Arabic. I looked from one to the other as Gary, scowling, pulled the cape off his shoulders. "What's going on?" I asked.

"My brother will be late if he doesn't hurry. I don't know what he's doing here since he knows he's scheduled for an ESL test at four-thirty." English as a Second Language.

"Reschedule it, Gary," I said.

Gary shrugged, handing me his jacket, speaking angrily in Arabic to Magda.

I turned to Magda. "People have paid money to see him perform this afternoon," I said.

"He should have mentioned the conflict to you," Magda said, her nostrils flaring. "He is not enrolled in an academic program because he has not passed the ESL exam. If he doesn't take the test and matriculate, he will have to leave the country anyway, tea or no tea. It's up to him." She threw her hands up. "Do you want to go home?" she asked Gary.

Gary walked past me, unbuttoning his shirt.

"Bring me the costume before you go," I said.

"When you work with amateurs—" Magda started to say, but I interrupted her.

"Please excuse us." I pointed to the hallway, allowing tension full rein in my voice.

With them gone, Omar in his street clothes returned to focus. "Not a single word from you," I said. "Go and dress in your costume and come back here immediately. Or I will kill you with my bare hands."

How to replace Gary fifteen minutes before teatime? Perhaps an actor could be persuaded to do it. I ran to the Freezer hoping someone lingered from the last scene but found only Gary, who placed his costume in my arms. "Sorry," he said. Mrs. Russell and Stephen Jervis practiced lines in the tiny butler pantry. Tea patrons lined up in the hall waiting to be let into the ballroom, men and women in period dress, little girls in tea-length dresses and jumbo hair ribbons. What would we do without a Count Cassel? The buffoon of the skit. Without his humor, it would fail. I would fail. Nigel and Vera arrived happy and excited, expecting a tea-theatre.

"Are you ready?" Vera asked, before noting my expression. "What's the matter?"

I told her about Gary. "Do you think Nigel would be up for a part?"

Vera frowned. "Not Nigel," she said, "but what about this line of potential actors?" She gestured toward the tea patrons standing against the wall as if we'd put out a call for Regency extras. "You said patrons should be allowed to join in the acting. Here's your chance."

A giant iron door opened, allowing me entry into the next level. What a great idea, and it was my idea. They were even dressed in Regency attire, ready to go on stage at a moment's notice. "Ladies and gentlemen," I said, as the crowd silenced and all eyes turned to me, "Literature Live believes that patrons should participate in performances. We have arrived at the moment when one of you will be chosen to play a role in our production. Who among you will play the part of Count Cassel?"

The line buzzed, several women pushed their blushing men to the fore, but my attention fixed on a tall, blustery man who announced, "Count Cassel, at your service." He removed his hat and executed a deeply dramatic bow. He reminded me of self-important Mr. Rushworth.

"Come with me," I said, taking his arm and leading him to the music room.

We ran through Count Cassel's lines and played vinyl LPs in the music room while volunteers served the three courses in the ballroom: scones, sandwiches, and tea cookies. The ballroom filled with noise of conversation, people laughing, enjoying themselves at our tea, excitement building for the entertainment. Once the play began, I watched from the butler pantry as Mrs. Russell embraced her long-lost son, Stephen Jervis. I saw how convincingly Mrs. Russell admired her son's physique as he said, "I will never leave you. Look, Mother, how tall and strong I am grown. These arms can now afford you support." Of course, we'd seen him without his shirt.

"I think Mrs. Russell has a crush on Stephen," I remarked to Omar, but he was busy looking over his lines. Just then

Sixby walked in and stood at the back of the room, the spot Magda usually occupied during productions. But no Willis.

Omar and I took the stage to perform the scene where Anhalt, the tutor, is sent to instruct Amelia, who is secretly in love with him, on the good and the bad aspects of matrimony. Amelia manages to wrangle a proposal of marriage out of him before the scene ends. Omar looked a bit green. He spoke his first line and I knew we were in trouble. I wished Sixby wasn't watching, nor Nigel and Vera. Omar's eyes never left the floor. He shifted his weight from one foot to the other and his fingers fiddled with the side seam of his breeches as he forgot to ask why my character had been crying. "If you please, we will sit down," he said. I feared he would not remember the next part of his line but it came to him. "Count Cassel is arrived."

"Yes, I know," I said.

Omar took a deep breath, looking sideways at nothing. Then he skipped the next ten lines, proceeding directly to his very long line about matrimony as "the meeting of sympathetic hearts" which I knew he would never finish. I wanted to stop the show. I saw myself interrupting the scene with an apology or tears. I couldn't look at Vera. Magda was right; I should have bought a Eurail pass. As I scrambled to improvise and stop Omar's misery, I saw Sixby walking through the tables with a wild look in his eye. Perhaps he would stop the show for me.

"Miss Wildenhaim," Sixby said, dismissing Omar with a flutter of his hand. "I come from your father with a commission. Count Cassel is arrived."

"Yes, I know," I said.

"And do you know for what reason?" Sixby asked. My hero. He knew all the lines, of course, and we sailed along, improvising where he wasn't familiar with our condensed script.

Willis walked in. My heart jumped as our eyes met and he sat in a vacant chair near the door. The room came to life. "You may tell my father—I'll marry," I said.

"I must beg you not to forget that there is another picture of matrimony," Sixby said. "When convenience and fair appearance joined to folly and ill humor forge the fetters of matrimony, they gall the married pair with their weight," Sixby continued, "till one of them sleeps in death. The other then lifts up his dejected head, and calls out in acclamations of joy—Oh liberty! Dear liberty!"

"I will *not* marry," I said.

"You mean to say that you will not fall in love," Sixby said.

"Oh no!" I said. "I am in love." We sorted through Sixby's professed confusion until reaching the line where I accept his unintended proposal of marriage. "If you love me as you say, I will marry; and will be happy," I said. "But only with you." I glanced at Willis over Sixby's shoulder. "It will soon be known that I am your bride, the whole village will come to wish me joy, and heaven's blessing will follow."

The skit succeeded from the moment Sixby joined in. My Jane Austen especially enjoyed the baron, played by a volunteer's husband, who turned out to be an improv comedian, roasting the guest who played Count Cassel. The rhyming butler closed with his moral:

> *Then you, who now lead single lives,*
> *From this sad tale beware;*
> *And do not act as you were wives,*
> *Before you really are.*

The audience finally cleared out so the volunteers could pack up the china. As Stephen carried Mrs. Russell's boxes to her car parked behind the Carriage House, I ran to the attic.

"A smashing success!" Willis said. "You must be very happy."

"I can't believe it."

"It was every bit as professional as anything Magda's ever put on a stage."

"Vera and Nigel loved it. Vera said Lady Weston would have enjoyed it immensely. Perhaps a less formal approach was what Lady Weston envisioned in the first place."

"I had no idea you were such a good actress."

"Neither did I!" I laughed.

"So, you'll do it again?"

"Every Wednesday at four. We've already got a waiting list for next week. Vera says we need to add more tables or do a second seating." Willis joined me on the window seat. "I'm so glad you were there," I said. "I wanted you to see it."

"I enjoyed it very much," Willis said. I watched as his face assumed a more sober expression, evolving into a question. "I thought you said *Omar* was playing opposite you as Anhalt."

"That was the plan." I smiled. "But we had to let him go before he fainted on stage."

Willis straightened. "I was surprised to see Sixby."

The next time I went to the attic, ratty green cushions had been stuffed into the window seat for my comfort. We met almost every day except Wednesday afternoons. Attic time operated on a different basis than the lower floors of the manor house, a phenomenon I assumed would transfer to any venue where I experienced intense pleasure. Whoever controlled time had decreed that if *I* were allowed to be happy, I would be allotted half the normal time in which to be so. Each day I anticipated Willis's casual greeting, hunched over his keyboard in the afternoon light when I arrived—the comfort of being expected, as if we were a married couple living in an attic. When he got to a stopping point, he would hand me the laptop and sit back to listen while I read what he'd written. My Jane Austen seemed equally content, sitting beneath some cobwebs in a shadowy corner compiling an alphabetical list of all the male heroes of her books—she'd gotten as far as Edmund Bertram.

"You'll have to dedicate your book to Lady Weston," I said, "in gratitude for her attic."

I wrote to Karen, telling her of the tea-theatre's success. After selling out the first event, we added more tables at the second tea, and cut the scones smaller to feed more people, easily seating sixty. Magda threw a fit when tea patrons lined up in the hall and made noise before her scene was over. In fact, the tea-theatre attracted more people than her professionals-only scene. I told Karen about Willis, leaving out the parts about meeting in the attic and the vampire novel. The only thing bugging me was that I really didn't know what Willis was deciding about. I assumed it had to do with his ordination, but he'd never come right out and said so. I'd replayed the conversation many times in my head, unsure what he meant, afraid to bring it up again for fear of provoking a decision that might go against me. I told Karen I was in love. She replied in bold letters: BE CAREFUL.

"What exactly is the decision you have to make?" I asked him one afternoon.

My Jane Austen fell violently off the stack of boxes she occupied nearby, sending a cloud of attic dust into our midst. His face fell as if I'd broken his laptop and I instantly regretted my impulsive question. If only I could rewind the conversation back to a comfortable subject, like my childhood in Texas and his at boarding school, me being chosen last for the softball team and Willis claiming speed reading as a sport. His gaze left me as he focused inward to form a response. Willis rose from his desk and joined me on the window seat, another sign that something bad was coming. Why hadn't I left things alone, happily learning of his master's in theology at St. Stephen's House, Oxford, and how he'd written only two pages of his thesis, now displaced by the vampire novel? This was starting to feel like the time my dad apologized for missing my high school graduation. I didn't want pity. "I'm afraid I haven't been fair to you," he said.

My blood froze. Dust particles paused on their inbound sunbeam. This *was* about me.

"I haven't been thinking clearly," he said.

I shivered. My future as Elizabeth Bennet, assured twenty seconds ago, vanished. "What is going on?" I whispered, searching his face.

"There is someone else," he said.

Someone Else. The room spun as his words reverberated and pain spiraled downward in awful glory. I stared at the cushion; its particular shade of lime green seemed so unfair, then folded my arms and held myself. "I can't believe it," I said.

"You must understand, my situation is complicated." He gestured. "I've known her for years; I've known you for weeks."

I didn't know what to say. At first he looked past me, out the window. When I didn't speak, he stood as if he might leave. "I don't want you to go," I said. The news was too difficult to accept, it circled around me, retreating as denial prevailed and then reappearing for another punch in my gut. "I'm so confused," I said, shaking my head as he stood at his desk, packing his things. "Why didn't you tell me?"

He faced me, his hands in his pockets. "I think that's obvious."

"Does she know about me?"

"No." He shook his head. I imagined her asking why he seemed so distant and Willis reassuring her everything was fine as he silently resolved to stop the attic meetings before things got even more difficult. Only he didn't stop the attic meetings.

He was gone for two agonizing days. On the third day, I ran into him, as if by accident, as I entered Newton Priors. "Will you be up later?" he asked. I went as soon as I could and every day after that, holding my questions and staying on safe topics in his company. We never spoke of the Someone Else but she was present, looming in the background, raising the stakes. My Jane Austen sat frozen in her corner, observing my cautious behavior, flinching when she thought I might fall off my wagon. He behaved like a monk; his reserve over the past weeks made sense now. We talked about his vampire novel and my tea-theatre, and we never touched. But the longer we carried on in this "trial basis" manner, the closer I felt to him emotionally, the more I began to think he might ditch the Someone Else. If Willis wanted to be with her, why was he with me? I spent every minute of my workdays calculating when I could go to him. Precarious life flourished in the attic. Fed a diet of forbidden fruit, everything around Willis grew, from the story under his fingertips to the organic matter thriving beneath the damp boxes and rotting wood, to me.

"Doesn't this place remind you of Anne Frank's attic?" I asked. "Nobody knows we're up here." When we got hungry I snuck into the music room where the volunteers kept leftover tea refreshments, filling napkins with scones and cookies to eat in the attic. I helped myself to bottled water kept in reserve for festival speakers. I borrowed a lamp from one of the parlors and set it on an upturned box we used as a table. Willis brought a green plastic chair for me so that we could both sit with our feet on the bench and look out the window. "Why is there a window seat in this attic?" I asked.

"So the imprisoned heroine can look out the window and see her lover approaching." A smile played around Willis's mouth and we shared The Look. But I was thinking: *My prince is always in the attic. Had I imagined that kiss so long ago?* Our interaction was so restrained that any light touch of his hand, the contact of our fingers when we passed the laptop, or lingering glance when I looked up to find him watching me at the end of a chapter, carried a force far greater than its own weight. I cherished each subtle gesture, hoping they would eventually accumulate into something tangible again. I didn't push. I proceeded with cautious optimism based on the fact that Willis felt like my best friend and he no longer left town. The regular absences to London stopped occurring. I didn't ask why, just allowed myself to hope.

Until one Sunday, as Newton Priors buzzed with festival activities, everyone seemed mildly peeved. Patrons lining up for tickets stomped away mad when they learned the tea-theatre had sold out a week in advance. Nigel expressed irritation that someone had put Mrs. Russell onto the mystery of "several letters still in private hands." Claire said a thief was helping herself to water bottles, and Bets complained of nasty perfume on her favorite black blouse. I didn't tell Bets that the nasty perfume came from her own cosmetics bin. Finally, Mrs. Russell barged into the office complaining that the lines in the scene had been changed and someone needed to do something about it—Fanny Price and Sir Thomas were explicitly discussing slavery. I escaped to the attic.

Opening the door triggered the conversion from one world to the next. Once past the door, I inhaled the musty damp brick- and wood-scented air. I heard the tick-tack of his keyboard—confirming Willis's presence—as I ran up the steps, each stair creaking under my footfall.

"Did Father Kitt bite her yet?" I asked routinely.

"No." He put a hand out to touch me as I passed, the casual gesture I'd come to love and anticipate. I could pretend nonchalance at the contact of our fingers, but goose bumps on my bare arms gave me away. I sank into my window seat, opened my copy of *The Monk*, and read while Willis bent over his keyboard. I'd had no idea when Omar gave me *The Monk*, saying I couldn't possibly understand Ann Radcliffe's novels without reading it, that it would be so racy—an abbot seduced by a woman disguised as a monk. Taking care to hold my book so My Jane Austen couldn't read over my shoulder:

> The woman reigns in my bosom, and I am become
> prey to the wildest of passions. Away with friend-
> ship! 'tis a cold unfeeling word. My bosom burns
> with love, with unutterable love, and love must be
> its return.

Willis spoke and I jumped, caught reading a racy novel. "Do you think Luna is a convincing female?" he asked. He turned in his chair to face me and I put *The Monk* facedown on my bosom, my heart pounding, while I focused on his question.

"Luna?" I took a deep breath and stretched my arms languorously, the way that had always distracted Martin from

ESPN. "You might make her a bit more affected by Father Kitt."

Willis nodded, encouraging me to elaborate. "What do you mean?"

"Luna's passion is not convincing because it's all intellectual; she's not engaged enough." I paused, hoping I wouldn't have to spell it out for him.

"I'm not getting it."

"Physically."

"A cheesy love scene?" Willis looked at me. "You don't want them to have sex in my book, do you?"

"Well," I said slowly, "why don't you let him hold her hand and see where it goes from there."

He looked back at his screen and I resumed reading. I hadn't finished another page when Willis turned to me again, "Don't you think there's a metaphor in there for marriage? Doesn't everyone have to make a decision to take the bite? Plunge into the unknown abyss with one person, or be lonely forever?"

"Willis." I laughed. "That's such a pessimistic view for a priest."

He smiled. "I suppose you prefer happy endings." Willis turned back to his computer.

I closed *The Monk* and sat up to look out the window. Three stories below, all was quiet. Far down the lawn a young couple posed for a photo, the abyss of the pond in their background, swans slinking in and out of the picture. Willis hadn't noticed I'd stopped reading, so I sighed aloud.

"Everything okay over there?" he asked without turning.

"No," I said, wanting more than anything to drag him to my window seat and replay the black blouse incident once more with feeling.

Willis stopped typing and turned to face me. "Something the matter?"

"Are you sure you want to be a priest?" I asked.

His face changed and he smiled to himself as if I'd stumbled on an inside joke. "You don't waste time on small talk, do you?"

I shrugged. "I'm just curious." I was intensely aware of the texture of the foam cushion under my fingers, the sensation of my feet touching the dirty floor. My stomach clutched in nervous anticipation.

"Just curious," he repeated playfully, rising from his desk, taking the four steps to join me on my cushion, my stomach fluttering with each step. "Just probing a man's deepest thoughts and fears is all."

"You've dropped a few clues." I faced him, my head tilted back, presenting an extended view of my neck and cleavage.

"Such as," he said, stretching.

"Well, there is the vampire novel for one." He was so close I could smell him, soap mingled with perspiration.

"Yes." He smiled.

"And the consideration of impending doom and the business of the abyss."

"You've got me there."

"So, I just thought perhaps there's some discontent generating these ideas." I struck the pose that always made Martin kiss me, but Willis looked out the window. Inching closer, I looked out the window with him so that our faces were perfectly positioned to touch when we turned back. But he moved away so it didn't happen.

I left early that day.

On Monday, I thought about not going to the attic. I dressed slowly and took my time reading a story written by one of

Omar's workshop participants. The festival was closed that day, Newton Priors deserted when I arrived in the attic much later than usual. Willis met me at the stairs as if he'd been waiting.

"Did he bite her yet?" I asked.

Willis almost took my hand. "No," he said. "But he's giving it serious consideration."

"That's progress." I touched his arm as he moved away.

"I want to show you something." Willis led me between boxes to a place halfway down the room where he pulled a rope hanging from the ceiling.

"Are we going to escape from this attic?" I sighed.

He smiled as a wooden ladder unfolded, not unlike my attic stairs at home. "They forgot to lock it the other day." Climbing, he lifted the heavy trap door in the ceiling, exposing us to the wan light of the outdoors, and then reached down for my hand.

"How wonderful," I said, climbing the rickety steps behind him. "No one's ever shown me a rooftop before." Emerging, I sat on the roof and swung my legs up. Willis held on to me as I steadied myself; but once standing, he let go. All around me were the tops of trees, leaves rustling in the chilly breeze. Holding the hair out of my face, I walked across the flat roof, tar mixed with rough bits of stone. The wind felt much stronger at this altitude. The entire perimeter, crowned by a stone balustrade, itself broken in places, patched with concrete where the blocks joined, lay covered with dusty gray lichen. Dry leaves accumulated at the balustrade's base. Three stories high, we had a good view of St. James's roof and the stained glass window; two people walking on the lawn looked like little dolls playing in an architect's model, and the herb garden revealed its careful blend of textures and patterns.

"I thought you would like it," he said, gazing toward the

pond where the grass appeared weed-free and the trees spaced themselves precisely. My Jane Austen paced the perimeter nervously. "Being up here reminds me of you," Willis said.

I couldn't have predicted that remark. "I remind you of a roof? What does that mean?" I asked. My Jane Austen stopped pacing and held her breath.

He turned to face me, not joking at all. "You offer me a new perspective."

I waited.

He looked out to the view and then back at me. "Would you mind terribly if I wasn't a priest?" he asked.

"No," I answered too eagerly, thrilled he had asked for my opinion on a matter of such importance to his future and what this meant about us.

He shrugged and shoved his hands in his pockets as he turned away from me. After a silence, as if reconsidering, he spoke to the sky. "You'll be gone soon." The wind rustled the leaves warning me to hush, and My Jane Austen stopped breathing again.

"Willis," I whispered, "how long must we know each other?"

He looked at me, surprised. A single green plastic chair sat vacant in the garden. St. Francis stood frozen in concrete, watching naked birds bathe. I'd gone too far. *Backtrack*, I told myself. *Think of something.* But I couldn't stand it anymore. I refused to spend another day imprisoned in the attic.

"You're not working today?" he said, choosing to ignore my question and push past the awkwardness.

"No," I said.

Willis hesitated while a bird hopped on one pediment and then another.

"I'm hungry." I frowned at him.

"So am I." He frowned back.

"And I'm going down to get a cookie," I said. "If you don't come with me, I'm going back to my room. You'll starve up here by yourself." He said nothing but followed me down the folding ladder, past his desk, and down the attic stairs to the second floor landing where anything could emerge from the closed doors without notice. We descended the stairs leading to civilization, although, being Monday, Newton Priors was deserted. As a precaution, we tiptoed down the last steps, passed the front door where tourists got in, and the Freezer where Magda fired people. Willis was still with me when we passed the ballroom where adaptations of her prose daily tortured My Jane Austen, and the butler pantry where Mrs. Russell played footsie with Stephen Jervis. I pulled Willis into the music room and shut the door.

"This," I whispered, "is where the volunteers hide the tea cookies." As I bent to open a cupboard, Willis turned away. When I looked up, he stood at the door with a hand on the knob. "Oh, don't go," I said, disappointed, extending a hand offering a cookie, "I haven't played my song for you."

Willis turned the bolt. Then, without looking at me, he walked purposefully to the other door and turned its bolt, as if he were in charge of festival security. Willis took the cookie from my hand and laid it on a low table. His face bore a hint of shy amusement I'd never seen before, as if he acknowledged the force of resistance he'd put up for so many weeks as well as the act of removing that obstacle between us. Part of me wanted to shake him and demand an explanation for his arbitrary behavior. But that impulse was overcome by the wonder of a breakthrough and the idea of exploring mysterious new territory.

He straightened to look at me. "I'm starving, too," he said, a slight tremor in the word too.

The eye contact, the step toward me, and the hand reaching out offered tangible signs that I hadn't been delusional all those days in the attic. I had been waiting for *this*. My affection was returned. Willis felt what I felt: the anticipation of receiving intimacy. Never had being *me* granted such possibility of joy, a room such comfort, a person such completion. Not just because of his appealing physical chemistry and his subtle, intelligent manner, but the way he thought about things; his seriousness of purpose. As Willis kissed me, I experienced the sensation of falling into the right place. No other place existed. He walked me to the ratty sofa, my arms around his neck, and we fell on it together. But then Willis hesitated, raising himself on his elbow and looking into my face. He gently touched my hair as his eyes formed a question, utter fulfillment of The Look. He would not use words, nor would he proceed lightly.

"Yes," I said. "Yes, yes, yes." I pulled him to me, trusting him with my happiness; ready for what would come next because I believed whatever happened with him would be good and carry the same meaning for him that it carried for me. As we lay together I experienced the kind of happiness I never believed would be mine—not complete enough to be chosen for this. The cosmos fit together perfectly, everything related to something else and everything belonged, especially me. I felt utterly connected, a part of the deep unknowable universe.

"You are lovely." He kissed me.

We lay together for a long while, my head on his shoulder, listening to his pulse, smelling his sweat, feeling the hair on his skin, and I kept moving; every new touch or slight shift of position satisfied a craving to get closer and renew the sensation of his physical presence. He brushed the hair out of my eyes and ran his hand lightly over my back and down my thigh. And I remember thinking he was more wonderful than a really good book, or music.

"Oh," I said. "My song." I rose, and went to the old record player. I pulled the vinyl LP from its sleeve and loaded it onto the turntable.

"You're well made," he said, watching me from the sofa.

The first fluttery notes of a harpsichord played. "I think of you when I hear this song," I said. I lay back down and Willis covered me with his shirt.

"Bach," he said.

I closed my eyes to listen but opened them again, needing to see Willis, the damp hair on his brow, the clothes on the floor, curling shreds of wallpaper in the upper reaches. Willis held me while the music played and I memorized all the details, although it was hard to concentrate, worried that anything that made me feel this good would surely not happen again.

"I can't resist you, Lily," he said.

"Thank God for that." I kissed him as if he were mine.

Thirteen

*W*illis was gone. When I climbed the attic stairs the next day, excited to resume our relationship under its new M.O., hoping to discuss the lease problem like a couple, he wasn't there. He should have told me he was leaving. Why would Willis disappear without an explanation after what had happened between us? Where was he? I'd never experienced such excruciating loneliness. In my head, Miss Clavel said, *Something is not right*, but in my heart, I cherished the hope that he'd gone to London to break up with the Someone Else.

I sat at my desk, staring at the pad on which I'd written the heading, "Business Plan for Dummies." Vera said we needed to accelerate our strategy since Magda had supposedly received a letter of interest from her funding source at Michigan. Vera proposed visiting Lady Weston in the hospital on Friday. But the Consummation in the Music Room had transformed me into a total blissful wreck, taking my daydreams to a new level. So far, I could generate only the words "Mrs. Willis Somerford" in lovely copperplate, especially swirling the W and scrolling the S. My Jane Austen doodled on her list of heroes as if she didn't know what to do with herself.

I couldn't bear my loneliness. I put my pen down in preparation for another run to the attic when a plump mother and three toddlers with runny noses toddled into my office, followed by Omar.

"Here we go," a ghastly, frightened Omar pushed the last baby body through my door and closed it behind them. The six of us looked at each other. "Where's Vera?" Omar asked as if a gun were pointed at his temple.

"In the ballroom," I said, "policing the script. Did you take the slavery lines out like Nigel told you?" I asked, hiding my "Business Plan for Dummies" beneath my other list: ideas for new tea-theatre entertainment—a one-woman show, *The Lost Letters of Jane Austen*.

"No," he said.

"Why not?" I asked. The woman snagged the arm of a child headed for the door.

"I'm scared of Magda," Omar said. "She has the original script; she refuses to use it." Omar pulled a chair up for the woman to sit. "Let's make this our base for now," Omar said, but she remained standing. "Do you have any, um, crayons?" Omar asked me, clearly resorting to his last idea, staring as if I should know what was killing him. The mother smiled, oblivious.

"Crayons?" I had colored markers but they were the permanent kind. Instead, I extended my hand to the plump woman. "Hello," I said. "I'm Lily Berry."

She returned the smile and gave me her hand. "I'm Sheila Porter," she said. "Archie's wife."

The situation focused. This would delay my next trip to the attic.

"Triplets?" I asked her, smiling at the three busy babes tangled in her legs.

Sheila's eyes sparkled as she shifted the very large diaper bag on her shoulder. "No," she answered, touching the shoulder of the tallest boy, "twins and a big brother."

Upon closer inspection, the age difference was obvious. "How can you tell them apart?" I asked, stalling for time, weighing the ins and outs of Archie's wife attending the same lit fest as Archie's mistress.

"A mother knows." Sheila touched one of the small ones. "Teddy had a pointy head at birth and Roger's was much rounder," she said.

Teddy was moving about but I thought I could see a little point on him. And it occurred to me that the wife's presence might be the train wreck needed to end Magda's takeover.

Sheila continued, "And Roger has a birthmark above his right bum." Sheila touched the place on her own body but thought better of showing her flesh. The extra pounds she carried and the hairstyle dating from the year of her marriage both added years to her appearance.

Omar crossed his arms, blinking rapidly.

"How can I help you?" I asked Sheila.

"I'm here to see Archie, of course," Sheila said. "I know my way to the ballroom." She moved toward the door but Omar blocked it with his body.

"I'll get Archie and bring him here," Omar said. "He's watching the scene." Omar stared at me again. "Don't go anywhere," he said.

"Oh no, I want to surprise him," Sheila said, unusually calm for someone about to confront her husband's mistress, a look I'd seen before. Perhaps my mother had confronted Sue and I'd lived through it, oblivious.

"I don't think that's a good idea." Omar shook his head, beseeching me to back him up.

At that moment, Archie would be in his usual position in the back of the ballroom, heads together with Magda's scarf, defending Magda's adaptation of the text. The last thing he expected to see was his wife.

Sheila lifted a fussy twin, while the other put fuzz from the floor into his mouth. She lowered her eyes as she spoke. "The same individual who invited me here today made certain I understood the lay of the land."

"Vera invited you?" I asked.

Omar closed his eyes.

The oldest boy tugged on her arm and Sheila pulled a tiny board book from her diaper bag. I would have backed off at that moment like a sensible person, but something about the mother sharing the little book with the baby made me want to act on her behalf. As if doing something for Sheila would help my mother.

"Let's go," I said. "Archie's in the ballroom, I'll take you."

Omar slumped into the chair he'd pulled out for Sheila. "I'll wait here," he said.

Sheila stood just outside the ballroom door, her face flushed; perhaps finally understanding the risk of confronting her husband and his mistress. Up to this moment, the affair was in the abstract, she could deny it. Now the horror she'd imagined would reveal itself in the flesh. Her eyes darted from her children to the threshold while inside a chorus of actors pressed Fanny to cooperate with the theatricals. I peeked around the door to see Archie and Magda against the back wall, arms touching, oblivious, right where I wanted them.

Suddenly Nikki, playing Julia Bertram, flashed through the hall, rushing past me, the force of her stage presence displacing the mother and children to the side where all five shared the threshold. Nikki called out in her professionally trained voice, turning every head in the room—actors, directors, and patrons alike, to see who spoke so urgently:

Julia: *My father is come! He is in the hall at this moment!*

That should have been the end of the scene, where patrons give the actors a round of applause, but it didn't happen that way. The boy in the doorway distracted the patrons from their obligation to applaud; speaking as though he were part of the cast, his line confusingly fit the action as he said, "Father!"

But the boy wasn't speaking to the actors. He and his mother were looking at the back wall where the entire audience turned their curious gaze—where Archie Porter stood blushing furiously. After hesitating, as if to consider his options, Archie walked away from Magda to kiss his wife on the mouth and lift one of the babies. Patrons responded with warm applause and murmurs as the upstaged actors retreated to the Freezer. When Archie put one baby down and picked up another, Sheila beamed. Archie's ponytail didn't look nearly so hip next to Sheila. It looked gray. In the context of his three kids, it looked silly.

I stood on tiptoe and craned my neck to see Magda's reaction. She turned on her heel and retreated out the back door, her scarf billowing in her wake like a flag on an enemy ship.

Fourteen

ixby complained I was preoccupied when he arrived to brainstorm our follies act. "You need to snap out of it," he said when I failed to respond. "We need a clever act."

I didn't want to snap out of it. I wanted to be alone with Willis in my recent memories. "How about a one-woman show: *The Lost Letters of Jane Austen*?" I said absently, as I added numbers on my pad.

"Ooh, I've never done a one-woman show," he said, leaning back in Claire's chair, flipping through his book. He'd dressed in Regency breeches and white cotton shirt—on his day off, his jacket flung on the chair. "What would Magda say?"

Magda was busy at the moment, putting up a fight. Hard to believe she would fight for scruffy old Archie. But sometimes it seemed Magda was winning, displaying her exotic charms, exposing an inch of firm brown flesh as she abandoned her modest garb in favor of tight jeans and cropped tops. Omar's comment: "Forget scarves and veils. The attire-oppressed women of the world are on hold while the future of Archie Porter is decided." And Vera worried that since Archie had moved back into his own rooms with his wife and children, Magda clearly had more time on her hands to pursue her funding goals.

Sheila's campaign suffered on the appearance front although her loose black pants and paisley tunics performed the public service of concealing her motherly midriff bulge. However, on another battlefront, Sheila was the Mother of His Children, a winning strategy she engaged at every opportunity, launching the children in the ballroom where they talked during scenes, the pub where they screamed, and the Freezer where they jumped on the furniture. Sheila's tactics were hard to ignore.

Accelerating her own battle plans, Vera urged me to prepare a real lease and business plan for Lady Weston by the end of the week. I tried to make her understand that Randolph would have to sign it this time around. I wanted to discuss this with Willis but he was still absent. He'd never been away this long and I had no way to reach him. The secretary at the church said he'd gone to London and she didn't know what his plans were.

"What are you doing?" Sixby asked, standing and walking to my desk where he sat on the corner.

"I'm calculating the proceeds from the teas."

"How much?"

"I'm still adding. I'll let you know." I suspected an exchange rate mistake because the total was running well over six thousand dollars so far. We charged twenty GBP per person for tea and sold scone mix the volunteers packaged and donated, but the total seemed high. If we held a tea every Wednesday, we could clear over fifteen thousand dollars before the end of August. Unless the volunteers grew tired of providing scones.

"I know." Sixby snapped his fingers. "Why not borrow one of your roommate's gowns," he said. "We can go up to my room and improv: Anhalt and Amelia Unchaperoned."

Sixby's remark made me realize how my life had changed. In a previous version of me, an uplifting piano sonata would have been playing in my head as I basked in the attention of this handsome actor. A month ago, I would have jumped at the chance to improv with Sixby. Back then Sixby was Shakespeare, Darcy, and all the male protagonists I'd ever fallen for rolled into one. Now, Willis was all I could think about. And Willis was nothing like Sixby. My Jane Austen sat on the other side of the desk making an alphabetical list of all of the unsavory men in her novels. She'd gotten as far as Mr. Collins.

"What's the book?" I asked Sixby.

"Love poetry. I've been contemplating the mysteries of love." Sixby sighed. "Shall I read?" he asked.

"Only if you are very quick," I said, ready to run upstairs again. Willis could have returned in the last hour.

"Here's a good one," he said, marking the place with his finger. His exquisite voice conveyed the poet's apology over the grave of a lover who'd been dead fifteen years. As the last syllable resonated, a lovely minor tone, I knew exactly how the poet felt. " 'Once drinking deep of that divinest anguish, How could I seek the empty world again?' "

"Beautiful," I said. "You made me forget where I am."

"Emily Brontë." He closed the book. "I know how to reach you," he said, smiling, activating his dimples. "Have you ever been in love?" he asked. "Rather personal question, no?" He paused. "You needn't answer. Just curious." He reached for my hand but I stayed where I was. My feelings existed between me and Willis and no one else. Private and serious, deep and considered, to speak of them with Sixby would be a profanity. I didn't answer.

"As for me," he said, "I'm afraid I'm too much a master of my emotions to experience the spontaneity of love."

"That's so sad," I said, employing mild sarcasm so My Jane Austen would know I was not falling for his line.

"Oh, it's very sad." Sixby laughed. "I can't tell you how many women have offered to help me."

My Jane Austen put her list down and stood, as if she would leave.

"But *you*, Lily." He gestured with both hands. "You're different. Let's try something," he said. "Stand up while I read. Close your eyes and feel a character, an alter ego building in your imagination."

I closed my eyes, conjuring Willis while Sixby read, sounding more and more like Willis. The delivery was so beautiful that I let go, carried away to the roof, the wind in my hair, the escape to the music room, and the presentation of the cookie. Willis stepped toward me, his hand outstretched; I felt Sixby's lips on mine yet the footsteps continued. And then the worst possible thing. Willis looked in at the door. Willis, who never ventured into the office. Our eyes met. My face burned.

"Oops. Wrong room," Willis said, vanishing as quickly as he'd appeared.

"Oh God," I said, hitting my head.

"We seem to have a knack for that," Sixby said, finally releasing me, oblivious to my distress. "That wasn't *me* by the way." Sixby cleared his throat.

"Who then?" I asked, angry.

"I confess; I was the dead guy in Emily Brontë's poem." He picked up his book. "But you see; this may work," he added.

"Next time you must borrow one of your roommate's lovely gowns and meet me in my room for some wicked improv."

I climbed the stairs to the attic, mentally rehearsing the explanation I'd been kissing Emily Brontë's dead guy, each step a reprimand. When I saw Willis, he was sitting at his desk, staring into space. When he saw me, he lifted the cover of his laptop.

"Did he bite her?" I asked.

He straightened and looked just past me. "Yes, he did."

I stood in front of him, his desk between us. "Where have you been?" I asked.

"London," he said, feigning preoccupation with his keyboard although he hadn't turned it on yet. "I've got a lot of work to do." He pushed the laptop's power button. His expansive reading selections sat abandoned in a stack on the floor, replaced on the shelf by serious spines that said Thomas Merton, Søren Kierkegaard, and Bishop N. T. Wright. Luminaries gathered, I assumed, to support him in the resumption of his thesis. I watched him pretend to be interested in his screen until he squinted, hands still poised on the keyboard, and looked up. "Why?" he asked.

I could resolve this simple comedy of errors by articulating a calm response. But I shivered, and surging emotion threatened to overwhelm the place my voice should control. "Willis," I said, borrowing poise from My Jane Austen, who looked more dead than usual at the moment. Willis continued staring into space. My Jane Austen opened one eye and waited for me to speak. "What you don't know about what you just saw in the office"—I inhaled, my voice slipping—"is that Sixby and I were rehearsing for the Founder's Night Follies."

Willis grimaced, glancing down immediately. I crossed my

arms. Priests should be more forgiving. "I have no interest in Sixby," I said, wishing to see his screen, unable to believe that he could type anything other than random keys under the circumstances. "Willis, this is important to me. There is nothing between me and Sixby. What you saw was theatre."

Willis stopped typing. "I believe you." He shrugged.

He didn't believe me at all. "Why are you doing this?" My protagonist voice got shoved aside, bullied by my default tendency to break down and cry.

"Doing what?" he asked, feigning perfect calm, utter reserve.

"Being so cold." Clearly, I could walk out. Part of me wanted to leave him, the early rumbling of thunder beat in my chest and I considered allowing the conflict to escalate, the pain to tear into me. Where were the people who found such happiness in the music room?

"What were you doing in London?" I asked.

Willis sighed, pushing his chair back. He looked different; he'd gotten his hair cut. He reluctantly raised his head; his expression revealed someone stuck in a difficulty. "Same things I always do," he said. "Collect mail, pay bills, water plants."

He hadn't been breaking up with his Someone Else. "Willis," I said.

He looked up briefly, the chair creaking. "Don't," he said, slowly shaking his head, closing his eyes. He was leaving me, closing doors we'd just opened. He'd gone to London for the big dose of *her*, necessary to counteract the effect of his great indulgence with *me*. And now he needed a reason to pull back from me. If he could just get a foothold in the opposite direction, he could backtrack and regroup, and my apparent bad behavior with Sixby provided the traction he needed. How could he be so indecisive?

"It doesn't matter," he said.

How could anything between us *not* matter? As if floods didn't matter. Or murder. "What doesn't matter?" I asked. "When you go, you take the air with you." I swallowed. "Color and light follow you out the door. When you're gone, my world is dead. *That* doesn't matter?"

He slumped in his chair, folding arms across his chest.

I couldn't keep the words down; they erupted like nature, out of my control. I sighed, speaking to the top of his head. "Willis, I love you."

In the ensuing silence, I pulled the green plastic chair opposite Willis and sat, my knees touching his legs, and took his hand. He offered his other hand, not speaking, not professing love he couldn't deliver. The torn expression on his face made me realize his struggle wasn't entirely about me. His conflict existed before he met me. He'd come to Newton Priors to resolve his issues in the solitude of this attic. I distracted him. The vampire novel and I together provided a safe haven where Willis could relax and forget the strife for a time. But cosmic soul mate notwithstanding, I'd managed to miss the iron wall dividing him. "What's her name?" I stopped breathing. Willis took his hands back and I braced myself, sensing that even in this foreign country where I barely knew anyone, I would recognize her name.

He looked me straight in the eyes for the first time. "Philippa Lockwood."

Not just a name but a whole world of obstacles.

"That explains a lot," I said. "Did you think I'd never find out?"

Willis breathed deeply and I sensed his relief. His arms reached for me, lighter, having shifted some of their heavy burden onto my shoulders. He pulled me onto his lap and when he kissed me, I felt not only his affection, but gratitude.

Fifteen

I set aside the lease I'd prepared for the next day's trip to the hospital as Omar walked into the office. "Go without me and save a seat," I said. "I'll be there in a minute."

"It's not just a lecture," Omar said of the evening's panel discussion, billed as "The Fanny Wars." "Sheila got a baby-sitter so she could go. And Magda will be there." Omar tapped his knuckles on my doorframe the way my boss once punctuated his gentle warnings. "You don't want to miss it."

"Save me a seat," I said. Even sequestered two floors above the Archie Wars, I grasped the dramatic possibilities of Archie, Sheila, and Magda in the same room. My Jane Austen was surely on-site already with an unobstructed view of the parties. All the same, once Omar left, I clicked on the e-mail I'd been ignoring for days, unwilling to sacrifice my happiness to the misery in Texas. But, now, one more hit could hardly matter. I clicked on Karen's message, "More Pictures." The page took forever to come up.

"Lily?"

Sheila Porter loomed in my doorway, a child in her arms and two more around her feet. She'd taken noticeable pains with her hair and makeup and I wanted to weep for her desperation. "Yes. Sheila. Hello," I said.

"Lily, I'm so sorry to bother you," she said, squinting from the pain of bothering me, "but could I leave the boys in here with you for just a bit?"

"Well, I—" I choked. "What happened to the babysitter?"

"She's delayed."

"How delayed?"

"Just a few minutes. I told her to fetch the children from you, here in the office."

"Well, it's all set then."

"If you don't mind." She squinted again and I didn't see any way out. "Thanks awfully, Lily." She closed the door.

The older boy grinned at me. One of the twins stood at the door crying and the other yanked an orange electrical cord as the e-mail radiated in my face. I grabbed the cord from the baby's hand and sat him in my lap as I read.

> **To:** Lillian Berry <verryberry7@hotmail.com>
> **Sent:** July 3, 5:45 A.M.
> **From:** Karen Adams <karen@adams.net>
> **Subject:** More Pictures
>
> Lily,
>
> I don't hear from you very often so I imagine things must be going better. I thought I'd save bad news for your homecoming but so much has happened that I don't think it would be right not to tell you.

Also, I'm worn out from dealing with it alone. It would really help me cope if we could talk.

I confronted Sue about the pictures she left out for me to find. She put one picture by the phone, one in the bathroom, and one on the mantel. The woman is twisted, Lily. She told me I had a problem. Me? When I spoke to Dad about it, he asked me to back off, that this had been hard on Sue as well as us. Can you believe it??!! I just want to scream. Anyway, I took the pictures to show Greg and to scan for you.

Do you think Mom knew? I can't believe she did. But the relationship has been going on for years. I just don't know what to think.

I'm still planning to attend the wedding, just to keep the lines open. Sue has a daughter who will be there. Not surprisingly, Sue and her daughter are estranged—information I got from Dad. So it will be a lovely event that I'm sure you're sorry to miss. Greg will be there to support me. He's been great.

I feel like we've lost both parents.

I miss you,
Karen

The baby slid off my lap and toddled over to his crying twin, tears mixing with mucus running from nose to mouth. I wanted to sit on the floor and cry with him. Older brother amused himself at Claire's desk, drawing on her blotter. "No," I said too emphatically, taking the pen away and setting him on the floor.

The e-mail had been sent a full week ago. I'd managed to

ignore reality for an entire week, which meant the wedding
was only days away. If I stopped now, ignored the pictures
she'd added as attachments, I might recover with minimal
damage. But I clicked on the first picture and waited. The
shot Karen had described filled the screen: my dad kissing
Sue at a New Year's Eve party. No mistaking the shirt, my
Christmas present to him, dating the shot precisely. Her arms
clasped behind his neck, his hands on her lower back, behav-
ing badly while the cancer grew in my mother. The damage
done, I began shivering from the inside out.

I clicked on the second picture, then rose to fetch Sheila's
oldest boy from Nigel's desk. He pulled paper and notebooks
from a bottom drawer. I relocated him to the front of the office
where I could see him while the next picture filled my screen:
Sue standing near a "Welcome to California" sign, like a thousand other vacation pictures in family scrapbooks. Posing in
a sundress, Sue smiles suggestively at the photographer. One
arm extends toward the little Karmann Ghia my father drove,
the car my mother called his "mid-life crisis." He *sold* the car
ten years ago.

The oldest boy had found a highlighter and drew long fluo-
rescent lines on his brother's arms. "Oh no, you don't," I said,
swiping the marker from his hand, ignoring his startled expression. Both boys cried.

Unable to stop with the pictures, I clicked on the last link.
My head felt hot, my insides like lava as though I might
vomit, while the oldest boy made noise at Claire's desk. The
last picture was obviously older, the color faded. Sue's hair
is darker and permed; her eyes still have the spark of youth I
recognized in younger pictures of my mother. They are sitting at a restaurant table, his arm around her shoulders, her
head leaning toward him, his mouth forming a word beneath
his mustache. Sue had included this shot because of the mus-

tache. My father had a mustache in his late forties. My father knew Sue at least twenty-five years ago.

The office door opened and I looked up at the babysitter. The twins were sitting on the floor crying. The oldest boy called, "Felicity!" from Claire's desk, where he rattled a box of breath mints in welcome. The babysitter ignored me, picking up a twin, staring strangely at the oldest boy. "What are you doing?" she asked him. She left the baby and grabbed the mints out of the oldest boy's hand.

"What happened?" I asked, turning my chair, still reeling from the emotional burden of an affair conducted over my entire lifetime.

"Sit still." Felicity spoke calmly, ignoring me.

"Iwanmymummy." The child began crying.

"He's pushed a mint up his nose," Felicity said, scowling. "At least one."

"No," I said, as if it couldn't have happened, as if I'd been paying attention.

"Be still," Felicity said. "I can't see it." She poked up his nose and the child screamed. "Oh shit," she said.

"How about if I ask him to blow his nose?" I said. I found a tissue and held it up to the child's face, demonstrating how to blow. Then I tried counting: "One, two, three, blow!"

"Mummeee," he cried, and I wanted to cry, too. Then a mint dropped on the floor. Mints were rolling all over the desk and it could have been one of those.

"Did that come from his nose?" I asked.

"Yes," she said.

I didn't know how she could be sure.

"Mummeee," he wailed.

When I arrived at the Fanny Wars panel discussion, one of the men was citing Lionel Trilling's famous comment,

"Nobody, I believe, has ever found it possible to like the heroine of *Mansfield Park*."

The audience laughed; a few clapped or made comments.

"With all due respect." A woman pointed her pen and took the microphone they passed among themselves. "I keep going back to John Wiltshire's essay suggesting Fanny is a radically traumatized personality, thanks largely to the abuse of Mrs. Norris and neglect of everyone except Edmund. Fanny turns inward, creates a life for herself from her reading, an intense inner world that cannot be reciprocated by those around her."

Someone else took the microphone and said, "Jane Austen's own mother thought Fanny insipid." The audience laughed. "But seriously," the new speaker continued, "I think Jane Austen messed up on this one."

Sheila was there for the discussion, sitting alone.

Sixteen

*H*aving spent the drive to London imagining Philippa Lockwood, I now prepared to meet her in the flesh. Somewhere within the teeming warren of the hospital, Willis's beloved stood at her grandmother's bedside, dreaming of her happy future with Willis. She persisted in her mistake, oblivious to the fact he'd spent days in the attic with me, introduced me to the roof, and made love to me in the music room.

In the hospital, Vera approached the information desk while I watched people coming and going, any one of whom could be Philippa. I walked the brightly lit halls like a spy, studying the block and diamond pattern in the tile floor, breathing the mix of chemicals and sick body odors. Fortunately, I had no appetite to lose; I hadn't eaten much lately and my clothes felt loose. Vera looked nervous, too.

"Do you have the lease?" Vera asked.

"For the last time, yes." She'd asked every five minutes, as if she had no memory.

Vera looked at the numbers on the doors and then the paper in her hand. She stopped and my stomach lurched. I'd harbored a fear of the horror behind hospital doors from my childhood service projects, delivering whatnots to elderly patients in declining stages of death and decay. Now the door concealed a new horror: my competition. A sensible person would have fled. I, on the other hand, having accepted the role of Other Woman, entered the room. At first, it seemed I had nothing to fear. A very thin young woman wearing tight jeans stood facing the bed, her back to us, coaxing Lady Weston to eat.

Nigel and Willis had been right. Lady Weston could hardly speak, so frail the part below the sheets didn't stick out in the places you would expect, no indication she had an awareness of things going on around her. She was busy getting ready to die and our festival concerns were inappropriate. I knew immediately I wouldn't press a legal document on this woman.

"Philippa," Vera said. "I bring greetings from Nigel." The young woman turned at the sound of her name. I gawked at her.

"Vera," she said. "How thoughtful of you to come." Outwardly gracious, I sensed something private cautioning us not to make a habit of showing up here. I studied her for what made her different from the rest of us. Her scoop-necked sweater did not come from the mall. It fit as though by magic, its shade of blue from a palette reserved for aristocrats. Every shift of her torso struck a pose; each movement released a fragrant breeze of her natural scent and revealed a new aspect of her perfection: white teeth, thin wrists, soft brown earlobes. *Pictures of perfection make me sick and wicked.* She looked for Randolph, who spoke with a doctor in the far corner of the private room while Vera and I stood against the wall like peasants, both chairs filled with Philippa's and Randolph's things.

As hard as I tried, I couldn't imagine Willis telling her about me.

Philippa returned to her task, coaxing Lady Weston to eat applesauce. "If you don't eat, they'll come and stick more tubes in you, Nana," she said, in a British head voice, blatantly denying Lady Weston's prerogative to die in peace. "You won't like that." Philippa glanced at Randolph, still huddled with the doctor. "Would you like me to get you a pudding, Nana? Would that be better?"

Lady Weston closed her eyes and I remembered when my mother looked like this. Close to the end, she no longer smiled at her grandchildren or listened to the details of my day, preoccupied with her inward progress away from us. And then, two days later, she stopped making sense. She left us many days before she actually died, a blessing, because how else could she bear to go?

Vera startled me. "I'd like to introduce my colleague, Lily Berry."

"I'm pleased to meet you," I said, "and so sorry about Lady Weston's illness." I stepped forward and extended my hand but retracted when Philippa nodded to the applesauce and spoon, so obviously straining her present capacity.

"Rand," she called; the doctor had left.

"Yes, Pippa." Randolph stood at comic attention.

"Would you mind fetching a pudding? We must find something she'll eat."

Sad, she thought food would bring her grandmother back at this point. As Pippa placed the applesauce on the tray table, I noticed a tiny sparkle on her left hand. I almost failed to draw the obvious conclusion but Vera, having also seen it, remarked, "Congratulations on your engagement. Nigel told me you've set a date."

Pippa wore an engagement ring; not flashy like Texas diamonds, but humble and serious in a way that made me ill. "Yes, we did." She smiled fondly, then glanced at the bed. "But we'll just have to wait for Her Ladyship to be well enough. And Willis is finishing his thesis."

Rand stood looking at me, waiting. I extended my hand again. "Lily Berry," I said, from the depths of active trauma.

"Pleased to meet you." He took my hand, lingering over it, so that I pulled out before he loosened his grip. "Are you with the festival?"

"Yes," I said, not sure what festival he was talking about, or what planet I happened to be visiting at the moment, still processing the information that Pippa wanted to get married before her grandmother died and Willis was stalling until his thesis was finished. And I was playing the part of Sue. How easily I'd slipped into the role.

"An actress?" Rand asked.

But Willis had been writing a vampire novel for most of the summer.

"Yes," Vera answered when I hesitated. "From Texas," Vera added meaningfully.

"Ah," he said. I saw him connect with Philippa in a quick glance I would have called The Look except I never thought of The Look within the sibling context. His eyes rested on me longer than seemed normal and I tried to pull myself together.

"Rand," Pippa said; a trifle pushy. "A pudding?"

"But where should I find a pudding?"

Pippa took Rand into the hall to point the way, and I found myself alone with Vera and the dying Lady Weston. I touched Vera's shoulder and shook my head. "Don't do it," I whispered.

Vera frowned and reached for the lease document; I backed away, worried Philippa would see us arguing.

"Don't do what?" Philippa asked, returning.

Vera shushed us and pointed toward the bed. I turned and left the room in an act of self-preservation, the lease still in my JASNA bag.

Busy people in white coats and blue scrubs moved about the hall; charts and pens in their hands, ducking in and out of doors, saving people. A doctor's surgical mask dangled jauntily from one ear as if he'd just emerged from the front. He passed behind the nurse's station, the border separating medical professionals from the masses, reminding me of an altar to which the humble could approach and beg for things like pudding. It seemed to me hospitals were portals for birth and death—the place where people come into the world for the first time or leave forever. Surely this hospital had a chapel.

I couldn't believe Willis had not told me he was engaged.

I pulled the *Acting* book out of my bag in a desperate effort to disguise my panic. Holding it open, I stood in the hall and stared at it blankly, reeling from confusion. But even the *Acting* book conjured Willis. He'd taken it from my hand one day and said, "Looks like a much-read book." He opened it and flipped through the pages, releasing the musty paper smell of my adolescent summers: pool chlorine mixed with *David Copperfield*, the soothing smell of raindrops on hot concrete mingled with the desolation of the moors, lake-house mildew like musty Manderley, newly mown grass merging with longing and tragic endings. Willis had looked at me, there in the attic, his eyes smiling as if he heard everything I was thinking and agreed. "Nothing like the smell of old paper," he said.

My Willis would never hurt me like this.

"Can I get *you* anything?" Randolph said, back from the cafeteria, a plastic cup of vanilla pudding in his hand. His manner toward me felt inappropriately familiar, especially considering his reserved British gene pool. While he spoke, his eyes followed a nurse's backside to the counter, breaking contact when she turned to reveal a bad complexion.

"Oh," I said, "no, thank you." I closed the book.

"Say, Vera's told me about you," he said. "You're working on the business plan?" His expression was perfectly serious, as though he spoke with a legitimate business consultant.

"Yes," I said. "We understand the need to rethink the festival to meet financial demands more effectively." Not knowing what the financial demands might be, I was winging it to a major extent. But Randolph nodded, the pudding hanging at his side. My Jane Austen began coughing so furiously that, if she weren't already dead, she would have required medical assistance. Pulling what felt like the draft of ideas out of my JASNA bag, I found some entirely unfamiliar papers; Bets's stuff. "I don't wish to add to your burdens," I said, holding the unfamiliar papers as if they were the beginnings of a plan to save Newton Priors and Literature Live. "However, with our agreement expired and future operation depending upon the use of your house, we're developing a plan that promotes everyone's best interests." My Jane Austen had turned purple.

"Well." Randolph touched his breast pocket as he straightened. His eyebrows arched seriously at the paper I held up. "That's not your business plan, is it?"

I looked at the paper, scrunched from having been in my bag, a photograph of some scruffy people posed gloomily around a bare-chested man. They wore lots of black stuff around their eyes like vampires. Superimposed over the picture were the words: "I'll Find You." I pushed the photo back into my bag. "My roommate, Bets, used this bag," I said. "She forgot to take her papers."

"Bets. She's my cousin, you know." Randolph folded his arms, manicured fingernails peeked around his biceps; the natural ridges of his nails smoothed. "Say, how about if I call you after things have settled a bit. And perhaps we could meet and take a look at your plan together."

"Yes," I said. "I know this is a difficult time."

Randolph looked into his grandmother's room. "Yes, difficult," he said.

"Rand?" Philippa called from the bedside.

"I'd better deliver this." He held up the pudding. "I've enjoyed meeting you." He extended his hand and I made certain not to withdraw prematurely. "I'll be in touch," he said.

Walking to the car, the truth hit and my world shifted: Willis misled me.

"I'm afraid this mission failed," Vera said, gazing straight ahead in search of the car. "There is no doubt in my mind we are in trouble."

"Yes," I said, tired. "But Randolph said he'd call. You think he'll forget?"

"I don't know, Lily." Vera sounded tired, too.

"Well, what's the worst thing that could happen?" I asked. "We have to get a new house?" We stopped walking.

Vera looked at me hard while her hand searched her bag for keys, and I remembered what Magda had said about Vera not thinking clearly. "Getting a new house, as you so casually put it, is not easy. And Nigel is not well." Vera paused to consider her words, unlocking the car door. "When you get older, Lily, your ambition declines," she said. "If we lose this house, Nigel will be finished."

"But there is hope." I opened my door, feeling no hope.

"Right," Vera said dryly, rolling her eyes. "You will marry Randolph and Literature Live will have use of the house forever."

Seventeen

"I think we should do a skit about the Fanny Wars," I told Sixby. We sat at the top of the second floor staircase. Tourists had been climbing the stairs since we opened that morning, hoping to view a nude portrait of Jane Austen allegedly hanging in the second floor hallway. No nude portrait existed and Vera sent me upstairs to fend off the curious and distribute fliers explaining the bogus Internet posting. Tourists expressed such disappointment that I nearly redirected them to Magda's room as a consolation prize. Magda and Archie fooled no one, arriving and departing separately.

"Did you hear the comments at the Fanny Wars discussion the other night?" I asked Sixby. "Some readers might enjoy voting Fanny out of the book." An old man wearing a beret huffed up the stairs; most of the nude portrait pilgrims were men. "So sorry," I said, handing him a flier as he looked past me into the hallway and I looked past him down the stairs.

The real reason I agreed to perch on the landing had more to do with the possibility of encountering Willis arriving or departing. Although I had mentally rehearsed our encounter, I had no idea what I would say if he appeared, and I felt sick with waiting.

"A Fanny Wars skit sounds deadly dull," Sixby said from the floor, slumped against the wall, arms on his raised knees, stifling another yawn.

"Why are you so tired?" I asked.

"Because," Sixby said, "I fell victim to the Regency skirt of a young fan who enticed me from the pub to her hotel room last evening."

"So you're in love."

"Not exactly; she wouldn't keep her dress on."

"Well, wake up. We've got to focus or we won't be ready."

"That's why they call it improv, Lil."

I offered fliers to a group of women. "So sorry," I said. "An Internet hoax." And then to Sixby, "What angle can we take to amuse our audience?"

"Let's amuse *me* for a change. How about a hot love scene; Edmund finds his groove."

"By the way, there's no kissing in this skit, Sixby. None."

Just then a woman with three little children struggled up the stairs, the children looking very much like Sheila's, but it wasn't Sheila; it was Bets, a baby in each arm, big brother following slowly. "Bets, are you babysitting?" I asked. Sixby sat up wide-eyed.

"Not for long," Bets growled.

"Where's their mother?"

"In her room crying." Bets plopped the babies on the floor next to Sixby, who jumped up.

"Why do you have them?" I asked.

"Because Sheila dumped them on Archie who dumped them on Magda who dumped them on Gary. And Gary is totally clueless about kids."

I looked at Bets and the babies.

"I was planning to dump them on you. I'm meeting Bella for lunch."

Sixby waved. "I'll see you later, Lily. Pleasure, Bets."

"No way," I said, the horror of my last experience with the little brutes still fresh in my mind. "I've got work to do. Where's Magda?"

"The visa office with Gary."

"Again?" I handed a flier to a portrait pilgrim without providing an explanation. "Hard work renewing a student visa if you're not in school." I stared into her eyes. "You're not going to marry him, are you?" One of the twins screamed, prompting the other two to do likewise, making it hard to hear.

"No," Bets said, turning to go.

Suddenly events blurred: Bets walking away, the children following her, the tourist who got past me searching for the nude portrait. I felt the first flicker of relief as my life burst into color and the earth resumed its revolutions without me having to pedal. I understood the ease addicts feel when the drug finally enters their bloodstream. Willis was coming up the stairs. He stopped at the top; no books in his arms, no question about the fliers in my hand, no amusement over the nude portrait. Willis knew that I knew. We locked eyes as the twins' cries receded down the stairs and the floor creaked under the tourist's footsteps. Slowly, I deflated, recalling the horror of the engagement ring.

"Today is my father's wedding day," I said, breaking the silence.

Willis drew back. "I'm so sorry." His hands in his pockets reminded me of my dad. He nodded to the attic door, "Coming up?"

I shook my head.

"I understand," he said.

"You understand what?" I asked, angry since I'd hoped for a denial, furious that he would give up without a fight. The tourist kept trying doors, going from one to the next, turning knobs relentlessly, finding them all locked. "There's no nude portrait," I called over my shoulder, my eyes still gripping Willis, the tourist's heels still clicking on the wood floor. "It's a hoax."

"Well," Willis said, stepping away from me, walking backward; gaining on the attic door as I silently dared him to leave me without an explanation, lusty despair rushing in to fill the emotional vacuum.

"What are you doing?" I asked.

The tourist opened a door behind us, the same closet stuffed with rotting curtains I'd found just before discovering Willis.

"If it's any consolation," Willis said, "I'm just as bewildered as you are."

Willis watched me drop the fliers on the floor. The curious could help themselves. I left the folding chair and walked away without giving him a second glance. Just as bewildered as I am. Not possible. He went up his stairs as I went down. Not the Willis I knew. No explanation; no words of comfort. No apology. Some priest. I cried for myself, familiar pitiful tears, dripping all the way down the stairs, crying as I passed Magda going up, crying as I walked through the entry, and crying as I exited the front door where Archie entered. The curious turned to watch me as I marched down the front steps and across the lawn, away from the house to the secluded hedge behind the Carriage House where Archie hid to smoke. Previous visitors had packed the earth into a hard dirt floor littered with butts. Overturned milk crates offered seating. I reached up and patted the dirty ledge until I found the pack holding cigarettes and lighter. Seated on the ground, I smoked an unfiltered cigarette, inhaling deeply, alternating between thoughts of self-pity and anger. I kept returning to things Willis had said to me in our conversations, unable to reconcile the good person I loved with the jerk hiding his engagement. I couldn't yet admit I'd been wrong about him or acknowledge my disappointment in him, but my anger ceased spinning as nausea took over. I lowered my head until the effects of the cigarette passed and I recovered enough to walk.

Making my way to the east wing, I avoided the stairs, crossing through the narrow doorway where the addition began and the pattern of wood planks dramatically changed direction. Closer to the office, a familiar sound emerged: the drama of crying twins. Claire sat at her desk, one ear on her phone, her hand to the other ear, struggling to hear. "I'm sorry, could you repeat that?" she said, her voice competing with the babies' rising howl. When she saw me, Claire gestured largely to Nigel's office. The twins stood by the door, noses and eyes running, crying for attention, the older boy crouched on the floor behind Nigel's desk, likely up to no good.

I approached the older boy slowly as if stalking a wild animal, but he didn't see me. His eyes fluttered open and closed like a child trying not to fall asleep. I grabbed Nigel's medicine box from his grubby hands. A chalky white pill lay in a pool of saliva on Nigel's chair; several other candy-colored pills lay about. All the pillbox doors of the weekdays were open, several pills remained in their slots but how many were gone and how many were in the boy's mouth? I pried his fingers open and discovered a small round red pill and a yellow and white capsule in his moist palm.

"Oh my God," I said.

Claire walked in. "What's he done?" she asked.

"He's taken Nigel's meds. Call Sheila," I said. "And Vera." Prying his jaws apart with one hand, I swept the interior of his mouth with my index finger, retrieving a partially melted blue pill and another that might have been one of the small red pills before the sweet coating dissolved in his tiny mouth. "And call Archie," I said, as the boy vomited on Nigel's threadbare carpet. "Oh my God, he's sick." I picked him up and his little body melted into my shoulder. "Don't go to sleep," I said, his eyes closing. "No sleeping." I shook him and thumped his back.

"Do you have 911 here?" I asked.

"Sheila and Vera are coming," Claire said. "I can't find Archie." Claire unrolled some paper towels and threw them on the floor. "And it's 999," she said reaching for the phone again.

"I know where Archie is." I jostled the boy on my arm to wake him. "Watch those two," I said to Claire. "Make sure they don't find any pills on the floor. I'll be right back." I ran down the hall, shaking the child as I went. "Don't sleep," I said. "No sleeping now." Every time I shook him his eyes would open before fluttering shut again. I ran up the stairs to the second floor and banged on Magda's door. "Archie," I said. "Open up, I have your son and he's overdosed on Nigel's medicine." The boy started crying and gagged as if he would vomit again. I held his shirt to his mouth.

The door opened and Archie stood there half dressed, eyes glazed, throwing his arms into his shirt. "What happened?" he asked, fingers trembling around buttons. "What happened!" he said again, louder, a madman in his distress, unable to button his shirt. "What happened!"

"He swallowed pills, I have no idea how many or what kind. Vera's on her way. The twins are in the office. Take him." I handed the child to Archie as Magda appeared behind him, pulling her long hair into a ponytail.

Downstairs one of the twins wandered the hall. "Really, Lily," Magda said, "what are you people doing down here?"

She'd picked the wrong moment to provoke me. I stopped in my tracks and stared at her. "What were you doing up there?" I hissed. "This is all your fault." I pointed at Magda. "You and Archie."

She closed her eyes.

In the office, Archie lit a cigarette with the hand not holding his son. A plume of gray smoke taunted Magda. "Is he going to be okay?" Archie asked. "Just a simple answer to a simple question," he said, frantic, his voice breaking. "Oh my God, baby," he said to the sobbing boy in his arms. "What did he swallow?" Archie asked me.

"I don't know," I said. "Nigel and Vera are on their way. "Don't let him sleep," I said.

Claire was still on the phone. "I'm speaking with the Poison people. They want to know what he took."

"Did you swallow any pills?" Archie asked the child tenderly.

"Did you eat the pills?" Magda asked, employing sign language with the child, bunching her fingers and touching her open mouth as she moved herself closer to the huddle, edging me out. I took the pillbox and my findings to another corner of the desk as Magda continued asking questions and Archie shushed her, putting his ear closer to the child's mouth. Actors and a few volunteers clustered outside our door, concerned expressions all around.

"Is his pulse okay?" Archie asked me, his cell phone hunched in his shoulder, trying to reach Sheila.

I touched the child's neck but I wasn't a nurse. The twin Magda held squirmed out of her arms and reached for Archie but Archie ignored the baby to focus exclusively on his oldest son, displacing everyone, including Magda. He dropped his cigarette into a paper cup half full of cold coffee where it emitted a quick hiss at Magda. She closed her eyes. I felt so angry at the two of them, or maybe all three.

"Does anybody know what exactly he swallowed?" Clare asked, her hand covering the receiver.

The other twin, Roger of the pointy head or Teddy of the freckled bum, jumped on the sofa as Nigel and Vera arrived and counted pills, hands trembling, struggling to clarify what the child had swallowed and what Nigel had already taken.

"Wake up, baby," Archie cried, prying the boy's eyelids open. "Oh God, where's Sheila. Don't die, baby. Don't die."

"But I forgot to take the Tuesday pills," Nigel said, clearly undone. "Why don't they go to the hospital?" he asked.

"Didn't you take them late?" Vera asked.

"Did I take today's pills?" Nigel asked.

"Yes. Remember? Right after you took the call from Tate. That's why we have the box," Vera shrugged.

Claire moved the phone away from her mouth. "You need to take him to the hospital immediately," she said.

My little mint up the nose seemed nothing compared to the deadly effect of Nigel's medication on this small child. Suddenly the crowd at the door parted and Sheila walked in. Not Sheila of the Frumpy Tunic but Sheila the Mother: fierce, all-powerful, master of the child's universe. The boy reached for her, sobbing as she took him. Archie automatically lifted the heavy diaper bag from her shoulder and took the car keys from her hand.

"Do we know what he swallowed?" Sheila asked Vera. She clipped her words to save time, already turning to leave as Archie lifted one twin and fetched the other from the sofa.

Vera handed her the paper indicating which pills remained in question while Archie looked on, balancing a twin in each arm, the diaper bag relegated to his back. Sheila folded the paper as Archie turned, allowing her access to the bag, movements like choreography, smooth from endless repetition.

"Keep us informed," Vera pressed her hands together as Sheila slipped the paper into the pocket. But Magda made the first move, her nostrils flaring as she abandoned ship, walking toward the door silently. Archie made no move to stop her; seemed unaware of her action as the affair ended in our presence. I felt we should not be watching; yet we did. Magda left without a backward glance. Oddly, I knew exactly how she felt.

"My car's in front." Sheila didn't seem the least bit frumpy now, having parked at the door of Newton Priors, passing carriages and crashing gates to get there. I patted the boy's back, wondering if I might suggest a simple X-ray of his nasal cavities for mints as long as they had him in the ER.

Eighteen

I did something I knew I'd regret. While waiting in the Freezer for the tea-theatre to start, I clicked on Karen's e-mail. I'd blown it off for the past week as part of my plan to avoid all things negative. Since the meeting on the stair landing when Willis gave me up without a fight, I'd struggled to keep my promise to myself not to go to him, avoiding stairways and detouring around any place Willis might surface, throwing myself into the tea-theatre and avoiding potentially depressing activities such as bad news from Karen. Idle moments such as I experienced just before clicking on Karen's e-mail undid my resolve.

To: Lillian Berry <verryberry7@hotmail.com>
Sent: July 16, 2:12 A.M.
From: Karen Adams <karen@adams.net>
Subject: Wedding Pictures

Lily,

I survived the wedding. Here are pictures to prove it. I didn't know anyone except Uncle Jim who was able to make it on the short notice. The rest of the guests were complete strangers although they seem to be very old friends of Nelson and Sue. (I don't feel like calling him Dad anymore.) They all knew each other and I begin to feel like there has been a parallel world existing all through our lives where these people got to know each other while we went to school and celebrated holidays, oblivious to the fact that we were sharing our father with a whole different dimension. Nelson's Other Life.

I tried to meet and greet, introducing Nelson's grandchildren to the strangers, but I finally quit trying and sat by the wall until I could go home. It was Sue's party, and her friends didn't want anything to do with me, or my children. I didn't exist for those people. Even Greg felt it. Greg has a terrible theory about Sue's daughter that I refuse to acknowledge. Check out the pictures and call me. Please.

Your whole sister,
Karen

I clicked on the first attachment just as a volunteer popped her head in the door.

"Lily, where are the programs?" The downside of the tea-theatre's success was to be constantly running out of things. Everybody wanted to come see the husband who played the baron. He was so good at gently roasting our guests, and patrons clamored to be chosen for the skit. Omar revised the script, adding roles he'd initially cut so that we could increase audience participation. But we had a job keeping up with the details.

"Top drawer of the ticket table," I said, willing her to go away.

"Are they folded?" she asked.

"No," I said. "See if Mrs. Russell and Stephen can fold them." They needed something to do with their hands.

The photograph dominated my entire screen, starting at the top and slowly working its way down, filling in hair before foreheads, noses before mouths, loading so slowly I feared it would not finish before I had to go. Finally, I recognized individuals. My father and Sue looked like themselves in an older version of the restaurant picture. But the person standing with them looked confusingly familiar. She looked like me. But I was an ocean away and the picture had been taken without me. It couldn't be me. And it wasn't me. But I saw my father in her face. I zoomed in to focus on the eyes, nose, and mouth, isolating the features as I had isolated my father's features in the rearview mirror when he drove me to school. I'd positioned my own face, without my hair, in the small mirror imagining I was my father. I looked just like him even then, with hair. And this person looked just like me, and just like him. At first, the discovery struck me as funny, an odd coincidence. I wanted to run and tell my mother and sister what I'd found, almost relieved, as if the doctors had finally, after a lifetime of tests and trials, isolated the mysterious cause of my ailment. "Miss Berry," they said gravely, "we have ruled out cancer, personality disorders, and missing organs. Your problem is a half sister." What relief!

I reread Karen's e-mail. She would be sleeping; still the middle of the night in Texas, with Greg to comfort her if the news of a half sister distressed her. I had to admit it was beginning to distress me and I felt the approach of an internal storm, thunder growing distinctly closer.

Mrs. Russell stepped in, waving folded programs. "Lily, we're waiting for you."

"Amelia, you have a brother," the baron spoke the same line I'd heard many times, but today it resonated.

"I have just heard so, my lord," I said, thinking of all the years I'd felt something was wrong with me, when in fact my father had split his attention between two families, building half of his life with people I didn't know.

"What return can I make to you for the loss of half your fortune?" the baron asked.

"My brother's love will be ample recompense," I said. Sue could finally have the husband she'd been denied all those years.

The baron and Anhalt delivered their lines, after which the baron handed me over to Anhalt to be his wife. It felt good to lean on Sixby. "Oh my dear father," I said. "What blessings have you bestowed on me in one day." If this discovery was such a relief, why did I feel so sick? The wave that had brought a bounty of truth to my life began to recede, taking as much as it brought. As if in delivering a half sister, it demanded my own self in exchange.

When the skit ended I did not stay to autograph programs for the children in the audience. Temporarily willing to disregard the entire issue of Pippa, I ran to the attic, desperate to see Willis.

"Hello," I called up the stairwell. All the years I'd spent pondering my affliction, searching for what was lacking in me, and it wasn't *me* at all. The half sister filled in so many blanks. Like the missing letter in a game of hangman, when finally inserted, suggests words, and those words associate instantly, causing an entire phrase to fall effortlessly into place. The absent father, the wistful mother, and the proprietary appearance of the mysterious woman: I didn't have a zillion unrelated problems; I had one.

"Hello," I called up the stairs. But the attic was silent; no clicking of the keyboard. "Hello," I called again, running up the stairs to the landing where I'd first met Willis. His chair was gone and his table lay bare, pushed against some boxes. My green cushions sat in the window but they'd been turned on their sides as if someone had checked beneath them for stray belongings. The books were gone. Every last volume of theology as well as *1000 Places to Visit Before You Die* and all its lighthearted friends. Only my half-read copy of *Anna Karenina* remained.

Pushing the cushions back into place, I sat in the window seat, inhaling the musty attic air, feeling the damp chill. Willis hadn't been avoiding me. He'd moved out. My Jane Austen sat in a dark corner making a list of her heroines and I felt grateful for her company, although I'd never make it onto her list. There *was* something wrong with me. A freak of nature, destined to be alone forever because of something deep down wrong with me that made me unlovable. No man ever stayed in my life for long.

Nineteen

On the evening of the follies, workers adjusted the stand-up microphones arranged on the stage, "testing one, two," followed by a squawk. I entered the ballroom dressed as Fanny Price for the evening's follies, wearing period attire from Bets's closet, including Bets's unused elaborate under-garments handmade by a seamstress who reenacted Regency romances on weekends. If Father Kitt, the vampire priest in Willis's novel, could see me now, he would be unable to resist the pillows of flesh bulging just south of my jugular. Claire inspected the name tags I'd arranged in alphabetical order. She expected a big turnout this year based on her assessment of the fragile state of affairs. Vera said, "Nonsense. The Founder's Dinner is always highly anticipated. Everyone *always* comes."

Everyone except Willis.

"Oh, there you are," Claire said to me. "Would you make another name tag? Your handwriting is so much better than mine." She handed me the nearly dead calligraphy marker I'd been chewing all week.

"What name?" I asked, pen poised over the white square.

Claire called to the sound person, "It's not centered on the stage." She gestured, scooting air to the left.

"Claire," I said, straightening. "Whose name?"

"Oh." She looked past me, blinking, struggling to recall. "Somerford. Willis Somerford."

We *would* meet again. The room shifted and the stage, tables, even the workers looked different, now that Willis was coming. I wrote the familiar letters of his name and placed the name tag between Sadonek and Stewart, my mind racing to organize the things I wanted to say to Willis. How to speak to him in a ballroom filled with people? How to be alone with his fiancée present?

Regulars began to arrive; several participants from Omar's writing workshop claimed a table. Magda held court. Her affair officially over, she'd announced plans to return to Michigan to hammer out the details of her seminar. Her announcement came the same day Archie let us know he would be staying close to home for the rest of the summer, offering gratitude for his child's survival. Although I disliked Magda, losing both Archie and Magda seemed a sorry blow for the festival. Like *Mansfield Park* losing Aunt Norris and Henry Crawford. The summer had been a riotous expansion. But now things around me were contracting, matters settling, people returning to their regular orbits. I'd soon be back in Texas.

Mrs. Russell followed Nigel around the room, wearing her Anne Elliot dress for mature heroines only. Vera kept signaling "go ahead" to Nigel from the head table where she sat next to the old woman who always brought her dog. But Mrs. Russell stalled, waiting until all the VIPs were present before she officially welcomed festival alumni and guests, inviting all to proceed to the buffet. I fixed my eyes on the door Willis would use for his entrance; my pulse surged at the arrival of every tall man.

Philippa stood near the bar. She lifted a single cracker from the basket and broke it into tiny pieces, placing crumbs in her mouth one at a time. It might take her an hour to eat one cracker. No wonder she was so thin. And her skin was so white the veins were visible to the naked eye. Father Kitt could drain her so easily. She waved as Willis arrived, then touched a napkin to the corners of her mouth. I looked away so I wouldn't have to witness the kiss.

Mrs. Russell's microphone squawked and Pippa led Willis to their place at the head table. I walked from table to table, unaware of my actions, lighting candles in little glass jars, my hand shaking, wondering if Willis had seen me yet. The earth kept shifting under my feet, rearranging my world again before I could adjust to the last shift. I poured myself a large glass of wine.

"You look awful," Omar said. "You want to go outside?" He grabbed a wine bottle and I followed him.

In the herb garden, where light from the ballroom illuminated St. Francis, who was blatantly eavesdropping, I told Omar about Willis. Once I finished my story, we sat quietly, listening to the hum of the party. When Omar spoke, it wasn't about the things I'd said.

"You did a great job with the tea-theatre."

"Thank you," I said, clinking glasses with him.

"It was just the kick in the butt this festival needed."

"Thanks to the volunteers. But once they tire of baking, our profit margins will shrink."

"Have you ever acted before?" Omar asked.

"Small parts in high school. No one is more surprised at my acting than me." I shifted on the bench. "I don't want to talk about business," I said. "I want to obsess over Willis." I rested my hand on my forehead. "Do you think I'm needy?" I asked.

Omar choked on his wine and coughed. I handed him a napkin. "Lily"—he locked eyes with me and touched my hand—"if you have to ask . . ."

I made sure to refill my wineglass and Omar brought me a plate of food before Nigel began his talk. Claire had led me to expect "Nigel's Last Words on Jane Austen." She made it sound as if Nigel would reveal the answer to the great mystery of Jane Austen's undying appeal—that aspect of Austen's work which provoked, not only Magda's activism, but Mrs. Russell's wardrobe expansion and my possessive friendship with someone dead two hundred years. Even though I refused to believe Nigel was retiring, I would listen to every word, just in case. But Nigel's talk was not long enough or serious enough to be his swan song. Not a funeral, just the Founder's Night talk that he gave every year and surely believed he would give next year. He reviewed the story "The Janeites," by Rudyard Kipling. *You take it from me, Brethren, there's no one to touch Jane when you're in a tight place.*

When Nigel's talk ended, the follies began. I looked at the plate of food Omar had brought me while listening to a man read a screenplay of his *Northanger Abbey* adaptation that went on way too long. Even the little dog got restless and wandered the room. Feeling sick, I put my plate on the floor and the dog wandered over, first sniffing, then gently biting into the chunks of lamb. He ate while, at the podium, Henry Tilney reminded Catherine Morland of the similarities between marriage and dancing. The dog licked the plate until it looked perfectly clean.

Next up for the follies, Sabrina played Jane Austen hosting a talk show, interviewing Patricia Rozema, director of a film adaptation of *Mansfield Park*. "What were you thinking, girl-friend?" Sabrina said; a joke that would never connect out-side of this crowd.

Sixby arrived somewhere between the end of my second glass of wine and the middle of my third, wine establishing a military dictatorship in my head, dispatching directives to my extremities, my reason completely overthrown.

"Ready, Lily?" Sixby asked, my dearest, oldest friend. I wished to fall into his embrace and be carried far away, skip the performance, blow off my plan to address Willis.

"I love your dress, my dear," Sixby whispered, his eyes on the bodice of Bets's spotted muslin.

"Thank you," I said, kissing the air.

"I'm going to change now." He winked. "I'll meet you back-stage in a tick." He adjusted the sleeve of my dress downward, revealing a bit more shoulder. I posed for him, naughtiness fueled by too much wine and outrage. As he left, touching my cheek affectionately, I caught Magda watching us; she never missed a thing. I bent low to retrieve my plate from the floor, hoping to escape, but Magda crooked her long finger, beck-oning me to the dessert table.

As I drew near, she glanced sideways and whispered, "Have you read *Mansfield Park*?" Her question was the great-est insult anyone could inflict on a fellow at this place. She touched my arm. "Do the words *amateur theatricals* mean anything to you?" she asked. "Sixby is a professional actor. You need to be careful." She took the plate from my hand just as she took everything as her due, even a plate lacquered with dog spit. She shook her head. "I'm warning you, as a sister."

"Magda," I said, as she moved closer to the fruit salad, "have *you* read *Mansfield Park*?" I'd drunk too much wine to bother with inhibitions.

She spooned a serving of fruit onto the plate. "What is your point?" she asked, the berry juices instantly reactivating dried dog saliva.

"I find your ideas about slavery *traduce* the text." I'd looked up the word Nigel used in conversation, meaning: to expose to shame or blame by means of misrepresentation. Still, I hoped my assertion was coherent, wished I'd had an opportunity to run it by Willis.

Magda frowned, exasperated, as she speared a pineapple chunk, slogging it through the juice. "Lily, you haven't been paying attention this summer."

Disarmed, I'd fired my only bullet.

She popped the dog spit fruit into her mouth and spoke while chewing. "The text skillfully reveals not only the complicity of Austen's society with the slave trade, but equates slavery with the status of genteel women: 'I cannot get out, as the starling said.'" Magda spoke in slow motion for the learning impaired.

"I don't think that's what Austen meant," I said, slurring.

Magda swept a melon slice through the juices, scraping the last stubborn dog germs. "She *meant*," Magda said, "to demonstrate that women were sold like mere chattel on the marriage market."

"When are you leaving?" I asked.

I watched the famous-looking man with abundant gray hair play his ukulele through a crack in the door. He sang "Dear Jane," an original composition sung in sincere falsetto to great amusement at Vera's end of the table. Another time I would have found him highly amusing but not this evening. Sixby appeared behind me as Nikki took the stage to begin our skit.

Willis and Pippa were seated front and center, eyes on Nikki. This performance might be my last opportunity to speak frankly to Willis; as a captive audience. Sixby squeezed my hand. I didn't want to be alone when this ended.

"The Fanny Wars have raged since 1814 when *Mansfield Park* was first published," Nikki said in her glorious stage voice. "After two hundred years of fighting over whether Fanny is insipid or merely dull, we offer a format whereby you, the readers, have an opportunity to end the battle. We present two Fanny Prices. Each Fanny will answer a series of questions. By your applause, you will choose which Fanny stays in the novel. First," she said, "please welcome Traditional Fanny, straight from the stacks, just the way she was written."

I entered the stage, smiling shyly, my character as loath to participate in the follies as to consider amateur theatricals in her uncle's absence. Willis sat directly in my sight, underlit by candlelight, free to stare if he so desired. He clapped and smiled as if he'd forgotten every wrong thing at the moment. Then Pippa reached over and took his hand, and envy plunged me deep into pain.

"And now, ladies and gentlemen"—Nikki spoke with greater enthusiasm—"the Fanny you've been craving these two hundred years. The Future Fanny of *Mansfield Park*, as Jane Austen really *meant* to write her, please welcome Forward Fanny." Applause and laughter exploded as the audience realized Forward Fanny was none other than Sixby in drag. Wigged and flat-chested, he air-kissed the audience, his arms and shoulders clearly straining the jumbo gown, a wolf in sheep's clothing.

Nikki cleared her throat but people were still laughing and

Sixby milked the moment. "For our first question," Nikki said, waiting for quiet.

Sixby and I turned to Nikki.

"We'll start with you, Traditional Fanny."

I stepped forward, taking care to balance myself.

Nikki read from a card. "Please tell the audience what you would say if Mary Crawford rode your horse—without asking. You have ten seconds to respond."

"I would say"—I cleared my throat—"I have been out very often lately, and would rather stay home." This was straight from the book. "I would not wish to appear rude or impatient or create suspicion of either emotion, but," and here I was improvising, "I would concede my horse, confident that Edmund would recognize the slight and privately offer me his reassurance." I stepped back and then added, "I would wait in my attic garret for such private reassurance." I did not dare look at Willis.

Nikki's eyebrows rose and the audience smiled. "Forward Fanny, same question. Take your time responding."

"I would say," Sixby said, jutting his lower jaw and bobbing his head like a tough girl, "Bitch. Off my horse." His delivery was perfect.

The audience laughed and then applauded.

"Thank you, Forward Fanny," Nikki said, smiling in spite of herself. As Nikki read the next question, I watched in horror as Philippa, charmed by the skit, gave Willis a little kiss on his cheek. I spoke my line and the skit moved on but it was all a blur as I struggled to recover basic faculties.

"Traditional Fanny," Nikki said, "is there any chance you would marry Henry Crawford?"

"No. How wretched and how unpardonable, how hopeless and how wicked it is to marry without affection," I said. *Take that, Willis.*

"Forward Fanny, would you marry Henry Crawford?"

"Interesting question," Sixby reflected. "I've been imprisoned in this manor house, living off the wages of sin for so long, I don't even know if I like men!"

Laughter and applause.

"Last question," Nikki said. "Are you in or out?" Nikki looked at me. "Traditional Fanny, you're first, two seconds."

"If you refer to my social status, I was presented at a ball given by my uncle to honor my brother William and me. Otherwise, I am *in* love with a would-be clergyman, *out* of my mind with jealousy of the competition, *in*creasingly lonely in my attic room, and *out*raged at the discovery of a new half sister in the colonies." Now he knew everything.

Nikki grimaced and the audience laughed politely, as if they got it.

"Forward Fanny?"

It was the way he said it. "I'm in *and* out." Sixby extended his arms, caressed the words, and the audience loved him. "I like Edmund *and* Mary. They hooted. "Even better"—Sixby played them along—"I can play Anhalt *and* Amelia. And back to your earlier question, there's room for both of us on that horse."

Under cover of Sixby's performance, I dared peek at Willis. He was smiling.

"And now"—Nikki's voice projected above the crowd—"each of the Fannys will present their closing remarks. By toss of the coin"—we paused while Nikki threw a coin over her shoulder, announcing, "Traditional Fanny goes first. Keep it short."

I took a deep cleansing breath and launched myself. "I am Fanny Price," I said, "no more and no less than the character Jane Austen lovingly drew to play the protagonist in *Mansfield Park*. I will never change. Adaptation and reinterpretation are futile protests against prose consigned to posterity. Long after you have sung your last alleluias, I will be cutting roses in the hot afternoon and walking to the parsonage in the rain. And even though I am shy and Mary Crawford is witty, Edmund will choose to love me for as long as readers engage the text. The novel is mine. I win. I stay."

The audience applauded. I dreaded the end of the skit. They would leave together and I would be alone in a way I hadn't been since meeting Willis.

Nikki sighed. "Closing remarks, Forward Fanny?"

Sixby drew closer to me, his male sweat and his stubble dead giveaways if anyone had doubts. "I concede," he said, taking my hand. "I concede *Mansfield Park* to *this* Fanny Price." As he raised my hand in victory, I saw a way not to be alone, a way out of my pain. "And I think I'm in love," he added. Sixby lifted me off the ground and kissed me; the unrehearsed spectacle of the two Fannys embracing created a fitting end of hostilities for the Fanny Wars. The audience hooted and whistled; there was more laughter and applause. Sixby and I left the stage together, holding hands as if we both knew what came next. I could lose myself in him, numb the pain at least for a while.

We passed through the butler pantry and into the main hallway where My Jane Austen waited, pacing nervously. People lingered, stepping outside to smoke. But as Sixby ducked into the Freezer to drop off his dress, Willis approached from the ballroom door, walking straight to me.

"Are you all right, Lily?" he asked, very serious.

I shivered. I wanted him alone in the music room, not here in the crowded hallway with Pippa on her way. I had two seconds to decide what to say. Continue playing Fanny Price and say yes, absolve Willis, and suffer in silence awaiting a miracle? I played myself. "No," I said and stared him down.

When he left, it would be over. Once he was gone, I wouldn't be able to breathe.

"There you are," Pippa said, walking up, pushing her arms into her sweater. She handed Willis her purse while she arranged herself. I shivered again. "You were just delightful," Pippa said to me. "Weren't they, Willis?"

"Yes," Willis said without conviction.

"Are you cold?" Pippa asked. She heard my teeth chattering. "Willis, give her your jacket, she's freezing."

I wasn't cold, just nerves hyper tensing.

"We don't want anyone freezing to death." She removed the jacket from Willis's back herself. "We'd never sell this old house with the frozen ghost of Fanny Price wandering the halls." She smiled.

I slipped into Willis's still-warm jacket, the armpits damp from perspiration, folded papers in the pockets. Surely he'd do something to spare me the grief of watching him walk out with her. But he just looked at me, waiting, as if *I* were at fault. I thought I might speak my mind in front of everyone, right there in the hallway, but Sixby rejoined us and Omar appeared from the ballroom as applause signaled the end of the follies.

"That was fun." Pippa stifled a yawn, touching Willis's arm. "But it's getting late," she said. Willis stood watching as Sixby stood behind me, both hands on my waist.

"Nice jacket," Sixby said, lifting me slightly as if I were a ballerina.

I spoke recklessly over my shoulder to Sixby, certain that Willis could hear me. "I feel like improvising some more."

"You've got my attention," Sixby said.

Willis turned away and the agony began. He touched Pippa's shoulder and she nodded, stepping away from us, a thick curtain drawing around their casual intimacy, separating them as a couple.

"Let's go," a no-nonsense Omar said to me as people distracted Sixby to autograph their programs, but I swatted his hand, watching Pippa wave to us as Willis ushered her out the door. Once Willis was outside, I ran. My Jane Austen followed close behind. I disappeared into the darkness beyond the gathering, moving through halls by memory, hiding behind a door until I could be sure Omar wasn't looking for me.

Twenty

*F*loundering in the dark, I gathered candles from the office stash since the orange cord did not power my destination. A candle lit my way past dead people in portraits as I climbed the stairs to the second floor, holding on to the rail to keep from falling. At the top, I sobered, remembering where I was and entertaining second thoughts. By the time I found the door I sought, my second thoughts had receded, replaced by surging desperation of pain. Plunging into disaster felt so much better than lame suffering.

Inside, my candle illuminated the *Romeo and Juliet* poster taped to the wardrobe door, assuring me I'd found Sixby's room. I placed candles strategically, the floorboards creaking as I relocated myself to another time and place in a different body. It wasn't me doing this. Removing Willis's jacket, I buried my face in the fabric, taking a good hit of his masculine scent before placing the folded jacket on a wicker chair. And then, rather than picture the engaged couple walking home together, I sat on the iron bed, once painted white, and unlaced the ribbons around my ankles, removing my slippers. Instead of imagining their good-night intimacy, I peeled the knee-highs off my legs and swept a dead fly off the covers.

My Jane Austen worked on another list in the candlelight: "The Bad Men in Lily's Life," and there, at the top of the page, I read my father's name. Yes. I'm so glad someone finally had the courage to call a spade a spade. I wanted to see whose name followed. Willis? Surely not Martin. But I'd never seen My Jane Austen so dim and I worried she'd grow too faint to finish the list.

I unfastened Bets's dress and by the time I laid the spotted muslin on top of Willis's jacket, My Jane Austen had completely vanished. For the first time since my arrival at the literary festival, I felt her absence. Not her cup of tea, this. Heedless, I placed my short stays, shift, and pantaloons on top in a neat pile, wondering if My Jane Austen was mad at me for doing this. She'd never faded away like that before. I couldn't help it; I'd drunk too much wine. My fingertips ice cold, I shivered, catching a glimpse of my naked torso, candlelit in the cracked dusky mirror over the chest of drawers; the word *sacrifice* came to mind, the image of an Aztec maiden preparing for her death.

You see, Willis, I said to myself, *I'm not thinking about you at all now*, as I pulled down the bedspread and climbed between the sheets, wondering when they had last been changed, reminding myself not to think realistic thoughts. Waiting, I studied the shadowy molding on the ceiling, decoding patterns in the water spots like Madeline in her hospital bed. Footsteps in the hall indicated my wait was over. As I listened for the final approach and watched for the turn of the shiny black knob on the yellow door, the footsteps passed and all sounds stopped. After that, I wondered what had happened but my thoughts drifted, and for a while I forgot where I lay, thinking about my mother and what she would say if she saw me like this.

When the door opened at last, it took a moment to remember what I was doing there.

"Ah, who is this?" Sixby's voice sounded playful.

Silent, my eyes closed; my heart beat. I craved the feel of his body on me, heavy and obliterating. *Take me away*, I pleaded silently, longing to fold myself into his arms and let him help me deny what was happening. Sixby carefully lifted the covers and found the answer he expected from the evidence on the chair. "The right idea, Lil, but the execution's all wrong. Let's take it from the top."

I opened my eyes and sat up, pulling the covers up to my neck.

"I'll be back in five minutes," he said. "Put all your lovely clothes back on and sit in the window seat. When I come in, you don't say a word. Here's the scene: We're in the drawing room and your husband is visiting a sick tenant in the neighborhood. We have very little time before he returns." He spoke quickly, as if he was directing an experienced actress, but his audible breathing gave him away.

"Can't *you* be my husband?" I asked.

"That would ruin everything, my dear." Sixby smiled, a hyped look in his eyes.

I let the covers slip, exposing my naked breasts in the candle glow, attempting to break through his fantasy; I didn't care for the story in his head; and didn't particularly want to end up there. But my naked breasts did not break his enchantment and he left, pulling the door shut behind him. Alone again, dressing myself, I marveled he had been working up to this.

★ ★ ★

Sixby didn't look at my face. His hands moved over my dress, his eyes boring into the fabric illuminated by candlelight. Was his fantasy supported solely by the drape of my muslin? Neither of us had removed a single item of apparel from either body, duly noted by the dear departed, watching from sepia portraits suspended from high moldings. Sixby knelt between my knees, the hem of my skirt still touching the floor, his head resting against my fully clothed bosom; I was a body in a dress.

I watched the table, wardrobe, chairs; the hole where the wall had settled leaving a crack large enough to reach through, where tendrils of vines grew inside like the bedroom in *Where the Wild Things Are*, one of my childhood books. Sixby's hands bored under my skirt and I felt him touching my actual legs. He *did* need my flesh after all. But he changed course and his hands returned outside my dress again, gripping my waist. From my position, I could see nothing but darkness out the window.

I would not have guessed there would be no dialogue in our love improv and the bed would be an unnecessary prop. Sixby bit my breast through the dress. It hurt; the nipple area had less protection than other parts of my body. Then Sixby's arms reached behind me and up my back. His hands grabbed my shoulders from behind and his head burrowed into my bosom. He held me so tight my body left the seat of the chair, but I could think of nothing except the image of Willis and Philippa turning to each other. And then Sixby dropped me abruptly, fumbling with his Regency buttons, releasing himself, burrowing into my skirt. He thrust himself against me, saying, "Thank you, thank you, thank you."

I began to cry as Sixby rested his head in my lap, his breathing slowing to normal.

"And what would you like, Lil?" He looked up and noticed my wet cheeks.

"Is there a menu or something?" I asked.

Sixby's head rose from my lap. "Are you hungry?" He backed away from me, confused, adjusting his clothing. I had no desire for further debasement with Sixby. I sat up now that his weight had lifted. Hearing noise in the hall, Sixby looked toward the door, wanting to get out, but knowing it wasn't the right thing to want at that moment. I could have made it easy for him since I wanted out as badly as he, but I'd never seen him stuck in an improv situation and I wanted to watch. Was he a vampire, too? Sucking the superficial out of people, never connecting with the soul? I couldn't spend another ten minutes of my life with this person—odd how I'd found him attractive before meeting Willis.

"Do you want to get something to eat?" he asked, confused by my menu remark.

"We just had dinner," I said impatiently.

"Are you sure?" He knew from my tone he could push safely, appear to care.

"Yes, I'm sure we just had dinner." Fully dressed, there wasn't much for me to do in order to walk out. I stood and put my arms through Willis's jacket. "Good-bye, Sixby."

He looked up from his seat on the floor. "Good-bye, Lily." And then, "I'm sorry."

"Oh, nonsense," I said, taking a candle.

"About your dress."

"Oh, that." The muslin was now spotted, indeed.

Proceeding directly to the attic, shielding the flame of my candle, despair took hold when I saw the exposed brick of the stairwell and smelled the musty rot. Wood stairs creaking beneath my feet gave comfort and the darkness recalled evenings with Willis, the moon in the window.

I lay down on the cushions in the window seat, grateful

for their familiar greenness, and gazed out the window into the darkness. Then I sat up and stared out the window and listened to the small night sounds. My Jane Austen was not there, either. A draft extinguished my candle while I moved Willis's table and chair back to their regular summer places. I sat looking at them in the almost darkness, growing thirsty from the effects of the wine.

Perhaps it would rain. The idea that I could collect rainwater on the roof led me to try the door, hopeful that no one had bothered to lock it. Pulling on the rope, the stairs responded, unfolding like always. Climbing to the top, I pushed the trap door open, exposing myself to the cool night air, thankful the breeze was not so strong at night.

The world from the roof looked different in the dark. I sat on the tar and stone mixture and let it cut into my palms. Then I lay down on the stones, curling my legs up to my chest, protecting my head from the stones with my arm. When it began to sprinkle, I covered my face with my other arm. I'd done this before.

I'd held a yard sale to finance the purchase of my airline ticket before coming here. Late on the afternoon of my sale, I was hauling more junk out to the yard when my friend Lisa parked her Saab behind a pink Mary Kay Buick. Sympathetic Lisa, who'd met me in the office stairwell for details and tears after my termination, had come to get my cat, Boris.

"You're not selling everything, are you?" Lisa asked without looking me in the eye.

"Yes, I am." I couldn't afford to pay rent so I decided to sell it all and let the apartment go. I sold all my big furniture to a plump woman in cowboy boots before I even got out of my nightgown. The only things I would keep were the two large suitcases I'd packed, and the chest that held the childhood books my mother collected for me. I planned to store the chest of books in the trunk of my car while I was gone.

"Do you have any Hummels?" a gnarly man with a smoker's voice interrupted.

I had a vague memory of brownish figurines in my mother's china cupboard. "No," I said; Sue had surely tossed them.

Lisa exhaled noisily. "I'm going to say something and I'm counting on you not to fall apart," she said, as her eyes finally met mine.

We glanced to the street as a truck pulled up behind her car.

"Wait a minute." I held up a hand. "That truck is here for my furniture. I have to deal with this first." I pulled up one of the landlord's rusty metal lawn chairs for Lisa. "Would you mind being cashier while I show them what to take?" I handed her the money box as the movers lumbered up to my porch, dirty from whatever work they had done all day. I positioned another rusty chair to keep the screen door open and the driver looked at me sheepishly as if I were the high school social studies teacher he had disappointed.

"Wife says to get the stuff she bought," he said.

"Down the hallway." I took them back to the bedroom and pointed to the bed and the dresser.

"That go?" The other guy pointed to a lamp table in the corner.

"No," I said, and then reconsidered the business of hauling it out myself. "Yes, take it. Get it all out of here." I spoke too quickly, my restless mind struggling to predict what Lisa had to say. I couldn't imagine what she thought would make me fall apart at this point. What was left? I waved a hand and showed them the sofa and the table they were supposed to take. But instead of watching the men, I went to the porch where Lisa made change for my lava lamp.

"So what is it?" I asked; arms folded across my chest, cars slowing as they drove by. Most of my good stuff was sold.

Lisa said, "I think you should reconsider this move."

The men grunted under the weight of the sleeper sofa, passing behind me.

"Now?" I gestured to the people in my yard.

Lisa sat back. "You can still change your mind."

"Why would I want to?" I moved out of the way as the men went in for more furniture.

Lisa spoke. "You've had so many setbacks recently. I just don't think this is a good time to make a big change."

Someone stamped a cigarette on my front walk; a fat woman held one of my shirts up for size. I couldn't wait to get out of this place. As much as I filled my days with personal connections and my evenings with volunteer activities and social events, I was as lonely as the gray-haired widows at the early church service.

"You should consider seeing someone," Lisa said carefully, "as in a mental health professional."

Those were the words she had come to say; we were having an intervention. I shielded my eyes from the sun's glare and watched the men close the back of the truck. One of them waved. "We got it," he called, waving as he pulled away.

"You need time," Lisa said.

I often recited a litany over girl lunches and happy hours: It takes the average single woman two years to get engaged, one to get married, and three to have kids. A woman who has just broken up with her boyfriend is looking at anywhere from four to ten years before she can live happily ever after. Without exceptional beauty or wealth, it would take me ten years. I had no time. "I'm going to England," I said.

At midnight that night, every overhead light in my apartment blazed. I leaned against the bathroom wall and slid down to the floor. I would have fallen asleep on the floor had my phone not rung in my bedroom. "Hello?" I looked at my watch. Lisa enunciated as if a kidnapper held a gun to her head or she spoke to someone whose native language was not English. "Boris escaped when I opened my front door to get my mail. He has been missing ever since. Do you want me to come over?" she asked.

"No," I said. What good would that do?" Boris had made a break with his past. *Good-bye Boris*, I thought. *I hope you find what you're looking for, too.*

"I'm going to put up signs in the morning," Lisa said. "I'm so sorry."

"He's a cat," I said, rearranging the future without my precious Boris who had lounged on me through endless novels over the past years. If he were here he would be walking across this barren room to sit on my lap. *Barren room.*

An alarm went off; my room should not be empty.

I dropped the phone on the floor and ran. "Oh my God. Oh my God." I could barely catch my breath. I ran through my apartment from back to front, searching in case they had moved it somewhere, knowing in my heart it was gone. Just like Martin. Just like the job and the cat. I opened the screen door and ran into the street where their truck had been parked. "No," I cried. "No, no, no, no."

I collapsed on the curb, the heel of my hand landing on a shard of glass, a cockroach scurrying for cover. "Oh my God," I cried, in bursts of grief, rocking back and forth, my hair tangling in my face. I had no way to track them down. They had paid in cash. The blood from my hand got in my hair and on my clothes and I could feel it mingling with the tears and getting in my eyes.

They had taken the little chest and the books it held. The stories my mother had read to me were lost in some rural resale shop. I had not paid attention and now her voice was gone. I tried to remember the sound of Miss Clavel exclaiming, "Something is not right," and the old woman whispering, "Hush" as I'd snuggled into my mother's side, tracing the roses on the floral chintz love seat, wondering how there could be so much purple and blue in the pink petals. When she read, my mother's voice mixed the lush sofa roses with the soft reading light and the romance of storybook heroines. So when I opened the books she saved for me, I could hear not only her voice but everything she told me, using the words of the stories like a special code between us. All for me. Even though she was dead, I'd cherished this last connection to her. The collection of books offered me comfort and hope. Now the books were gone. How could I have let this happen? I sat folded in the grass by the curb and cried; I couldn't hear her anymore. I stared at the stars and a bug crawled onto my arm. Did I remember the feel of the soft inside of her arm as she turned a page of *Goodnight Moon* or was I creating memories?

I stood and walked to the front edge of the roof. Lifting my arms to my sides as if preparing to dive, the chilly air blew my skirt, my unquiet spirit gnawing from the inside. *What if I just go away?* Three stories below lay the great stone steps. Jumping would bring immediate and certain death. No more loneliness; no more pain, no more aching spirit.

Thick dark curtains separated me from the life I had known, curtains to guard the privacy of my self-destruction and reinforce my feeling that nothing waited for my return. Nothing lay behind me but darkness and nothing before me but the void.

Two spooky eyes looked at me as the picture crawled down my screen, the familiar nose and the smile for her father. What started the affair? My father nurturing a vague complaint that something was missing. Sue playing along; willing to be a secret. Karen said Dad cheated because he could get away with it. Did Willis think he could get away with it?

The three of us had made a sharp triangle at the follies; me on the stage, Willis below, and Philippa next to him, as oblivious as my mother. I was the secret of the triangle, willing to take any covert part Willis allowed me to play in his life. Willing to play the part of Sue in the story of my own life.

My toes hung over the edge, a black breeze blew my skirt. Karen says we all have problems. Take it in stride and keep fighting, she says. Not the end of the world. Look at your wonderful life. I looked at myself, perched on the edge of a roof at a failing literary festival, in the middle of the night, in England. Fanny Price beckoned to me from the trap door, no indulgent pity in her voice or manner. "Come along," she said. My Jane Austen wasn't there, wouldn't bother, obviously. No patience for nonsense.

Two faint stars struggled in the sky, and something fiercer, a satellite, blinked; perhaps it could see me. I remembered the feeling, lying with Willis, when the cosmos came together and everything belonged to something. Maybe normal people always felt that way. I don't want to be Sue. I don't want to be my mother. My mother no longer makes sense. I bent down to pick up a broken piece of concrete, once part of the balustrade. *You should have dropped the code, Mom. You should have talked to me while we sat there all those months reading and dying. Hiding behind books instead of working past your shame to tell me. You should have tried harder.* I threw the concrete as hard as I could and watched it smash into bits on the steps three stories below. *I don't want to be like you.* "I want to be normal," I cried from the rooftop. "I just want to be normal."

Twenty-one

$\mathcal{T}$wo mornings later, I lay in bed while Bets did her five-minute prep for work: the thong, the dress, the kerchief.

"Time to rise and shine, Cellmate," Bets said.

I'd seen no one for three days. Not Omar, not Sixby. My Jane Austen had been absent since she faded out in Sixby's room. I'd suspected she might be prickly, but never imagined she would ditch me for good. A dead person should take a more godlike approach and cut me some slack. Maybe Magda was right; the real Jane Austen would swallow me whole.

Being Wednesday, Mrs. Russell would come looking for me if I didn't show up. "I'm sick," I told Bets, still recovering from the rooftop spectacle. Thank God no one but Fanny Price witnessed my drama. Now Fanny was gone. Perhaps Maria Bertram would haunt me. Maria and I could compare stories about self-destructing over the wrong men scene after scene, but that would cease to amuse her once she claimed the high ground of being ink on a page, lacking in the opportunity so abundant to me, of learning from mistakes.

Gary came to the door with coffee and Bets shushed him. "She's sick," she whispered as they closed the door behind them. One thing I was sure of: they were up to something. Last night during a commercial, Bets said, "Why not now?" She used a few Arabic words I missed, but Gary shook his head, clicked his tongue, and said *lah*, Arabic for no. I fell asleep breathing fumes from their Indian food.

I opened my eyes and pulled Willis's jacket out from under my pillow. Had he gone to London for good? His abrupt absence felt like death, a giant iron wall preventing further communication. I could never tell him one more thing or ask him one more question. I lay in my bed, staring at the plaster wall, seeking a pattern in the faint swirls.

The messy room had begun to stink; I knew I would find dirty food cartons if I bothered to look. They'd left cellophane wrappers on the floor. Biscuit tins, bottles, cans, newspapers, and bags littered the room. Bets had thrown her clothes on the floor as they left her body. My follies costume lay spread on the table to dry. I got up and opened the window to let air circulate; gray and rainy outside.

Not having bothered with my appearance since the night with Sixby, I looked awful. I sat on my bed in my nightgown, holding my script. With Magda on her way out, I needed to know the lines and I'd been reading the part where Fanny refuses Henry Crawford's proposal of marriage. Even though I'd read it many times, the scene never failed to create anxiety that *this* time Fanny would cave, fall prey to Henry Crawford's superficial arts, be seduced by the comfortable life he offered. I considered reading *Sense and Sensibility* instead.

The rain rallied and I had to consider the possibility that *Sense and Sensibility* might get wet on the windowsill. I rescued the book, using my nightgown to wipe it dry. To my utter surprise, Willis appeared, walking toward my dormitory. I ducked down and watched over the sill like a spy, the rain spattering my face. Willis walked purposefully, eyes downcast, the hood of his jacket protecting him from the rain. He headed for the parking lot but turned as if he were approaching the entrance of my building, a place he'd never been. My room! I quickly bolted the door, turned off the lights, and regretted the unmade beds, clothes covering the floor, dirty dishes in our little sink. Every horizontal surface lay buried under junk, drawers stood open. Impossible to clean the room in the short time he would spend climbing the stairs. And even if I could straighten the room, what would he think when he saw *me*? I brushed my teeth in record time and crawled to the far corner of my bed to wait; my heart pounding.

I knew he'd come—as instructed by my follies portrayal of Fanny Price. Willis was back from the dead; here was my chance to ask one last question, to understand the truth about what happened between us and say good-bye to him perhaps forever.

His knock penetrated my bones. I asked all blood rushing to my heart to please resume its normal speed and direction. If he saw me now—he'd remember me forever like *this*! My nightgown! Just to be safe, I stopped breathing.

He knocked again. I could clean up and find him later.

"Lily."

The sound of my name in his voice melted my resistance. If he knocked again, I would open up. Again, please. We both waited. Every rustle of his rain jacket traveled over the open transom. I froze, not risking a creak of the floor or mattress. What would I give for an opportunity to speak with my mother one more time?

He gave up. Willis walked away, his footsteps growing softer as they receded to the stairwell until I couldn't hear them anymore. Deep regret set in. The mess didn't matter. This was my last chance. He would be long gone by the time I cleaned up. The mattress and floor creaked and moaned as I jumped up and ran to the door. I threw it open and shouted, "Willis!" The dimly lit hall was not vacant, he had not walked away, and I screamed when he stepped out of the opposite wall.

He smiled. "The old diminishing footsteps trick."

"You scared me to death." I touched my heart.

"Well, then we're even, Fanny," he said, pausing near the threshold.

I stepped aside allowing Willis into my room. "We had a hurricane in here," I said, folding my arms in front of me as he noted the devastation. "I'm surprised you didn't hear about it on the news."

"I'm too busy for news." He turned, appraising the extent of the disorder. "So this is where you live." He took in the dirty clothes and unmade bed. "Ah, my jacket," he said.

I handed him the jacket and he tucked it under his arm. We stood looking at each other; me still catching my breath while raindrops tapped nervously.

"That was quite a performance with Sixby." He shifted his weight and the floor creaked. "I didn't much care for the ending."

"It was theatre," I said, frowning. If hc only knew. But he would never know.

Willis draped his jacket over a chair and then stepped to the window. "What a mess," he said touching his forehead on the frame. He ran a finger along the wet sill; hard to know if he referred to the weather, the mess in my room, or the two of us. "You're not working today?"

"Later."

We stood silent while the rain fell, dark and dreary outside. My legs felt weak. "Would you like to sit down?" I gestured to a chair holding a big box of Bets's stuff but Willis stood his ground on the opposite side of the table, his rain jacket rustling when he moved.

"I can't stay. I wish I could," he said, hands in his pockets.

Bits of sorrow gathered near my throat. His hands seemed so far away in those pockets, as if they didn't know me. "How are you?" I asked.

He shrugged, and took a step away from the window. "How are *you*?"

"I have a half sister," I said. "And I find the news overwhelming."

"So do I," he said, connecting my words with the news Fanny delivered from the stage. "How are you dealing with it?" he warmed, his empathetic manner emerging.

"I keep remembering what you said about forgiving my dad," I said, "but I don't know where to start. And it keeps getting bigger." I did not share the reflection I'd caught of myself in the family mirror; mistakes could pile up quickly without a single bad intention.

"You don't have to condone his behavior," Willis said as he lifted the box off the chair and sat at the table he didn't have time for. I moved the spotted muslin and sat across from him.

"The forgiveness is for you," he said. "Let go and move on."

"I've already done that part." I waved a hand in dismissal.

Willis looked at me, skeptical, almost smiling. The messy room coughed. "I've missed you," he said.

"I've missed you," I said.

Willis straightened. "I should tell you I'm going to London." He touched the table as if to push off. "Lady Weston is comatose and I need to be with them."

A wave of the jealousy rolled through my stomach. "To be with *her*." I immediately regretted my words, small and petty.

Willis frowned at me. "You of all people should know I can't walk out when her grandmother is dying. The only mother she's known."

"I *do* know," I said, my voice competing with the wind and rain against the window. "But *I'm* trying to get to the other side of all *this*." I gestured to the space between us. "Can you help me make sense of it?" I leaned into the table to emphasize my need, early tears blurring my vision.

"I'm sorry," he said, glancing away, silent, until he added, "I've made promises I need to keep."

"Can't you tell her about us?"

Willis drew himself up. "Look, I'd like to follow this thing with you. But it won't work on your schedule." Willis looked at the ceiling and took his time; the music room seemed impossibly far away. "We planned the wedding for June," he said softly.

Lightning flared behind my eyes. "*Last* June? A month ago?"

"Yes. But postponed, obviously." He shrugged. "Her grandmother's health." His sleeves rustled as he shifted in his chair and unzipped his jacket. "And I wanted time to think. I used my thesis as an excuse to be alone." Willis pulled the jacket apart as if he were hot.

"Think about what?" I asked.

"Everything." He shook his head, not willing to elaborate further. "But then you showed up." He looked at me and smiled as if that were the end of the story.

"So?"

He swallowed. "So." He gestured. "You were fresh and vulnerable, delivered directly to me in my attic. And very

attractive in your costume, I might add. Upset about something. No trace of artifice."

No trace of artifice? He'd never met *Cosmo* me.

"And you appeared to believe *I* invented the written word."

I nodded.

"I wanted to *know* you," he whispered; the shy amusement lit his face. "I wanted to see where it would go." He
cleared a path through the junk on the table and took my
hand while the rain rallied outside and tears pooled in my
eyes. "I couldn't decide if you were sent to me as a gift or a
test." He kissed my palm. "I started writing the vampire story
the day after I met you."

"Why?"

Again, Willis looked at me as if I should understand from
context. "Because I was afraid."

"Afraid of what?" I asked.

Willis shook his head uncomfortably. "Afraid of what
would happen if I failed to honor my commitments," he said.
"Afraid of what would happen if I *did* fulfill them." Willis
leaned into the table and pulled my forearm to him. His face
was slightly flushed from emotion, the muscles around his
mouth not quite under control. He looked straight into me
and I knew he spoke from his heart. "I was afraid you would
give up on me. That you would stop coming to find me." He
closed his eyes and kissed the inside of my wrist, the white
place where the veins meet close to the surface.

Tears fell down my cheeks. I rose from my chair and stood
before him, my bare feet on the old wood floor, shivering in
my thin lavender nightgown.

"I like looking at you." He sighed.

"Hold me," I said.

He pulled off his raincoat and let it fall, then opened his

arms and took me on his lap. I fit myself into him, sliding my arms around his back, savoring the essence of this person who attracted me so ferociously, whose existence connected me joyfully with my own life.

He spoke into my hair. "Is this what you wanted to know?" he asked. "Does it make things better? Or worse?"

"I love you." I moved my lips, barely making any sound, knowing my words would be met with silence.

He held me tighter. "I don't know what to make of you, Lily. We should have met in our secret attic years ago."

"I won't be your secret," I said softly.

He kissed my hair. "Of course you won't."

I listened to the rain through his arms.

"I'll try and sort things out," he said. "Can you give me some time?"

I told myself that if I let him go, he would come back to me. But I sensed My Jane Austen somewhere, making a list of silly ideas. Certainly some Austen character had agreed to wait for a man. Fanny waited for Edmund, sort of. Marianne waited for Willoughby. Sue waited for my dad.

"I'll wait for you," I whispered.

"You won't run off with Sixby?" he said.

"Heavens, no."

Once Willis was gone, I staved off regret and despair by cleaning furiously, feeling like a secret in spite of assurances to the contrary. I made the beds, threw Bets's dirty clothes into her closet, and disposed of trash, all the while contemplating the news that Willis almost got married in June. He had forgotten to take his jacket, again.

In the bathroom, I filled the tub with just enough water, blending cold and hot from separate faucets, to wash my hair and get clean. Leaning forward and rinsing under the cold-water faucet, I felt exhilarated by my newfound *lack of artifice*. A large quantity of soap foam quickly melted to milky scum and I was about to stand up when urgent footsteps sounded in the hall; distant knocking. I waited, not moving in the tub. He couldn't be back already. Gray scum clung to the side of the tub.

The knocker struck again; a new voice called my name.

"Lily," Vera said.

"I'm in the tub," I yelled, quickly lifting myself out of the water, wondering what excuse I would offer for being AWOL.

Her footsteps grew nearer; I grabbed my towel.

"Lily?"

"I'm in here." I opened the door of my stall and Vera leaned against the frame, a book in her hand. Her face had lines today that hadn't been there before.

"Are you okay?" she asked. "Everyone's asking where you are."

"I'm fine."

Vera hesitated, catching her breath.

"What are you reading?" I asked.

Vera looked at the book. "Magda left this for you."

A copy of *Mansfield Park*. Bitch.

The drip from the faucet plopped in the dirty water.

"Lily," Vera said. "Lady Weston is in a coma."

"Yes," I said. I clutched the towel around my shivering body as Vera took a breath, leaning her head forward as if praying. I reached into the tub and pulled the plug as Vera watched. "Is Nigel okay?" I asked.

"I haven't told him yet," she said, somber. "I thought I'd practice on you."

We looked at each other, tears pooling in Vera's eyes.

"I can't tell him." She shook her head.

"It doesn't have to be the end," I said.

"It certainly feels like the end." Vera stared at the water draining so slowly one could probably fill the tub without plugging it. Vera backed out of the stall as I gathered my things and followed her out.

"We still have Randolph and the business plan," I said. A terrible wave of loneliness crashed against itself and stretched away from me; the anesthesia of our last meeting was wearing off.

"Yes, there is that," she said in the hallway, turning to me. "Before I tell Nigel," she said, "I just wanted to see if you'd heard anything from Randolph."

I looked at Vera. "No, I haven't heard from him since we met at the hospital."

Vera tried to smile. "I just thought he might get in touch with you, and let you know what we're to do."

"We're probably not a high priority at the moment," I said, imagining them waiting, and how waiting for death felt a lot like waiting for a birth, a suspension of ordinary life. I imagined black cars and gravesite umbrellas. "You'll be the first to know if he calls."

Vera sighed. "You might make a point of remembering to keep your phone with you."

"Yes," I said. "Can I help you tell Nigel?"

"No, she said. "I'll do it. You need to get to work on your play." I'd told her about my one-woman show.

I shut my door and sat at the table, still wrapped in my towel recalling the look on his face. Away from me, Willis might get the distance he needed to lose his resolve and marry Pippa.

Maybe Vera was right. This *did* feel like the end.

Twenty-two

Bets and Gary executed their plan on Saturday. They drove up in her tiny car as I was walking back to the dorm in the late afternoon, having spent the day selling tickets in order to give the scheduled volunteer—who also managed scones for us—some well-deserved time off. Naturally, Sixby was the first person I saw that morning. "I love your dress," he'd said. We would both pretend the scene in his room never happened.

I waved to Bets in her driver's seat. "Where are you going?" I asked, relishing the prospect of an empty room and my book.

Bets whispered, "I'm taking Gary to London, losing him there."

London? She hadn't been to London in weeks as far as I knew. She'd had no chance to look for my necklace. "Will you find my necklace?" I asked.

"Not likely," Bets said. "I'll be busy."

"Please," I said. "I'll be going home soon."

"You come and look for it yourself." Bets nodded to the backseat and rolled her window up.

"But I have to change clothes, I can't go like this." I was still wearing Mrs. Russell's Elinor dress, white empire with a high-collared gauzy blue overlay that reached from behind to tie like a scarf around my bosom.

"Get in, we're leaving right now."

I crawled into the tiny backseat, an accessory to the crime. As she drove, Bets brought me up to speed on Gary. He had not managed to solve his student visa problem via matrimony or matriculation, so Bets masterminded a plan to conceal him in the mighty chaos of London. The genius was in the timing, hiding him one day before his scheduled flight to Lebanon and Magda's departure for Michigan. No time to search for him.

Bets said Magda had covertly planted the idea to hide Gary, "Although she would have preferred that I marry him." I wanted to ask Magda if she'd read *anything* by Jane Austen. So cavalier with other people's commitments, she seemed to believe the institution of marriage existed solely to manipulate at her discretion. Escaping Hedingham, passing charming green hills littered with sheep, I pulled out the copy of *Mansfield Park* Magda had left me. I read her note to me on the title page.

Lily,

This is the critical edition my freshmen read. I assign all of the materials in the back. I'm assigning them now to you. Read.

Magda

Opening to the first essay in the back, I tried to read but Willis interfered with the text, his last words playing in an endless loop. *I'm going to try and sort things out.* Brits are always sorting things. To *be* or not? To get married or not to get married? That was the question. I imagined Willis sorting socks in his head as he drove toward home that rainy afternoon.

I wanted to know you. I wanted to see where it would go. By the time we left the country of green meadows and quiet villages, slipping into fringes of the city, I lost myself in imagined scenes of reunion in the music room.

Bets looked in her rearview mirror. "You look like you could use a drink," she said.

We drove through neighborhoods of seedy hotels and slummy bed-sits followed by districts of embassies and multinational corporate headquarters. In the private domain of the rich, flowers billowed out of window boxes; hotels' discreet Georgian exteriors hardly looked like hotels. Every possible light turned red as we navigated the unfamiliar streets. Bets struggled to interpret an old map. "It's been a while since I lived in this neighborhood," she said. Gary sat quietly confused and I struggled to suspend my conversation with Willis in order to focus on street signs. But loud trucks shifted gears, buses spewed familiar exhaust fumes, people rushed in all directions, and Willis kept repeating: *It won't happen on your schedule.*

We pulled up to a storefront with "Mediterranean Bakery" written on the window in both English and Arabic. Bets had found Gary the bakery job and a temporary place to stay. I moved up to the front seat as Bets opened the trunk and Gary hauled his bag to the curb, on schedule, as planned. He already had some of the Wallet's money to tide him over.

"So long, buddy." She said something in Arabic, calling him Gamal, slapping him on the arm. "It's been real."

Gary looked at the bakery and then smiled wanly. "Thank you," he said, and nodded, watching us pull back into traffic.

Bets exclaimed over the traffic noise, "Next: a necklace for Dorothy!"

We parked near Tommy's apartment building in the neighborhood of grimy urban lofts, rent compliments of the Wallet. My stomach fluttered, as if sensing proximity to the necklace. I'd seen it everywhere lately: on the bodies of strangers or in billboard advertisements, as if my necklace had been folded into God's being—existing in all times and all places.

We climbed his stairs and reached Tommy's door, me in Regency dress like an early nineteenth-century time traveler. Standing heads together over the doorknob, Bets sorted through her key ring and pushed the chosen key into the lock while I tried to breathe normally.

"Shit." She dropped her purse on an overturned milk crate, scattering fast food trash into the hallway and spilling the remains of a soda.

"Key not working?" Pangs of disappointment hit me; I should never have allowed myself to hope.

"Wait a minute." She held the key up to the light.

"Is it the right key?" I asked.

She banged on the door. "Tommy!"

No answer. She banged again.

"Not home?" I asked.

"No." She looked hard at me. "He's not fucking home and the fucking lock's been changed."

I felt panic creeping in. "Can we call the landlord? Pick the lock?" Something. Anything.

Bets didn't dignify my desperation with a response as I followed her back to the car. "He could have fucking told me."

★ ★ ★

By the time we arrived in Camden and parked, several blocks
from the King's Castle, darkness encroached and I felt very
homesick for My Jane Austen and Newton Priors. Everything:
the city lights, walking among strangers, the goth clothing
hanging outside shops felt alien to my nineteenth-century
sensibilities and heightened my longing for affiliation with
Jane Austen. Simply existing near her immortal blaze had
made me bigger than myself. Approaching the sign over the
door, a faded shingle featuring redcoats in action, I wished
I could feel that deep sense of communion with her again.
Given another chance, I would work harder at maintaining
the relationship.

The pub smelled of cigarettes, mildew, and spilled beer.
Ancient air handlers circulated the nasty air like an endless
repetition of Maria Bertram's foolish lines. The interior was
black, as if they spray painted the floor, walls, light fixtures,
ceiling, boxes, and contraptions before hanging the glossy
photographs of performers schmoozing with pub owners. A
food service lamp warmed popcorn in a recycled aquarium.
At the bar, I took a deep breath and asked my question.

"Where is your lost-and-found?" I crossed my fingers and
visualized my necklace, in a random jumble of sunglasses,
scarves, and misplaced keys. "I'm looking for a necklace."

"Ah, soo am I," the bartender answered as he turned to the
next customer. "Lemee know if you find it."

I asked again when another bartender looked my way. After
that, they stopped looking my way.

We sat in bright orange and aqua bus station chairs around
a small table. A dark-skinned man with long glossy hair parted
down the middle arranged microphones on the stage and had
just said "testing" when some scruffy people whose names

I faintly remembered from Bets's caller ID joined us. The one named Nick kissed Bets and commented on my clothing. Bets lifted my dress to display the pantalettes. "Crotchless," she said. I slapped her hands and grabbed my skirt. They stared at me as if I were a time travel porn star.

Bets lit a cigarette and exhaled as Nick pointed to a blond woman at another table. Bets slammed her glass on the table. "That asshole," she said.

"What's wrong?" I asked.

"Tommy's new chick." Bets nodded toward the woman standing near the table directly in front of the stage, welcoming people like a hostess. New Chick had long blond hair with bangs, back-teased and gathered. She wore a black top decorated with rhinestones and very large half-moon dangly earrings that reflected stage lights. She hugged someone, grabbed an extended hand that passed her table, and laughed big. Probably fancied herself a young Linda McCartney.

"I'm free," Bets said, launching her beer bottle in a toast as band members took the stage and picked up their instruments. The room darkened as the house lights went down and city lights sparkled in a high window. Someone turned off the heat lamp in the aquarium and it got even darker. They played stray notes and then Tommy sauntered onto the stage. Ruggedly handsome, the author of music written on napkins, blinding stage lights reflected off his guitar. The air felt full of possibility. Tommy gave the beat, and then—boom. The big sound generated raw energy; the music carried us away. Tommy closed his eyes and sang, his powerful male voice calling us, interpreting mysteries for us, preparing our emotional climax. The musicians savored the music, blue and yellow filters casting a zombie vampire glow on their skin. They watched each other for cues as they moved in and out of a riff and reprised the main motif.

"Do you have any paper?" Bets shouted in my ear.

I pulled a scrap out of my JASNA bag.

"Do you have a pen?" she asked.

I gave her a pen as Tommy announced, "This one is for Fanny, from Edmund," and something familiar took life in the music. The bass resonated in my chest as I recognized the song inspired by Bets's script. Tommy's voice cried out not to worry, he would find me. I thought of Willis, following where the darkness cast me.

"Thanks," Bets shouted, returning my pen; then grabbing her keys. "Bye," she waved. Nick stood and followed her just as the music opened up. I had to listen; it was the good part. "A night such as this—neither sorrow nor wickedness in the world." I thought of the original author of those words as the momentum ramped, chords modulated stressing each word, Tommy took a breath, and the drums caught me. I was a mild-mannered girl from Literature Live who'd come to listen to the band, a reserved member of the audience. But on the inside, I felt all the protagonists I'd ever known surging in the singer's voice, and in one tremendous bodice-ripping crescendo he delivered the payoff and I was with him, our sensibilities merged: "So long the beloved of such a heart." The swell of emotion made me feel like flying, seduced me with the idea that I could just go, like my mother or Lady Weston, progressing in endless modulations. *Godspeed, Willis.*

The band stopped and I decided to postpone my metamorphosis into music to look for Bets. Crossing the pub floor in my dainty satin shoes, I watched for beer puddles as well as cords or contraptions. I didn't find Bets in the serenely quiet ladies' room, but I heard her voice.

"Nasty," she said, and Nick laughed.

They were sitting in a backstage room that smelled of male sweat mingled with essence of marijuana. Instrument cases and discarded amplifier boxes littered the floor, beer bottles and fast food cups lay in the corner and a wadded up T-shirt draped a chair; but no necklace anywhere. Sensing My Jane Austen sitting in the darkest corner of the black room, I looked directly but she disappeared. This had happened before; I'd hear a little rustle and imagine My Jane Austen lurked in the fringes, but it would come to nothing. In an effort to explain my bad behavior with Sixby, I'd told My Jane Austen, *I don't know how to have a relationship with a man. With my father never home, and my mother unhappy most of her life, my entire knowledge of happy relationships came from books. You raised me, Jane. So forgive me this mistake. I know what I did was wrong.*

"Hey, I'm free." Bets and Nick clinked beer bottles.

"Free from what?" I asked.

"Free from Literature Live," she said, rolling her eyes and stressing each syllable in ridicule of books and the clueless people who discuss them. "Apparently Tommy doesn't need money anymore—so the deal is off. I'm free." The deal had been with her dad: Bets spending the summer at Literature Live in exchange for her father's financial support of the band for one more year. "You know what really pisses me off?"

"What?" I asked.

"That I've been running around in a nightgown for no good reason. Tommy didn't bother to tell me he'd moved out."

"You're not going back to Hedingham?"

"Never." She shook her head, relishing the pronunciation of the word.

This news was not entirely bad. No more of her TV at all hours of the night, no more ethnic food cartons behind her bed. No one to play Maria Bertram.

"What about your stuff?" I asked.

"You can have it. Or give it to the poor—some starving actor."

I imagined myself distributing Bets's possessions to the long line of actors who'd waited at my door since dawn: her popcorn popper, her torn black shirt, her thongs, her TV, and the carton of cigarettes. "But how will I get home?" I asked.

"Don't cry; there's a lovely train that will take you to the heart of lovely Hedingham, darling," Bets said, in character, the best acting she'd done all season. She pulled train fare from her wallet. "A parting gift." Bets kissed me dramatically on each cheek and I felt not only the end of something, but a tiny blossom of freedom in my own breast. Tommy walked in, followed by grungy band members lighting cigarettes, and his new chick.

"Bets." Tommy extended his hand—optimistically, I thought—but instead of shaking, Bets gave him the folded paper, like serving a subpoena.

"This is where you drop the car—unless you have it with you now." She picked up her purse and beer, preparing to leave. "Nick can help me take it," Bets said, businesslike, not screaming profanity at Tommy or having a hair-pulling cat-fight with the new chick. Tommy's face fell. Maybe he hadn't realized Bets would take the car. He had counted on losing the operating budget and her brilliant companionship but— the car? Perhaps he should reconsider.

The new chick dug into her bag, furiously displacing lip gloss and credit cards, the car keys falling on the floor. Bend- ing over to retrieve the keys, gravity acted on her blouse, not only exposing her wonderwear-induced cleavage, but freeing a gold chain that had been tucked beneath—*my* gold chain. I froze for a split second while my brain released a heady shot of adrenaline.

"Here's the keys," she said, bypassing Tommy and hand- ing them directly to Bets.

The room's dim light reflected off the cross and I stepped

closer to where it hung on her neck. My arms and legs moved in slow motion as if fighting the huge resistance of an invisible underwater current. One more step and I could touch the cross, although I couldn't afford to linger over a reunion with my property or risk a claim dispute—only action would do. I sensed My Jane Austen behind me, gathering her skirts to prepare for our getaway, urgent for me to take my necklace and run.

The clasp had worked its way to the side, halfway between the back of her neck and her front. I distracted her by exclaiming, "What a beautiful necklace." While she responded, I grabbed the cross in my fist and held it while I worked the clasp. Knowing the clasp intimately helped because she balked, raising her hands to fend off my arms. I had one instant to pull it from her neck and run. "This is mine; you can't have it," I said, bolting for the door.

I ran out the backstage room, through the maze of tiny tables and bus station chairs, past the bar and the popcorn aquarium, and into the street. Choosing the path of most resistance, I burrowed into the crowd, losing myself in the throngs of people who were walking, pointing, getting in and out of cars, crossing and recrossing my path, until, exhausted and breathless, I emerged far away.

My Jane Austen and I walked the ancient streets of London searching for a train station and I felt akin to protagonists who had lived their stories on these same streets, haunting the air I breathed, folding me into their rich, deeply layered existence. I felt Willis's presence just as surely as I felt my mother's cross in my fist; my memories of both belonged to me completely.

Not until the train left the station did I open my hand and allow myself to experience the reunion with the cross I thought gone forever. I fastened the chain around my neck in a brief personal ceremony during which I vowed not to remove it again. Settling into my seat and closing my eyes, I recited from memory every line of Maria Bertram I could remember.

Twenty-three

*N*oise increased as the audience accumulated in the ball-room awaiting the debut of my one-woman show, *The Lost Letters of Jane Austen*. Patrons crossed legs and chattered, fanning themselves with programs, making plans for later while I hovered in the butler's pantry. Breathing slowly and deeply to calm my nerves, I struggled to recall what impulse had compelled me to produce a one-woman show. I blamed Vera, encouraging my ideas, glad for the money from extra events, and, from the success of the tea-theatre, convinced that I could pull this off. But taking the stage alone to deliver my homemade script from memory seemed half-baked and lonely at the moment.

Sabrina passed me on her way out. I smiled at her; we were buddies now. The departures of Magda and Bets removed all obstacles between me and the role of Maria Bertram, which I performed now, in addition to my own productions. Sabrina jerked her head, indicating my bonnet. In my nervous state,

I'd forgotten to remove it. I untied the bow under my chin and removed the hat, stuffing the ribbons inside the crown, placing it on the countertop.

When the time came I entered the ballroom and took my place, front and center, in the chair with the spindly gothic arches, the sort of chair that might moonlight in a prison, hired for especially high-profile electrical executions. Claire sat near the front, waiting, perhaps she suspected me of harboring clues in the Case of the Missing Letters, a mystery originating in her mind. Stephen Jervis operated the spotlight I'd rented.

I bowed my head and took a deep breath, noting, in my downward gaze, the tiny drawstring bag hanging from my wrist. Too late to do anything about that now, a hundred pairs of eyes fixed on me, actively waiting. I raised my face, looked straight into the audience, and exercising the full power of my diaphragm as taught by Sixby, said, "My Dear Cassandra."

The familiar salutation incited such a reaction from the audience of Jane Austen fans that I might have been mistaken for a rock star launching into a greatest hit. In the commotion, My Jane Austen appeared downstage, one eyebrow raised. I hoped she'd brought her sense of humor. Repeating the words, "My Dear Cassandra," I continued, "I'm writing to you from Oblivion where I've been detained nearly two hundred years by the public's persistent interest in a certain number of my letters which are now said to be lost." The audience responded to my lead as if I were the driver and they the car, savoring every lingering consonant and nuance of expression, holding their laughter for my pauses. "Thank you, Cassandra, for your diligent attention in censoring and burning so many of my letters. Imagine the consequences had you not made such good use of scissors and fireplace. But back to me.

"Perhaps," I said, "if the public knew the content of the Lost Letters, I might be released from their curious grip and allowed, finally, to proceed to my eternal rest. To that end, I will now work very hard to recall their content. It is my hope that in so doing, we may *all* move on." I glanced at Claire before closing my eyes.

"My Dear Mark Twain," I said, squinting with the effort of remembering. The audience seemed to understand where I was going. My Jane Austen stepped closer, cautiously amused. "If you so much as touch my shinbone, I'll use it to beat sense into your head. If you don't like *Pride and Prejudice,* stop reading it!"

The audience waited for more. My Jane Austen scribbled on her ivories as if she might add her own remarks.

"My Dear Tom Lefroy," I said. "It wasn't good for me, either. P.S. I meant what I said about your morning coat."

I lifted the water glass I'd placed near my chair, feeling the audience with me even as I sipped.

"My Dear Charlotte Brontë," I said. "Passions unknown to *moi*?" I placed my hand near my heart, confidence surging, the audience eating from my hand. Maybe I could take this show on the road. "Have you seen Colin Firth in the wet-shirt version of *Pride and Prejudice*?" Pause. "I didn't think so. Pity." I wished Willis were here to witness this. But I could not think about Willis while on stage. Whenever the deacon peeked around the corner of my subconscious, I tended to leave my body and climb stairs to the third floor where I entertained him with witty observations, causing Willis to be immediately overcome, etc. When I detected Willis creeping into my head I had to look the other way and focus on something scary like my half sister. "My Dear Kingsley Amis," I continued. "Sorry to miss dinner at your house but I have to wash my hair that night."

While addressing My Dear Andrew Davies, demanding information leading to the apprehension of the party or parties authorizing the Harlequinization of my novels, I felt My Jane Austen more intensely than ever. I corresponded briefly with My Dear Lionel Trilling to recommend counseling with an emphasis on sensitivity training. Taking big curves now, audience laughter cushioned the turns. As I roasted My Dear Seth Grahame-Smith, warning him not to travel alone in dark alleys, or for that matter, anyplace it might eventually get dark, like his personal bedroom, I felt as if I had become Jane Austen. She hovered so close to me, and I so close to her, that a sideways glance would not scare her away. I experienced such fusion with My Jane Austen, sensing the words she scribbled on her ivories as if she wrote in my mind. If I let go, her words would come out of my mouth. "My Dear To Whom It May Concern," I said. "Regarding the issue of failing to include slavery and war in my novels, what part of writing about the doings of a few country families do you *not* understand?" And then it happened; her words came from my mouth. I felt slightly buzzed, as if a dentist's anesthesia had numbed body and soul for my own protection since the words felt different, sharper.

"You are very kind to offer advice as to the sort of composition which I might have undertaken," I said. "I am fully sensible that a historic account of the Napoleonic Wars or Evils of Slavery might have been much more to the purpose of profit or popularity than pictures of domestic life in country villages as I deal in. But I could not sit down to write a serious history under any motive other than to save my life. And if it were indispensable for me to keep it up and never relax into laughing at myself and other people, I am sure I should be hung before finishing the first chapter." The audience sensed the change in the language, condescending. I wished to go back to my own script but I couldn't get there, speeding too fast to change direction without crashing, and I sensed more dangerous terrain ahead.

"My Dear Faculty of Literature Live," she spoke through me. The audience stopped breathing and raised their collective eyebrows. Some looked over at Nigel. "I must thank you dear teachers, for the very high praise you bestow on my novels. I think I may boast myself to be, with all possible vanity, the most unlearned and uninformed female who ever dared to be an authoress. While I am too vain to wish to convince you that you have praised my novels beyond their merit, I must warn that your intellectual endeavors on my behalf have been extolled so highly that future generations shall have the pleasure of being disappointed." Some audience members laughed but they weren't laughing *with* me anymore; we were out of sync. I'd been abducted, forced to perform. My Jane Austen was showing her true self. Prickly, she suffered no fools and wasn't cutting us any slack now. Her words felt mean, born in pain and subtly intended to inflict the same. I once *imagined* feeling the sharp end of her pen; now I *felt* it.

"My Dear Janeites," I said, knowing this was going to be bad, unable to stop because Jane Austen was driving, recklessly. "Why do you insist on another stupid party?" Several people gasped and I sensed a low rumble, unrest in the audience. Would someone please call the police and have me arrested? "Can you conceive that it may be possible to do without dancing entirely? Instances have been known of women passing many, many months successively, without being at any ball of any description, and no material injury accrue either to body or mind. But when a beginning is made—when the felicities of rapid motion have once been, though slightly felt—it must be a very heavy set that does not ask for more. Obsession working on a weak head produces every sort of mischief."

No one laughed. I kept my mouth shut to make sure no further damage occurred. I conveyed harsh thoughts to My Jane Austen: *How could you use me like this? We were best friends but you've gone too far. Return to my rear periphery and either stay there or go away. If you can't respect boundaries, you need to get help.* Nigel's face bore frail amazement. Vera looked stricken. Omar's fist supported his nose, obscuring his expression. Just as I thought things couldn't get much worse, the muffled electronic wail of a cell phone interrupted the horror, the sound originating from the tiny fringed bag on my wrist. The unmistakable ringtone played the first line of Tommy's new song, "I'll Find You," as a rush of panic crashed against my chest. I answered the phone, why not? Perhaps Lionel Trilling was calling to get the last word. "Hullo?" I said. The audience waited, stifling black laughter as I listened to the halting voice.

"Oh, Lord Weston," I said, "I'm so sorry."

The audience hushed, watching intently.

"She's here with me, actually," I said, looking up at Vera. I listened. "Yes, I'll let her know." I nodded and closed my eyes. "I'm so sorry." I powered off the phone and looked at Vera. She sat stiff, prepared for the worst as I spoke the last line of my last one-woman show. "Ladies and gentlemen, I'm terribly sorry to be the bearer of bad news," I said. "Lady Weston died early this morning."

Twenty-four

$\mathcal{T}$he memorial service looked more like *Masterpiece Theatre* than a funeral. Mrs. Russell and the entire corps of volunteers filled our church with their Regency best, thankfully distracted from the insults of my one-woman show. Volunteers who had served tea, sold tickets, and passed out programs over the years, now gathered to celebrate Lady Weston's life. Even the sun presented a robust rendition of its English version—nothing you could fry an egg on—but the cobalt and emerald in the church windows sparkled like tumblers inside a kaleidoscope.

Surrounded by a multitude of glorious hats, I would see nothing unless I stood on the pew. I would miss the first glimpse of Willis when the clergy processed down the aisle. The organ thundered a prelude and my heart beat faster at the immediate prospect of existing in the same room with him. Only here, at the memorial service for a dead woman, would the world come alive for me. Breathing deeply to calm myself, holding his jacket to return to him, I failed to suppress the dangerous hope that he was sorting Philippa out of his life. My anticipation grew and I desperately needed a sign from him to sustain me.

The woman next to me fanned herself with the bulletin as the small assortment of gray-haired Weston relatives filed into reserved seats in the front. The actual funeral had been held elsewhere, making family attendance here optional. Philippa wore black except for the gold purse chain slung over her shoulder; her dark glasses, worn inside the church, compelled her to lean on her brother to avoid running into things. Randolph, in a somber suit, looked like the polished bankers or lawyers that rode the elevators to the upper floors in my old office building.

With a great rustling of fabric, the congregation stood for the opening hymn. I leaned forward for a view of the verger leading the procession, followed by an earnest young acolyte hefting an ornate brass cross, flanked by two torch bearers. Behind them, the small choir followed, and finally the clergy. A star zapped me when Willis entered, the center of the lovely universe; the only one who mattered. I saw the world through him, saw myself through him, and knew I wanted to get *in there* with him forever.

Music stopped and the priest said, "I am the resurrection and the life." The mighty words resonated. I heard them for the first time. Fear took note and fled the premises, snagging my personal tangle of dread and beating a hasty departure. Once freed, my spirit surged and I met myself in clarity, suddenly unafraid of being alone. I wiped tear-filled eyes with my bare hands until the woman next to me offered a tissue. I turned the pages of the prayer book feeling new and strong. What was so hard about this and why was I only now feeling this lightness? Fresh confidence sustained me all the way through the Great Thanksgiving.

When the time came, I approached the rail for communion, eyes downcast and hands folded, passing the family, including Philippa, without looking at them. Aware that Willis could see me, I knelt at the rail, head bent. If my mother's spirit were here, as Willis had assured me it was, there must be so many others, a great swirling mass of ethereal beings hovering above us like spirits in an Italian Renaissance painting. In their parallel plane of existence, they welcomed the new arrival—Lady Weston—and supported me as I knelt. Outwardly, I projected calm, but beneath my composed exterior I harbored the entire heavenly company, their voices joining with angels and archangels in a chorus of eternal forgiveness. I *could* be free.

Willis came closer every moment. His shoes entered my downcast vision, only two people away as the priest put the wafer in my hand saying, "The body of Christ; the bread of heaven." Willis stood before me and I looked up at him. "Lily," he said, putting the cup to my lips. Then, providing the sign I craved, he touched my hand supporting the base of the cup. "The blood of Christ, the cup of salvation." He lingered a beat longer in front of me than with any other communicant. I made the sign of the cross over my chest while the wine blazed a warm path to my heart.

As I left the church, scattering birds, it occurred to me I'd left without reciting the funeral liturgy for my mother. I could still go back and say the words for her, but it seemed unnecessary. My mother had moved beyond the need for a funeral. Perhaps I should recite the liturgy for my father next time. I sat on a bench outside the church with My Jane Austen and some birds. Our relationship had been cool since the *Lost Let-*

ters debacle. Now we all waited; his folded jacket in my arms, birds pecking nervously in the pebbles. Willis would be shaking hands with the congregation as they filed out to join the reception at Newton Priors. He would remove his vestments in the sacristy. My Jane Austen stood and paced once birds began landing where her lap would be, and I focused on shedding any artifice I might have recently accumulated.

It seemed Willis and I shared The Look at communion but I couldn't be sure. He should be here by now. Sun and breeze conspired, causing leaves to flicker in my peripheral vision. Perhaps he had departed by another exit and missed me altogether. But then I saw him in the door, shading his eyes, looking toward Newton Priors. At that instant, the clock started. Time sped recklessly and I resented the passing of every precious second.

"Willis." I ran to meet him, slipping on the pea gravel.

"Lily." He came down the steps and held out a hand.

"You left this again," I said, surrendering the jacket.

"Yes, another abrupt ending, I apologize." I denied his expression and ignored the word *ending*.

"Look what I found." I held up my necklace. "Can you believe it?"

"No." He held the cross; examining the piece he'd heard so much about. "Where was it?" he asked, genuinely curious.

"Around a neck in a London pub."

"Naturally," he said. And then, "How is your Jane Austen?"

"The same," I said, "timeless and sparkling, swirling in my subconscious, folded into my existence."

Willis smiled and reached for a lock of my hair blowing across my eyes.

"Although she did get me in big trouble," I told him, birds eavesdropping under cover of pecking nearby, the breeze blowing my skirt.

"How?"

I tried to communicate how she'd spoken through me at my one-woman show but Willis wasn't listening. Talking to him felt like running in a dream without making forward progress. The connection failed on his end and I heard desperation propping up my voice.

"Are you all right?" he asked quietly.

How to answer that? I would be all right if he'd give me a sign. I could bear anything as long as the promise of Willis secured my future. But I wasn't all right. I was terribly *not* all right, on the brink of suffering emotional torment as ferocious and debilitating as an abscessed tooth because Willis wasn't listening to me and he hadn't been looking for *me* when he stepped out the church door just now.

I asked him quietly, "How's the sorting going?"

His expression reminded me of Martin when he said he didn't want a scene.

"This has been terribly awkward for you." Willis shook his head.

"Yes," I said. My Jane Austen stood behind me, revisiting her hero list with a cloth for erasing in one hand. I looked hard at Willis, memorizing his features for future recall. Even as he asked about my well-being, sincere and penitent, he would leave me as soon as I answered. He'd gotten the distance he needed to carry on with his original plans. He'd done his sorting and I was out. Only he wouldn't tell me. He'd join Philippa at the reception and beyond, suppressing all the fear he'd entertained in the attic, and I would start the waiting again, far less certain than I'd been before the service, the black abyss seeping into my future. Waiting forever.

"Willis," a voice called.

"Over here," he said, without turning.

Philippa stood in the church door looking down at us. In

the moment our eyes met, I understood two things: Although Philippa had perhaps sensed that something in her relationship was not right, she had not known what, and now she knew. Willis had told her nothing. What she knew, she inferred from the tension around my eyes and the stress in my jaw. "I lost track of you," she said, smiling, scattering birds with the snap of her heels on the stone steps.

"Pippa," Willis said, eyes still on me, "you remember Lily."

"Of course," she said, both hands busy adjusting her purse strap.

"I'm so sorry about your grandmother," I said.

"Thank you." Even behind her dark glasses, I could read her fearless expression. She whispered to Willis, "I'll go on. The costume drama awaits us," patting his arm to fortify him for what he must do to me. A clergy wife braces herself for these things, all in the line of duty.

Willis looked at me, tilting his head in silent question, but this was not as complicated as I would like it to be. Quite simple really, Willis would soon walk away and I would be alone. I moved my mouth, speaking very quietly, watching Philippa in case she should turn around and catch me. "I can see where this is headed." I touched my heart and shook my head. "I'm not going to wait for you."

His eyes widened and his smile faded. He understood.

"Good-bye, Willis," I said, releasing him.

Willis rubbed his nose, looked at the ground in a helpless way I couldn't bear, and then whispered, "I understand." Time came to a screeching halt. Birds froze, the breeze ended, the sun dipped behind a cloud, and all color drained as Willis turned away from me and followed Philippa down the path to Newton Priors.

Twenty-five

*O*mar joined me in the library one week after the memorial service. We sat at the table we'd occupied two months
ago. I lost myself in Brontë while Omar read books on Shaw,
working on his dissertation. I spent all my time in the library
now. As soon as I was free, I retreated to the east wing, traveling the same worn planks, passing Nigel at his desk discard-
ing papers into a large metal waste bin, passing Vera calmly
typing schedule revisions. Only cloistered in the library, reading from the endless supply of mind-altering smelly books,
did I find peace. Any page of any book would do.

"Omar?" I asked.

He looked up, obviously straining to return to England and
place me. "Yes?" he said, turning a page.

"I owe you an apology," I said.

He looked up again with less effort. "For what?"

"For avoiding you after the follies."

Omar waved a hand, dismissing the sentiment, although

he had been cool and distant since that evening almost three weeks ago.

"I know you were trying to help," I said, routing a cuticle on my left hand, "and I appreciate your concern."

Omar closed his book and removed his glasses. "You're crushed, aren't you?"

"Yes." I pressed my lips as tears filled my eyes.

"That was pretty brutal of him," Omar said.

I couldn't speak.

"I don't know what his problem is." Omar took my hand. "Willis did not treat you well, Lily. If this were the olden days, you'd be a ruined woman."

"I don't think he meant to mislead me," I said.

"Right." Omar smiled and shook his head.

We looked up as Vera opened our door and stuck her head in. "Randolph's here," she said. "Come quickly." She gestured with one hand, glancing behind her as if he were in the hallway. I scooted my chair out, noting Omar's disapproval. "He's in the front," she said, leading the way.

Randolph's silver Jaguar sat parked outside, just beyond the window where Vera and I watched through the swirly glass and pouring rain. Like Sheila, he'd crashed the gates, passing horse-drawn carriages to park outside our door. *His* door. "Look at his car," Vera whispered, her head suddenly next to mine.

"Hmm," I said.

"Why isn't he getting out?"

"It's raining." My breath fogged the window.

"Perhaps we should take him an umbrella."

"That would be awkward," I said, *awkward* being my new favorite word since Willis used it on me.

"Or maybe he's on the phone." Vera grabbed my hand and we both gazed at the silver auto against the majestic landscape, dreamlike through the distorted glass. Lately, as things seemed more desperate, the adrenaline from her ideas had been going straight to her mouth. "You could hold your wedding at Newton Priors," Vera said. "Your children could grow up playing on this lawn."

I said, "This is a business meeting." She'd become so inflamed by her hope of saving the organization that the line between business and self-delusion blurred.

Vera whispered, "You made an impression on him. And, as the book says, 'A young man in possession of a fortune . . .'" She looked at me earnestly. "The world needs a new Lady Weston."

"He probably has me mixed up with someone else he met in the hospital that day. He must meet many people. If his face falls when he meets me, we'll know it was a mix-up," I whispered back.

"Nonsense." She smiled insanely, confident I would save Literature Live, congratulating herself on having brought me to England in spite of the *Lost Letters* embarrassment.

Randolph's door opened.

He had arranged that, after a tour of the festival and a meeting with Nigel, we would discuss my ideas for Newton Priors. His visit provided the incentive necessary to force the business plan into existence. Pages had been finalized that morning in a panic as Vera flitted like a nervous moth, contributing helpful remarks such as, "Randolph *must* produce an heir; they say the House of Lords will be extinct by the year 2047."

Randolph stepped out of his car. There was no turning back. The unlikely social phenomenon—me mixing with an English lord—was about to happen, plausible or not. And Vera blanched as if it suddenly occurred to her that she might have been wrong. Maybe he *did* have me mixed up with someone else. "An English lord, for God's sake. In a silver Jaguar," she said, touching my hand.

He locked the car and then ran toward our door. "He's taller than I remember," I said. His hairline had receded since I last saw him and his shirt looked like something my father would wear bowling. Must be really expensive. My hand flew to my mouth as he ran through raindrops. Suddenly, I was in over my head.

"Go." Vera pushed me.

Randolph approached, his gaze lowered and a faint smile graced his lips. He appeared far away in thought. Near the door, he looked up; his brow arched mildly, a peer of the realm coming for me. I grasped the doorknob as our eyes met through the window; his warm smile encouraged me, but the knob left its socket and fell out of my hand. I pointed to the floor. Randolph looked down. I knew *then* that Jane Austen would never eat me for lunch for the simple reason there would be nothing left to eat after I finished with *myself;* she'd starve to death if she were counting on me for a meal.

"Oh, the door." Vera rushed over. "Lord Weston, welcome," she said through the glass. "If you don't mind, just pushing on the frame will open the door from your side."

Randolph pushed and the door cooperated.

"These old doors," Vera explained.

"House is full of them." Randolph's easy smile calmed me. "Lily." He reached for me and I gave him both hands, too late to bow or curtsy. I had been right in expecting strong aftershave; it seemed to go with first dates, even when they were business meetings with peers of the realm.

"Vera," he said, extending both hands and kissing her cheeks.

Nigel joined us and quietly offered condolences while I studied Randolph's confident manner, his polished exterior, a man who knew life's secret rules. I slid my eyes sideways to enjoy Vera's reaction. Randolph's face had not fallen when he first saw me.

Vera guided Randolph on a tour of Newton Priors, his ancestral home, engaging the usual suspects, all of whom had been prepped. Although Randolph had grown up around Literature Live, it was his project now, and Vera wanted him to see it in a fresh light. Randolph leered at a volunteer wearing a flimsy, almost see-through gown. Vera dismissed his blatant behavior later, saying, "Their clear understanding of the changing world in 1890 caused the Westons to divert investments to overseas equities and save the family from early extinction. Randolph descended from people who evaluated opportunities; of course he's going to leer at provocative volunteers."

Vera served us to Sixby, who appeared to be leading a last-minute rehearsal of several cast members in the Freezer, something he'd never done. We watched Alex pretend not to know how to deliver his line, and Sixby coach him. "Place the emphasis here," Sixby said, pointing to the script. We watched, in the room where Magda and Archie's unquiet spirits felt especially strong to me, until Vera decided Randolph had seen enough "behind the scenes."

The ballroom appeared to be buzzing with patrons when I recognized people from the volunteer staff posing as tourists. Mrs. Russell had wisely joined her considerable resources with Vera's to save the house. Their partnership implied the obvious truth: no house, no ball. And the ball remained the ultimate goal, in spite of undead Jane Austen's admonitions to the contrary. The appearance of a new male volunteer, conspicuously uncomfortable in period attire, did not escape my notice. *Mr.* Russell had taken to working the ticket desk *on Wednesdays.*

Randolph touched my arm, leaning in to speak to me. He treated me gallantly and I grew to expect opening of doors and the pressure of his hand on my back as we entered a room. He couldn't possibly be interested in me—a girl totally lacking in artifice chaperoned by her prickly Jane Austen—but pretending he was made me feel better, even temporarily. "You're not on stage today?" he asked.

I couldn't remember if we had decided on a response to that question when we scripted the afternoon, but Vera, hovering nearby, said, "We recast the scene today to free Lily for meetings." Then she added, "But you'll see her perform Amelia in the tea-theatre."

Randolph winked at me and I began to see a way out of missing Willis. But when the actors took the familiar stage and spoke the familiar lines, I couldn't concentrate because, for one thing, I sat next to the owner of Newton Priors, and for another thing, he was not paying attention. Almost immediately, he began jiggling his knee. He stopped jiggling to shift position, but he started again and completely missed the line when Henry Crawford says: "I will not be tricked on the south side of Everingham any more than on the north; I will be master of my own property."

Two full hours past the time we'd set to discuss my business plan, Vera summoned me to Nigel's conference room where Randolph and Nigel were sharing a bottle of wine. They had not attended the tea-theatre.

"I was hopeful the numbers would look better," Randolph said as he swirled his wine.

I accepted the glass Nigel poured for me and took the chair next to Randolph. While they met, I'd rehearsed the basic premise of my business plan: the idea was tourists living in a Jane Austen novel. I ignored my gnawing anxiety he'd not been interested in the festival. Now, Randolph looked at his watch and shoved papers into his portfolio. "I'm afraid we've gone a bit long. And now something's come up in London." He looked at me.

Something had changed while he met with Nigel; the ground had shifted.

"Could I persuade you to join me for dinner another night this week to go over your plan?" he asked.

"That would be fine." I smiled, knowing it would never happen, ripping off a cuticle.

"I expect you're rather busy now," I said as we walked to his car in the gathering dusk, warm and humid after the rain. I couldn't imagine how he spent his days. Vera said people like Randolph sat in the House of Lords, observing august traditions far older than anything in Texas.

"Yes, quite busy."

"Will you take up politics?" I asked, imagining Randolph inheriting a robe, the pesky hairline problem concealed beneath a wig.

"Can't," he said, folding his arms.

"Why not?" I asked.

"Tony Blair. House of Lords Act, 1999." He smiled.

I would have to look it up.

"But I *can* reserve an excellent table at just about any restaurant." He looked at me as if he noticed my presence for the first time that evening, causing me to wonder where he stood on girls without artifice. "Right now I'd like to take up acting."

"Did you have a chance to look at my plan?" I asked.

"Not yet." He patted his portfolio. "But I will, before we meet again."

Just then, a tourist snapped our photo: *Aristocrat and Texas Girl Outside English Manor House with Jaguar.*

"Good," I said, "because I have some marketing ideas that might be lucrative for Newton Priors."

"I'm glad to hear that, because I'm quite torn actually," he said as he threw his portfolio on the seat. He looked past me into the evening air where I imagined pieces of torn Randolph floating out of order. "Quite simply, I find I'm the steward of a burdensome asset in which I have no real interest."

My Jane Austen smiled knowingly as I sighed over the unwelcome piece of information. "But it's such a magnificent house," I said.

"So I'm told." Randolph leaned against his car as if we had all the time in the world.

"Do you ever think about living in Newton Priors?" I asked, wondering what the house looked like to someone who'd known it from birth.

"Not a chance," he said, frowning, as if I should have known better. "Nobody lives in these houses."

"Your grandmother was quite fond of it," I said.

"Oh yes, sentimental really. In her backward thinking, the economics would reverse, and all of England would return to an agrarian economy, with servants."

I'd assumed he had servants.

"I don't subscribe to that cult of country house nostalgia," he said.

I didn't hold out much hope that Pippa did, either. "But you said you were torn."

He paused, choosing his words carefully, his hands supporting his weight on the car. "Regardless of my personal inclination, I must be mindful of my stewardship," he said, "to both past *and* future."

I imagined him at the deathbed, accepting a golden orb from his failing grandmother, while the past—Newton Priors—and the future—equities in Prague—waited nervously, to see what sort of steward he would be.

"I must hold up my end." He smiled. "That is, not let the house and its content go on my watch."

"Yes," I said, nodding.

"Nor let the house and its content deplete the trust."

Odd, he had so much time to talk while London waited on hold.

"At any rate, the house must support itself; that much is certain." Randolph squinted in a thoughtful way that reminded me of Willis, a welcome contrast to his earlier jiggling knee. "And from the look of things, Literature Live can't begin to pay the bills."

Vera had not thought to cook the books. She had done a lot of maneuvering in preparation for Randolph's visit, but she had not, as far as I knew, played with the numbers. We were off the script again. "Well." I swallowed. "Perhaps you'll think differently after you read my plan."

Randolph nodded and looked at me carefully. He asked, "Is this the sort of thing you're interested in?" His arms gestured big and at first I thought he was referring to himself. Was I interested in *him*. But then he added, "Making a country house pay its way?"

I remembered my mother asking me, as a child, if I wanted a toy badly enough to spend my own money on it. Couched in those terms, my interest always faded. "Of course," I said. "I believe there is a market for escape vacations; a place where people can go to live in a novel. And the premise of my business plan is: tourists living in a Jane Austen novel." My Jane Austen would not be a good hostess. She'd hide the extra pillows and run out of coffee and then feign disappointment at early departures, "Leaving my novel already?" She'd install locks on all her books, like diaries, and hide all the keys.

"I must say I'm impressed with your ideas," he said. "I had no idea actresses were so resourceful." In one very smooth gesture he stepped forward and kissed me. A brief and efficient kiss—a husband kissing his wife as he left for the office, as if we'd become a married couple without the work of getting acquainted, without the terrifying exposure of being known. Perhaps he wanted an abridged, intimacy-free version of me: *Lily for Dummies*. It would be much easier that way. But I knew that would be cheating and My Jane Austen knew it, too.

I smiled and tucked my hair behind my ears. "It's all in the plan," I said. We'd been standing there talking long enough for the sky to grow completely dark.

"Let's look at it together," he said. "In fact, come with me. Do you have time?"

"Now?" I imagined Vera's rapture at the news.

"My sister's getting married and there's a party in their honor tonight."

A camera flash reflected off the silver hood like a flare of lightning, illuminating my expression for anyone who was paying attention. *Texas Girl Horrified Outside English Manor.* I wished I could replay his comment to make sure I'd heard correctly. Did he say the wedding was *on*? I wanted to ask Randolph if he'd spoken with Willis *lately*. Are you *sure* they're getting married? He watched me struggle to look normal as my cosmos shifted once again. Willis at society parties in his honor, something he'd never have had with me. Maybe he wanted society parties.

"Could you come to London?" he asked again.

Yes," I said. Although I wasn't stupid; this dinner party
didn't *just come up.*

"Excellent."

Color came back and the clock ticked once more.

Two hours later, my knees secretly weak, I entered a chic
London apartment where people stood in small groups holding wineglasses. No one met us at the door. Randolph winked
at me and we walked in, his hand guiding from the small of
my back. I searched every face, seeking one person, afraid
of finding him. Randolph steered me into the kitchen where
we discovered his sister leaning against a granite counter, her
wit animating the faces of three enchanted listeners. I felt
Randolph's eyes on me, like a protective shield in this foreign
place. A caterer shuffled large plates of leftovers into storage
containers and a dark-skinned woman in a maid's uniform
rinsed plates. Judging from the direction the food was headed
and the stack of dirty dishes, we'd missed dinner.

Pippa stopped speaking when she saw me. She looked from
me to Randolph and back. "Well, hullo." Her mouth spoke
to Randolph but her eyes stuck on me. Her enchanted listeners broke Pippa's gravitational pull to shake Randolph's hand.
Then all three peered at me as if I were an alien invader from
dark space. I looked to see if I'd remembered to change out of
my Regency gown. I had.

"She's agreed to run away with me," Randolph announced
to the little group.

"Where are you running away *to?*" asked a man.

"Old novels," Randolph told him. "We'd like to live in one.
Preferably Jane Austen."

"Ah," the person said. "Clever. No one would think of
looking for you there."

"Although I'd prefer a racy French novel," he whispered

to me as Pippa's moons resumed their orbits. "Austen's so tame," he said, "might get boring for a guy."

I faux frowned. "Well, maybe Forster," I said, lifting a warm glass of champagne off a parked tray, feeling surreal. Randolph's friends made the trek to the kitchen to say hullo, most of whom observed me suspiciously after Randolph tried to pass me off as his evil twin, recently convicted of misshelving books in a Texas library. He told a persistent guest that I wasn't "out" (in society) yet, keeping one hand on my back as I disregarded his conversations to search faces. The open kitchen allowed a view of the room beyond but Willis was not present in the room beyond. How many rooms were there and where was the guest of honor?

"How did he propose?" a woman behind us asked Pippa as Randolph turned to shake another hand.

"You mean the first time?" Pippa asked. "We were sixteen and he chased me into the girls' bathroom at our school." Pippa sighed. "It was so long ago, but I *do* remember reading some gothic novel at the time, or maybe it was *The Thorn Birds*, and agreeing to marry him if he would swear to be a priest when he grew up."

I disengaged Rand's hand and ventured into the next room. A window wall turned out to be a sliding glass door revealing guests on a balcony. A woman stepping into the room from the balcony tossed a remark to the people behind her and I saw Willis, big as life, his head rearing back to laugh at whatever she'd said. How odd to see Willis so exuberant. *My* Willis brooded over his laptop in melancholy confinement on the third floor. As I approached the sliding glass door, the panorama opened up, glamorous London at night. Willis saw me. I stepped onto the balcony, closing the door behind, and my time began elapsing. "Still seeking rooftop perspectives?" I asked.

"What a surprise," he said. "Lily." He extended a hand and I prayed he wouldn't squander our private seconds sorting out my presence at the party.

"No small talk," I said quickly, touching the cross around my neck.

"Never, with you," he said, his face still lit from the last round of levity. My Attic Willis was make-believe; this Society Willis was real.

"How are you?" I asked, meaning the big picture.

He reached for a more serious expression, unable finally to engage either a smile or a frown. "Well, since you asked, I'll tell you." He lifted his glass from the low table, avoiding my eyes. "I've decided to leave my degree program."

"What does that mean?"

"I'm not seeking the priesthood." He sipped his wine, relieved, as if he'd finished the thesis and won an award, rather than abandoned his life plan.

"Congratulations," I said. "You've struggled with this. And how is your fiancée taking the decision?"

"It's still new to her." He watched a blinking light make its way across the dark sky.

"So what will you do?" I asked.

"That"—he laughed—"is a more difficult question." He opened his mouth to speak. Certainly his lips formed the word *you* but the unbidden grind of the door, sliding open along its metal track, admitted party chatter onto the balcony and ended our privacy. We'd been a fairy tale with a beginning, middle, and end, and we'd reached the last page sometime in July. Tonight felt more like an epilogue.

"They're looking for you," Randolph said to Willis. "Time for the toasts," he added, offering me a champagne glass, extending a hand to Willis.

"Ah, duty calls," Willis said. "Excuse me." And passing me, he left without a good-bye.

I started to follow Willis back into the noisy room, not sure I could bear to hear tributes to the lovely couple, when Randolph gently tugged my hand. "Let's stay out here," he whispered, nodding at the sparkling skyline, taking my glass and setting it on the rail. Willis had forgotten to take the stars and the moon when he left. Rand's arm found my waist and I gratefully leaned my head on his shoulder.

"So, it's Forster for us," he said.

Four days later in my library, I reached up to touch the spines of the old books on the shelves, a light touch, the way Randolph touched my back or my hand. I thought about decoding the shapes of ink, the alphabet blooming into people and places in my mind, regardless of book or page number. But mildewed pages were out of character for an aristocrat's dinner date. Rather, I should brush up on foxhunting and afternoon tea. While staring at the shelves, halfheartedly seeking a book on peerage laws, my cell phone went off, igniting my pulse. But it was Vera again.

"Has he called?" she asked.

"No," I reported once again as I pulled an old encyclopedia off the shelf. "The Eleventh Baron of Weston has priorities and we have to wait." I'd fed Vera's frenzy, sharing Randolph's comments about my interest in making a country house pay its way and the talk about running away in Forster. "Do you think he's really interested?" I asked, purposely imprecise, allowing her to address either question: his interest in keeping Literature Live in his house or his interest in Lily. I faced the bookshelf so my voice wouldn't carry into the room, deceiving myself that My Jane Austen wouldn't hear the question.

I knew which way Vera would go, which made me think she also understood, at least subconsciously, that Literature Live was doomed.

"Of course he's interested. He's always been especially fond of American actresses," Vera said. Her response triggered a memory of something I couldn't place.

Omar joined me, throwing books and papers on the table. "What are you reading?" he asked.

"I'm looking up the 1999 House of Lords Act," I said. "Do you know anything about it?"

Omar sat. "It restricted the number of hereditary peers allowed to govern; no more than ninety-two can sit in Lords. The rest are appointees with life terms." He guessed why I asked. "Randolph is not entitled to a seat."

"I see." Like learning that nobody lived in country manors nowadays or had servants. "Speaking of," he said, "how's Lord Randy?"

"I haven't heard from him. I'm a bit worried for Literature Live's future, really."

"You should be." Omar pulled a newspaper from his pile of stuff. Rifling through the pages, he found the section he looked for and tossed it to me. "Have a look."

"What's this?" I scanned photographs of people in evening attire, society types posing for the camera. "What am I looking for?"

"Your Randy Lord." Omar pointed to a picture in the middle of the page and folded his arms across his chest.

There, posing in aristocratic understatement, stood my Randolph with a demure socialite. The caption read, *Lord Weston and Sara Stormont at the Benefit for the Sick Dentists' Trust*. I studied the picture, wondering who she was, how serious their relationship might be; another Someone Else.

Omar wagged a finger at me. "You're not letting Vera use you, are you?"

"I don't think so."

"Good. Don't let her pump you up so you can't think for yourself. You can't save Literature Live for Nigel, so don't let her convince you it all hangs on you snuggling up with the lord of the manor. It doesn't."

"No?"

"Look at Vera. Look at her life. Lonely as can be, married to a gay man, no family to call her own." Omar leaned forward. "I know how charming she is, but you need to *only connect* yourself."

"Let's talk about something else," I said. "When are you leaving?"

He looked at his watch. "Midnight, why?"

"No," I said. "When are you going home—to Michigan?"

"Friday," he said, opening his laptop.

"You're not staying through the end?" I asked.

"It's over," he said.

I sat back and folded my hands.

Omar removed his glasses and asked me, "Why don't you come with me?"

"And do what?"

"Continue your work connecting disjointed personalities; the university is full of them." He smiled. "And spend evenings amusing me with your stories."

I rolled my eyes.

"No, really. Why don't you come to Michigan? Go back to school." Omar leaned back on his chair's hind legs. "Get your MFA."

"No money." I bit my lip.

"You can work on campus. Human resources, isn't it?" He wiped the lens on his shirt.

"I don't remember."

"You can stay with me until you get your act together."

I took a deep breath and looked at him. Without glasses, he appeared younger and more vulnerable. "That's a very tempting offer, Omar."

He rested on all four chair legs. "Think about it," he said.

"I'll think about it."

With less than a week of literary festival left to me, I sat on my bed, holding Magda's book, staring at Bets's mattress. I'd stripped her bed, folding the matching bedspread and stuffing it in her closet. The naked ticking satisfied in a mildly punitive ascetic sense. Bets's side of the bureau was bare, as well as her side of the sink and table. I'd removed the things she'd stored under my bed and stuffed all of it in her closet and forced the door shut. I wanted to be completely alone.

I'd spent all day Monday and Tuesday, festival days off, reading in my room. Books accumulated in stacks around my bed. Not novels, but critical essays about Jane Austen and *Mansfield Park*, the type of thing Vera had encouraged me to read back in June. I discovered back issues of *Persuasions*, a scholarly journal published by JASNA, the existence of which blurred my understanding of the distinction between academics and Janeites. Essays about *Mansfield Park* referenced names I'd heard in Nigel's conversations and in lectures, and I worked backward to the primary sources listed in bibliographies. Most books were on our shelves, and the deeper I read, the better I understood what I'd been doing all summer.

I survived by eating Bets's leftover cheese crackers and drinking water from the sink in my room. By Tuesday evening, when I began reading the slavery essays in the book Magda had left me, a week had passed since Randolph said he'd call. So tired, yet unable to sleep, I struggled to understand how anyone could believe that Jane Austen was complicit with slave-owning society. No way.

But then I read, and reread, that Jane Austen's father was trustee of a plantation in Antigua. The godfather of Jane's oldest brother owned the plantation, and details of his life bear striking similarity to those of the Bertram family. Jane Austen drew on details from her family to create *Mansfield Park*. This information wasn't in anything else I'd read about her life. Jane Austen had secrets. Or maybe her father had secrets. But she discovered them. And she never told me. I would have told her something that important. I told her everything. Perhaps we weren't as close as I thought. Perhaps the person in my peripheral vision wasn't Jane Austen at all.

I answered my phone that evening, the last Tuesday of the season. "Hello?" I said, groggy, hung over from the reading binge.

"Hullo?" A male voice. Not Willis.

"Randolph?" The depth of his voice stirred me. Vera would be relieved at the news of his call.

"I've been meaning to call you," he said.

I should be careful. Hold back.

"Can you have dinner tonight?"

Don't do it, I told myself. "Um, yes," I answered.

"There's a small problem," he said. "I'm afraid I'm engaged, but should be free by seven. Any chance you can meet me at my hotel?"

I responded without thinking. "Yes, of course."

"Seven then?"

"Yes."

"Excellent. See you then."

My Jane Austen dimmed in the corner.

Twenty-six

$\mathcal{B}$y the time Vera drove into Knightsbridge and stopped at the richly beveled glass door of Randolph's hotel, I was unfashionably late; Vera had been too involved coaching me to concentrate on making the lights. "And the most important thing," she said, wagging her finger like a gothic villain, "leave him wanting more." Thanks to Vera's talking and driving I was also unfashionably nervous.

"Where's the business plan?" I asked.

"Here it is." Vera pulled the envelope from the gap between the seats. "Good luck, dear," she said, as if I were a finalist in the Lady Weston Pageant, stepping onto the stage rather than the curb. "Of all the women in this city, Randolph chose to have dinner with you," she said.

The doorman in long coat and derby hat held the door as I entered, my head high, prepared to meet the Eleventh Baron of Weston. *Glamorous Actress Enters.* Chandeliers glittered overhead and a grand bouquet of white flowers, roses and hydrangeas, graced the entry. Crisp black and white marble tiled the floor and a lamp trimmed in ebony and gold suggested Napoleon slept here. Perhaps Randolph was watching my entrance from just beyond the double doors to the salon. Although he mentioned a previous engagement, I nursed a romantic vision of a handsome nobleman stepping forth to claim me, anticipating the feel of his hand on my back. I stalled, pretending to consult my envelope, allowing Randolph every chance to emerge from the cigar brown lair of tufted club chairs. Finally, it became necessary to concede his absence, but without Vera's enthusiasm, I began nursing a less romantic vision of Randolph held up by a press photographer: Sara Stormont, the real candidate in the Lady Weston contest, posing possessively at his side.

At the high mahogany desk, the young attendant smiled and slipped an envelope across the cold marble countertop before I'd said a word. Apparently he'd been expecting me. Another young male, perhaps the concierge, watched from the nearby desk as I pulled a plastic access key and a thick square of the hotel's cardstock from the envelope. A note in Randolph's handwriting said, *Please wait in my room. So sorry to be late.* I touched the embossed hotel name and studied Randolph's one-word signature at the bottom: Weston.

In the elevator, my reflection revealed every angle of the diaphanous ankle-length empire gown, borrowed from costumes and accessorized with Bets's goth jewelry. It looked like something an actress would wear. Vera had thought to send a shawl, beneath which I shivered, cold and nervous. My Jane Austen slipped into the elevator behind me. Inserting the access card into the slot on the door handle, a frightening vision flashed before me: my new friend Weston waiting inside, naked in the bed. But the door opened to reveal a large silent room where an unoccupied bed waited in the soft yellow light of a table lamp. I closed the door and entered carefully. What if Randolph was one of those people who jump out and scare you, then think it's funny. Although the hotel was quite old, the room's furniture was contemporary and masculine. A framed photograph of a man laboring at a desk, perhaps the hotel's founder, hung on the wall. A bottle of mineral water from Blenheim Palace (home of Churchill) and a bowl of cherries (me) posed together on the bedside table. The digital clock said 7:38.

Unsure where to wait, the bed and a single chair provided limited seating options. When Randolph arrived, one of us would have to sit on the bed. I chose the chair. My Jane Austen hovered in the background with the drapes. I laid the business plan on the table next to a phone, a laptop, and personal papers. Seated, I smoothed my gown over my knees and began waiting. The clock read 7:41. What should I be doing when he arrived? What tableau should I create for his pleasure? *Woman Reading Scary Essay on Fanny Price* offered itself as a possibility, except I'd left my book at home. *Woman Reclining* seemed like a bad idea. Leave him wanting more. I glanced at the debris littering the table. Would I hear him before he opened the door? If I jumped he would think I had been snooping through his papers. How unromantic. But his personal things lay on the table for anyone to see: papers, envelopes, a portfolio. *Don't look*. I listened carefully for footsteps in the hall. Nothing.

The clock said 7:44. I wondered what he was doing, and with whom. Were there others besides Sara Stormont? Lots of others? It didn't seem so when we were together. Perhaps I would gain insight into this man's life if I looked at the papers on the table. Under those terms, it wouldn't be snooping. Of course it would. *Don't look*. 7:47 P.M. The room was so very quiet except for my beating heart.

My Jane Austen was creating another list. I was getting a little tired of her lists. Who was she to divide the world into good and bad? Where would her own name fall on one of her lists? "I don't even know you," I said to her. "You're not Jane Austen. Who are you and what are you doing in my head?"

I stood and walked to the bathroom. Oddly, this bathroom had no shower stall. The whole bathroom was the shower. A narrow slice of glass acted as barrier between sink and shower head but water would flow directly into the room. Unless the drain could work really fast, it appeared the room would flood with every shower. The sink offered no counters. No place for a woman's things. And the only electrical outlet was an oddly configured plug for "shavers only." Must be the Caveman Suite. I opened my tiny bag and pulled out my lipstick. Well—Bets's lipstick, I liked the color and Bets had abandoned it. Would he open the door and find me applying lipstick? I leaned in to examine myself in the mirror. Was that me? The real me or the fictional me? Willis would know. Some people understand you so clearly, and others just don't. Most don't. Why is that? I dropped the lipstick into my bag and drew it shut, then checked my breath and decided I could stand a mint, which I didn't have. Toothpaste. Surely he had toothpaste in here, but where? I looked for a Dopp kit but the maid had obviously cleaned; nothing lay about, no razor, toothbrush, or comb. Towels hung neatly folded. I imagined him opening the door just now and finding me embracing the chrome towel warmer for heat.

The last essay I'd read was still talking to me, saying, *Nobody falls in love with Fanny Price.* "Nonsense," I said to the mirror as I found toothpaste hiding behind shower gel. "Edmund falls in love with Fanny Price." I pointed to make sure the mirror understood. "I'm wrestling with this," I continued. "Don't tell me Edmund doesn't love her. I felt the chemistry. You felt it, too, Willis? That fizz of connection? Just curious: Do you feel it with Philippa?" I squirted a tiny dot of toothpaste on my finger and rubbed it around the inside of my mouth. What if I spit in his sink. Better not. But I could collapse in a puddle of Regency gauze and cry on the lovely caramel tile floor. "I miss you, Willis." My Jane Austen looked up from her corner. She seemed a bit dimmer, as if she might faint again.

I left the bathroom and struck a pose near the window where I could stare at the London night sky, eyes relaxing, casting the sparkling lights into a blur, wondering if Jane Austen had completely tricked me about *Mansfield Park*. "Did I miss something? Was I *supposed* to dislike Fanny Price?" I asked. "Was this your joke on us—designed to separate the lightweights?" But the black window made me feel abandoned and alone. Like the window at day care when I was five, waiting for my father to pick me up. Other parents had claimed their children and gone home for dinner and bedtime. My teacher and I waited alone, her purse and keys on her desk. Most of the lights were switched off and her lips pressed together as she searched the darkness for my dad's headlights. I watched her, feeling the deep isolation of the night, wishing my dad would come so she could go home. But my dad's real life happened somewhere else where the people were more important than me. I'd always known this. And because of the unimportance of me, my teacher had to wait.

7:51. Randolph should be here by now. I went back to my chair by the desk. Funny how the bathroom looked so neat and the table was such a mess. Perhaps the maid didn't touch papers. Or maybe he messed them after the maid cleaned. I looked in the trash can and found several crumpled papers indicating he had worked in here *after* the maid cleaned. *Woman Examining the Evidence:*

"And where were you at 7:51 on the evening of the eighth of August?"

"I solemnly swear I spent the evening in Lord Weston's hotel room, going through his trash."

The phone rang and I jumped. The moment of truth. Should I answer? Two rings. 7:53. My pulse raced. What if Randolph was calling me? If a woman answers, hang up. My Jane Austen and I watched like cats as the ringing stopped, another sound took its place, and paper ratcheted into a printer. The fax machine zipped into action, feeding the paper into the waiting trough. My Jane Austen read the paper as it spooled through the printer. Could I read his faxes? No. But I could read his trash. Trash is considered public domain.

I stopped talking to myself, proceeded directly to the trash can, lifted the three crumpled balls from the bottom, and recognized the sensation of seeking painful truth. Where was my dad when I waited all those nights in the dark day care center? If she knew, my mother never told me. She put me in the car and drove in silence, the green freeway signs communicating distance. I feigned sleep, imagining the story of her grief.

Shaking, I dropped the three crumpled balls on my lap. One fell to the floor. I didn't even look at the time. No time to look at the time. The first trash item was a pink carbon copy of a claim check from a tailor, Savile Row. Name rings a bell. The second trash item was a phone message from Chris, no last name, no call back number. I recrumpled the two trash items, and rethrew them into the bin. I fished the last ball off the floor and smoothed it in my lap. A transmission report from the fax machine. 14:38. I endured the snarky glare of the fax machine on military time. I threw the last ball back into the trash. I'd made no progress in my quest for insight. But having crossed the line into reading trash, I felt compelled to move on to bigger things. 8:01. Time flew. The idea that a paper in this room would tell me everything I needed to know about Randolph Weston and the role I played in his life consumed me.

Or did I seek a hit of familiar pain?

8:05. *Woman Reading Personal Papers*. I helped myself to the personal papers on the table. A bill from Pratt's. Bank statement (still in the sealed envelope). An invitation to a dinner benefiting the Osteopathic Centre for Children, a newsletter still folded from Alliance of Independent Retailers, a fax from Tony Palmer Investments "looking forward to meeting on Tuesday." I carefully restored every paper to its exact original position.

No dance card, no love letter, no broken engagement. Nothing about me. 8:11. I sat perfectly still, but my heart pounded, blood raced through my veins, thoughts skittered in all directions. Looking up, I saw the girl from Texas reflected in the mirror on the opposite wall. *What are you doing here?* I asked her. *Do you crave love or pain and are they the same thing to you?* She leaned over and lifted the fax out of the trough. Reading, she found a listing agreement for Newton Priors signed by Tony Palmer.

This wasn't my novel. I wasn't the protagonist. I was a secondary character hidden in the hotel room. Sara Stormont didn't know about me. I was the secret; the bad surprise that ruins the main character's day—the mad woman in the attic, the villain destined for a disastrous end. 8:21.

The door opened and I jumped.

My tableau was realized: *Crazed Woman Sitting on Chair*. "Hullo, Lily."

Randolph smiled at me. "Did I frighten you?" he asked, very handsome in his black tie, in spite of his hair loss.

My hand flew to my heart and I assumed an innocent

smile. "Hullo, Wes— Randolph." A man who considered his opportunities, of course he would entertain listing agreements. He hadn't signed anything. Perhaps I had been wrong again. I extended a hand and he pulled me into an embrace. He smelled of alcohol and I sensed myself numbing, the walls blurring into once upon a time. Letting go of me, he loosened his tie. "What a bore, knowing you were here, waiting." He tore the tie out of his tuxedo shirt—eyes on me—and tossed it into the lap of the other chair. "You look lovely," he said.

What would it be like—beloved of an English lord? We were slipping into the faux familiarity again, conveniently holed up in the Royal Bachelor Pad. I watched to see if he would stop with the tie as My Jane Austen asked, *What about dinner? What about the business plan?* Sitting on the bed, he touched a panel on the bedside table and a soft electronic buzz sounded as a very large television emerged from the surface of the desk. *The 007 Suite.* He touched again and the drapes began to close, flushing My Jane Austen from her hiding place. He switched on the TV and a cricket match filled the screen.

"Aren't you hungry?" I asked, standing midway between the bed and the TV.

"Only for you, love," he said, eyes on the cricket match.

"I thought we were going to dinner," I said, touching my elegant dress.

"I'm sorry, I've eaten. But we could call for room service," he said, fondling the remote. Randolph removed cuff links and studs, placing them on the surface of the bureau. He threw the shirt and tie onto the chair and then looked at me, his chest bare. Obviously, I was dinner. He held his arms open and I knew if I went to him, I would lose My Jane Austen. "I appear far more committed to this relationship than you," he whispered, referring to his state of undress.

The slightly aloof prince. I crave this. Part of me wanted

to go to him and see what it would be like—happily ever after with an English lord. What if this was the real thing—or could become the real thing? If I backed out now he would be mad at me. My Jane Austen grew withered and pale, less vivid every moment, fading while I stressed. She chose that moment to turn her completed list so I could see it, but I already knew what the list said. She'd written across the top: "Lily's Life." And made two columns: one for protagonists, and another for secondary characters. The list of protagonists in my life was very long, among them Sara Stormont. But the list of secondary characters was short; only one name and it was mine: Lily Berry, playing herself over and over in other peoples' lives. When I backed away, my shawl fell to the ground and My Jane Austen vanished. Gone. I bent to retrieve the shawl and restore it to my shoulders but she didn't reappear. I kept blinking hopefully, searching for her in my peripheral vision. Whoever she was, a projection of myself, my mother, bits of the great writer thrown in, she never returned after that moment.

Randolph worked around my shawl, "What do you look like under all this?" he whispered, searching for the zipper of my gown. He found the secret seam under my armpit. He held at the top and tugged with his other hand. "Any calls while I was out?" He smiled, removing my sleeves from my shoulders, but had to stop there since I crossed my arms in front of me. "Lovely." He bent to kiss the breasts bulging over my folded arms. I held my clothes on, resisting the urge to fall into this familiar place, to please a virtual stranger. And things around me weren't transforming. My shoes wouldn't stop being real. The chair and desk remained firmly real and the bowl of cherries sat there slowly rotting. I felt a little pressure behind my eyes, a touch of nausea, and I began to understand how I would feel when this ended.

"Just one call," I answered automatically, before registering his smile and the joke that he was undressing his secretary. "But it was a fax."

He grew sober and left me to fetch his fax. I pulled the gown back over my shoulders as Randolph lifted the paper from the fax trough. The soft light shone on the floral bedspread, recalling the chintz sofa where my mother read to me. Here I was at last, the roses, the soft light, and the prince, all for me. Randolph pursed his lips the way Omar did when he read books on Shaw, the way Willis did when he typed. Randolph signed the paper and loaded it back into the fax machine. He looked up the number and pressed the buttons. The signed document went flying back to Tony Palmer. Then he stood and removed his trousers, throwing them on the chair. "Come now, forget about all that." He reached for me, "Let me help you out of that tangle of clothes."

He would sell Newton Priors. Without even telling me. He pulled the floral bedspread down, the prince bedding Rapunzel. My mother knew. Of course she knew.

"Come now, forget about all that," Randolph repeated, reaching for my hand, no longer smiling. But without "all that" I was just a face, just a body—how little he understood me; my total lack of artifice. I wasn't Rapunzel and he wasn't the prince. Everything about me was the same as always and I could see that after this ended, I would feel bad. Randolph took the shawl from my arms and tossed it at the foot of the bed. Tears pooled in my eyes as I stood, confused. He sat on the bed and searched my face, clearly at a loss with my behavior. But I was *better* than Maria Bertram, who fell for Henry Crawford every time we played the scene. We play it over and over, five times a week, and she never evaluates her situation; she never thinks about approaching her life with a different end in mind. She can't learn from her mistakes because she is nothing but ink on a page. Fanny Price got in my head. *A sensible girl would flee.* Sounded so familiar, my own words, unheeded again and again. *Fear like yours is not normal.*

"Is something wrong?" Randolph asked.

"Yes," I said. "I'm not a professional actress."

"I know. I Googled you; you're an address in Texas," he said. "Vera's little friend." I remembered now: The Look Randolph and Philippa had shared across the hospital bed when Vera announced I was an actress. The information held particular significance for the three of them. He reached to pull down my sleeves, but I grabbed his hands and pushed them to his lap, holding them there. "We don't know each other," I said. Reaching for the zipper of my gown, I pulled up, catching tender flesh. I saw myself returning my Regency gowns to the costume wardrobe, folding the undergarments and tucking them into their drawer before Suzanne arrived. "You're going to sell Newton Priors, aren't you?" I said.

He smiled, falling back on a pillow, his palm on his forehead. "Do you *really* care?"

"I care very much. So do Nigel and Vera and a lot of others."

He sighed, staring at the ceiling, and I recognized the look of someone planning the best way to deliver bad news to me. "The truth is I can't afford Literature Live," he said, sober. "My accountant has reviewed everything, including your ideas, and advised me to sell the estate if I want to avoid ruin."

"When were you planning to tell us?" I asked.

He paused, rubbing his temples. "Perhaps this is a disappointment to you. But, believe me, Nigel has known for some time." He turned on his side, propping his head on his elbow, patting the bed next to him. "I want you," he said.

I threw the shawl around my shoulders and gathered my business plan. "No," I said.

"That's it? The house is out—so now you're going?"

"Of course not." I could see myself leaving this hotel and leaving Newton Priors, as if I stood on the roof watching myself go, a normal girl. "I've realized something that actually has nothing to do with you."

"So we can still have fun together."

"I'm afraid not." I lifted Vera's fringed bag from the chair, willing to concede a civil good-bye, sparing bridges for the good of the organization. But then he wrapped his arms around a pillow and lowered his voice to a whisper.

"Just think what you can tell your friends when you get home."

I walked to the door and paused; turning to face him, I saw his cell phone in his hand. He slipped it behind his thigh and out of my view, assuming an innocent expression when our eyes met for the last time. "Call me when you grow up," I said. I walked out before he could punch the next girl's number in my presence. 9:06 P.M. *Texas Girl Escapes London Hotel.*

Twenty-seven

*V*era answered her door. "Lily, you're back," she said; a bright smile lit her face, the room behind her somber, perhaps kept dark for Nigel's benefit.

"Can I come in?" I asked. I'd had enough time alone in the station and on the train to be conflicted over everything that had seemed so neatly resolved when it happened. Now that I had to deliver the bad news to Vera, I considered returning to the scene of the crime and retrading the deal for her sake, offering my body for a lease agreement. Anything but inform her that Newton Priors—Literature Live for the past thirty years—was gone.

"You can't imagine how distracted I've been, thinking of you, wondering how it went with Randolph," she said, searching my face for a sign.

"Not well, I'm afraid." The dream had ended not only for Nigel, but for me. The train ride to Hedingham was my last trip "home" to the festival. Next time, home would be Texas.

My new self would return to my old self, even though my old environment no longer fit. Back to a job in a gray cubicle where people don't care what Jane Austen thinks. No lectures, no scenes, no endless stacks of books. My Jane Austen would melt in Texas.

Vera dimmed her tone. "Is there a problem? Come in," she said, arching her eyebrows as she opened the door enough for me to enter. Clearly, I had never been invited into Vera's rooms because a visitor had no place to go. Things cluttered all horizontal surfaces of the tiny apartment used by a dorm mother during the school year. Boxes of Nigel's worldly goods filled the room awaiting further instructions. Perhaps without Literature Live, Nigel would be homeless, like me. The bedroom door remained shut but pillows and blankets lay on the sofa, a good indication of where Vera had slept all summer. I moved a box to the floor, making room for myself on a chair.

Vera sat among blankets on the sofa, her lips pursed. "So, we're all going home, are we?" she asked, not meeting my eyes, fidgeting with the hem of her blanket. Blinds closed, a cockeyed lampshade directed light onto Vera's lap where a book would usually sit. A tablet of paper—Vera had been composing a list with Claire's name at the top—sat on the lamp table. Crumpled paper, distractingly similar to the trash I'd recently searched, littered the table. The suitcase she dragged through Heathrow waited near the wall.

"*I* am," I said.

Inhaling deeply, she shaded her eyes, and I noticed a tremor in her little finger. "What went wrong?" she asked.

Her question implied I'd messed up the drills she'd carefully taught me. Anger released a hit of adrenaline. "It's not about anything going wrong," I said, a bit too loud, noting the crux of the problem with Vera—always insisting dissimilar things fit together, her own brand of reckless creativity. "It simply wasn't meant to be," I said. "*Ever.*" If I was not careful, I would break down. Not about Randolph, but the whole summer, about the lost possibility of connecting with an ideal life. I tried to remember how I had planned to tell her about the house but I lost my way and then the door opened and Nigel walked in.

Vera raised her hand. "Lily's back."

"Hullo, Lily." I was sorry he was here; now I'd have to deliver the bad news to both of them.

"There's a message from John Owen on your bureau," Vera said, sitting up straight, moving her blankets to make room for Nigel on the sofa. "But come and sit now." She patted the cushion next to her. Nigel opened the little refrigerator in the tiny kitchen casting light into the room. All those years of working to build an organization; who was I to tell him it had ended? Surely, someone could find another house.

"What, Lily? Tell us what happened." Vera's arm braced the sofa. Nigel concentrated on the refrigerator's interior as I did whenever the nurse gave me a shot; don't look and it will soon be over.

"Randolph's accountant has advised him to sell Newton Priors; he has hired a broker."

Vera struck herself in the heart. "I can't believe it," she said.

"Yes," Nigel said, his face still turned away.

"We assumed"—Vera clutched her throat—"that Randolph would require changes, perhaps even major changes in funding and direction such as Magda had pushed, but I never really anticipated he'd sell the house from under us."

"I did," Nigel said, retreating to his bedroom, closing the door behind him.

Vera leaned forward. "What happened with Randolph?"

she asked, her eyes narrowed, seeking a place to lay the blame. "He asked if restoring old houses was the sort of thing you wanted to do, only a few days ago." She frowned. "He seemed so interested."

"Interested yes," I said. "In one thing."

"But he invited you to dinner. What happened to make him change so quickly?"

I stared at her. "He Googled me."

"Really."

"You told him I was an actress, remember? He discovered the truth."

"So much has changed since I was your age," she said, backing off now that her share in the crime lay exposed. "I don't understand romance these days."

"No, Vera," I said. "Things have not changed. They never change. Have you read Jane Austen?" I asked. "Inheritance laws change but human nature *never* does. Even dead, Jane Austen understands that." My voice grew too loud as desperation crept in. Why was Vera's recklessness only now clear to me? I deserved blame for not reading her more closely. "You knew. But you fed me to him anyway, like a throwaway orphan, hoping he'd let you stay in the house a few more years."

"Lily, what are you talking about?" Vera's face became ugly. "I wanted this for *you*." She spoke very slowly. "I desired with all my heart that it would work out for you—*somehow*—this time."

Tears came and I felt hopelessly tangled in my own losses.

"Lily," Vera said, rising, coming to my side.

I held up my hand. "Don't talk to me," I said. She tried to put her arm around me but I stood.

"We're all upset," Vera said as I walked out.

★ ★ ★

The next night I had dinner with Omar. Tomorrow, he would be gone, along with Archie, Magda, Bets, and Willis. And My Jane Austen. We met in the pub, Omar looking spiffier than usual in an oxford cloth shirt, his rough hair watered down and combed.

"I brought you something." He handed a book across the table.

"Omar, how sweet," I said, regretting I had not thought of a gift for him. I read the cover. *English Manor Houses.* "It will remind me of our summer," I said, aware it wasn't a straight-forward gift; some irony existed that I was too anxious to grasp.

"Read the inscription." Omar smiled so hard his cheeks pushed his eyes into little slits behind his glasses. He waited for the punch line to occur to me, optimistic that it would.

> *To Lily,*
> *Repeat often:*
> *People live in houses, not novels.*
> *People live in houses, not novels.*
> *Omar*

"Very funny," I said, failing to match his mirth, turning the pages. I wouldn't be able to focus on the gift until much later, alone in Texas. We walked to Newton Priors and sat on the steps of the house in the twilight. "I once assumed Jane Austen was mistress of a grand house like this," I said. "One of my early mistaken impressions."

"Now you know," Omar said, smiling.

"Wouldn't you love to see all the letters Cassandra destroyed?" I asked. "Knowing what she *really* thought might solve your Jane Austen problem."

"Nah, I'd be disappointed, as usual." Omar shrugged.

"Probably," I agreed.

We were watching bats fly overhead, little black specks that surely slept in my attic during the day, when Mrs. Russell appeared. I almost missed her, dressed as she was in twenty-first-century jeans. "We're saying good-bye to the house," I said.

"Oh my dear," she said. "You'll miss the ball."

"The ball?"

"You didn't hear? Nigel called me last night and I rushed right over"—she indicated her attire—"dressed as I was"—she covered her mouth—"with a toothbrush in my purse." She laughed confidentially. "I slept upstairs last night," she said. "I've no time to turn around. The ball's Sunday and we're all pitching in to make it happen."

"I'm so glad," I said. "You've worked for it so long." Nigel's parting gift to the volunteers.

"Now or never." Mrs. Russell shrugged and I realized how alike she and I were, each of us projecting ourselves into dead Jane Austen. Mrs. Russell's need illuminated my own need to create my personal heroine. The real Jane Austen was unknowable. She was not the creature of perfection the family memoirs put forth, their lack of particulars allowing us to imagine her in our own image. I considered giving Mrs. Russell a copy of Magda's textbook.

"You know what I think I learned this summer?" I said, after Mrs. Russell left us.

"You can act," Omar said.

"Besides that."

"What?" Omar turned to face me, expecting something really interesting.

"I think I'd never make it in a Jane Austen novel; the experience might be worse than real life."

"Congratulations, Dorothy. You can tap your ruby slippers and go home now," Omar said.

"For example," I said, setting the book on the step in front of me and hugging myself in the evening chill, "Henry Crawford could crook his little finger and I would be a ruined woman before the story had a chance to begin."

"No you wouldn't," Omar said. "Not anymore."

I turned to look at Newton Priors in the waning light. How long would its details remain crisp in my mind? How would it appear from the distance of my humble gray cubicle? "I used to imagine myself as the protagonist in every novel I read," I said.

"Don't we all? Hard work being a protagonist."

"You can say that again."

"Hard work being a protagonist."

I socked him in the arm.

Omar smiled big and patted my knee. "Lily, I'm going to miss you."

"I'm going to miss you, too, Omar." My eyes filled with tears.

Omar departed for Michigan; I didn't see him again. I had hoisted my suitcase onto my bed packing everything I would not need before departure, when a knock sounded on my door.

"Can I come in?" Vera asked, her voice flowing over the transom. We had not spoken since my meltdown and I knew we needed to reconcile before I left. I'd been rehearsing potential lines in my head. Vera sat across from me on Bets's bare mattress, and from the way she leaned forward I sensed she had an agenda.

"What will you do, Lily?"

"I'm going home peacefully," I said. "I'll probably stay with my friend Lisa until I get a job," I added.

"But what will you *do* there?" Vera repeated, irritation in her voice I found out of place, considering.

"I haven't figured that out yet," I said. "For starters, I'll probably gather courage to deal with my new wicked step-mother and then hope a gray cubicle offers me a paycheck and benefits." I waited. "Why are you asking?"

"I've been thinking," Vera said. "And I have a couple of ideas." I watched from my bed as Vera stared into middle space. "The first idea is rather ambitious, really." She looked at me. "Perhaps we could move this whole thing to Biblio-phile Books—do it in Dallas." Vera's eternal creative opti-mism surprised me as she waited for my reaction, the old spark waiting to connect.

"Produce Literature Live in your bookstore?" Perhaps the problem was not Vera alone. Perhaps the combination of her eternal creative optimism with my indiscriminate hopeful longing equaled danger. She hadn't meant me harm; she was reckless and I was naive. I sat up straight. "You're right," I said, "that's very ambitious."

"Yes." Vera rested her chin on her fist. "And I'm needed here," she said, looking at her feet, clearly expecting me to understand her meaning.

"Is Nigel okay?" I asked.

"No," Vera whispered. She looked up and shook her head, eyes glistening.

"I'm sorry," I said, my voice catching, my own eyes filling with tears. Perhaps I'd used her just as much as she had used me, casting her as my new mother, expecting her to lead me to a safe place where I could belong to someone again.

"I can't keep him alive, no matter what I do, no matter how hard I wish it away," she said, clearly worn down by the resis-tance campaign she'd mounted over the last months.

"I'm so sorry," I repeated.

"Nigel is going to stay in Hedingham and I would like to stay with him," she said, stopping to compose herself. "You know"—Vera looked at the ceiling, wiping her tears with her hand—"our marriage wasn't ideal," she said, "but I never imagined being in the world without him. And I'm quite beside myself."

I searched my drawers for a tissue. "Is there anything I can do to help?" I asked, handing her a towel I pulled out of my suitcase.

"Well," Vera said, wiping her eyes, "that brings me to my second idea." She paused. "And that is—why don't you manage Bibliophile Books for me?"

I imagined leaving my gray cubicle to spend entire workdays in the stacks.

"You remind me so much of myself at your age," Vera said. "You know, I married Nigel with the understanding I'd never have children. But if I'd had a daughter, I'd want her to be like you."

"Thank you," I said, touched by the tribute, but still thinking about a day job surrounded by books, talking about books, touching books; freely reading through my lunch hour. Working in a bookstore would be an all-day party with a diverse guest list: Natasha Rostov and Prince Andrei, Daisy Miller and Miss Havisham, Nick Adams and Captain Wentworth. Jane Austen might join us.

She looked at her hands. "Nigel and I will be sorting through the books here, deciding which to send to the store," Vera said.

I imagined Nigel ending his days scanning the titles of hundreds of books, opening his favorites and reading a line to Vera, saying good-bye to old friends. I thought of them sharing this distraction, quite happy, in a way I didn't have the experience to understand.

"Some will be sent to Texas as inventory for the store. It would be very helpful if you could be on the other end to receive them. Chutney can't cope with large shipments."

I imagined Chutney sneaking out to the Dumpster after hours, tossing entire boxes of musty books into its pit. "I would love to," I said. "What a privilege."

"You know," Vera said, "when the books started coming in, he gave them all to me. He never said so, but I think the books are my compensation."

I would have to think about that.

"And Lily," she said, fixing my attention. "I'm sorry for the way things went with Randolph."

"Oh, Vera."

"It was a farfetched idea." She stood and reached for my hand. "And I was being very selfish."

Without considering, I used my best British accent and channeled Mary Crawford, "Selfishness must always be forgiven you know, because there is no hope of a cure."

"Touché," Vera said.

Twenty-eight

$\mathscr{B}$ack in Texas, I drove through my former neighborhood, air-conditioning turned full blast. The changes in the season of my absence shocked me. The med student's little duplex on the left now sat vacant awaiting the bulldozer. A developer's sign in the next yard indicated imminent demolition, and a McMansion was going up where my duplex had existed, its construction begun during the summer. Gone were the casual days of twin porches offering two doors, two mailboxes, and two free neighborhood newspapers. The new regime dressed up; urgent flaming carriage lanterns and buxom petunia beds flanked solo porches whose portals could grace a temple. Titanic SUVs posed in driveways begged me to ask, *What master of the universe dwelt therein?* A Hispanic nanny pushed a double stroller out a front door.

I drove slowly past my dad's house, taking note of the "For Sale by Owner" sign in his yard. Dad always said doing it yourself was the way *not* to sell your house. Maybe he wasn't so keen to move.

I lived in Vera's apartment over the bookstore, managing the store by day, and reading from the unlimited supply of books in the evenings. Having sold my possessions before leaving for England, except for the box of keepsakes still locked in the trunk of my car, I kept remembering my things the way an amputee would remember a lost limb. *It's in my closet*, and then I would remember I gutted that closet and I didn't live there anymore. I had no clothes and no costume department to raid for just the right outfit.

I visited Karen and her family and we worked through our grief together, sorting through what china and photos she was able to save from the wreckage. Karen helped me with my project to donate copies of all my lost books to the Pediatric Oncology Ward of the Children's Hospital. We inscribed them in honor of our mother and whenever I had a new set to deliver, I arrived with enough time to read to whatever seven-year-old child, nauseated from chemo, felt well enough to listen to a story about twelve little girls in two straight lines or a monkey calling the fire department. I would pause briefly to compose myself each time I recognized my mother's voice.

Vera and I e-mailed regularly but the flood of new inventory required overseas phone calls for guidance. Several estates had donated books over the summer, and Chutney had parked boxes wherever she could find space, stacking books in the upstairs apartment when she ran out of room in the store. And now that Vera was shipping from Literature Live, we were drowning in books. Boxes piled in the aisles required narrow canals to travel to the cash register or my office.

"How are you, Lily?" she asked.

I immediately choked up. I'd declined my friend Lisa's happy hour invitation in order to be alone with a stack of musty books culled from the boxes of new arrivals—the smell of Newton Priors in their pages. Lisa would never understand falling in love with a clergyman I met in a deserted attic where we discussed his vampire novel-in-progress while My Jane Austen took notes.

"Lily? Are you there?"

"Yes. I'm here."

"Are you okay?"

"I'm fine," I said, knowing she could hear the sharp intake of breath, even if she couldn't see the tears, "just lonely."

Vera sighed. "Did you call any of your old friends?"

"Yes," I lied, twisting the phone cord around my finger.

"Well, I suppose it will take some time to find your way," Vera said.

Omar e-mailed as promised, attaching an application to a dual MFA/MBA degree offered by the University of Michigan. So glad to hear from him, I responded immediately, asking how Magda's seminar was going, but he must have been busy because he didn't write back. Hearing from Omar brought a rush of memories from the summer. I felt homesick for Newton Priors and My Jane Austen summer. But she'd surely gone to someone who needed her presence—the reader experiencing the shock of separation after finishing Number Six for the first time, an agony I understand clearly. And regardless, her books are with me always—in my office, near my reading lamp in the apartment, and at least one in the car for those moments I need to hear her voice—timeless and sparkling, swirling in my subconscious, folded into my existence.

I was thinking of calling Omar, just to hear his voice, when his e-mail arrived. This time his message brought a far more interesting attachment: a picture from the *London Times*, Court and Society Pages. "Hey, what's up with your old friend?" Omar wrote, and I could almost hear the snark in his voice. I read the caption, *Sheila Bates and Peter Davidson celebrate Ziva's birthday at the Tate Modern*. I'd never heard of these people and puzzled that Omar sent it to me until I recognized a familiar face in the middle ground. There, in strapless splendor, posing next to a giant apple core sculpture, was none other than Philippa Lockwood. My heart raced because the tuxedoed man at her side, his hand possessing her bare arm, his mouth open to speak, was not Willis. If My Jane Austen were here she would be looking over my shoulder, suggesting Pippa might simply be chatting with a mystery man while Willis fetched drinks from the bar.

"Lucky for you, I keep up with the foreign press," Omar wrote.

Foreign gossip, I said to myself.

"*Mansfield Park* belongs to so many people and can be read on so many levels," I said to the Bibliophile Book Club regulars seated around the table for our January meeting. Magda loomed heroic now, so safely distant I was willing to entertain the possibility that Jane Austen might have been experimenting in Romanticism when she wrote *Mansfield Park*.

"Slavery, feminism, and incest?" Michael asked, tossing his girlfriend The Look as if I'd exceeded their expectations this time. Michael, formerly a drummer, spent mornings on his laptop writing a book, borrowing from the stacks for his research. He watched all of us, seeking material for his characters. Occasionally I offered him new words from the summer: *mindful*, *knickers*, and *bad form*.

"Feminism, I love it!" Charlotte, the former actress-turned-single-mother spoke rapidly, as if her babysitter might expire before she articulated her thoughts. "I can live without the incest and slavery, however."

"I always wanted to live in *Mansfield Park*," I said, remembering how Willis said he once wanted to live in a book called *The Pirate's Cove*.

Avery the psychiatrist, who sometimes missed meetings due to emergencies, spoke directly at me, his highlighter paused mid-flip. "What do you mean, Lily?"

"Aren't some characters so real you feel as if you could slip into their lives?" I asked before turning to the group. "Hasn't anyone ever wanted to live in a novel?"

Julia shook her prenuptial curls and adjusted her engagement ring. "I wouldn't want to trade my life."

"You would always know what was going to happen next." Charlotte smiled at me apologetically.

If Omar were present he'd speak up to sharpen the point he'd made giving me the book about English manor houses. I could hear him. *You don't want to* live *in a novel*, he would say. *You want to* hide *in a novel. You say you want to experience the passion of life, but you camouflage yourself in ink and paper. Connect* yourself, *Lily*.

I wanted to warn Avery that his brow, furrowed so deeply, might freeze like that.

Charlotte looked at her watch.

"Actually, I don't think it would be much fun to live in a novel, either," I said. "Inasmuch as I can get into Jane Austen's mind—at least my interpretation of her mind—I can never get anyone else in there with me. And that is the problem. Life in a novel is a lonely proposition."

★ ★ ★

When I finally ran into Willis, it was midnight and I was lying in bed with a publisher's catalogue. Almost a year in Dallas, I'd settled into my job, books no longer filled my apartment or obstructed the paths of the store. But spending so much energy arranging *old* books, we hadn't taken time to order *new* books. Vera, still in England, suggested I investigate the catalogues clogging my in-box and place some orders. But these days, I was more concerned with the Amazon in the living room and how little indies like us might avoid getting swept under the carpet.

As I kicked off my covers, enjoying the open windows, soon to be shut for the summer, my gaze snagged a title at the top of the page. *Vampire Priest.* I sat up to focus the words under my reading lamp. *Debut fiction by Willis Somerford: a vampire priest hides his curse from his beloved and ultimately must sacrifice either his love or her mortality.* I clutched my throat and read it again. Descending to the dark office, I checked online and learned that Willis's book had been published two weeks earlier. Looking the other way, I clicked the one-day delivery option.

When the slim brown box arrived, I left Chutney in charge of Vera's empire and locked my apartment door. Once the phones were silenced and Vera's floral quilt dragged to the sofa, I sat shivering beneath the warm glow of the reading lamp, nervous, as if I might meet Willis in the flesh after all this time. I tore open the box and removed the brand-new hardback. The perfectly smooth dust jacket featured two people dressed in black: a man whose head is cropped just above his priest collar and a woman playing a cello. *Vampire Priest* by Willis M. Somerford. The stiff binding and crisp title page offered subtle resistance as I turned to the dedication:

To Lily, who dreams of living in a novel

I heard the words in his voice. The essence of Willis emerged from the blurry distance, recalling his powerful attraction, the joy I'd found in my own life through him. Pressure started in my chest and pushed like a hot wave into my head, leaving my eyes wet and my throat aching. As I turned pages, Willis spoke to me through the story of two people who sounded much more like Lily and Willis than they had when I'd read the pages on his screen last summer. Luna plays Bach in F Minor for Father Kitt, the same music I'd played on the old record player for Willis that day in the music room. She seeks Father Kitt after every concert, oblivious to the fact she's fallen for a vampire. On a backstage tour of the dark music hall after closing, she lures him to the undercroft and asks, *"How long must we know each other before our relationship can move forward?"*

Father Kitt is dangerously tempted by the hope of sharing his immortal doom . . . *"She has no idea how I burn to be with her, how close I am to marking her as my own forever."* Tortured by the guilt of his deception, he tells her, *"I'm not strong enough to resist you."* But when she tells him she loves him, he remains silent. In anger, she announces she won't wait for him, but will leave to tour with the orchestra at the end of the symphony season. Desperately torn, he watches from his seat in the audience, seeing her for the last time, knowing he cannot allow Luna to forfeit her soul, to make the irrevocable decision to become something she could not possibly anticipate. Afraid of losing his resolve, he leaves the concert hall before the performance ends and returns to lonely despair.

He never meets her again. But even so, he never stops feeling her presence.

Long after her life reached its mortal end, she still comes to find me at the musicians' entrance. Wisps of brown hair blow across her eyes, her smile beckons me inside—a timeless, sparkling memory, swirling in my subconscious, folded into my existence. And every time I find her at the stage door, I tell her I love her.

Willis Somerford lives in London. Vampire Priest *is his first novel.*

After a long while, faint sounds of life rose from the bookstore below.

Selected Bibliography

Austen, Jane. *Mansfield Park: Authoritative Text, Contexts, Criticism*. Claudia L. Johnson, ed. New York: W. W. Norton & Co., 1998.

Fleishman, Avrom. *A Reading of Mansfield Park: An Essay in Critical Synthesis*. Baltimore and London: Johns Hopkins Press, 1970.

Le Faye, Deirdre, ed. *Jane Austen's Letters*. New York: Oxford University Press, 1995.

Persuasions: The Jane Austen Journal, no. 28. Susan Allen Ford, ed. Jane Austen Society of North America, www .jasna.org.

Tomalin, Claire. *Jane Austen: A Life*. New York: Alfred A. Knopf, 1998.

Wiltshire, John. *Jane Austen: Introductions and Interventions*. New York: Palgrave Macmillan, 2006.

Wiltshire, John. *Recreating Jane Austen*. New York: Cambridge University Press, 2001.

Acknowledgments

Many people helped launch my debut novel. I am fortunate that Mike Lankford was my first serious writing teacher. For careful reading and comments, I thank: Kathleen Kent, Bill Swart, and Ellen Moody. Many thanks to my writing groups: Jana Swart, Erin Burdette, Larry Campbell, and Brett Levy. For helpful assistance: Shilpi Gowda, Lori Reisenbichler, Cindy Corpier, Lori Ingram, Deborah Sundermann, Sarah Lunzer, Will Clarke, Amy Bourret, Bob Jones, Leslie Callahan, Philip Theophilus, and Alma Garcia. For the trip: Justus Sundermann.

I am grateful for everything The Writers' League of Texas and The Squaw Valley Community of Writers offer aspiring writers. The online discussions groups, Austen-L and Janeites, were a constant source of information and I have learned much from my association with the Jane Austen Society of North America.

I am grateful to my wise and talented agent, Laura

Rennert, for patient guidance, and to my unflappable and enthusiastic editor, Lucia Macro. Esi Sogah and the team at Avon/HarperCollins have been an absolute pleasure to work with. Thanks to my parents, Dan and Sally Sundermann, with extra gratitude to my mother for reading multiple drafts. Love and appreciation to my sons: George, Daniel, William, and Robert. I would not be thanking anyone were it not for my husband, George, who is also my best friend, first reader, and the person who goes to work every day so I can write.

A+
AUTHOR
INSIGHTS,
EXTRAS &
MORE...

FROM

CINDY JONES

AND

WM

WILLIAM MORROW

Your Private Austen:
Six Steps to a Closer Walk with Jane

Prerequisite to friendship. You must read all six novels. The films are beautiful adaptations but they lack the sparkling narrative that is the essence of Jane Austen. Choose your edition and start reading—or rereading.

Step 1: Getting to know Jane Austen. Not easy since her relatives enforced a posthumous rebranding, establishing Aunt Jane as a saint. Contemporary biographies do a good job of bringing her to life, conveying an awareness of her poverty and dependence, and describing the struggle of her homeless years. Imagine Jane Austen hand-carrying hard copies of her unpublished manuscripts each time she moved. The story of how she nearly married a man she didn't love in order to have food and shelter will establish instant sympathy.

Jane Austen: A Life by Claire Tomalin.
Jane Austen: A Life by David Nokes.

Step 2: Trade confidences. Consider your favorite Austen novel and listen to what she has been saying to you between the lines of her text. For instance, my favorite is *Mansfield Park:* Jane Austen and I totally agree that it is hard to be Fanny Price in a Mary Crawford world. And we both believe that men should fall deeply in love with intelligent wallflowers.

Which Jane Austen heroine are you?
Which novel would you choose to live in?

Step 3: **Do things together**. Become a Janeite. Join the Jane Austen Society of North America (JASNA) and get involved in the activities of your local chapter. Or visit Jane in England. Gaze upon her writing desk, walk where she walked, find her grave in the floor of Winchester Cathedral, and knock on her door in Bath. Dress in period attire and celebrate at one of the many Jane Austen festivals around the world:

Jane Austen Society of North America: www.jasna.org
Jane Austen Festival in Bath: www.janeausten.co.uk
Jane Austen's House Museum:
    www.jane-austens-house-museum.org.uk
Jane Austen Festival in Louisville, Kentucky:
    www.jasnalouisville.com
Old Mandeville Jane Austen Festival in Louisiana:
    www.janeaustenfestival.org
Jane Austen Festival in Pittsburgh: www.janeaustenpgh.org
Jane Fest in Fresno, California: www.jasnacenvalcal.com
Jane Austen Festival in Australia:
    www.janeaustenfestival.com.au

Step 4: Get obsessed. To get even closer, find out what Jane Austen *really* thought; read her correspondence. Discover what she *really* meant when she wrote the novels; read the criticism. Find out what other people are saying about *their* Jane Austens; lurk online and listen to discussion groups. Surf the Web, subscribe to blogs, friend her on Facebook. She's everywhere!

www.austenauthors.com (cooperative blog for Austen-inspired
    authors)
www.pemberley.com (good starting place, see the links page)
Austen-L Discussion Group/Archives at McGill University
Janeites Discussion Group/Yahoo

Step 5: Bear the inevitable disappointment. If some of Jane's letters seem mean-spirited, if the criticism contradicts beliefs you hold dear about your favorite novels as well as their author's intent, and if it appears that Other People's Jane Austens are completely unrelated to yours, it may be time to pull back. If you have begun to fear Your Jane Austen is laughing *at you* for wanting to be her best friend, you should probably give the relationship a break. Reconsider the Brontës. Or read something from a current best-seller list.

Step 6: Establish boundaries. Don't give up. Reconcile the person who traded secrets with you in Step 2 with the Irritable Supernova reconciled in Step 5 and remind yourself that Jane Austen is dead, therefore unknowable. What *is* knowable is the sparkling narrative, the wit and irony, and the joy that comes with every reading of The Six. Allow distance for the real Jane Austen, whoever she was, to rest in peace. The novels live forever.

Questions and Answers

Where did this story come from?

My Jane Austen Summer started when I read a review of Karen Joy Fowler's *The Jane Austen Book Club* in the *New York Times Book Review* years ago. The review inspired me to reread all six Austen novels, saving Fowler's book for dessert. But when I came to the end of the last Austen novel and realized Jane Austen was dead and would never write another word, I went into withdrawal. I tried to wean myself with Austen's novel fragments and juvenilia, read Austen's contemporaries, picked at the sequels and fan fiction, but nothing satisfied. I wandered the Internet and found many lost readers like myself, struggling with the void.

Thank goodness for Fowler's book. She led me to realize that I could bring Jane Austen back to life through my writing. I imagined the book I wanted to read: *The Jane Austen Book Club*, relocated to *Howard's End*, narrated by an American Bridget Jones. I envisioned Gothic elements and characters immersed in enactments and discussion so immediate it would seem Jane Austen were present. I found myself inventing a literary festival where Jane Austen's novels assume relevance in the life of a troubled young woman. Spending five years writing *My Jane Austen Summer* thoroughly satisfied my Austen craving.

Where did you get the idea for Lily's imaginary Jane Austen?

The first line of the prologue in *The Jane Austen Book Club*, "Each of us has a private Austen," as well as an essay where John Wiltshire, quoting Katherine Mansfield, suggests that readers imagine Jane Austen speaking to them between the lines of her text, intrigued me, especially since I was certain Jane Austen was my new best friend. I read biographies and criticism, getting to know her really well. But I was surprised when her human side was eventually revealed: irritable and prickly. And shocked by what seems to be a secret: her father's trusteeship of a slave-owning plantation. With the heated debate over the meaning of *Mansfield Park* and no one to define the truth for me, I had to wonder: Who is this person? Finally, the explanation that our heroine functions for us as a blank slate, upon which we can project our hopes and dreams, allowed me to understand the underlying dynamics of her relationship with fans, put it to rest, and simply enjoy reading her books.

However, the best friend experience demonstrated that a person could carry on a complete relationship, from initial infatuation, to blow-up, to establishing boundaries, with someone who has been dead two hundred years! Thus Lily's relationship with the imaginary Jane Austen embodies my idea of the dynamics of a contemporary woman's relationship with Jane Austen, taken to its end.

Why did you choose to shadow *Mansfield Park*?

Mansfield Park is my favorite Austen novel. A later work, it seems darker and more mature to me and I like the Romantic elements. However, my favorite aspect is that Jane Austen favors the quiet, reserved Fanny Price over the witty, gregarious Mary Crawford. I like to think of Jane Austen as a Champion of Introspective Women.

Where do you stand in the Fanny Wars?

I love Fanny Price. I completely identify with a person who creates an interior world through reading, and I admire her courage in taking such a strong stand against Henry Crawford and Uncle Bertram. I do sometimes wonder if it is probable for her to endure with such determination, considering her miserable upbringing. And it would not have bothered me if she didn't marry Edmund, as long as Edmund didn't end up with Mary Crawford. Lily Berry is my contemporary riff on Fanny Price, with Lily indulging in more failure than Fanny was allowed in her story.

How did you research this book?

I'm no scholar, so the task of depicting a literary conference required some work on my part. Aside from a lot of reading (my favorites are listed here in a selected bibliography), I spent years lurking on two Internet discussion lists listening to erudite conversation, learning how it sounds when Austen scholars discuss her work. One could almost get a free graduate degree in Jane Austen Studies by paying attention online. New threads of discussion arrive via e-mail daily, strong positions are constructed and defended, and further resources are regularly suggested.

What were the fun parts to write?

No one in the real world would hire me to develop a Jane Austen literary festival. But in my imagination, I'm in charge. From the volunteer check-in desk, to opening day enactments, I created every atom of my characters' world. And it was fun. I went house hunting on the Internet, seeking the perfect English manor, not too Palladian but big enough to house a literary festival. I have no practical interest in houses or decoration, but on a virtual level, I found it fascinating, poring over books on Georgian architecture, old house renovations, antique furnishings, and floor plans to create the perfect house—in my head. I used my experience at Squaw Valley Writers Conference as a reference for people gathered blissfully around the written word. I drew on memories of growing up in a family of educators where raised voices usually meant my grandfather was making his point. I chose scenes from *Mansfield Park* and *Lovers' Vows* to illuminate the action in *My Jane Austen Summer*. I enjoyed creating the flow of activities at the festival and the intellectual texture of a literary conference.

Which part of this book is written from the heart?

I wanted to write about a woman who breaks her cycle of unhappiness. This was the one aspect that was not negotiable in the many revisions. We all know people who repeat mistakes over and over, as if they were characters in a book, ink on a page with no second chances. But I believe people can change if they can imagine themselves differently. And the first step to imagining a difference is to see oneself truthfully. Self-knowledge is gained through observation, introspection, and examination of experiences.

Novels are a shortcut to examined experiences. Anyone who reads has a head start because the author does all the work, producing a story where complex characters act under pressure and either succeed or fail. The truth of an accurate portrayal in a novel resonates, as if to say: *This is how life is.* Like a cautionary lesson, sometimes I see myself reflected in the characters' situations, sometimes I see people I know. But when an author shines a light on a situation, and it resonates, and I can relate the experience to myself, I am saved a lot of time and trouble: disasters from which I learn, without having to experience them for myself. Jane Austen is expert at portraying human nature. True life resonates on every page, big scenes and small exchanges. I admire Jane Austen, agree with her judgment, and can't think of a better teacher for a young woman struggling with Lily's issues. Even though reading on the job got Lily fired, the examined experiences in Jane Austen's novels help Lily imagine a better way to confront her problems. Through learning from failures, guidance from Willis, and immersion in Austen's literature, Lily becomes a more stable person. Books are good for you.

What about the ending?

All of Jane Austen's novels end with a wedding. Although the ending of *My Jane Austen Summer* is not conventionally happy, Lily gains a sense of identity and the confidence to eventually write her own happy ending. Like the *Don't give a man a fish* proverb: Don't give a character a wedding; teach her to love herself and she'll find happiness for a lifetime.

Discussion Questions

1. After being fired for reading on the job, Lily warns that reading can be dangerous to one's mental health. But the literary festival is all about books! Discuss the theme of reading in *My Jane Austen Summer*. How has reading shaped Lily's hopes and dreams? What role do books play as Lily confronts her demons?

2. Describe Lily's relationship with her imaginary Jane Austen. How does the relationship change as the story progresses? Would this story work if Lily's imaginary friend had been Charlotte Brontë or Edith Wharton?

3. Her mother's death is very hard for Lily. How does it affect her relationships with Vera and her imaginary Jane Austen? What is the significance of the necklace and why is Bets so cavalier with it?

4. Lily wants a relationship so badly that she keeps squeezing herself into undersized romances. Why is a good relationship beyond her reach? When she discovers Martin with Ginny, Lily says, "I could have done *earth* for him." Why does she make this comment and what does it say about Lily? What are Lily's demons? When does she finally confront them? What advice would you give her?

5. Discuss the meaning of *only connect* from *Howard's End*. According to Omar, it's about connecting one's thoughts with one's deeds. According to Lily, it means relating to people

with greater gusto. Omar suggests that Lily join him at his university once the festival ends and spend her time connecting disjointed personalities. But can Lily connect herself? Do any of the characters in this story *only connect*?

6. Willis has secrets. He tells Lily he's working on his master's thesis but Lily discovers he's writing something completely different. Willis's other secrets are hurtful to Lily. How should Willis have behaved differently? Does Lily bear responsibility for not reading him more carefully?

7. Discuss Lily's family secret. How has it shaped her character and how does it impact her behavior at the literary festival? Discuss parallels between Willis's relationship with Lily and her father's relationship with his mistress. Archie and Magda? Maria Bertram and Henry Crawford? The baron in *Lovers' Vows*? Lily faults her mother for not confiding the truth before she died. Do you think Lily's parents should have told her? How much do children need to know about their parents' private lives?

8. Omar tries to prevent Lily from pursuing her self-destructive urges on the evening of the follies, but Lily runs away from him. Magda tries to give Lily sisterly advice, which Lily ignores. What makes for a healthy friendship? Is Omar a good friend to Lily? Is Bets a good friend to Gary? Is Lily a good friend to anyone?

9. Discuss the different approaches to understanding the meaning of *Mansfield Park*. Is *Mansfield Park* about slavery and feminism—or the importance of self-knowledge? Where do you stand—with Magda or Nigel? How does the novel *Mansfield Park* illuminate the story of *My Jane Austen Summer*?

10. Compare and contrast Lily Berry and Fanny Price. Where does Fanny get the strength to resist Henry Crawford? Would Lily, as she fears, have fallen prey to Henry Crawford on page 1? Is Fanny Price insipid or heroic? Take a side in the Fanny Wars and defend your position.

11. Does the play *Lovers' Vows*, about a woman whose baby daddy is a baron, speak to modern readers? How did it speak to Lily?

12. Janeites are a very diverse group of fans, evenly distributed along age lines and listing a wide variety of professions. Discuss the contemporary fame of Jane Austen. What is the reason for her great appeal to readers? Will it last, or, as she once said, will future generations be disappointed?

13. Consider the elements of traditional gothic fiction: castles, foreign settings, attics, death, secrets, overwrought emotion, mystery, tyrannical men, women in distress, grief, and hereditary curses. Which elements are present in *My Jane Austen Summer*? How do they enrich setting and story?

14. Have you ever wanted to live in a novel? Lily believed that attending a literary festival might be a way to accomplish her dream. Are there other practical ways to "live in a novel"? What novel would you pick and how would you move in?

15. Consider the ending of *My Jane Austen Summer*. What will happen to Lily? Willis? Will some characters repeat the same mistakes for the rest of their lives? Did the ending satisfy you?